"No matter in what time period Joan Wolf writes, the results are the same: a superb story with wonderful characters and romance that touches the heart."

—Fayrene Preston
author of *Storm Song*

"Joan Wolf is absolutley wonderful. I've loved her work for years. She's an extraordinary storyteller and her characters stride boldly from the pages, complex, sympathetic and vibrantly alive."

—Iris Johansen
author of *Beloved Scoundrel*

"The only thing that could be better than one of Joan Wolf's wonderful romances, would be two of them! She writes with such grace and ease that you're halfway through her book before you know it—and sorry it will have to end so soon. It's time for her intelligent, well-crafted modern romances to be read and re-read."

—Edith Layton
author of *Love In Disguise*

BELOVED STRANGER

SUMMER STORM

by

Joan Wolf

A SIGNET BOOK

SIGNET
Published by the Penguin Group
Penguin Books USA Inc., 375 Hudson Street,
New York, New York 10014, U.S.A.
Penguin Books Ltd, 27 Wrights Lane,
London W8 5TZ, England
Penguin Books Australia Ltd., Ringwood,
Victoria, Australia
Penguin Books Canada Ltd, 10 Alcorn Avenue,
Toronto, Ontario, Canada M4V 3B2
Penguin Books (N.Z.) Ltd, 182–190 Wairau Road,
Auckland 10, New Zealand

Penguin Books Ltd, Registered Offices:
Harmondsworth, Middlesex, England

First published by Signet,
an imprint of Dutton Signet,
a division of Penguin Books USA Inc.
Previously published in two volumes.

First Printing, October, 1994
10 9 8 7 6 5 4 3 2 1

Foreword

Dear Reader:

I'm writing to you this time not to get you cranked up for one of my novels, but to give you wonderful news about Joan Wolf, one of my favorite authors of all time, bar none.

Perhaps you remember that Joan and I wrote Signet Regency romances back in the late seventies and early eighties. Then Joan went on to write seven contemporary romances in the mid eighties before turning to historical novels, while I continued with historical romances.

Now the time has come to treat you to two of Joan Wolf's contemporary romances in one package. It's your chance to fill out or start your collection of these almost impossible to find books. The only other person I know who has the complete set of Joan's books is Linda Howard, and she wouldn't agree to part with any of her first editions for any price. Even I am missing one of Joan's novels, and now, thanks to Signet and Hilary Ross, it's coming soon to my bookcase.

You are in for a real treat. Signet intends to re-issue all seven of Joan's contemporary romances in three collections over the next year and a half. Vintage Joan Wolf. It doesn't get any better.

Why, you might ask, is she so wonderful? Why am I carrying on about her as if she's better than my sourdough bread recipe? Joan Wolf has a unique way of making each of her characters very real: what they say, how they feel, what they do—she presents everything to you directly, clearly, and with deceptive simplicity. I've accused her of using smoke and mirrors and magic, but it's just a very special talent she has. The result is that you know her characters, care about them, and never want the story to end.

Now, if you've never read Joan Wolf, I feel very sorry for you, considering all the enjoyment you've missed over the years, and excited for you as well, because now you'll have a wonderful opportunity to curl up with these terrific romances.

After you've read these two romances, do write both Joan and me. Write her to say you've fallen in love and are a fan for life. Write to me about what great taste I have and how lucky I am to have good friends who are also great writers.

Catherine Coulter

Author's Preface

Dear Reader:

Whenever I conceive the idea for a new book, I never picture just a hero, or just a heroine. I always think of *two* people. I suppose this is because what really interests me is relationships, the emotional reaction of one person to another; in short, the dynamic that we call love.

"Opposites attract" is an old and honored saying, and like many old and honored sayings, it is true—at least superficially. My books are often about people who, on the surface, appear to be direct opposites. And yet, as the two love stories in this collection show, deep inside, where the truth of a person lies, they are more alike than not. I have always thought that it would not be possible to interchange the heroes and heroines in any of my books. They are especially matched, not just sexually, but emotionally as well. There's something in his nature that answers a need in hers, and vice versa.

One could hardly imagine two more dissimilar people than Ricardo Montoya, gorgeous Colombian superstar center fielder for the New York Yankees, and shy and insecure Susan Morgan, who has lived her life in the shadow of her brilliant parents and her beautiful and intelligent sister.

In *Beloved Stranger* these two seemingly incompatible people marry for the sake of a child and discover that, in some deep and wonderful way, they are exactly the right people for each other.

In *Summer Storm* you will meet Christopher Douglas, movie star, and Mary O'Connor, college professor. On the surface, Kit seems to have been born for the big screen. Not only is his face worth a fortune, but he can act too. And Mary is a bona fide intellectual, daughter of a conservative New England doctor and professor at a prestigious Connecticut university.

But all is not as it seems—and during a summer theatrical workshop Mary discovers, much to her surprise, that the early marriage between them that had foundered on seemingly irreconcilable differences is really based on solid bedrock.

I have always been particularly fond of the people in these two books, and I hope you will enjoy reading their stories.

Joan Wolf

BELOVED STRANGER

Chapter One

The snow was coming down harder and harder and Susan Morgan was beginning to worry. She had left the White Mountains ski lodge of a school friend a few hours earlier, when the snow had been light and flaky. Now, however, it was beginning to look like a blizzard, and she was afraid she had been foolish to insist upon leaving. She had been traveling the side roads; she decided she had better try to get over to 91 instead.

Half an hour later she knew she wouldn't make it. She couldn't see a foot in front of her and there had been no other cars on the road. "I'm the only one idiotic enough to come out in a blizzard," she muttered as she hunched over the wheel of her old Volkswagen and tried to keep on the road. Two minutes later she slid into a ditch and the car stalled. She could not get it started again.

Susan could feel her stomach clench with fear. She tried the car one more time and got no response. "Well," she said aloud, trying to be calm, "the choice is to sit here and freeze to death or to try and find help." She did not want to get out of her car but chill was already beginning to set in and she knew she couldn't stay. She leaned over to her suitcase in the backseat and fished out ski mittens, goggles, hat and scarf. She bundled herself up as warmly as she could and then resolutely stepped out into the raging storm.

She walked for twenty minutes without seeing a house, a car or a gas station. She had never been so cold in her entire twenty-one years. The only thing that kept her going was the thought of her mother. *I can't die,* she kept repeating fiercely to herself. *I can't do that to Mother. Not after Sara.*

When she was absolutely certain that she couldn't walk another step, she saw the lights of a house at the top of the hill on her left. It took the last remnant of willpower to get her to the door. She leaned against it for a moment, summoning the strength to knock. When the door opened she almost fell into the room.

"*Dios!*" said a startled male voice.

Susan tried to say something but her face felt frozen. Her teeth were chattering like castanets. "All right," the deep voice said practically, "first let's get you out of those wet clothes."

Susan's fingers didn't seem to be moving and so the stranger efficiently stripped her of hat, scarf, gloves, coat and one sweater. Her wool slacks below her jacket were caked with snow. He said, "Wait here," disappeared for a minute and came back with a large terry-cloth bathrobe and a pair of wool socks. "Come over to the fire and let me check you for frostbite," he said, and she followed on trembling legs.

"Can you get those slacks off?" he asked.

"I—I think so." Her face and fingers were beginning to tingle and she managed to unzip her wet plaid slacks.

The stranger handed her the bathrobe. "Put that on and sit down," he said matter-of-factly.

She did as he asked and he knelt to pull off her socks and inspect her toes. His hands felt very warm against her icy feet. He put the wool socks on her and looked up. "Let me see your hands." She held her hands out and he took them in his own large warm ones and carefully inspected first one side and then the other.

"Another five minutes and you'd have been in trouble," he said. "Sit right there and I'll get you a glass of brandy."

Susan huddled inside the warm robe, flexed her feet inside the warm socks, and slowly the feeling returned to her body. The brandy burned going down but she finished it all and then looked over at her rescuer and attempted a smile. "I don't know how to thank you. I thought it was all over for me."

"It almost was," he said noncommittally, and reached over to feel her hands. "I'll run you a bath. That should finish thawing you out. And then you can tell me what the devil you were doing wandering around in a blizzard."

"I was being stupid," she said bitterly. He gave her an assessing look before he went inside. In a minute she heard the sound of running water.

The bath was hot and wonderful and she could feel all her muscles relaxing. She stayed until the water began to cool off and then she got out. The collar of her turtleneck cotton jersey was wet and cold and she couldn't stand the thought of putting it on again, so she put on only her bra and panties and wrapped the bathrobe firmly around her. It was enormous. She put the wool socks on her feet; they were enormous too. She looked in the medicine cabinet and found a comb with which she smoothed out her shoulder-length hair.

Then she opened the bathroom door and went, with a little uneasiness, toward the living room. All she had noticed about her host before was that he was very tall and dark and that he had a deep, mellow speaking voice that seemed to hold the very faintest trace of an accent. She stepped into the living room. "That felt marvelous," she said to the man who was sitting comfortably in front of the fire.

He turned at the sound of her voice and looked at her out of eyes that were very large and very brown. He saw a small girl, whose slenderness was almost comically swathed in the folds of his terry-cloth bathrobe. Her delicate face was framed by curtains of straight, pale brown hair. He grinned. "You look lost in that robe," he said.

Susan smiled back. He had the darkest eyes she had ever seen, and the most beguiling smile. His teeth were very white against his warm olive skin. "I know," she replied. "But all my things were wet."

"We'll hang them in front of the fire to dry tonight," he said, and gestured. "Come over and sit down."

He was sitting on one end of the worn, comfortable-looking sofa and she walked slowly across the room and seated herself on the other end. She tucked her legs under her, sedately arranged her robe and turned to look at him.

"Let me put another log on the fire," he said, "and then you can tell me your story." He stood up and went to get wood from the basket. Susan watched him silently. He was a spendid-looking man, in his middle to late twenties, tall and dark-haired, with glowing golden skin. The hips that were encased in a worn pair of jeans were slim but the shoulders under the plaid flannel shirt looked enormous.

He dropped the wood on the fire, poked it a few times and then came back to the sofa. He sat down where he had been before, turned to her and said, "Well?"

She sighed. "My name is Susan Morgan," she began dutifully, "and I was staying with a college friend at her family's ski lodge up in Franconia Notch. When I left this morning it was only snowing lightly. I had no idea it was going to get this bad."

"You should have gotten off the road hours ago."

"I know." She looked embarrassed. "I was—kind of preoccupied and I didn't really notice how heavy the snow was becoming."

A look of faint amusement settled over his face. "Women," he said. "They shouldn't be allowed behind the wheel of a car."

Susan sat up a little straighter. "I was—thinking of something else," she said defensively.

The amusement on his face deepened. "You must have been if you didn't even notice a blizzard."

Susan bit her lip. "Please don't try to make me feel stupider than I do already. I can't thank you enough for rescuing me."

He shrugged. He had the widest shoulders she had ever seen. "*De nada,*" he said. "I am glad I was here."

"Is this your lodge?" she asked curiously.

"No. I'm only renting it for a week." He smiled at her, that unbelievable smile, and said softly. "My name is Ricardo."

"Hello, Ricardo," Susan said, and smiled back. It was impossible not to smile when he did, she thought. "You're here all alone?" she asked.

"Yes."

She looked at him gravely and the large, incredible

brown eyes looked back. Susan nodded her head. "It's nice to be alone sometimes," she said softly. "That's why I like cross-country skiing better than downhill."

He looked interested. "I have never done cross-country."

She smiled dreamily, her widely spaced gray eyes shimmering in the firelight. "It's lovely. So quiet. Only the trees and the sound of the skis. All the rest is just beautiful white silence."

"It does sound nice." He looked suddenly a little rueful. "Sometimes it's very hard to be alone, I find. I'll have to try cross-country."

"I'm sorry I barged in on you," she said a little awkwardly.

"You I do not mind." There was a note in his voice that made her breath catch suddenly. "Susan," he said experimentally, trying her name as if it were a foreign word. "Are you warm now?" He reached over to feel her hand. His own was lean and brown and very hard.

Susan had never been this physically conscious of a man in her entire life. The touch of his hand had been like an electrical charge. She cleared her throat. "I'm fine," she said. Then, feeling it necessary to say something. "Do you do a lot of skiing?"

He had removed his hand but he was now sitting halfway across the sofa. "When I get a chance, which is not often." He grinned at her. "I have a boss who is paranoid about my getting hurt. And I do like downhill. I like the speed of it."

A strand of straight dark hair had fallen over his forehead. She had a sudden urge to reach out and smooth it back. She retreated a little farther into her corner and searched for something else to say. Good manners forbade her asking him what his job was.

"Would you like something to drink?" he asked.

"If you're having something."

He got up from the sofa with the liquid grace of a dancer—or an athlete. She stared for a moment at the narrow outline of his hips in the low-slung jeans and then raised her face to his. "Some wine?" he asked softly.

"Okay." Their eyes met and for the first time there was tension between them. He turned to go to the kitchen and Susan looked into the blazing fire. He returned with two glasses of red wine and handed her one. He sat down next to her and stretched out his legs.

"I think the snow is stopping," he murmured as he sipped his wine.

"Is it? Good. I'm anxious to get to my mother's. I only have a few more days before I'm due back at college."

"Mmm?" he said deeply. His long lean body seemed perfectly relaxed. He was only inches away from her.

I should get up, Susan thought. She knew what was coming next. I should make it perfectly clear that I have no intention of falling into bed with him. But the fire was so drugging in its warmth; it made her feel so safe, so secure. She sipped her wine slowly and stared at the flames. When she finally turned, it was to find him watching her. He said nothing; neither did his eyes drop. They were filled with the light of the fire.

She gazed back, her small head tilted back, exposing her slender neck, her fine, shimmering hair spilling all around her shoulders. He slid his fingers into that hair. "It's like a child's," he murmured softly. "So soft. So very fine."

She drew back from him a little and he smiled at

her, a lovely smile that quite turned her heart over. "Su-san," he said, *"querida*. You needn't be afraid of me." She was getting lost in his eyes. His hand moved down to caress her throat and she closed her own eyes. The smoky smell of the fire filled her nostrils. The brandy and the wine ran warm in her veins. She had never felt this way before in her life. His hand slid down between the robe and touched her breast. Susan's eyes flew open and he bent his head to kiss her.

It was as if she were drowning in sensation. The thought flashed across her mind: I must be crazy. I don't even *know* this man. But his mouth on hers was warm and gentle, his body against hers was broad and strong. All sense of strangeness left her. His eyes were brilliant in the firelight. His arms around her felt very secure. He is so big, she thought, so warm. The touch of his fingers on her breast was exquisite. He kissed her again and she relaxed against him, her arms sliding around his chest with a naturalness that would have amazed her if she had been capable of rational thought. The flannel of his shirt was soft under her palms, but she could feel the hardness of muscle through the fabric. His mouth was hard now as well, demanding, urgent. Susan's lips parted sweetly for him and one hand went up to caress the strong column of his neck.

The only light in the room was the glow given off by the fire, and when he laid Susan back against the cushions of the sofa and began to unbutton his shirt, she looked at him out of eyes that were wide and won-dering. His skin was coppery in the glow of the fire-light, his eyes dark with mystery and with promise. In that enchanted moment he seemed to her almost as a god, a strange and mythical being, enormous and overwhelming, before whose power she bent as a reed before the wind. But the feel of his warm brown body was very real against hers as was the growing, throbbing ache his touch was arousing deep inside her. The warm air from the fire was hot on her bare skin, the fabric of the sofa rough under her back. She held him close, all the length of her slim body pressed against him. Her mouth sought his again and a small whimper formed deep in her throat.

He heard the sound and pressed her back into the cushions of the sofa. Susan obeyed him blindly, seeking desperately for a release from the unbearably sweet ache he had wrought inside her.

"Dios!" The muffled exclamation from him came at the same time she felt a sharp shooting pain tear through her body. Her eyes flew open in shock and she tried to pull away, but he held her firmly. "It'll be all right," he muttered. "Hold on." And then, mixed with the pain, came a flooding wave of pleasure that made her body shake and her fingers press deeply into his back. "Oh," she whispered. "Oh."

There was silence in the room, then a log cracked and fell on the fire and he raised his head to look down at her. "You were a virgin," he said in an odd voice.

She felt sleepy and warm and peaceful. "Mmm," she answered dreamily.

"But why?"

She didn't pretend to misunderstand him. She smiled up into his puzzled face. "I don't know," she said simply.

He had been watching her steadily, seriously, but now he smiled as well, a slow smile that was as intimate as his touch had been. "It was magic," he said softly.

So he had felt that too. "Yes." Her eyes were very heavy.

He picked her up as if she weighed scarcely anything. "You are falling asleep," he said. "Come." And he carried her into the bedroom, wrapped her once again in his bathrobe and tucked her under the covers. "Good night, *querida*," he said. "Sleep well."

She awoke to the bright sun streaming in her bedroom window. It was ten-thirty according to her watch and with an exclamation of alarm she jumped out of bed. The snow had stopped and the world outside the window looked like a fairy tale. She walked into the living room rather tentatively, but Ricardo was gone. He had left her a note on the kitchen table. "The roads are plowed and I've gone to try to locate your car. Make yourself some breakfast." There was no signature. She walked back into the living room. Her clothes were spread on several chairs in front of the fire. When she felt them, they were dry. She looked at the blanket and pillow on the couch and knew where he had spent the night.

She dressed and went back to the kitchen, made herself a cup of instant coffee and sat down at the table. She should be horrified with herself, she thought. She had just slept with a man she didn't know, a man who was obviously anxious to see her on her way as quickly as he could. And yet she wasn't sorry. It had been—as he had said himself—magic.

It wasn't magic two hours later, however, when Ricardo returned. He brought a gust of cold air in the door with him and the grin he gave her was good-natured and slightly cocky. He stood by the door and stripped his gloves off. "We've got your car going," he said.

"Oh good." She walked slowly into the living room from the kitchen, trying to conceal her uneasiness. "How did you know where to look for it?"

"Simple," he replied. He came across the room tracking snow all over the floor. "You said you were coming from the Notch and I knew you couldn't have walked far. Not in that storm." He unzipped his jacket. "It's down at the garage in town. I'll take you there after lunch."

"Fine," she replied quietly, "but I'm afraid there's nothing to eat. You only have coffee and bread and butter."

He fished in the capacious pocket of his jacket and brought out a small brown bag. "Ham and cheese." He handed it to her. "You can make some sandwiches."

She accepted the package. "All right." He followed her into the kitchen, talking cheerfully about her car. She made the sandwiches, listening to him with half an ear and trying to deal with her own sense of shock. It was hard to believe that the tender lover of last night was the same person as this tall and obviously tough young man who was lounging carelessly at his ease, waiting for her to serve him. She put a sandwich in front of him. "I'm afraid there isn't any mustard," she said expressionlessly.

"I eat out," he said, and bit into his bread with strong white teeth. "Where do you go to school?" he asked after half the sandwich was gone.

"Melford," she answered, naming a very old and very prestigious women's college.

"I see." He looked amused. "And are you studying political science so you can change the world?"

She looked at him levelly. "No. I'm studying English literature."

"Ah." He started on the other half of his sandwich.

"What do *you* do?" she asked to turn the tables.

He regarded her reflectively as he chewed. Then he said easily, "I play baseball. For the New York Yankees."

Her eyes widened and she put her coffee cup down. He had said his name was Ricardo. "You—you can't be Rick Montoya?" he said breathlessly.

"I can be and I am," he replied. He grinned at her engagingly. "You don't follow baseball, I take it."

"I knew your name."

He drained his coffee cup. "But not my face." He got up, went over to the refrigerator and took a piece of paper from the top of it. "These are my addresses," he said. "I'll be in Florida for spring training until April." He pointed to the Fort Lauderdale address. "The rest of the year I live in Stamford, Connecticut." He looked at her soberly. "Let me know if you need any help."

She stared at him blankly for a moment and then brilliant color stained her cheeks. Her eyes fell. She couldn't think of a thing to say.

"Come on," he said, "and we'll go get your car."

"Yes," she answered, and jumped to her feet. "Just a minute and I'll get my coat." Two minutes later she walked out the door with him and it slammed behind her, slammed forever on her night of magic.

Chapter Two

Susan reached her mother's house in Fairfield, Connecticut, by early that evening. Mrs. Morgan was surprised to see her. "You shouldn't have traveled in all this snow, dear," she said after Susan had kissed her at the door. "If I had known you were on the road, I would have been extremely worried."

"The highway was plowed all the way down," Susan said with a smile. "It wasn't bad at all. But I *could* use something to eat."

"Of course. Come into the kitchen." Susan followed her mother and watched as she efficiently prepared a cheese omelet for her daughter. "Did you enjoy your skiing?" Mrs. Morgan asked as she sat down across from Susan at the kitchen table.

"Yes. The Fosters are very nice people. I felt a little guilty about leaving you, though."

Her mother made a gesture of dismissal. "You mustn't worry about me, dear. I've been very busy. The Talbotts had a dinner the other evening and then there was a meeting of the university women I had to attend."

Susan ate and listened to her mother chatter on. Apparently she had resumed her old busy schedule of meeting and lunches and teas and dinners. She was in-

domitable, Susan thought. The uncharacteristic leth-
argy of Christmas week that had so worried her daughter had quite disappeared.

"Are you teaching a full load this semester?" Susan
asked.

"Yes." When working, Mrs. Morgan was Dr. Helen
Morgan, Professor of Anthropology at the University of
Bridgeport. Susan's father had also been a professor at
the university before his death a few years ago.

They moved into the living room and Susan curled
up on the sofa. "I was so pleased to hear of your ac-
ceptance into the Honor Society, Susan," her mother
said warmly. "I'm proud of you. You worked hard for it."

"I know." Susan made a face. "I may be just a member and you and Sara were presidents, but I'm pleased
with myself. It took me so *long* to finally get the
grades."

"I don't see why," her mother said briskly. "You're a
bright enough child."

Susan sighed. "I have such a hard time *finishing* a
test, Mother. I'm always still there when the time has
run out and usually I'm only half done. I think too
much and write too little."

Mrs. Morgan smiled abstractedly, her mind obviously
elsewhere. "I've gone through Sara's clothes," she said
after a minute, "and there are a number of things that
should fit you. The dresses will all be too big, but the
sweaters should be all right. And the suits could be altered. And her new black coat. I've packed a bag for
you to take back to school with you."

"Oh Mother," Susan said weakly, "how can I wear
Sara's clothes?"

"She would want you to. I want you to." A shadow

crossed Mrs. Morgan's face. "I don't want to just give them to the Salvation Army, Susan."

Susan had a brief vision of her sister's beautiful, vital face. She had loved clothes, loved shopping. "Of course you can't give her things to the Salvation Army," she said quickly. "I hadn't thought. I'll take them. They'll remind me of Sara."

For a brief moment it seemed as if Mrs. Morgan's eyes went out of focus and Susan knew it was not she that her mother was seeing. "It doesn't seem possible that she's gone," the older woman said at last in a low voice.

"I know." Susan sat still, helplessly watching her mother. There was nothing she could say, nothing she could do to comfort her. Sara was gone, killed instantly by an out-of-control trailer truck on the New England Thruway, and no one could fill her place.

Mrs. Morgan forced a smile. "You must be tired, dear, after that drive. Don't let me keep you up."

"I am rather tired." Susan rose slowly and went to kiss her mother's smooth cheek. "Good night, Mother."

"Good night, dear. Sleep well."

"I'll try," murmured Susan; the memory of how she had slept last night flashed into her mind. She wrenched her thoughts back into the present and slowly, resolutely, climbed the stairs to her bedroom.

Susan looked out the window of her dorm and sighed. It had been raining for five days and the new leaves on the trees looked heavy and green and limp. The weather was a perfect reflection of her mood. She stared blankly for a few more minutes at the paper she was trying to write for a poetry course and then reached into the desk drawer and drew out, once again, the lab report. There it was clear and inescapable, the unwelcome news: she was pregnant.

Her first reaction had been anger. How could she have been so *stupid*? Her second reaction had been self-pity. Why me? I only did it once. From self-pity she had progressed to her present state of mind, which could be summed up by one question: what am I going to do?

Ricardo had foreseen this possibility. He had told her to get in touch with him, and given her his address. The regular baseball season had opened a few weeks ago. Susan, who had never followed baseball in her life, had taken to reading all she could get her hands on about the New York Yankees and about Ricardo Montoya in particular. Consequently, she knew that he had signed a multimillion-dollar contract in February and that he had had a sensational spring. The Yankees were universally expected to win the American League Pennant this year.

Ricardo would be home in Stamford. Should she write him?

She took out a fresh sheet of looseleaf notebook paper and began to compose a letter. After three sentences she stopped, looked at what she had written and tore it up. "I sound like an idiot," she muttered disgustedly. She stood up. "I *am* an idiot." She got her raincoat from the closet and ran down the stairs. She needed to get away from her own company.

The student lounge was more filled than usual due to the rainy weather. Susan spotted a group of friends and went over to join them. One girl had a copy of a national news magazine on her lap and Susan felt a jolt of shock when she looked down and saw the picture on the cover.

"May I see that for a moment, Lisa?" she asked rather breathlessly.

"Sure," the other girl answered. "You can join in the general drooling if you like. We've all just decided that *that* is the man we would most want to be stranded on a desert island with."

"Would you?" asked Susan, and stared down at the picture. Ricardo was wearing his baseball uniform but not the hat. His thick, straight, dark brown hair had fallen slightly forward over his forehead. He looked lean and brown and his smile was the irresistible grin that she remembered so vividly. But it was the eyes that caught and held you, the large, beautiful, thick-lashed brown eyes.

"You could travel halfway round the world and you wouldn't find another man like that," one of the girls was saying.

Susan cleared her throat. "Where is he from? I mean, he's not American, is he?"

"He's Colombian. Or his parents are Colombian. He was born in the States, so that makes him an American citizen. It's all in the article."

"May I borrow the magazine, Lisa?" I'll give it back to you."

Lisa grinned. "Susie! Now we know why you find all your dates so uninteresting. You're holding out for Rick Montoya."

Susan could feel herself flushing and the other girl reached over to give her hand a quick squeeze. "Of course you can borrow it. But I do want it back."

"Lisa wants to hang Rick's picture over her bed," one of the other girls teased, and everyone laughed. About ten minutes later Susan made her escape, clutching the magazine securely under her arm. Up in the solitary shelter of her bedroom she read the cover story through. Then she went to lie on her bed and stare out at the rain. Rick Montoya. It was impossible to make herself believe that the man she had just read about was the same man who had given her shelter from the storm and had made such tender and rapturous love to her.

She couldn't write to him. Everything the article said had removed him further and further from her. He was wealthy from baseball, she knew that, but according to the article, he had been born wealthy. His father was a director of Avianca Airlines and he had grown up partly in Bogotá and partly in New York. He had been drafted by the Yankees after college and had consistently been one of the best hitters in baseball ever since. He averaged thirty-eight home runs a season and had a lifetime batting average of .320. Susan didn't know much about baseball but she gathered from the article that these were highly impressive statistics. He was twenty-eight years old. He was unmarried, but according to this article, he never lacked for feminine companionship. The names of two or three of the world's most beautiful models were listed as his frequent companions. No, she couldn't write to him. She felt sure that all he would do—all he *could* do, really— would be to offer her money for an abortion.

Susan closed her eyes and blotted out the view of the rain. An abortion. The temptation was so great. It would solve all her problems. No one would ever have to know. It was so easy, she thought, to be opposed to abortion in general. It was so hard when the particular case was you. She thought of her mother. How could she hit her with this? And after Sara. It wouldn't be fair. It was, in fact, unthinkable. Morgans just did not have babies out of wedlock. Period.

But she knew, too, deep in her soul, that she would not have an abortion. It would solve all problems except one. She would have to live with the knowledge of what she had done.

She remembered then having seen an advertisement in the *Bridgeport Post* for an organization called Birthright. It was a group set up to help girls like herself. Susan got up off her bed and washed her face. She would get the number from information and call Birthright, she thought. She'd make an appointment and go home this weekend. It was time to stop bemoaning her fate and do something about it.

Susan relaxed gratefully in the cool air conditioning of the small restaurant and sipped her iced tea. Outside the downtown Hartford street shimmered in the heat of August, but inside it was pleasantly cool and uncrowded. It was two-thirty in the afternoon, well past the regular lunch hour. Once she had finished her drink she could go home.

Home. Well, it *was* home, she thought, for two more months at least. She could only feel gratitude toward the middle-aged single woman who had provided a shelter home for her for the duration of her pregnancy. The people at Birthright had found her the home and a part-time job that enabled her to give Elaine something toward her board and room.

The baby inside her gave a kick and she shifted a little on her chair. She glanced up as the door opened and then froze in her seat. There was no mistaking that tall, lean figure, that shock of very dark brown hair. Almost instantly she bent her head and gazed furiously at the table, trying to hide her face. Consequently she didn't see the man notice her, frown and then start a leisurely but purposeful approach toward her table.

"Susan?" said a low, deep, mellow voice that was unnervingly familiar. And she had to raise her head.

"Yes," she said. "Ricardo. What a surprise to find you here." She was surprised to hear how composed she sounded.

"I had to see someone in the immigration office about a friend of mine." He gestured. "May I sit down?"

"I suppose so." She made her voice distinctly unenthusiastic but he didn't appear to notice. He pulled the chair out opposite her and sat. She stared resolutely at the saltshaker. She didn't have to look to know that those shrewd brown eyes were assessing the bulkiness of her stomach. If it had been winter, if she were wearing a coat, then she thought she might have hidden it. But in a light cotton dress she didn't have a chance.

He reached out and caught her left hand as it moved restlessly on the table. They both stared for a long minute at the slender, delicate hand, so conspicuously bare of rings. He raised his eyes to her face. "Is it mine?" he asked tensely.

She bit her lip. "Yes."

"*Dios!* I told you to let me know if this happened. I knew there was a chance of it."

His hand was still grasping hers and she tried to draw away. He didn't let go and she stared once again at the strong tan fingers that were gripping her wrist so efficiently, remembering the last time they had touched her. "There was really nothing you could do for me, Ricardo," she said, she hoped calmly. "I'm managing quite well on my own, thank you. There is no need to concern yourself about me."

He smiled at her words and it was not a smile of good humor. "How are you managing, *querida?*" he asked.

She pulled her hand again and this time he let it go. She flattened her back and said evenly, "I went to an organization called Birthright. I didn't want to tell my mother what had happened. She would have been terribly upset." She put her hand up, from long habit, to push back her hair but it was already neatly tied at the nape of her neck. She let her hand fall again. "My older sister Sara was killed last year in a car accident," she explained flatly, "and Daddy died of a heart attack three years ago. So, you see, I'm the only one Mother has left. I've never been as bright as Sara, or as pretty and vivacious, but still I'm all Mother has left now. I just couldn't come home pregnant."

"Your mother would have been angry?" he asked noncommittally.

"No. Not angry. She would have been marvelous. But, underneath, she would have been so disappointed."

"You would be a failure in her eyes."

Startled, she looked up at him. Those remarkable brown eyes had a very understanding look to them. She put her elbows on the table and rested her chin on her hands. "I suppose so," she said ruefully. "I suppose it wasn't just Mother's feeling I was sparing."

"So you went to this Birthright," he said. "Why did you not get an abortion?"

"I just couldn't."

He nodded. "And so?"

"And so the people at Birthright were absolutely

marvelous. I couldn't stay around home, for obvious reasons. They found me a shelter home here in Hartford. I came here after graduation." She smiled a little painfully. "I made it through graduation all right. I didn't start to really show that much until the fifth month. After graduation I told Mother I had an opportunity to go to Europe with a family as a combination nurse-tutor for two children. That's where she thinks I am. A friend of mine, who *is* in Europe, is periodically mailing postcards I wrote in advance. So there it is."

"Not quite." He looked at her levelly. The lines of his cheek and jaw looked suddenly very hard. "What are you planning to do with the baby?"

This was the hard part. A look of strain crept across her face, tightening the skin, making her nose look more prominent. She was very pale. "I'm going to give him up for adoption," she said in a very low voice.

There was a long silence during which she refused to look at him. Then, "Why?" he asked in a clipped kind of voice.

"Because it will be the best thing for the baby. It may not be the best thing for me, but it's not my interest I've got to look out for in this." Now she did look at him. "My best friend in high school was adopted. Her parents were two of the greatest people I've ever known. It is not possible to love a child more than they loved her—and her two adopted brothers as well. A child needs a stable loving family. He needs a mother and a father—not a full-time day-care center, which is all I could offer him. The agency I'm going through has a list as long as your arm of couples who are just *longing* for a baby." She compressed her lips. "I've thought about this long and hard, Ricardo, and it hasn't been an easy decision, but I know it's the right one. I'm going to give him up for adoption."

"You keep saying 'him.' Do you know it is a boy?"

"Yes, actually I do. I had an ultrasound and the way the picture came out you could tell."

He leaned across the table toward her and took her hand once more in his. "Susan." No one else, she thought, made her name sound as it did when Ricardo said it. "If you could keep the baby," he was going on, "would you?"

"Of course I would," she answered instantly. "I don't *want* to give him away, you know."

"Then marry me," he said.

Her eyes flew wide open in shock. She stared at his face. It looked perfectly serious. "What?" she said.

"You heard me. Marry me. Surely it is the obvious solution."

"To you, maybe, but not to me," she got out. "I hardly *know* you."

He laughed, a sound of genuine amusement. "You know me well enough," he said, and she felt herself flushing furiously.

"Don't be clever," she muttered. "You know what I mean."

"Listen, *querida,*" he said patiently. He was very obviously the reasonable, intelligent male dealing with an unreasonable and very silly woman. "You said yourself that it is not your interest that concerns you. It is the welfare of the child. Well, I am the child's father. I am wealthy. I will take good care of him." He stared into her eyes and his own were suddenly commanding. "I do not want *my* son to be brought up by another man."

She felt the force of his will, of his personality, bearing down on her and, instinctively, she resisted. "I don't know," she said.

He sat back a little in his chair. "I could simply take the child and let my mother raise him," he said. "She would be delighted to have a grandchild to live with her. And, unlike your mother, she would not think I had disappointed her." His dark stare was unwavering, almost inimical. "Would you prefer that?"

She stared back, her own eyes clearly reflecting her confusion and her hurt. She couldn't answer him. Quite suddenly he smiled and his whole face was transformed. "Listen, *querida*," and now his voice was gentle, "I know this has been a very hard time for you. I am as much responsible as you and yet you have had to bear all the worry, all the pain. Let me take care of you now. I know you will be a good mother and, who knows, you may even come to like being a wife." His eyes sparkled. "I am not so bad, you know. Now what do you say? Do you want to keep this baby?"

Of course she wanted to keep her baby, more than anything else in the world. But what would the final price be? "Yes," she said. Her widely spaced gray eyes searched his worriedly. "What—what kind of marriage did you have in mind?"

He looked surprised. "Marriage is marriage," he said. "I didn't know there were different brands."

She could feel herself flushing. "I meant—did you expect it would be permanent?"

"Permanent?" he echoed. And then his eyes narrowed as comprehension struck him. "So you mean would I expect to divorce you after the baby is born?"

"Well," said Susan. "Yes."

His mouth thinned. "No," he said flatly. "I would expect you to be my wife." He looked at her assessingly and she was terribly conscious of her bulky figure. "What are you afraid of?"

She closed her eyes for a minute. "Everything." Her voice was barely audible.

When she opened her eyes again his face had softened. "You are afraid to trust your future to me," he said very gently. "Don't worry, little one. I will take good care of you." He reached out and touched her cheek lightly. "We will have a son—the son we made together." He picked up her hand and kissed the inside of her wrist. "You did not find me so disagreeable once. It will be like that again."

The touch of his fingers, his mouth, brought back disturbing memories. "We really *don't* know each other. Do—do you still think we could make it work?" she asked uncertainly.

"Of course. Why ever should we not?"

Why ever? Susan thought blankly. And, really, what was her alternative? She looked up into his dark eyes. "Well—all right," she said.

He smiled at her and she felt the corners of her mouth lifting in response. "Good girl," he said. "We will do very well together. And now, why don't we go along to your shelter home and collect your things? You might as well come back to Stamford with me now." He signaled the waitress for her check.

Susan was a little nonplussed. She had been making her own decisions for so long now, it was a little bewildering to have someone move in so efficiently. It was also, she thought a little wryly as he paid her bill and pulled out her chair, rather pleasant. She wouldn't at all mind being bossed about for a while. She was very weary of managing on her own. Nevertheless, she said firmly, as they stepped out into the heat of the city street, "I have to go talk to the people in the agency first. They've been very good to me."

"Do you want to go now?"

"Yes."

"Very well," he said, and, putting a hand on her back, guided her toward a forest-green Mercedes. "I'll come with you. I don't want anyone trying to change your mind."

God, Susan thought, what were they going to think at the agency when she turned up with Rick Montoya? It really would be easier if he stayed in the car. She glanced sideways at the set of his mouth and decided not to argue. She didn't have the energy. "What is the address?" he asked, and she gave it to him.

Chapter Three

The following week was one of the most stressful and unsettling times in Susan's entire life. It started with the ride to Stamford in Ricardo's car. They had left Susan's old Volkswagen behind; Ricardo assured her easily that he would have someone pick it up.

"What are we going to tell people?" she asked him as she sat back against the comfortable beige upholstery of the Mercedes.

He flicked a glance at her before he went back to watching the road. "What do you mean?"

She felt horribly embarrassed. "I don't want people to know the truth," she said unhappily. "Couldn't we say we've known each other for a while?"

"Oh, I see." A faint smile touched his mouth. "I don't see why we couldn't say that, *querida*. We'll say we met in the autumn and quarreled in January. All the rest can be the truth—your keeping the news of your pregnancy secret and so forth."

"Yes, I suppose that would do." She felt her cheeks grow hot. "What are people going to *think* of me?"

He chuckled. "People will think very well of us. After all, we're doing the proper thing."

"They will think well of *you* for making an honest

woman of me. They won't think so well of me, I'm afraid."

He shrugged. "It is not important what other people think." He glanced at her again, his eyes warm and bright in the late sunshine. "*I* know what kind of woman you are, *querida*. That is all that matters."

Susan felt a sudden flash of gratitude. After all, he had never even questioned whether or not this baby was his. She wondered how many other men would have behaved so gracefully under the present circumstances. She sighed a little and he reached out to cover her small hand with his strong, warm one. "Don't worry," he said easily. "It will all work out."

They were married four days later in Stamford. Joe Hutchinson, the second baseman on Ricardo's team, and Maggie Ellis, Susan's closest friend, stood up for them. It was accomplished very quietly, with absolutely no press leaks, and the only other person present in the church was Mrs. Morgan.

Susan had been extremely apprehensive about breaking the news to her mother, but the reality had not proved as dreadful as her imagination had predicted. Mrs. Morgan was visibly shocked by the sight of her pregnant daughter, but Ricardo had taken charge, and almost before she realized what was happening, Susan found herself sitting on the porch while her mother served them lemonade.

"It was a foolish quarrel," Ricardo was saying gravely. "And it was very wrong of Susan not to have contacted me when she knew she was to have a child." He gave her a reproachful look and sipped his lemonade. "But now we are reconciled and all will be well." He looked serenely at Susan's mother out of large dark eyes. "May I have some more lemonade? It's very good."

"Of course," Mrs. Morgan moved to rise but Susan forestalled her.

"I'll get it, Mother," she said hastily, and disappeared in the direction of the kitchen. When she returned, after a rather longer time than was necessary, Ricardo and her mother were talking comfortably about South America. Both Susan's parents had been anthropologists and when she was a child they had periodically disappeared for stretches of a year at a time into the jungles of the Amazon.

"I have never been to the Brazilian jungle," Ricardo said as Susan settled down again into her chair. He had accepted his drink with a perfunctory smile. He's used to being waited on, she thought, as she sat back and prepared to listen.

The discussion was pleasant and civilized, and from the way her mother looked at him, Susan realized that Ricardo knew what he was talking about. When they left he gave Mrs. Morgan a smile that visibly moved her. Susan was beginning to suspect that he got a lot of mileage out of that beguiling grin.

"Mother liked Ricardo," she wrote in her journal that evening. She had been keeping it ever since she was sixteen, as a way of sifting through, assimilating and comprehending the raw material of her life. And life for Susan, daughter of two educated and brilliant super-achievers, had never been easy. She loved her parents dearly, she had admired and adored her elder sister Sara, but she was different from the rest of the family, slower, more introspective, more deeply feeling. The journal had become essential to the daily routine of her life.

She looked now at the sentence she had written and then added, "and what is perhaps more surprising, she was impressed by him. There is an extraordinary quality about him that goes beyond his looks. He simply sat there on our porch, drinking lemonade and wearing perfectly ordinary-looking clothes, and one somehow had the impression that he was conferring an honor on us by his very presence." She frowned a little as she thought. "It's not that he's conceited," she wrote then. "He's not. But he has—perhaps presence is the best word for it. Whatever it is, it did a job on Mother. She's coming to the wedding and she never even objected when she learned her Protestant Yankee daughter was going to be married by a Catholic priest. I suppose the fact that said Protestant daughter is also seven months pregnant had a lot to do with her compliance."

Susan put down her pen and looked out the window of her bedroom. The stars were very bright in the moonless sky. Ricardo was playing a night game and wouldn't be home until after midnight. She thought now that it was odd she hadn't thought of staying with her mother until the wedding. Her mother hadn't suggested it either. They had both simply fallen in behind Ricardo like good soldiers, nodding yes to whatever he suggested.

Extraordinary, she thought, and yawned. She was very tired. She looked one more time at her diary entry and then closed the book. She got into the wide bed in the big bedroom Ricardo had given to her and tried to get comfortable. He hadn't even suggested that she share his room. The baby kicked, hard, and Susan smiled ruefully. In her present condition she was scarcely alluring, she thought. And then she fell asleep.

* * *

The wedding went very smoothly and afterward Ricardo took everyone out to lunch in a very expensive Greenwich restaurant. Then Joe Hutchinson, Maggie and Mrs. Morgan left and the new Mr. and Mrs. Montoya returned home. However, Ricardo only stopped long enough to drop Susan and change clothes. The Yankees were playing a twilight double header that evening at six. Ricardo had to be at the stadium by five. "Don't wait up for me," he told her pleasantly as he dropped a kiss on her cheek. "I'll be late."

"All right." She stood at the door as he walked toward the Mercedes he had left parked in the circular drive in front of the house. "Good luck!" she called, and he gave her a grin before he slid in behind the wheel.

Susan closed the door and slowly walked back to the living room. Maria, the Colombian maid who did the cooking and cleaning for Ricardo, had been given the afternoon off in honor of the wedding, and Susan was alone. She stood silently in the middle of the living room and stared at the lovely marble fireplace. This was "home." It didn't feel like home, was nothing at all like the comfortable old clapboard house she had grown up in, but she was going to have to grow accustomed to it, she told herself firmly. She looked carefully around the large, high-ceilinged room. It was lovely, she admitted. The molding and wainscoting were beautiful, as was the shining wood floor. It just was far more elegant than what she was accustomed to. Far more rich.

Ricardo's home was a stately Georgian colonial, built of brick and slate and set on a wooded couple of acres in north Stamford. He had bought it two years ago, he told her when she first arrived home with him, and his mother had furnished it for him. The furniture was not the style Susan would have chosen, but she found herself liking the carved Spanish pieces very much.

Perhaps it was a good sign: she would have something in common with the mother-in-law she had yet to meet. Ricardo's mother lived in Bogotá since his father's death and came north only once or twice a year to visit her son. Ricardo also had two sisters, both quite a bit older than he, and both married and living in Bogotá. "When the season's over we'll go visit them," he had told her casually.

"Ricardo, the baby is due in October," she protested.

"We'll go for Christmas, then, and bring him along. My mother will be thrilled. You know how women are about babies."

It was not a visit that Susan looked forward to. Ricardo's mother might be thrilled to see the baby, but Susan very much doubted if she'd be thrilled to see the bride her son had so hastily wedded.

Oh well, she thought, as she walked slowly about the downstairs rooms of her new home, no use borrowing trouble. I'll cross that bridge when I come to it. She passed through the large dining room, which also boasted a marble fireplace, and into the two rooms she was most familiar with: the breakfast room, where they ate their meals, and the family room with its lovely french doors leading out to the slate patio. "It's scarcely what one would call a starter home," she said out loud with a laugh of real amusement.

There was only one room on the first floor that she hadn't been in and that was the study. She walked in now and looked around slowly. The room was paneled and lined with bookshelves. Susan went over to one wall and looked at the titles; they were almost exclusively nonfiction. There were a number of books, both in Spanish and English, about Latin American politics. There were quite a lot of books on sports; not just baseball but soccer, tennis, golf and skiing. There was an Encyclopedia Americana and a full set of Sherlock Holmes. There was a small assortment of best-selling thriller-type novels. My God, thought Susan. There is so much I don't know about him. She collapsed heavily into a comfortable leather armchair and stared at a photograph of Ricardo that was hanging on the wall. It looked as if it were a newspaper photo that had been blown up and framed. It showed what was clearly a moment of victory; the three men in the picture were all laughing and one of them was pouring a bottle of champagne over Ricardo's head. His face, dark, vibrant, filled with triumph, was the dominant point of the photograph. Susan looked at that thoroughly male picture and inwardly she quaked.

How on earth were they going to build a marriage, she thought almost despairingly. If she had searched the earth over, it would have been impossible for her to find a person so utterly opposite to her. She was quiet and introspective, reserved and shy. That night in the blizzard had been completely out of character for her.

She thought of that night now and wondered with deep bewilderment how she had ever come to behave as she had. Over the last months it had become only a hazy memory, a dizzy recollection of warmth and smoke and the deep timbre of a man's voice. Her body heavy now with child, her senses dulled by advanced pregnancy, she couldn't begin to understand what had possessed her.

It was because of that night, however, that she was here, in the home of Ricardo Montoya, a man whose way of thinking and looking and relating to things was completely opposed to hers. It was frightening.

She left the library and went upstairs. There were five bedrooms on the second floor, each with its own bathroom. Susan had been using the one next to Ricardo's and now she hesitated and went into the empty room that belonged to her husband. She had peeked into it swiftly during the tour of the house he took her on when first she arrived, but now she looked around more carefully.

It was a thoroughly masculine room, with large oak furniture and colorful woven material on the bed and at the windows. An oil painting hung on the wall facing the bed, a picture of a house nestled among high, green mountains and very blue sky.

There was a clutter of loose change and papers on the dresser, and on the floor, in front of the closet, lay the suit that Ricardo had just taken off. His socks and shoes were on the floor in front of the big upholstered chair. Susan, who was innately tidy, bent awkwardly to pick up the clothes. They were all creased from lying in a heap. He might have hung them up, she thought irritably. Now they would have to be sent out to the cleaners. She folded the clothes neatly and laid them on the bed. There was a book on the night table and she went to look at it. *Report on El Salvador,* she read. She picked it up, read the cover and then replaced it on the table. She looked one more time around the large, sunny room and then went next door to her own bedroom.

There was a large mirror hanging over the dresser in this room and Susan walked over to look in it. "Some bride," she said ironically as she regarded her own reflection.

She actually looked very nice. Her skin had tanned to a pale honey from sitting out in Elaine's small yard and her shimmering light brown hair framed a face that had filled out a little with imminent motherhood. She looked, Susan thought, disgustingly healthy. But not even the expensive pale pink suit her mother had bought her could disguise her advanced pregnancy.

Susan kicked off her shoes and sighed with relief to stand barefoot again. She felt so small in comparison to Ricardo that she had bought much higher heels than she was accustomed to wearing. She took off her suit and hung it carefully in the closet. Then, wearing only her slip, she went over to the bed and lay down. There was a lovely breeze coming in the open window and she suddenly felt very tired. In two minutes Susan was asleep.

When she awoke it was dark and she was feeling hungry. She showered, put on a smocked sun dress and thongs and went downstairs to the kitchen. She made herself a sandwich and then went into the family room and switched on the television. She looked at her watch. It was almost nine o'clock. The second game of the doubleheader should still be on.

It was the first time Susan had ever watched Ricardo play. Baseball had not been a sport anyone in her family ever watched and she was entirely unfamiliar with the routine of major league ball. She knew the basic rules of the game, had learned them almost by osmosis as does every American child, but the names and the tactics and the teams and the rivalries—all of these had remained obscure. She had refrained scrupulously from watching Ricardo before now; it had been almost a superstition that she should not allow him to come even that close to her. But now she sat back, munched her sandwich and prepared to watch.

It took her awhile to sort out what was happening. It took her awhile as well to sort out the strange feeling she had whenever Ricardo appeared on the screen, swinging a bat, looking relaxed and confident and surprisingly graceful.

"Montoya's the key to the pennant," the announcer was saying. "As long as he stays healthy, the Yankees are practically unbeatable."

"It's his consistency that's so amazing," another voice put in. "Day in, day out, always the same. It's pulled the club together, that evenness, that reliability."

"Yep. George was saying the other day that he doesn't grudge Rick a penny of what he's paying him."

The pitcher was peering in at the plate now and then began his windup. The ball was released and Susan watched in horror as Ricardo flung himself to the ground. She pressed her hand to her stomach and held her breath as he climbed slowly to his feet. He signaled to the bench that he was all right and began to dust his clothes. The entire stadium was roaring its disapproval at the pitcher. Ricardo looked perfectly calm.

"Carter doesn't want Rick to crowd the plate," commented the announcer. "He's moved him back a step with that pitch."

The pitcher went into his windup once more. Ricardo swung, a smooth, almost elegant motion, and there was the sound of a sharp *crack*.

"That's it!" the announcer cried jubilantly. "That one's gone." Ricardo began to jog around the bases, seemingly oblivious to the uproar of hysteria that had filled the huge stadium. When he crossed home plate there was a lineup of teammates to meet him. He shook hands, grinning that now familiar irresistible grin, and then he tipped his hat at the crowd. He never once glanced at Ben Carter, who was standing on the mound looking extremely unhappy.

"That'll be the last time Carter tries to brush Montoya back," the announcer said with a chuckle.

"Rick *does* have a way about him," the other voice said. "And now here's Price. The score is two–nothing, Yankees."

Susan sat through the remainder of the game, becoming increasingly fascinated. It was such an orderly sport, she thought; there was something very satisfying about the precision of all its movements, the way each man functioned individually yet as part of the whole. She watched the way the infield shifted as one to accommodate the different players. She watched the way Joe Hutchinson stepped out of the way to allow Ricardo, the center fielder, to take a high fly ball unimpeded. She watched the swiftness and precision of the Yankee infield effortlessly executing a double play from third to second to first. It was, she thought, an immensely satisfying spectacle. She had always understood the satisfaction of playing a sport. Now for the first time she was beginning to appreciate the pleasures of watching.

After the game was over Susan went upstairs and wrote in her journal for over an hour. When she finally put down her pen she went over to the window and looked out. There was no sign of Ricardo. She began to feel sorry for herself. This was certainly not the wedding night every young girl dreams of. She was very lonely.

As she was leaning forward to pull down the shade

the lights of a car lit up the drive. Ricardo was home. For some inexplicable reason, Susan began to feel apprehensive. She stayed sitting at the desk, immovable, until she heard the sound of his feet on the stairs. The footsteps stopped outside her door.

He must have seen that her light was on for he called softly, "Susan? Are you still awake?"

"Yes," she called back. Her voice sounded strange and she cleared her throat.

Her door opened and he stood on the threshold. She noticed a little nervously how wide his shoulders were. "Will you make me a sandwich?" he asked. "I'm starving."

Quite suddenly she relaxed. "Of course I will," she said, and smiled at him. "Haven't you eaten since lunch?" she asked as they walked down the stairs.

"No. I don't like to play on a full stomach." He seated himself comfortably at the kitchen table and watched her cut up some cold chicken.

"I watched the game," she said as she put the sandwich in front of him. "What would you like to drink?"

"Milk, please." He took a bite and chewed. "I didn't think you watched baseball."

"I haven't—until now." She put two glasses of milk on the table and sat down herself. "Why did that pitcher throw that ball at you? The announcer seemed to think it was deliberate."

"It was." He swallowed some milk, looked at her expression and chuckled. "Don't look so horrified, *querida*. Baseball is a constant war between the pitcher and the batter and one of the battles is over who has control of the plate. The batter likes to get close because it makes life more difficult for the pitcher. When the batter gets too close, however, the pitcher has to try to move him back."

"By throwing the ball at him?"

"Well, that is one way."

Susan drank some milk. "That was when you hit a home run," she said.

He raised a black eyebrow. "I do not like having a ninety mile per hour fastball thrown at my head."

"I should think not," she replied fervently.

They sat for a few more minutes in silence as Ricardo finished his sandwich. Then Susan said, "Did you ever think that this was how you'd be spending your wedding night?"

He laughed, his teeth very white in his tanned face. "No. But I'm not complaining." He finished his milk. "Are there any cookies?"

She got out some cookies for him and refilled his glass. He looked up and caught her gaze. "We are not exactly a romantic duo, are we?" he asked humorously.

Susan's face suddenly lit with laughter. "No, we're not." She laid her hand on the pronounced curve of her stomach.

His eyes followed her hand. "You are carrying my child. You've fed me and listened to me." His dark eyes held twin devils in their depths. "The rest can wait," he said.

Susan felt her breath catch in her throat and her body tensed. Then he leaned back in his chair and stretched. "Come," he said. "It's late and I've kept you up too long." She started to tidy up and he made an impatient gesture. "Leave it. Maria will clean up in the morning." He held the kitchen door for her. "Your job, *querida*," he said as they went up the stairs, "is to take good care of my son."

Chapter Four

Susan's baby was born on the day the Yankees won the American League Pennant. Ricardo took her to the hospital at five in the afternoon and then left for the stadium. She didn't see him again until five in the morning, after the baby had been born.

It had been a long, painful and lonely labor. There were two other women in the labor room with her and both had been panting and puffing in great Lamaze style with supportive husbands at their sides. Susan had suffered in silence and alone.

Ricardo had never even suggested that he might be present when the baby was born. The thought, she had come to realize, simply never crossed his mind. Childbirth, in his view, was woman's work. After two months she had come to learn a few things about the man she had married and one thing had become increasingly clear. He was *not* a liberated male.

He must have been waiting at the hospital, though, because he came into see her as soon as she was brought back from the delivery room. He came across to the bed immediately and picked up her hand. "How are you feeling, *querida*?" he asked softly.

"Tired." She gazed up at him gravely. His hair was

tousled and the shadow of his beard was dark and rough. He looked tired, too, she thought.

"It took a long time," he said.

"You're telling me," she answered, and at that he smiled at her, not the quick irrepressible grin that so beguiled strangers but a slow, warm intimate smile that lit his extraordinary eyes as if from within. Her own face softened and for a brief moment the weariness disappeared. She smiled back, a bewitchingly beautiful smile. "Have you seen him yet?" she asked.

"No. I'll stop by the nursery on my way out. I wanted to see you first." Susan felt an unaccountable stab of joy when he said those words. "The doctor wanted me to come into the delivery room," he was going on, a note of horror in his voice. "Can you imagine? He seemed very put out when I said no."

The look on his face made her giggle. "A lot of husbands do, you know."

"A lot of husbands are crazy," he said firmly. He bent to kiss her gently. "Get some rest, *querida*. I'll see you later."

He had reached the door before she thought to call, "Did you win?"

"What? Oh." He turned and grinned. "We did, one to nothing. I hit a home run. Good night, Susan."

"Good night, Ricardo," she answered softly, and looked for a long time at the empty doorway before she closed her eyes and fell asleep.

Two days after his son was born, Ricardo flew to Los Angeles for the opening game of the World Series. Susan watched the game on TV in her hospital room. The Yankees lost, 5-4, in extra innings. Ricardo had singled twice and doubled.

The next day Mrs. Morgan came down to Stamford and brought Susan and the baby home from the hospital. She was clearly entranced by her grandson and talked enthusiastically about the play-offs and last night's game. Susan stared at her mother in astonishment. To her knowledge, Mrs. Morgan had never watched a baseball game in her life.

Maria, Ricardo's maid, was almost as ecstatic about the baby as his grandmother, and before she could say a word, Susan found herself being tucked up in bed while her son was kept downstairs in his port-a-crib, vigilantly guarded by two doting would-be nannies. At first she was a little annoyed—he was *her* son, after all. But then her sense of humor reasserted itself. She'd get him back fast enough when he was hungry. In that respect, he was remarkably like his father!

The Yankees lost the second game in Los Angeles as well, 4-3, after holding a 3-1 lead until the ninth inning. The game was over at eleven p.m. Los Angeles time, and immediately afterward the team got a plane back to New York. Consequently, Ricardo arrived home at ten o'clock the following morning without having been to bed. Susan was bathing the baby in the sunny bedroom she had made into a nursery when he walked in the door. He stood for a minute in silence, watching her deft, gentle hands manipulate the squalling infant. Then, although he had made no sound, her head swung around and she saw him. Her gray eyes widened. "Ricardo! You're back."

"I'm back." He came into the room and regarded his son in some astonishment.

Susan laughed. "He's not overly fond of water." She scooped the baby up, wrapped him in a hooded towel and handed him to his father.

"Dios!" said Ricardo, startled and clearly uneasy. "He's awfully small."

"Actually, he's rather large. Nine pounds, as I remember to my sorrow."

Ricardo began to rock the baby and the crying stopped. His eyes sparkled as he looked at Susan. "I think I am a natural," he said. He looked so extremely proud of himself that Susan had to stifle a giggle.

"Make sure you support his head," she said. "Here. Like this." Ricardo's strong brown hand was larger than the baby's head but he was cradling the child with instinctive tenderness. Susan felt her eyes mist over and she blinked hard. "Say hello to your father," he was saying to the small face of his son, and Susan had to blink again.

Ricardo slept for a few hours and then in the afternoon he raked some leaves. "I'll have to have a pool put in," he said over dinner. "I never did before because I was gone half the time and there was no one to look after it."

Susan felt a flash of irritation. "And now you have a wife to take care of it for you."

"Yes." He smiled at her serenely. "Wouldn't you like a pool?"

She would, of course. She just didn't like to be regarded in such a utilitarian manner. "Yes," she said a little unwillingly. "I suppose a pool would be nice."

"I'll see about it."

"All right." She hoped, belatedly, that she had not sounded sulky.

They went to bed early, as both of them were decidedly short of sleep. Susan had the baby in a bassinet in her room so she could hear him when he awoke, which he did promptly at midnight. She picked him up and was preparing to sit down in the chair to nurse him when her door opened and Ricardo appeared. "What's the matter?" he asked. "I heard the baby crying."

Susan looked up at the tall figure of her husband. He was wearing only a pair of pajama bottoms and she stared for a moment in wonder at the great muscles of his chest and biceps and shoulders. She looked up further and met his eyes. Without her shoes, the top of her head reached barely to his shoulder. "He's hungry, that's all," she said in what she hoped was a calm voice. "He needs to nurse every four hours."

"Oh. I was afraid he was sick or something."

"No. It's nothing like that." She sat down in the chair and hesitated for a moment. He hadn't moved and she found herself reluctant to nurse the baby in front of him. Slowly she unbuttoned the front of her nightgown and put the baby to her breast. The crying stopped instantly. She glanced at Ricardo. He was staring at his son, looking absolutely fascinated. "You'd better get some sleep," she said. "You have a game this afternoon."

"That's true." He moved to the door with obvious reluctance. "Good night, *querida*."

"Good night," she answered softly.

The Yankees opened in New York at two o'clock that afternoon, two games down in a series where one team had to win four games in order to take the championship. It was essential, Ricardo had told Susan, that they win all three games in their home ball park. The last two games would be played at Dodger Stadium in Los Angeles.

The baby was sleeping peacefully when Susan and

Maria Martinez sat down in front of the TV. The stadium was packed with over sixty thousand fans, the announcer informed them. As the camera panned around the park all one could see was an unending sea of faces: old and young, male and female, rich and poor, all smiling and waving and brandishing signs.

The Dodger team was introduced first, drawing mixed applause and boos from the New York fans. Then it was the turn of the home team. "Batting first and playing second base, Joe Hutchinson," the loudspeaker boomed. Applause swept over the ball park as the first three men came out of the dugout and onto the grass. Then, "Batting fourth and playing center field," the announcer said and a roar went up from sixty-thousand throats. *"Rick Montoya,"* the announcer shouted into the microphone, and Susan watched her husband jog onto the field and shake the hands of his teammates. The uproar showed absolutely no signs of subsiding and Ricardo tipped his cap in acknowledgment. Good God, Susan thought in stunned amazement, I had no idea it would be like this.

The crowd finally quieted enough for the rest of the team to be introduced and then the Yankees took the field and a famous opera singer sang "The Star Spangled Banner." An illustrious old Yankee player threw out the first ball and the game began.

It was the kind of game baseball fanatics dream of. The lead changed hands twice, and going into the ninth inning the score was six–five, Yankees. The first Dodger up hit a home run and the score was tied. The next man singled and the Yankee manager brought in a new pitcher. The next two men flied out and then Frank Revere stepped up to the plate. Revere had forty home runs to his credit during the regular season and with the *crack* sound of the bat on the first pitch, Susan thought he had notched forty-one.

Then the camera picked up Ricardo in center field. He was back against the wall and at the very last instant he leaped, impossibly, dangerously high, and the ball landed in the webbing of his glove. The ball park exploded into pandemonium.

"What a catch!" the announcer was shrieking over the bedlam. "I don't believe I saw that!"

"I don't believe it either," Susan said a little numbly. Maria was screaming at the television is Spanish and Susan turned to her with a grin. "Ditto for me," she said, and laughed.

The Yankees came to the plate in the bottom of the ninth with the score tied. The leadoff man singled, but then Buddy Moran hit a hard line drive right at the first baseman and the Dodgers made a double play. When Ricardo walked up to the plate, Susan thought the stadium had gone mad. Her palms and her forehead were damp with sweat. My God, she thought, how is it possible for anyone to perform under that kind of pressure? Her stomach heaved and she felt slightly sick.

Ricardo swung his bat with the even, elegant, iron-wristed swing that had become so familiar to her over the last two months. He looked intent and very serious in the close-up camera shot. Knocking the dirt out of his spikes, he stepped up to the plate.

The count ran out to 3 and 2 and Susan's feeling of nausea increased uncomfortably. I can't stand this, she was thinking as the pitcher went into his windup. Ricardo swung.

"That's it!" the announcer shouted. "That's the ball game!"

And indeed it was. As sixty-thousand hysterical and delirious fans pounded each other on the back and threw things onto the field in their ecstasy, Ricardo jogged around the bases, a huge grin on his face. There had never been any doubt about that ball being caught; it had landed far back in the upper left-field grandstand.

The Yankees won the next two games in New York as well and then they returned to Los Angeles, ahead of the Dodgers three games to two. Susan felt that her whole life was divided between taking care of the baby and watching baseball. One of the things that struck her as she watched the games was the way the television camera would zero in on the faces of the players' wives. She was very glad she had the excuse of a nursing infant to keep from attending in person. She would hate to be singled out like that, broadcasted and exposed. It was bad enough watching at home.

They lost the first game in Los Angeles, 7-6. In the second game, the game on which the championship depended, the score was tied in the ninth, 4-4, and the game went into extra innings. The Yankees' relief pitcher, Sal Fatato, got into trouble in the bottom of the tenth inning and only got out of it when Ricardo threw a perfect strike all the way from center field to cut down Frank Revere. In the top of the eleventh, Joe Hutchinson singled, moved to second on a sacrifice and Ricardo doubled him home. The Yankees were the new World Champions.

"This World Series was finally won," wrote noted sports columnist Frank Winter in the *New York Times* the next day, "by the hitting, the throwing, the fielding, the sheer blazing brilliance of Rick Montoya. Rarely has a World Series Most Valuable Player Award been more thoroughly deserved."

"Congratulations," Susan said when Ricardo arrived home the following day. "I almost had heart failure half a dozen times and Maria was even worse. Couldn't you have won in a less *dramatic* fashion?"

He grinned. "It wouldn't have been as much fun."

"Fun," Susan said faintly. She thought of the dreadful pressure of all those screaming fans. "You call that fun?"

"Absolutely."

"Oh, Señor Montoya," came a high-pitched voice from behind Susan, and Ricardo laughed.

"Oh, Maria," he mimicked, and catching her in his arms, he kissed her soundly. Maria's worn face glowed with pleasure. Ricardo had not kissed his wife.

"Where's my son?" he asked.

"Upstairs asleep," she answered slowly.

"I won't wake him, then." He took off his jacket and threw it on a chair. Maria hurried to pick it up. "Did the paper come?" he asked.

"*Sí*, Señor Montoya." Maria picked the *Times* up from a table and handed it to him. Ricardo sat down in a comfortable chair, stretched his long legs in front of him and opened the paper. "I'll have some coffee," he said from behind the sports page.

"*Sí*, Señor Montoya," said Maria again, and disappeared in the direction of the kitchen.

Susan stood in the middle of the room and stared at the paper that concealed her husband. The baseball season was over, she thought, and here he was—home until spring. Maria returned with the coffee, which she set on a table at his elbow. He grunted a thank you. Quite suddenly she was furious.

"Perhaps if I knelt down in front of you, you could rest your feet on my back," she said in a voice she had never used with him.

He lowered his paper and stared at her in astonishment. "What did you say, *querida*?"

"You heard me." She stared back at him steadily, clear gray eyes like slate under the surprisingly dark and level brows.

"But why are you angry?" he asked in genuine bewilderment.

"You're so wonderful," she said acidly. "You figure it out." And she stalked from the room.

Chapter Five

A week after the World Series was won, the Yankees' owner threw a dinner party for his team. It was held at a very elegant New York hotel and Ricardo told Susan he expected her to attend with him.

"But I can't leave the baby," she protested feebly.

"Nonsense. Maria will stay with him for the evening. I'll drive her home when we get back."

"But what if he gets hungry?"

"He can drink a bottle. Or he can wait." He cocked an eyebrow. "You don't want me to invite someone else, do you, *querida*?"

Susan lifted her chin. "I'll come," she said.

"Good." He smiled at her engagingly, willing her to be pleased. "You'll have a good time. You need to get out more."

It wasn't that she wouldn't enjoy going out to dinner, Susan thought as she went through her wardrobe in search of something to wear. It was just that she quailed at the thought of meeting all those people who knew, who *had* to know, that she and Ricardo had been married only two months before Ricky was born.

She closed the closet door on her schoolgirl clothes and went over to look down into the bassinet at her sleeping son. Ricky's face, she thought with a flicker of extreme tenderness, was the surest proof of his paternity. He was a miniature of his father. Not that Ricardo had ever, in any way at all, even hinted that he might wonder if the baby she had been carrying was really his. She had always felt immensely grateful to him for that trust. She still did. It was one of the things she always remembered when she found his lordly masculinity getting on her nerves. He had believed her word, and on the basis of that word he had married her. She doubted there were many men—particularly men in his position—who would have done the same.

She settled a light cover on her sleeping son and sighed. She would have to buy a dress. And have Sara's black coat altered. Her old camel hair would not do for the St. Regis. She was going to have to talk to Ricardo about money.

Ever since she had come to live with him, Ricardo had continued the same financial arrangements he had always had. He gave Maria a housekeeping allowance and out of it she bought the groceries and took care of the laundry and the dry cleaning. Over and above that, of course, she got her salary. A salary that was extremely generous, Susan realized, when Maria told her what it amounted to. Ricardo had also bought his housekeeper a car so she could drive from her home in Norwalk to his in Stamford and so that she could do the errands. Maria thought that God was simply another name for Ricardo.

He certainly had never grudged his wife money either, but Susan didn't enjoy playing the beggar maid to his King Cophetua. The purchases she had made—which consisted mainly of furniture and clothing for the baby—he had agreed to immediately and generously. "How much do you want, *querida*?" he would say, and unhesitatingly hand over to her the amount she requested. The problem was, she hated having to ask.

She hated having to talk to him about this, too, but it was going to have to be done. She arrived downstairs just as he was coming in from raking leaves. "*Dios!*" he said to her humorously. "I think half the leaves in Connecticut have found a home in my yard. The more I rake, the more leaves there seem to be. At least I can dump them in the woods. I'd hate to have to bag them all."

"We used to burn them," Susan said nostalgically. "I loved the smell of leaves burning in the fall. It seemed like such a big part of the season."

"Well, if I burn them now I will get a summons," Ricardo said practically. He took off his down vest and dropped it on a chair.

"Ricardo," Susan said with exemplary patience, "there is a closet right behind you. Do you think you could hang that up?"

He looked surprised. "It doesn't go in that closet," he said simply. "It goes upstairs."

There was a short silence and then Susan decided to fight this particular battle another day. She cleared her throat. "I have to talk to you, Ricardo. Could we sit down for a minute, please?"

"Of course." He followed her into the family room. There was a chill in the air and he said, "I think we could use a fire."

She sat down on the sofa and watched as he expertly stacked wood in the stone fireplace. The shoulders under his plaid flannel shirt looked so wide, so strong, so—impervious. Could she possibly make him understand how she felt? He sat back on his heels and watched as the fire grew. Then he turned and looked at her. "So?" he said. "What do you want to talk to me about?"

"Well—I need a dress for the dinner on Saturday, for one thing," she began.

"Naturally." He sounded surprised that she should need to mention this obvious fact.

"Ricardo," and now her voice began to sound tense, "can't you see that I hate to have to come and ask you every time I need money? It isn't that you aren't generous—you're only too generous—it's just that, well, it's just that I hate it." She looked at him a little desperately, a mute appeal in her large gray eyes.

He looked back at her and his own face became very grave. "Susan," he said, "forgive me. Of course you should not have to come and ask me for every penny. I am sorry. I should have made you an allowance long ago." He gave her a faintly rueful, utterly charming look. "I was preoccupied with other things," he said. "Shall I give you a monthly allowance for you and for Ricky? How about . . ." and he named a sum that made her blink.

And that was it. It had been so easy. He had, surprisingly, understood. "Thank you, Ricardo," she said a little breathlessly. "Honestly, I don't mean to be a millstone around your neck forever, but I am rather tied down with the baby at present. I just don't think I can get a job right now."

"A job!" He looked utterly thunderstruck. "What are you talking about, Susan? You are not a millstone around my neck. You are my wife. The mother of my son. Of course I expect to support you. I won't hear of you getting a job."

She stared back at him, startled by his vehemence, even more startled by his point of view. Her own mother had always worked outside the home. She herself had always assumed that was what educated women did. "Not now, of course, while Ricky is still little," she began tentatively.

"Not now, not ever," he said firmly. "You have a job. You are a wife and a mother. You are a very good mother, *querida*. I always knew you would be. And we will have more children. You'll be busy enough, I promise you."

Susan felt her heart lurch a little at that mention of more children. She ran her tongue around suddenly dry lips. "Ricardo." She spoke very gently, very carefully, "I am twenty-two years old. I have a college degree. I had—I have—plans for my life that involve something more than being just a housewife."

Ricardo's mouth set in a line that was not at all gentle. "And what are these plans?" he asked in an abrupt, hard voice.

"Well," said Susan weakly, pushed to the wall and forced to admit out loud and to someone else what she had scarcely dared admit to herself, "I've always wanted to be a writer."

The set of his mouth got even grimmer. "On a newspaper?"

"No. Oh, no. I've wanted to write—novels." The last word came out as barely a whisper. She was desperately afraid that he would laugh.

His face relaxed but he did not laugh. "Oh novels," he said. He smiled at her, his good humor restored. "I have no objection to your writing novels, *querida*. That is something you can easily do at home."

"Yes, I suppose I could," she said slowly.

"We even have a library for you to work in," he said magnanimously.

She stared at his splendid dark face. He was humoring her, she thought. He did not take her at all seriously. "Thank you," she said, her voice expressionless.

"Not at all." He waved his hand in a gesture of magnificent dismissal. "And what is all this foolishness about being 'just a housewife.' You aren't a housewife, you're *my* wife." His eyes glinted at her and his voice became softer. "I realize we have been somewhat delayed in starting a normal married life." he went on, "but that should be over with soon. When do you see the doctor again?"

She could hear her heart hammering way up into her head. "In three weeks," she got out.

"So long. Ah well." He leaned back in the armchair and closed his eyes. "I've waited this long. I suppose another three weeks won't kill me." There was absolute silence in the room. Susan couldn't think of a thing to say. He opened his eyes a slit. "I'm thirsty after all that raking. Could you get me something to drink?"

It was definitely not the time to take up a feminist stance. Susan stood up. "What do you want?"

"Some ginger ale would be nice."

She nodded and left the room, shaking her head ruefully.

The dinner party turned out to be a very enjoyable evening. Susan had bought a pale gold dinner dress in Bloomingdale's and was conscious of looking really smart for the first time in almost a year. Her shining, fawn-colored hair, so fine that it wouldn't hold a curl, fell, sheer and glistening to her shoulders. She wore high-heeled gold sandals and Sara's black coat and she felt pretty as well as smart. It didn't hurt either, she thought as they went in through the doors of the hotel, to have an escort as impressive-looking as Ricardo. Even if he had never played baseball in his life, his tall, broad-shouldered figure would have commanded attention.

It was the first time that Susan had ever met any of Ricardo's teammates, with the exception of Joe Hutchinson, and it was fun actually seeing in person the people she had been watching so assiduously on TV. They sat at a table with Joe Hutchinson, Bert Diaz, Carl Seelinger and their wives. The conversation, after the first few minutes, drifted away from baseball and Susan found herself talking to the quiet, shy wife of Bert Diaz. Sonia Diaz's English was halting, so Susan, who had been getting in a lot of practice with Maria, spoke with her in Spanish. The Diazes had a six-month-old daughter, and the two women happily talked babies during the appetizer and soup courses. Susan's attention was wrested from this fascinating topic, however, when she heard Carl Seelinger ask Ricardo, "And what are you going to do this winter, Rick? If you do any more skiing, George will have a heart attack. He does not want you reporting to spring training with a broken leg."

Ricardo looked amused. "George is a worry wart." He sipped his wine. "We'll be leaving for Bogotá before long. I don't want to delay Ricky's christening forever and my mother and sisters are dying to see him."

"Are you having the baby christened in Colombia, Rick?" asked Jane Hutchinson.

"Of course. That's where my family is."

All of this was news to Susan. They hadn't even discussed the subject of Ricky's baptism. Susan had assumed that Ricardo would want him baptized Catholic and she didn't plan to object. She herself was Congregational, but her family had never been churchgoers.

She hadn't noticed that Ricardo was much of a church-goer, either, but he had made a point of their being married by a priest.

He might also have made a point of discussing his plans with her, she thought now as she watched his oblivious profile. Her chest felt tight, the way it always did when she was upset. "You never told me we were taking Ricky to Colombia," she said in a low voice to him a little later in the meal.

He looked surprised. "Of course I did, *querida*. I said we would go to Bogotá for Christmas. Don't you remember?"

"For Christmas. Not for a christening."

He shrugged and gave her his charming, boyish smile. She was getting to know his expressions very well. This one meant, Oh well, I didn't think it was important, but if you want to make an issue of it, I'll humor you. "I didn't think it mattered to you," he said patiently. "Would you like your mother to be there? I'll give her airplane tickets."

That wasn't the issue at all. The issue was that she wanted to be consulted before plans were made that involved her and her baby. It wasn't that she objected to Ricardo's plan; she just wanted to be part of the decision-making process.

"That's not it," she said softly. "We'll talk about it later, at home."

He looked a little surprised but then his attention was claimed again by Jane Hutchinson. In a few minutes the conversation had become general.

"You're different from the girls Rick used to date," Bev Seelinger said to Susan as they freshened their makeup in the ladies' room after dinner. "Somehow I knew you would be."

Susan fought a brief battle with herself and lost. "What kind of girls did he date?" she asked.

"Oh, the tall, sultry model type. But I never for a minute thought he'd marry any of them. In fact, I sometimes wondered if he'd ever marry at all."

Susan put her comb down and looked curiously at her companion. "Why?"

"I don't know," the other woman answered slowly. She flashed Susan a quick grin. "It's not that he doesn't like women. God, when I remember how those model types used to be all over him." Bev frowned. "It's odd, now I come to think of it, that I never pictured him as married."

"Perhaps he was too much the playboy type," Susan said with an effort at lightness. She felt guilty discussing Ricardo like this. She felt almost that she was betraying his privacy. But she couldn't help herself. She knew so little, even now, about this man she had married.

"No," Bev was saying decisively. "That's not it. He certainly had a lot of girlfriends, and he certainly has a sex appeal that would knock over your eighty-year-old maiden aunt if he turned it on her, but that's not it. It's just that—somehow, one always sees Rick as essentially alone."

Susan stared at Bev's healthy, outdoor face. It was not the face of a deeply perceptive woman but, Susan suddenly realized, that was what she was. "Yes," she said softly after a minute, "I know what you mean."

Bev smiled at her gratefully. "I don't know what got me started on this topic. I hope you don't feel I've been out of line."

"No, of course I don't." Susan put her comb back in her purse. "Are you ready? Shall we go?"

Susan thought about what Bev had said as the evening progressed to after-dinner drinks and a three-piece band for dancing. As she had watched the World Series on TV and read the ecstatic press reports, she had tried to comprehend, to analyze, the astonishing popularity of her husband. It was not just his baseball talent—other men were equally talented, she thought. It was something about him, something inherent in his character, that made him what he was: Rick Montoya, American idol.

She watched him now, relaxed and laughing among his teammates, and even here he stood out. He was one of them but he was still, always and incontestably, his own man, invincibly private behind all the outward good cheer. Susan, always deeply sensitive to the vibrations of another spirit, had long apprehended this solitariness in her husband. It was the thing in him that most frustrated and fascinated her.

"Dance with me?" Ricardo's voice broke into her reverie and she looked up into his dark eyes.

"Of course."

He took her hand and they moved out onto the floor. The band was playing "Moon River," and Ricardo's arms came around her and held her close. She had not been this close to him since that night in the blizzard, the night Ricky had been conceived. His body felt so strong against hers, so big. The music was slow and dreamy and she relaxed against him, supple and light, following his slightest move effortlessly. When the song was over he looked down at her, his eyes warm and very dark. "That was nice," he said softly. She didn't answer and the band began another slow song. "Again?" he asked, and she nodded and moved back into his arms. "What a shame we have to wait three more weeks," he murmured against the silky softness of her hair. And at that moment, seduced by the intense magnetism of his nearness, Susan had to agree.

Chapter Six

"I don't know what's the matter with me," Susan wrote in her journal one evening two weeks after the dinner in New York, "But I can't seem to organize my life and get down to writing anything. There's no excuse, really. Maria does the housework and a great deal of the cooking. I only have the baby to deal with. But somehow there never seems to be any *time*."

She sighed and looked out the window. The main problem, she thought, was Ricardo. He had spent the last few weeks building shelves in the baby's room and he had had the foundation poured for an addition to the garage. He had come home a week ago with a new Volvo station wagon for her, which needed garage space as the present two-car garage housed Ricardo's Mercedes and the new sports car he had won as MVP of the World Series. When they got back from Bogotá he was going to have the new garage addition framed out and then he would finish it himself.

All of these were Ricardo's projects but they seemed to eat incessantly into Susan's time. He needed someone to hold his hammer, to hold a board straight, to run to the store for sandpaper. She had to drive the new Volvo over half of Connecticut before he was satisfied she was competent to handle it alone. She wondered sometimes if it wasn't his strategy to keep her so occupied that there wasn't room in her life for anything else.

"The problem is," she wrote reflectively, "that I don't feel confident enough to demand time for myself. Who am I to say I'm a writer? Who am I to say I need time away from my husband, my child? Who am I—a mediocre scholar, a shotgun wife—to make any kind of demand of Ricardo? And yet—I feel I *must* make it, that if I don't, I'll suffocate."

She was sitting at the desk in her bedroom and now the lights of a car caught her attention as they swung into the drive. Ricardo was home.

Ricardo was home and she would go downstairs to greet him, to ask him about his dinner, about his speech, about the people he had seen. He would smile at her good-naturedly; that famous ingratiating grin that had charmed millions, and shortly afterward she would go to bed in her own private room.

Next week, of course, she would see the doctor and all of that would change.

It frightened her, the prospect of sleeping with him again. He had seemed so confident these last two weeks, so toughly competent in all his undertakings, so calmly dominant where she was concerned. And yet he scarcely touched her, never kissed her. She didn't like to admit it, but she was afraid of him. She was afraid, inexplicably, of his maleness, his capability, his way of "dealing" with her. When the time came he would take her to bed with the same casual expertise with which he did everything else. He would impose his own implacable reality upon the hazy memory of that night in New Hampshire, and she was afraid he would destroy it. For some peculiar reason she was unable to associate the Ricardo she knew with the Ricardo of that night. They seemed two separate and distinct people. She felt as if she would be going to bed with a stranger.

"You're just fine, Mrs. Montoya," the doctor told her reassuringly. "You can resume sex without any problem. Would you like me to give you a prescription for birth-control pills?"

Susan said yes and then had the prescription filled before she drove home. She also stopped at Lord and Taylor and did a little shopping. Ricardo was speaking at a Little League sports dinner that evening and Susan wanted him to be gone before she arrived home, so she delayed for as long as she could.

She was successful; the sports car was gone when she peeked into the garage before going into the house. Maria was waiting, ready to go home, and Ricky was indignant because his dinner had been delayed.

It was a very long night. Susan fed Ricky and put him to bed, then, knowing it would be impossible for her to write, she switched on the TV. At eleven she fed Ricky once again, took a shower and got into bed. Her room seemed very large and very strange. They had moved the baby's crib into the nursery a few days ago and she was alone. She closed her eyes and tried to go to sleep, but all her muscles were tense with waiting. At twelve-thirty she heard the sound of Ricardo's car on the drive.

It seemed forever before his feet sounded on the stairs. Then the door to her room opened and closed and Ricardo was standing there, his shoulders against it, motionless in the dim glow from the night-light Susan kept burning so she could see if she had to get up with the baby. His face was shadowed and he did not speak—or maybe it was that she could not hear him above the thudding of her heart. Then he came across the room and stood, towering, next to the bed. He said her name.

"Yes?" She hoped, desperately, that she sounded sleepy. "What do you want, Ricardo?"

"Really, Susan, what a question." He sounded amused.

She was aware of him standing there with every pore of her body. "How was your dinner?" she asked, and sat up, pushing her hair out of her face.

"I don't want to talk about my dinner," he said softly, and sat down on the bed next to her. "How did your checkup go?"

"All right." Her voice sounded squeaky in her own ears. "He said I'm okay."

"Now that is very good news." He raised a hand and lifted the hair from her neck. "It's been a very long wait," he said, and let the pale silky strands slide through his fingers.

"Ricardo." She moistened her lips with her tongue. "It's been a long day and I'm tired. Perhaps we could wait. . . ."

Her voice trailed off. He was taking off his suit jacket and undoing his tie. "No, *querida*," he said. "We can't wait." He dropped the jacket and tie on the floor and started in on the buttons on his blue dress shirt. In a minute the shirt had followed the rest of his clothes to the floor.

"They'll get all wrinkled," Susan croaked out of a dry throat. His bare chest and shoulders looked enormous in the dim light of her bedroom.

"It doesn't matter," he answered impatiently, and began to unbuckle his belt. Susan shivered and dragged her eyes away from him. She was breathing very quickly.

I'm being stupid, she told herself. It will be wonderful, just as it was the first time. The bed creaked as it took the brunt of his weight and her eyes flew up to his face. For the first time he seemed to apprehend that something was wrong.

"Susan," he said. "*Querida.*" His voice was deep, caressing. "You aren't afraid of me?"

It was the voice of the blizzard. "Ricardo," she said uncertainly, and he answered, "Shh, little one. It will be all right." And he bent his head and kissed her.

It was an infinitely gentle kiss, infinitely sweet. After a moment he eased her back against the mattress and stretched out beside her, gathering her close against him. She remembered instantly the feel of his body and slowly her arms curved up to hold him. "Susan," he said in her ear. His mouth brushed her cheek, her temple. "*Dios*, but it has been a long wait."

She arched her head back to look up at him. "Did you mind?" she asked wonderingly.

He made a sound deep down in his throat. "I am a man," he said. "Of course I minded."

"Oh," breathed Susan, and then he kissed her again. Her lips softened under his and immediately the kiss became more forceful, his mouth opening hungrily on hers in an erotic demand she recognized and involuntarily surrendered to.

It was like nothing else in the world, the feel of Ricardo's rough callused hands, so incredibly sure and delicate on her body. She melted before the magic of it, opening for him as a flower opens to the warmth of the sun. He seemed to sense the magnitude of her surrender, for his gentle caresses became something more.

She had the dizzy feeling of being violently overthrown and mastered, and then, astonishing, her own passion came beating up, answering strongly to his, overwhelming and all-encompassing. When it was over they lay still, locked together, not ready yet to return to their separate identities.

It was he who spoke first. "Do you know why I never tried to see you after that night in New Hampshire?"

His breath lightly stirred the silky hair on her temple. His voice was so soft, so deep, it penetrated her nerves. "No," she answered on a bare breath of sound.

"It was because I didn't want to spoil the memory of that night, and I was afraid that if we met again it would never seem the same." He chuckled. "It was rather like something out of a medieval romance, you must admit: the night, the storm, the beautiful young virgin."

She had never suspected him capable of such profound romanticism. "I know," she whispered. "It was— you said it was magic."

"It was." He rubbed his cheek against her hair. "I expected you to turn into a unicorn the next morning and gallop off into the mountains."

She sighed. "And instead I turned into a very pregnant lady whom you had to marry."

"Well, let us say rather you turned into a very pregnant unicorn," he suggested, and she giggled. "But I'm not sorry we got married," he was going on. "Are you?"

She was acutely conscious of his nearness, his maleness, his power and strength. He was the biggest thing that had ever happened to her. She knew that and she knew, too, in a sudden flash of intuition, that he always would be. Nothing else in her life would ever measure up to the importance of Ricardo. "No," she said, low and steady, "no, I'm not sorry."

"Good." He burrowed comfortably deeper into the bed and in two minutes he was asleep. Susan lay awake for much much longer before she finally drifted into a dreamless slumber.

The next few weeks slipped by for Susan, heavy with the haze of sensual fulfillment. All the minor discontents and irritations of the past weeks seemed simply to vanish. Her world both expanded and contracted and that world consisted of just one thing: Ricardo. Even the baby became somehow an extension of her husband. All of Susan's intellectuality and feminism died, drowned in the absorbing, purely physical life she was leading. For the first time in her life she was profoundly conscious of the pleasures of being female. She wrote absolutely nothing.

"I got our tickets for Bogotá today," Ricardo said to her one evening in early December. They were sitting in the family room in front of the fire, Susan curled up on the sofa next to Ricardo, her head pillowed against the hardness of his shoulder. She stirred a little and looked up at him.

"What?"

"I got our tickets for Bogotá. We leave in four days."

She sat up and stared at him. The glow from the fire cast golden shadows on his warm olive skin and high cheekbones. "Four days?" she repeated.

"Um." He looked at her and quite suddenly frowned. "You did update your passport, as I asked?"

She had done that months ago. "Yes. But, Ricardo, four days! I have to pack and get Ricky ready . . . Ricky! He doesn't have a passport!"

"Oh yes, he does. I got him one a month ago."

"You got him one. . . . But when?"

He looked a little impatient. "I had the photographer come to the house. Don't you remember?"

"No." She was quite definite. "I do not remember."

He looked even more impatient. "Well, perhaps you weren't home. As a matter of fact, now that I think of it, you were out getting your hair cut."

She stared at him, utterly flabbergasted. "And you didn't even think to tell me?"

He shrugged. "I forgot." He raised an eyebrow. "But what is all this fuss, *querida*? Ricky has a passport. You have a passport. I am so important that I have *two* passports. You throw some clothes into a suitcase, and we go. Why are you upsetting yourself?"

She expelled her breath in a sound of mingled exasperation and defeat. "I don't know. I suppose it's utterly weird of me, but I *would* like to be kept a little more apprised of your plans for us, Ricardo."

He looked surprised. "Don't you want to go?"

"Of course I want to go." She looked up at his splendidly masculine face and surrendered. "Why do you have two passports?" she asked.

He smiled, irresistible and charming now that she had given way to him. "I have both a Colombian passport and an American passport. When I am traveling to Colombia I use one and when I am returning to the States I use the other."

"How convenient."

"Isn't it?" He looked down at her. "But then, I have always liked convenience. I find having a wife is very convenient. If I had known how much I would like it, I might have married years ago. Aren't you lucky I waited?" He picked up her hand, turned it slightly and kissed first her wrist and then her palm.

"You mightn't have found another wife quite as convenient as I am," she said very softly. The touch of his mouth was causing her heartbeat to accelerate.

"That is true." He shifted his grasp to her wrist and pulled her closer to him. "Let's make love right here, in front of the fire," he murmured.

Susan's eye's widened with surprise. "Here?"

"Here." He bent his head and began to kiss her, slowly, seekingly, erotically. He pressed her back against the cushions of the sofa and her hands came up to hold him. The muscles of his back and shoulders were hard under her palms. He kissed her throat, her collarbone, and his hand moved up under her sweater toward her breast.

"Ricardo," she whispered. She kissed his cheekbone, his ear. "Let's go upstairs."

"No," he said. "Here." His fingers found her breast and his other hand began to move caressingly along her hip, her thigh. Susan's body responded even as her mind hesitated, her New England conservatism slightly scandalized by his behavior. This wasn't a ski chalet in New Hampshire; this was her home.

He sensed her indecision and pulled back a little to look into her face. He was so close he could clearly see the baby-fine texture of her skin. Her wide gray eyes were both unsure and voluptuous, her mouth was so soft, so inviting. . . . "Little puritan," he said, and then his weight bore her back against the wide cushions of the sofa.

"Ricardo . . ." Susan said protestingly, but her hands closed on his shoulders and held him close.

"*Cariña*," he said. "*Angelita*." Susan's eyelids felt

heavy as her body ripened under his touch. She helped him take off her clothes, conscious at last only of the rushing of her blood, the sweet melting desire that longed for him to take her and make her his. The fire was hot on her bare skin and he was deep within her. Her whole body shuddered with the intensity of the pleasure he gave her and she buried her face, her mouth, in the sweaty hollow of his shoulder. She said his name, and then she said it again. He rolled over onto his side, still keeping his arms around her, and they lay still. After a long while Susan raised her head and, bending, rained a line of tender kisses along his face, from temple to chin. Her hair swung forward, enclosing both their faces in a silken tent. She raised her head a little and he smiled at her, warm and peaceful in the glow of the fire. Later he carried her upstairs to bed.

Susan spent the next three days doing laundry and packing. On the day before they were to leave she put Ricky in his car seat and drove up to Fairfield to visit her mother.

"Why don't you come to Bogotá for your Christmas vacation, Mother?" she asked as they sat over a cup of coffee in the kitchen. Ricky was sleeping next to them in a port-a-crib Susan had brought along with her.

"I'd love to, dear, but I'm afraid I won't be able to," Mrs. Morgan said. "There's a whole calendar full of dinners and parties I've promised to attend."

"But what will you do on Christmas?"

"The Slatterlys have asked me for the day." Anne Slatterly was an old college friend of her mother's and the two had always remained very close.

"Oh," said Susan. She smiled and said lightly, "I can see I don't have to worry about your being alone."

"Of course not." Mrs. Morgan smiled down at her sleeping grandson. "I'll miss this little guy, though."

"Yes. Well, we'll be back sometime after the first of the year."

"When exactly are you coming home, Susan? I forgot to ask you the other day."

"I don't know." Susan sipped her coffee. "Ricardo hasn't said. But I'll call you when we get in."

Amusement lit Mrs. Morgan's face. "Ricardo doesn't know how lucky he was to marry you, Susan. There are very few American girls today who would be as accommodating to his 'lord of the manor' style as you."

Susan kept her eyes on her coffee. She tried very hard not to feel hurt, but she was. "That's just the way he is," she managed to say.

"I know. And you are—and always have been—a sweet, gentle and affectionate child. You'll suit him perfectly." Mrs. Morgan got up to take a coffee cake out of the oven. "What is Ricardo doing these days to keep himself busy?" she asked as she served her daughter a slice.

"He's been going into New York these last few days, to film a camera commercial for television."

"Oh? Good for him. There's a great deal of money to be made in that sort of thing. Does he do it often?"

"Once in a while. For products he really uses and likes."

"And what have you been up to, dear?"

"Well," Susan said feebly, "the baby keeps me busy." She looked down at her sleeping son. He didn't look as if he kept anyone busy.

"But you have Maria to help?" Her mother was prodding gently.

"That's true."

"You ought to join a few local organizations," Mrs. Morgan advised. "Stamford has some excellent civic groups." Mrs. Morgan herself was a member of various professional, political and civic organizations. All her life Susan could recall her mother going out to meetings.

"I'll think about it," Susan said with noticeable lack of enthusiasm. Her mother gave her a slightly baffled look and then, obligingly, changed the subject.

Driving herself home an hour later, Susan felt the old familiar sense of worthlessness sweep across her. She was bitterly hurt by her mother's assessment of her and yet she didn't know how to dispute it. All her life she had felt weaker, less vital, less interesting than the rest of her family. She had always seemed to be swept along in the bustle of theirs lives, trying desperately to reach out and touch them and never quite succeeding. She *had* touched people—a few high school and college friends, one or two of her teachers—but with her family, and in particular with her mother, she always seemed to fail. She had never doubted that the failure was her fault. And if she was so unsuccessful with her own mother, how on earth was she going to manage with Ricardo's. She would never admit it to him, but she was really dreading this trip to Colombia.

Chapter Seven

They flew first-class to El Dorado International Airport in Bogotá. Ricardo's sister Elena and her husband were waiting to drive them to the family home in Chico, the elegant new suburb in northern Bogotá. There was a great bustle of kissing and handshaking and Susan had the confused impression of a very attractive woman in her midthirties and a middlesized, stout man with a gray mustache, before they were all in the car, a deeply cushioned Citroen, and on their way through the darkness. Ricardo sat in the front with his brother-in-law, who had been introduced to Susan as Ernesto Rios, and Susan, holding Ricky, sat in the back with Elena. Up to this point they had all spoken Spanish but now Elena turned to Susan and said, in very good English, "Did you have a pleasant trip? How was the airplane?"

"Very nice," Susan said. Ricky began to fuss and she shifted him to her other shoulder.

"Flying bothers some babies," Elena said sympathetically. "Fortunately, mine always seemed to like it. At any rate, they always slept."

Susan patted Ricky's back and he quieted. "How many children do you have?" she asked.

"Five. But they are no longer little. My youngest is

eight." Susan must have looked her surprise for Elena chuckled. "Ricardo is the family baby, did you not know? I am forty and Marta is thirty-eight."

"I knew he had older sisters and nieces and nephews, of course, but that was all."

Ricardo turned around and spoke to his wife in English. "That's the university we're passing, on the right, *querida*." Susan obediently peered out the window but it was too dark to see much.

He smiled. "I'll take you on a tour tomorrow. We can leave Ricky with Mama."

"That would be nice," Susan said faintly.

Ernesto suddenly honked and then rolled down his window to shout something unflattering at the car that had just cut him off.

Ricardo laughed. "Home again," he said. He sounded very content.

The Montoya home in Bogotá was a very large, relatively new Spanish-style house with a walled courtyard on the street that protected it from the gaze of passersby. Ricardo's mother, Maria Montoya, was waiting for them in a beautiful, very formal living room. "Ricardo!" she cried joyfully at the sight of her tall son, and he scooped her up in his arms and hugged her.

When she was on her feet again, he said, "Mama, this is Susan, my wife," and Susan found herself looking at one of the most elegant women she had ever seen in her life. Maria Montoya was a few inches taller than Susan, with graying dark hair worn in a simple chignon and the slim supple figure of a much younger woman. She smiled now at Susan, warmly, and said, "Welcome to Bogotá, Susan."

Susan smiled back. "Thank you, Señora Montoya." She held out her arms. "And here is your grandson."

A look of unutterable tenderness came over the face of the older woman, and very gently, very competently, she took the baby from Susan. She peered down into the tiny face and laughed. "*Dios*, Ricardo! He looks just like you!"

"So everyone says," Ricardo took off his coat, and Señora Montoya said instantly, "Elena, go and get Francie."

Elena nodded but, before she went, she took Ricardo's coat from him. In a minute Elena returned with a maid who collected the rest of the coats.

"Julio has put your bags in your room," Señora Montoya said to Susan, "and I have put up Ricardo's old crib. Would you like to take the baby upstairs?"

"Yes," Susan said gratefully.

"I will show you," her mother-in-law said with a smile. Then, turning to her daughter, "Elena, see what your brother would like to eat and drink."

"Yes, Mama," said Elena, and as Susan left she saw Ricardo sit down on the sofa and stretch out his legs.

When Susan awoke the following morning, she looked out her bedroom window and saw the mountains. They ringed the city, the peaks of the Cordillera Central, clear-cut and beautiful against the brilliant sky. On the plateau was the capital city, Bogotá, with its curious mix of old Spanish and ultramodern architecture. But in the future, whenever Susan thought of Colombia, she would think of the mountains.

She enjoyed her stay in Bogotá very much. She found Ricardo's mother to be a warm, lovely and utterly charming woman. At first Susan felt very young and gauche next to the elegant perfection of the elder Señora Montoya, but her mother-in-law's quite genuine kindness soon had her feeling more comfortable. Both Elena and Marta were very like their mother and Susan spent many pleasant hours chatting with them about babies and child rearing.

Unlike her own mother, the Montoya women were not at all intellectual. They also catered unashamedly to the men of the family—and in particular to Ricardo. For the first time Susan understood why Ricardo expected to be waited on—his mother and his sisters waited on him constantly, hand and foot. He was the only son, and the baby. The whole household, quite literally, revolved around Ricardo. They ate when it was convenient for him. The car was at his disposal; if he was using it, his mother and his wife took taxis. His mother wouldn't dream of making a social engagement without first consulting him. During the whole time they were in Bogotá, Susan never heard Señora Montoya indicate the slightest opposition to a word he uttered.

He was very busy. Half the time Susan did not know where he was or what he was doing. "Business, *querida*," he would answer cheerfully whenever she questioned him as to his doings.

He did find the time to show her around Bogotá, however. They saw all the old Spanish sections of the city, starting with the Plaza de Bolivar. They went to a bullfight at the Plaza de Toros de Santa Maria, which Susan did not like, and they spent several mornings at the Museo del Oro, Bogotá's Gold Museum. Ricardo was very knowledgeable about the various Indian tribes and their workmanship and Susan found the whole place utterly fascinating.

"I ought to be a tour guide, eh?" he said good-naturedly as they left the museum after their third visit.

"Keep it in mind if you should ever be broke," she retorted, and he laughed.

"I don't think that will ever happen, *querida*. I have my eggs in too many baskets."

One of his baskets was a coffee plantation, a finca, on the mountain slopes three hours out of Bogotá. They went there for a few days the third week of their visit, bringing Ricky with them. Señora Montoya hated to see her grandson removed from her vicinity for so long, but as Ricardo had told his mother humorously, "We can't separate him from his food supply for that long, Mama."

Susan loved the finca. "When I think of Colombia, I shall always think of mountains," she told Ricardo softly as they sat together on the veranda one evening looking at the stars.

"The green mountains of Colombia," Ricardo's voice said next to her in the darkness. "They are the most beautiful in the world."

"And no snow," Susan said incredulously.

"Well, *querida*, we are in the tropics."

Susan laughed. "It's hard to believe that in Bogotá. Your mother has the fire going all the time and I've worn my coat every day."

"That is because Bogotá is at eight thousand feet. In Colombia, if you want a change of climate, all you must do is change your altitude. The finca is warm. Down at sea level, at Santa Marta and Cartagena, it is hot."

It was true. They had driven three hours down the mountains from Bogotá and the weather here was warm and summery. Susan sighed and inhaled deeply. "It's nice just to *sit*," She remarked after a while. "Your mother's energy is astonishing. Every day she has at *least* two social engagements for me to attend. I'm embarrassed to tell her I'd just like to stay home and do nothing once in a while. Has she always been this busy?"

He laughed and shrugged. "She has her clubs, her luncheons, her teas, just as any woman does." He looked down at her, his face shadowed by the darkness. "You will be just the same, *querida,* once you get a little more established in Stamford."

He reached out with one arm and drew her closer so that she was resting against him, her head falling naturally into the hollow of his shoulder. "I don't know," she said uncertainly. "Somehow, Ricardo, life for me is more—difficult."

"What can be difficult?" he murmured into the baby-fine softness of her hair. "I am here to take care of you now."

It was too hard to explain. But she knew, with great certainty, that she was not the social, urban, clubby person that Ricardo's mother was—or her own mother for that matter. She was the sort of person who needed a few friends, people she could really touch, really talk to and share with. The busyness of a large acquaintance and many social engagements was not for her. And, strangely, she did not think it was for Ricardo either. "*You've* only gone to a few dinner parties," she pointed out after a minute.

She could feel his shoulder move under her cheek in his characteristic shrug. "I don't have much patience for that sort of thing, *querida.*"

"No. You've seen the men you want to see during the day, haven't you?"

There was a hint of impatience in his voice. "One can't talk in the crowd of a party."

Susan sighed and closed her eyes. "No. One can't."

His lips moved from her hair down the side of her cheek. "Let's go to bed," he whispered.

And, "All right," she whispered back.

It was raining the day they left the finca. Susan sat in the front of the Fiat Ricardo had borrowed from a friend, holding Ricky in her lap and biting her lip. The road was very steep, narrow, winding and wet and Ricardo was driving much too fast. From time to time she stole a surreptitious glance at his profile. He looked calm, intent, relaxed. He had the car under perfect control. But, he's going too fast, Susan thought again. Ricky moved in her arms. "Ricardo," she said tentatively, "would you mind slowing down a little? You're frightening me."

The car slowed almost instantly. "Of course, *querida*. I'm sorry. I forget you are not used to our mountain roads."

They proceeded up the mountain at a more sedate pace and Susan, glancing again at her husband, felt miserable. He had been enjoying that drive and she had spoiled it. Why was she always so timid, so unadventurous? The only daring thing she had ever done in her life had been that night in the New Hampshire ski lodge when she had made love with Ricardo. She thought about things too much, worried too much. She always had. She supposed she always would. The prospect made her unutterably gloomy. She wished, passionately, that she could be like Ricardo's mother and sisters. None of them would ever have dreamed of asking him to slow down. He really *needn't* have slowed down. He had been in absolute control. But she had been afraid.

She wasn't like his mother or his sisters. She was fond of them. She admired them. But she wasn't like them. They all ran large households, were involved in charitable and church organizations and excelled at a variety of sports. Ricardo's nine nieces and nephews were all healthy, polite, charming children. His sisters were excellent mothers. But it seemed to Susan that the whole life of the Montoya women turned outward. There was nothing left for just themselves.

Perhaps they were right. Perhaps it was through others that one was fulfilled oneself. But she knew also that there was a need in her for something more.

The trip to Bogotá crystallized in Susan the determination to write. For years the journal had been enough; now she must try to use what she had learned and see if she could create something new. It was a need in her that she could not explain, but it was there, as intense as it was inarticulate. Ricardo had said he wouldn't object. She would remind him of that, and when they got home, she would set up a schedule and start to write.

Two days before they left Bogotá there was a very gala party at the San Carlos Palace, home of Colombia's president, which all the Montoyas attended. Señora Montoya took Susan to Bogotá's beautiful shopping center, the Unicentro, and in one of the most elegant and expensive little boutiques she had ever seen Susan got a stunning evening dress. It was dark green with a straight, slim skirt and bodice that showed off her neck and shoulders gracefully, tastefully but unmistakably. Ricardo loved it and took her out to buy her an emerald necklace and earrings to match. "All good Colombian women wear emeralds," he told her when she protested at the extravagance. "This is your wedding present, *querida*. Wear them in good health."

The emeralds were magnificent and Susan had her hair done in a smooth and sophisticated upswept style in order to better show them off. For the first time she felt as elegant as Ricardo's mother and sisters.

The party was very large and very glittering. All of Bogotá's social elite were there as well as many members of the diplomatic community. At first Susan felt a little overwhelmed by the jewels, the gowns, the darkly handsome men in evening dress. She stayed close to Marta, who introduced her to at least half the people in the room. And then Ricardo came up to her with an elderly, silver-haired man with the aristocratic features of old Spain. "Susan, I would like you to meet Señor Julio Merlano de Diaz," he said. "I know you have read his work."

Julio Merlano de Diaz was Colombia's most famous poet, a winner of the Nobel Prize for Literature. Susan's eyes widened. "I am so pleased to meet you, Señor Merlano," she said in her soft, careful, college Spanish. "I have read almost all of your poems. And I love them. It is a great honor to meet you in person."

Señor Merlano took the hand she had shyly extended and shook it warmly. "Thank you, Señora Montoya. It is my privilege to meet such a charming young lady."

"I reread *The Death of the Condor,* just before we left for Bogotá," she offered a little hesitantly, "and I've been thinking about it ever since. In fact, I've rather been trying to see Colombia through your eyes."

The old man looked at her curiously. "Have you?"

"Yes. It is so—difficult—to have a balanced view, isn't it? To see the dark and the light as well."

Señor Merlano's face was grave. "It is indeed, Señora."

They continued to talk for a few minutes and then someone came over and collected Ricardo to go and talk to the president. Susan and Julio Merlano moved to a couple of chairs along the wall and continued to talk. *The Death of the Condor* had made a very deep impression on Susan. A long poem about the extinction of a tribe of Colombian Indians, it told of a tragedy that had been perpetrated by a conglomeration of modern political and socially progressive programs. Yet the tone of the poem had not been that of outrage but of sorrow.

"And what have you seen of Colombia through my eyes?" the older man asked at length.

"I've seen a country very like your poem," she replied. She was sitting gracefully on the decorative gilt chair, and in the light of the chandelier her flawless skin glowed with a pearly sheen of indescribable beauty. Her large gray eyes were dark with thought. She tilted her head on its long slender neck and said, "There are things for celebration and things to lament. Ricardo didn't just take me to the tourist sights."

"He didn't, eh?" The famous poet, revered around the world yet regarded with uneasiness in his own country because of his unfortunate penchant for telling the truth, looked across the room at her husband. "Ricardo Montoya is a very extraordinary man," he said softly. "Even more so than his father, I think."

Susan's eyes followed the direction of her companion's. Ricardo was standing on the other side of the room talking to a woman Susan did not know. He was impeccably attired in black-tie evening dress and he looked elegant, assured, cosmopolitan. Yet, even formally dressed and standing perfectly still, he gave the unmistakable impression of strength and agility. As Susan watched he laughed at something the woman had said. His face was instantly transformed by that familiar radiant smile and, watching him, Susan felt something inside her turn over. She stared at her husband, and with that frightening yet unmistakable swerve of her heart all of her feelings of the last weeks crystallized and she knew that she was in love with him.

"I'm sorry," she said faintly to Señor Merlano. "What did you say?"

"I said that Ricardo is a very extraordinary man. I doubt there are five people in this room who have any idea of his activities in Bogotá, and yet all of them regard him as a personal friend."

"Ricardo can be—difficult to know," Susan got out.

"So you understand that," said Señor Merlano, and both of them watched as Ricardo came across the room toward them.

"You have been monopolizing my wife this last hour, Julio," Ricardo said good-naturedly. "What have you been doing?"

"I have been talking to her, Ricardo," the poet replied with gentle dignity. "It is not often I have the chance to converse with so sensitive and intelligent a listener." He smiled at Susan apologetically. "I hope I have not kept you from enjoying the party?"

"Oh no!" Susan was appalled. "It was wonderful talking to you, Señor Merlano. I shall never forget it."

"Nor shall I." The old man smiled at Ricardo. "I only came here tonight to please you, my son. I did not expect to enjoy myself. I must thank you for the gift of your wife's company."

Ricardo smiled back, the warm intimate smile he kept for so few people. "I am leaving on Wednesday, you know. I have left instructions with Ernesto."

"Very good. You won't be returning for a while?"

"No. Spring training starts shortly."

"I see." Señor Merlano looked amused. "You and your baseball."

"I like it," Ricardo returned simply. "It's fun."

"I know." The old man looked even more amused. "You are a constant source of wonder to me, Ricardo." He held out his hand. "Good night, my son."

"Good night, Julio."

The poet turned to Susan. "Good night, Señora Montoya. Ricardo is very fortunate in his wife."

Susan colored with pleasure. "Thank you, Señor."

When the old man had reached the door, Susan glanced up at her husband. She still felt a little dizzy from her discovery of a few minutes ago. She also felt suddenly shy. She looked away from him again and said softly, "He is a splendid person, Ricardo."

"Yes, isn't he? He was a good friend of my father's. I learned quite a lot from him."

"He said . . ." Susan hesitated and then went on. "He said you were doing some special work in Bogotá?"

"It is nothing so special," came the easy answer. "It is merely a matter of helping to fund a few projects." He changed the subject, elusive as ever about his own doings. "You must have bewitched Julio, *querida*. He is usually very quiet."

"He was very kind," she said sincerely. "I was afraid I was monopolizing *him,* that he felt he had to stay with me until someone came and took me off his hands."

Ricardo's dark eyes looked down at her and he did not speak for a minute. Then he said, very quietly, "You underestimate yourself, Susan. I have not seen Julio talk so much in a very long time."

"I do love his poems, you see."

"Yes." He smiled again, teasingly. "I see."

Once again Susan felt her heart give that disturbing jolt. She had thought, if she had thought at all, that Ricardo's attraction for her was purely a physical thing. He had a sexual magnetism that was as powerful as it was rare. It was a force felt by nearly every woman who met him. She knew that. She had seen it. She knew also that that was why she had succumbed to him that strange night in New Hampshire.

She had thought that, with effort, they might perhaps build a workable marriage. It had never crossed her mind that she could fall in love with him. He was the total opposite of the kind of man she had thought she could love. They were poles apart in interests, cultural background and temperament. But that moment of revelation at the ball had opened her mind to what her heart had known for quite some while. She loved this dark Latin stranger who had come so disruptively into her life and turned it upside down. She loved him, but she didn't understand him.

It frightened her, this love that had come up on her so unexpectedly. She was afraid of the weakness his presence produced in her. He had only to touch her and she melted; she had no strength to oppose him. He was pleased with her; she knew that. Why shouldn't he be? In all their relationship so far she had conformed to what his idea of a wife ought to be. She had been as docile and tractable as her mother thought her. She had bent before the overpowering force of Ricardo's personality, given in to all his wishes. But if the day came when she had to stand up for herself? If she stopped being what he thought a wife ought to be?

She shivered a little, suddenly cold in the pleasant heat of the ballroom. He put a warm hand on her bare arm. "Come," he murmured, "let's dance."

"All right," she said, and let him lead her out to the floor. As always, their movement together, to music enveloped them in a special world. His arms came around her and she rested her head lightly against his shoulder, her eyelids half closing with the sensuous pleasure of his nearness, the feel of his strong body against hers. When the dance ended, she raised her head and found him looking down at her, his eyes dark and unfathomable.

"Susan." It was Marta. "Do come and meet some friends of mine."

"Susan is tired, Marta," said Ricardo pleasantly. "I've just promised to take her home."

"But it's still early!" Marta protested to her sister-in-law.

"Early for you, perhaps," returned Ricardo, "but Susan doesn't like staying up to all hours of the night." Belatedly he turned to her. "Do you, *querida?*"

Her eyes laughed at him although her lips were grave. "No, I'm afraid I don't, Marta," she said. "But it's been a perfectly splendid party."

"I'm glad you enjoyed it," Marta said. "Take the car," she told her brother. "Luis and I will see Mama home."

"Shame on you, Ricardo," Susan said as they got into Señora Montoya's comfortable old Mercedes.

He chuckled and leaned forward to start the ignition. "The things a man must resort to in order to be alone with his wife."

"What if I had wanted to stay?"

"But you didn't," he said serenely.

He was right. She wanted the same thing he did. She watched his profile in silence as they drove through the darkened streets. When they reached his mother's house, he turned to her and said, "It will be good to get home. Then we won't have to find excuses."

She smiled at him, unspeakably pleased by his words. "I thought, perhaps, you regarded Bogotá as home."

He looked surprised and then thoughtful. "I used to," he said at last. "But not anymore." He opened his door and came around the car. "Come," he said. "They'll all be back before we know it." And she laughed.

Chapter Eight

They arrived home in mid-January, after having been in Colombia for over a month. "How was the christening?" Mrs. Morgan asked her daughter when she came to visit a few days later.

"Very lovely," Susan replied. "Ricardo's sister Elena and her husband were godparents, and Ricky wore a christening dress that had been in the family for generations. The archbishop did the job, and I must say it was all very impressive."

"The archbishop?" Mrs. Morgan raised her eyebrow.

"Yes. Ricardo's mother and sisters are very active in church circles. They are really a quite prominent family in Bogotá, Mother."

"I never thought Ricardo was from the barrio," Mrs. Morgan said dryly. "Nor did I think he was so religious."

"Well, actually, he's not," Susan replied a little unwillingly. "Or at least he doesn't go to church much. I think that's another one of those things he leaves to the women."

Mrs. Morgan smiled with real amusement. "I'll tell you, Susan, if Ricardo weren't so outrageously charming, he would be impossible."

"Yes," said Susan slowly, her eyes on her knees. "I know."

"Susan!" The front door banged and the object of their conversation came bursting into the living room, lean and brown and ablaze with life. "Oh, Helen. How nice to see you." And he came across the room to kiss his mother-in-law.

"Was that you I heard sawing wood?" Mrs. Morgan asked. Her face had become very bright and young looking.

"Yes." He grinned, cocky and irresistible. "I'm on my second cord." He shed his vest, which missed the chair and hit the floor. He turned to his wife. "I'm starving, *querida*. What have you got to eat?"

"Would you like some of this banana bread Mother and I have been having?"

"Um. Sounds good. I'll just go wash up first."

He left the room and Susan rose to go to the kitchen. She bent, picked up the vest and then met her mother's eyes. Quite suddenly her face dissolved into laughter. "It's no good telling him to hang it in the closet," she said. "He'll only reply, with irrefutable logic, that it goes upstairs."

When she got back to the living room with the bread, Ricardo had returned. She served him a large slice and a glass of ginger ale and had to refrain from reaching out to smooth back the thick dark brown hair that had fallen over his forehead. He had rolled up the sleeves of his flannel shirt to wash his hands and his forearms looked as hard as iron in the late-winter light.

"Susan has been telling me how much she enjoyed Bogotá," Mrs. Morgan said. "I haven't been there for many years. It sounds as if it's changed."

"It has. There's a lot more money in the city, for one thing."

"Drug money?" Mrs. Morgan asked bluntly.

He shrugged. "Of course, some of it comes from drugs." He took another bite of his bread. "And then in some ways Bogotá hasn't changed at all. There's still the poverty, the street children, the thefts. It will be many years before it approaches the social equality of this country."

Susan sat back and listened quietly to the conversation between her husband and her mother. When Mrs. Morgan got up to leave, Ricardo said, "But why don't you stay for dinner?"

Mrs. Morgan looked immensely gratified. "I'd love to but I can't," she said with regret. "I have a meeting at seven." She turned to her daughter. "I ran into Charlotte Munson the other day, dear. She lives in Stamford, as you know, and she was telling me about the women's club here. They are very active in a wide range of areas and they desperately need more people. And then there's the Junior League. They're starting up a project to work with foster children that sounds very promising."

"I don't think I'd have the time, Mother," Susan hedged.

"Why ever not?" her mother returned impatiently. "Really, Susan, you are so—immovable."

"She has just gotten home from a very long trip," Ricardo said pleasantly. "Give her a chance to catch her breath, Helen."

Her mother's face relaxed. "Yes," she said. "Of course." She kissed Susan and then Ricardo. "Take good care of that grandson of mine."

"I will," promised Susan. "Good-bye, Mother."

"Don't let her push you into doing something you don't want to do," Ricardo said sympathetically as they moved back into the living room.

"You see," Susan explained quickly, "I want to start to write, and if I fill up my life with other activities, I won't be able to find the time." She smiled ruefully. "Or the energy."

"You must do as you please," Ricardo said again, "not what your mother thinks you should do. You are all grown up now, *querida*."

In the end, however, it was not her mother who put obstacles in the way of her writing but Ricardo. He started out by being very helpful. "Of course you can use the study," he said when she inquired. "I'm starting to do taxes, but that will only last until April."

"Until April?" she echoed incredulously.

"Yes. I prefer to do my own, you see, and it takes time. But I don't work on them every day, Susan. You can use the desk when I don't need it."

"And what about Mrs. Noonan?" Mrs. Noonan was the woman who came in once a week to deal with Ricardo's mail. "Doesn't she always use the study?"

"Yes. But that is only once a week."

"Ricardo, between your taxes and Mrs. Noonan, I'm afraid there isn't going to be much time left for me. I'll find somewhere else to work."

She settled on her old bedroom and Ricardo helped to fix it up, bringing in a larger desk, a typewriter and some bookcases. She was able to get a start on her novel by setting up a schedule that allowed her to work three hours a day in the morning. She actually got the first chapter written.

Then Ricky got sick and she was up with him for two nights in a row.

Then Ricardo came down with the flu. He was used to being splendidly healthy and consequently was a wretched patient on the few occasions when he did become ill. He had a fever and he ached all over and he only wanted Susan. The baby still was not back to sleeping through the night, and after three days of toiling up and down stairs, taking Ricardo's temperature, bringing him medicines and juices and food that he didn't want after he had asked for it, she was exhausted. And frustrated as well. She had actually been *writing*. She had felt the book taking shape for her, the words obeying her thoughts. She wanted to get back to her book. But she hadn't the energy.

Ricardo's fever subsided to a little above normal five days after he first became ill and he seemed more comfortable. That afternoon Susan sat down at her desk and reread her opening chapter. She stared out the window and once more put herself back into the hidden, secret world of childhood. She picked up her pen.

"Susan!" came Ricardo's voice from the next room.

"Yes?" she called back, a hint of impatience in her voice.

"Will you bring me up my account books? They're on the study desk. I think perhaps I could work a little."

Susan sighed, put down her pen, and went downstairs. The books were not on the desk. After two more trips up and down stairs she located them on top of his filing cabinet. She sat down at her desk again, picked up her pen and Ricky woke up. She let him cry for a minute, hoping that Maria would come up to him.

"Susan!" came the voice next door. "I hear the baby."

Susan put down her pen. "Yes, Ricardo," she called

with resignation. "I'm going to get him." She did not get back to her book for three more days.

"We'll be leaving for Florida in a week," Ricardo said to her at dinner a few nights later.

"In a week!" Susan looked at him in astonishment.

"Of course. Spring training begins, *querido*. You know that."

"I didn't know it began so soon. I thought it began in the spring!"

He laughed. "The season begins in the spring, Susan. The training is *for* the spring season. And it has begun in February for years and years."

She put down her fork. "But, Ricardo," she almost wailed. "I've only just gotten home."

"I know." He didn't sound at all sympathetic. "But it is only for six weeks. Then we will be home for the rest of the year."

She picked up her fork again and pushed the rice around on her plate. "I feel like a nomad," she muttered mutinously. "Someone is always pushing me to *go* somewhere."

"Don't be so dramatic," he said coolly, and she looked up to meet his eyes. He was watching her steadily and for once there was no amusement in his face.

"I don't think it's being dramatic to resent being hauled off around the world without even having my wishes consulted," she said. There was bright color in her cheeks. "You gave me four days notice before we went to Colombia. I suppose I should be grateful that you've given me a week this time."

"Why do you need notice? Do you want me to give you a schedule for the year?"

At the tone of his voice all the brilliant color drained from her face. "No, I don't want you to give me a schedule," she said a little unsteadily. "I want you to *ask* me. I am your wife, not your slave."

Ricardo's face was closed and shuttered, his eyes cold. "You are my wife and you go where I go," he said evenly. "What is there to ask about? *I* do not have a choice. I must be in Florida on February twentieth." His eyes narrowed. "Or are you saying that you do not wish to come with me?"

"No, I'm not saying that." Susan had been gripping her fork tensely and now she forced herself to relax her hold and set it down. "Of course I want to go with you. But it—upsets—me to have unexpected things flung at me like this. I need time to adjust my thinking."

"So." He took a mouthful of chicken, chewed and swallowed it. "In the future I will try to be less unexpected."

It was not what she wanted but at the moment she knew it was the best she could hope for. She did not want to run the risk of angering him further. She forced a smile. "Thank you, Ricardo."

He shook his head in rueful bewilderment. Such a tempest in a teapot," he said. "I think I had better make out a schedule after all."

"Perhaps that wouldn't be a bad idea," she said softly.

From upstairs there came the sounds of a baby crying. Ricardo rose. "I'll see to him," he said. Left to herself, Susan collected the plates to bring them out to the kitchen. The crying upstairs stopped and she began to load the dishwasher. Ricardo came downstairs with the baby and sat down with him in a big chair in front of the fire. From the kitchen Susan could hear her husband talking to Ricky in Spanish. When she went into the family room, Ricardo was dancing the baby on his knees and Ricky was beaming. Susan laughed and went over to sit next to Ricardo on the ottoman. They played with the baby for almost an hour and then put him to bed. Susan and Ricardo then followed their son's example, but unlike Ricky, they did not go to sleep for quite some time.

Two days before they left for Florida Ricardo took Susan to the theater in New York. She was aware of the stir his presence caused as they walked through the lobby and could feel herself tightening up, self-conscious and nervous. Ricardo seemed completely at ease, and when a few people said things to him like, "Good luck this season, Rick," or "Are we going to win another series, Rick?" he would smile good-naturedly and make a brief, pleasant response.

"It's a little daunting, being out with such a celebrity," she said to him as they settled into their seats.

He was reading his program. "It's no big deal, *querida*. People in New York just like to wish me well. They are Yankee fans, you see."

The show was a Chekhov revival that had gotten rave reviews. At the intermission Susan turned to her husband and asked curiously, "How are you enjoying it?"

He was looking a little puzzled. "I am enjoying it very much, but it doesn't seem to have a plot. Am I missing something?"

Susan's large gray eyes danced. "Chekhov is short on plot and long on character," she said.

"Oh, I see." The puzzled look left his face and she laughed.

The play was marvelous and the acting superb. At

the end, when Sonya was comforting Uncle Vanya with the words: "We must go on living! We shall go on living, Uncle Vanya! We shall live through a long, long chain of days and weary evenings; we shall patiently bear the trials which fate sends us; we shall work for others, both now and in our old age . . ." Susan glanced at Ricardo and saw tears in his eyes.

It was raining when they retrieved their car from the garage and started through the city streets toward the East Side Drive. They were turning down Ninetieth Street when Susan noticed two men on the sidewalk. They were bending over a third man who was lying on the pavement in the rain. "Something's wrong!" Susan said, and Ricardo stopped the car.

"Wait here," he ordered tersely and got out, locking his door behind him. As Susan watched he approached the group. She couldn't hear and so she rolled down her window halfway. They were all speaking Spanish. Then Ricardo knelt on the sidewalk and Susan could see him feeling for a pulse. He spoke sharply to the other two, who Susan could see now were only boys. One immediately ran off up the street like a deer. On the pavement Ricardo began to apply CPR.

Susan reached into the backseat for her umbrella and got out of the car. She went over to stand next to Ricardo and tried as best she could to shelter the man's face with her umbrella. The rain was coming down hard and it was cold.

Ricardo was working very hard. "I don't know CPR, but can I help?" Susan murmured after a minute. He shook his head and kept on counting. The boy knelt next to Ricardo and his young face looked stricken. The second boy came running back. Susan understood him saying that he had called 911 for an ambulance.

It was fifteen minutes before the ambulance arrived and all during that time Ricardo worked ceaselessly over the unconscious man. After the ambulance workers had taken over, Susan heard Ricardo giving one of the boys their phone number. The ambulance pulled away and Susan and Ricardo got back into their car.

Ricardo started the engine and glanced at her in concern. "You must be freezing, Susan. I'll get the heat going as soon as I can."

She was shivering and her feet, clad in thin dress shoes, were icy. She looked at Ricardo. His hair was soaked and there was rain still dripping from the tips of his lashes. His coat looked sodden. He had gotten the least benefit of the umbrella.

"Do you think he'll be all right?" she asked after they had driven in silence for a few minutes.

"I doubt it. I couldn't get a pulse going. And I'm not sure how long he was lying there before we came along."

"A lot of other cars went by," she said slowly, "but nobody stopped." He shrugged and said nothing. "Who were those boys?" she asked.

"His sons. They were all walking home from work. Evidently he had been complaining of chest pains all evening."

"Oh dear. It doesn't sound good."

"No, it doesn't."

The heat began to come through and Ricardo turned the blowers on full blast. They were at the Larchmont tolls before he said, "What an ending to our evening out! And I thought I would give you such a treat tonight."

"It was a treat," she said quickly. "I adored the play. And the dinner. And I'm very glad we saw that man when we did. Even if he dies, at least his family will have the comfort of knowing that everything that could be done was done. At least they'll know that someone *tried,* that they didn't just have to stand helplessly by and watch their father die in front of them."

"I suppose so," he murmured.

"It's true. Why else didn't you give up on him.? You said you thought it was hopeless."

After a pause he answered, "As you said, *querida,* one has to try."

She watched the windshield wipers in silence for a few minutes. Then, "I heard you giving one of the boys our phone number."

"Yes. I'm sure they are a poor family. The loss of a father will probably hit them hard."

That was all he said on the subject, but Susan knew he would help the family financially. They pulled into the Greenwich tolls and she turned to look at the sudden illuminated face of her husband. He was like no one else she had ever known. On the surface he appeared so uncomplicated, so easygoing and casual. But under that surface geniality, he was a very complex man. He could be hard and demanding. He had a temper that frightened her when he was obviously holding it in check. She didn't like to think what he would be like if he were ever really angry. He had enormous magnetism and charm, yet he was a very private man. What he thought and what he felt he kept to himself. Yet he had had tears in his eyes tonight for Uncle Vanya.

He was an enigma to her, a stranger whom she lived with on the most intimate of terms. She loved him— deeply, irrevocably. But aside from liking to sleep with her, she had no idea of how he felt about her. After all, love had not been the reason for their marriage. The rain beat down against the windows of the car and Susan sighed and closed her eyes.

"We'll be home soon, *querida*," he said.

"Yes." The very cadences of his voice did strange things to her insides. He was so splendidly, competently male. Whatever the situation, she could always rest secure in the knowledge that Ricardo would handle it. He had known he might be walking into danger tonight. He had locked her safely into the car before he went to investigate. And if there had been danger, she was sure he would have handled that as well. She opened her eyes and looked at his shadowy profile. He was so self-sufficient. He seemed to need no one—certainly not her. The only solid achievement of her life was Ricky. And Ricky was what had brought her Ricardo. He had not even married her for her personal charms.

She closed her eyes again. How was it possible, she wondered, to be so happy and yet so miserable and all at the same time?

Chapter Nine

It was almost impossible to rent a house for only six weeks, so when they went to Florida Ricardo took a large suite in one of the best hotels in Fort Lauderdale. They had two bedrooms, a living room and a small kitchen area with a refrigerator and a hot plate. When they arrived Susan quickly made arrangements for a baby-sitter. "We're going to have to eat dinner out," she told Ricardo firmly, "and I do not want to have to drag Ricky into a hotel dining room every night."

He grinned. "True. His manners leave something to be desired."

"That's putting it mildly," Susan replied. She did not anticipate finding it easy to take care of a four-month-old baby in a hotel suite, but she forbode to press the point. They had had this out before. And difficult though it was probably going to be, she was glad she was here with Ricardo.

She accompanied him the following day when he went to report to the Yankee camp. The sun was shining, it was eighty degrees, and as she pushed Ricky along in his umbrella stroller, she felt the festive mood of the occasion.

They hadn't been at camp for five minutes before Ricardo was surrounded by reporters. He stood courte-

ously, answering their questions with absolute patience
and good humor. Susan came in for a small share of
the attention but she found the reporters to be polite
and their questions had to do with Ricardo and not
with her.

"What's Rick been doing all winter?" a wire-service
man asked her first.

"Chopping wood," she replied a little shyly. "Building
a new garage."

"He looks in great shape."

"Yes. He's been very active."

"Is this the pennant baby?" another reporter asked.

Susan looked startled and then she smiled. "Yes,
that's right. He *was* born on the day Ricardo won the
pennant, wasn't he?"

The reporter grinned. "It was the *Yankees* who won
the pennant, Mrs. Montoya."

Susan laughed. "It all depends on your point of view,
I suppose."

The reporter laughed back, his eyes bright with admiration. "I see what you mean. And you're probably
not far from the truth. Rick had an awful lot to do with
winning that pennant. And the series as well."

She smiled and didn't reply, and shortly afterward
Ricardo moved away from the reporters to go change
and she and Ricky walked over to where the other
wives were sitting to watch. This had been Susan's first
encounter with the press and it left her feeling more
comfortable than she had dreamed possible. It was the
nature of Ricardo's celebrity that protected her, she
thought. His personal life was a minor adjunct to his
fame. It was what he did on the field that counted.
There had never been a breath in any of the papers
about their hasty marriage or the quick arrival of Ricky.

The TV announcers had proudly imparted the news of Ricardo's son's birth, but no one had ever mentioned the fact that his parents had only been married for a few months. She had been enormously grateful for their reticence.

And yet Ricardo was one of the most famous men in America. Wherever they went in Florida, people came up to him, for his autograph, to shake his hand, to wish him well. Men and women, teenagers and young boys and girls: the whole world knew Rick Montoya. It knew him—and it admired him. Again and again Susan was struck by the regard in which Ricardo appeared to be held by all the fans who crowded to see him. And she was struck as well by the grace and the courtesy with which he accepted the pressing admiration of so many strangers. Her husband, she thought, was that rarest of all things—a hero deserving of the name.

The change of scene and of routine made it almost impossible for Susan to write. She did try, in the intervals when Ricky was napping, but she had a hard time finding the proper concentration. After an hour's work she would reread what she had written and it would seem terrible: stilted, awkward, childish. When Ricky woke up, she would take him down to the beach and wait for Ricardo to return. He didn't like the idea of her being "cooped up," as he put it, all day in a hotel room. He was such an active, outdoor person himself that he regarded any indoor, sedentary activity as a punishment.

She didn't know why she persisted in her fantasy that she could write. There was nothing to encourage her to continue; everything seemed to say give it up, be content with what you've got. Yet for her, not to write was not to be fully alive. Writing was the door into her deepest self. And so, though discouraged and feeling foolish, she struggled on.

Florida may not have been good for her writing but it proved to be beneficial in most other ways. Ricardo was happy and that was important to her happiness. And she made a new friend.

His name was Martin Harrison and he was a writer for a very respected literary magazine with a large national circulation. He was not a sports reporter, but he was, as he himself told her, a "baseball nut," and he had come to Florida to do an article on the Yankees for the *National Monthly*. He was in his early thirties, the kind of literate, intelligent, thinking man that Susan had always admired.

She met him about a week after camp opened. She had been sitting in the stands, rocking Ricky with one hand and holding a book with the other, when he came up to her and said in his soft voice, which held just the suspicion of a southern drawl, "Mrs. Montoya?"

Susan looked up from her book and saw a nice-looking man with brown hair and very clear hazel eyes. "Yes?" she said pleasantly.

"I'm Martin Harrison," he explained, "and I'm writing an article about the team for the *National Monthly*. I wonder if I could talk to you for a little?"

"Of course." Susan closed her book and gestured for him to sit down. The warm Florida weather had been good for her this last week. She had been feeling run-down and the sun and the beach had worked wonders. Her skin was tanned to the color of golden honey and her pale hair shone with the texture of spun silk. She was wearing a yellow sun dress and espadrilles and her wide-set gray eyes regarded him with charming gravity.

"I'm afraid I'm rather a novice about baseball, Mr. Harrison. Talking to me is likely to prove a dead loss."

"I doubt that," he said, the drawl more pronounced now. Then his eyes lit on her book. "Merlano!" he said. "Do you like him?"

"Yes. In fact," Susan said a little shyly, "I got to meet him last month in Colombia."

They talked for the remainder of the practice session and never once mentioned baseball. In Martin Harrison Susan felt she had met someone from her own world, the world of books and ideas and feelings. When he said, with a rueful laugh. "May I see you again tomorrow? I'm afraid I never got to the point of my interview," she had assented gladly. As she pushed Ricky's stroller across the grass to meet Ricardo she reflected that she had not realized how much she missed the company of people like Martin Harrison. She had let most of her friendships slide this last year—for obvious reasons, she thought wryly. Tonight she would begin to write some long-overdue letters.

She saw Martin Harrison the following day and this time they did talk baseball. They talked about Ricardo as well. "He's amazing really," Martin Harrison said seriously. "Very few people realize how tough it is to stay at the top of a professional sport. It's got to get to you, that constant pressure to do it again and again. After a while something's got to break—your performance or, in some cases, your willpower. Look at Borg—he just got sick of it all. And who can blame him?"

"Ricardo *likes* to play baseball," Susan said quietly. "He doesn't seem to feel a great deal of pressure."

"But that's why he's so remarkable, don't you see? He's a professional's professional in most ways. He does everything a ballplayer is supposed to do and he does it brilliantly: fielding, throwing, running, bunting. And hitting, of course. But he has the spirit of a kid who plays in the schoolyard for fun. That's why he's so enjoyable to watch, and why he's such a good model for kids. He's so clearly enjoying himself."

Susan looked thoughtfully at the thin, intelligent face of Martin Harrison. "Yes, that's true."

"And he's so—unruffled. No prima donna outbreaks. No temper tantrums. I've never heard him say a mean word about anyone. Since he's been captain, the Yankee clubhouse is a far more pleasant place."

Listening to Martin, Susan felt deeply gratified. It meant something, that a man of this caliber should appreciate Ricardo. When the writer joined her on the beach two days later, she was unfeignedly glad to see him. She was sitting talking to him animatedly when Ricardo arrived from practice. Susan looked up as his shadow fell across her and her small face lit with welcome. "Ricardo!" she said. "Are you out early?"

"No," he said. His dark eyes moved to Martin Harrison and then back to his wife. Susan was wearing an aquamarine maillot suit that showed off her slender figure and pale golden tan. Her loose hair was hooked behind her ears and she wore large dark sunglasses perched on her small, straight nose.

She smiled up at her husband from her sand chair. "We've been talking so much, I lost track of time."

"Did you, *querida*?" He looked at Martin Harrison, who was sitting cross-legged on the blanket next to a sleeping Ricky. "Have you been discussing baseball?" he asked politely.

Martin laughed and stood up. "No, we've been talking books. Children's books, as a matter of fact. Your wife and I have discovered we shared a common child-hood library."

"Oh?" Ricardo looked at Susan. "I'm going to take a swim."

"I'll come with you," Martin said. "It's hot just sitting here." The two men walked side by side down to the water's edge and Susan watched them. Next to Ricardo, she thought, Martin seemed a mere boy, even though he was certainly a few years older. Ricardo dove into the waves and after a brief minute Martin joined him. They swam for quite some time, and when they returned to her they seemed to be in perfect amity. Ricky had woken up and Susan was holding him on her lap when they got back to the blanket. As Ricardo dried his face and hair her eyes briefly scanned him, going over the wide shoulders, flat stomach and narrow hips. He was deeply tanned, his skin dark and coppery, showing, as he once said humorously, his Indian blood. He draped the towel around his neck and she dragged her eyes from his bare torso and looked at Martin Harrison. Next to Ricardo's splendid height and strength he looked pale and insignificant. Ricky began to fuss and Susan rose.

"The prince is hungry," she announced. "I'll go feed him and be back later."

"Why don't you just bring a bottle down to the beach?" Martin asked innocently.

Ricardo's eyes glinted. "Ricky doesn't like bottles," he said. "He likes his mother." The glint became more pronounced. "In that way he resembles his father," he added wickedly.

Susan could feel herself flushing. "Behave yourself," she said primly. "Martin has been telling me what a model of rectitude you are. You don't want him to find out the truth about your character, do you?" And shifting the burden of her son to her other shoulder, she walked toward the hotel as sedately as she could manage in a bathing suit and bare feet. Behind her she could hear Ricardo chuckle.

Martin stayed in Fort Lauderdale for the duration of spring training and Susan found herself seeing quite a lot of him. She didn't think it odd that he should seek out her company. She assumed he felt the way she did—pleased and delighted to have discovered a person who shared so many of the same interests, the same thoughts—and he said nothing to make her think differently. He talked about his writing, and encouraged her to talk about her own.

"You *must* write if that's how you feel," he told her firmly.

"Yes, I know." She smiled a little ruefully. "But it's so hard. Just living seems to take up so much time. And effort. I know now why there were so few women writers in the past. Its very difficult to be married and to write. I've been remembering quite frequently that Jane Austen was single."

"I'm sure Ricky doesn't mind your writing," he said carefully.

"Of course he doesn't," she answered quickly. Too quickly. "It's just that ordinary things seem to take so much out of me. But that's my fault, not his. Why, when I look at my mother, I realize what a mountain I make out of nothing at all. *She* had two children and managed to find the time to be a working anthropologist, a college teacher who has published a number of articles in her field, a wife and an energetic clubwoman. I often just sit back and look at her in amazement."

"You feel things more," Martin said slowly, his eyes on her delicate, wistful face. He resisted, with difficulty, the desire to reach out and touch her. "You give one hundred percent of yourself to everything you do. With you, nothing is part-time. You may not do as much as your mother, but I'll wager you get a lot more out of what you *do* do."

"Well," said Susan with an obvious attempt at lightness, "that's a comforting thought. I'll try to hold on to it." She gave him an apologetic smile. "I'm sorry to be boring you with my complaints, Martin. It's ridiculous. I have all the modern conveniences, all the help I want to ask for. I'm just making excuses."

They were together on the beach again and Martin's eyes were drawn irresistibly to the slenderness of her throat, the high fullness of her breasts. He lay back on the blanket and shaded his eyes from the sun. "You don't have the two things every writer needs," he said quietly from behind his shielding hand. "Uninterrupted time and a place to work."

Susan gave a heartfelt sigh. "I'll have it when we get home," she said. She too moved from a sitting position to lie on her stomach and prop her chin on her hands. "It's all this moving around these last few months that's thrown me so. I'm a dreadful creature of habit."

"Rick is a bird on the wing, isn't he?" Martin asked in an expressionless voice.

"He has to be, I'm afraid." She turned her head and he uncovered his eyes to look at her. "I'm enough of a writer to resent sometimes the upheaval of husbands and babies, but not enough of a writer to do without them." She smiled a little wryly. "It's the classic feminist dilemma, I fear."

Martin's hazel eyes looked gravely back into hers. Their faces were very close together. Then he glanced up. "Rick!" he said. "I didn't see you coming."

Ricardo didn't answer but stood next to the sand chair looking down at them. Susan smiled at her husband. "Did you win?" she asked. There had been a pre-season game that afternoon.

"No, we lost." He did not smile back but looked down at her out of half-shut eyes. She sat up and pushed the hair off her face.

"What was the score?" asked Martin with an attempt at casualness. Ricardo's eyes moved, consideringly, to his face.

"Seven–four," he said.

Susan picked up her sunglasses and put them on. She sensed the tension, Martin thought. "Ricky didn't wake up in time for me to come by," she said. "Did anything special happen?"

"No." Ricardo's eyes were very dark and there was a decidedly grim look at his mouth. Then his gaze shifted to Martin and the message in that dark stare was unmistakable.

Martin rose to his feet. "Well, I'll be pushing off. Good to see you, Rick." He looked at Susan. She was so very sweet, he thought. So very vulnerable. "Remember what I said," he told her.

She gave him a fleeting smile and then looked again, nervously, at her husband. Martin felt his stomach muscles clench. There was nothing he could do. He managed to return her smile and give a casual wave to Ricardo before he walked away, on rigid legs, down the beach toward the parking lot.

There was silence between Ricardo and Susan after he had left and then Susan started to lie down again. "What did Harrison mean, to remember what he said?" Ricardo asked, and she rose up again and looked at him.

"Oh," she answered uncomfortably, "he just told me to keep on writing. He was trying to be encouraging."

"And I am not encouraging," he said flatly.

"I didn't say that," she protested.

"I see. I'm glad to hear that." He looked at her, measuringly, and then said, "I'm going to swim and then we'll go back to the hotel. It's getting late." He looked at Ricky, who was lying in his basket under the umbrella waving his fists. "Unless you would like to swim first? You must be hot from lying here in the sun."

His courteous offer set her teeth on edge. He was out of temper, and she didn't know why. "No," she replied quietly. "I'm fine. Martin watched him for me before. You go ahead." She watched as he went down to the water's edge and dived in. What could have happened today to put him in such a rotten mood, she wondered. He was making her nervous. She hated it when he was annoyed with her. But she hadn't done anything, she thought in bewilderment. It must have been something that happened during the game. Oh well, she thought with determined optimism, he was hot and he had lost. A swim and dinner should cheer him up.

Chapter Ten

They went back to the hotel and Ricardo watched the news while she bathed and fed Ricky. He was still sitting in front of the TV when she came out of the bathroom from her shower and said, with determined cheerfulness, "The bathroom's free if you want a shower." He got up without a word and went inside.

Susan took special pains with her appearance, putting on mascara, which she rarely used, and choosing a hot-pink dress with spaghetti straps and a full skirt. It was a good foil for her tan and her pale hair and Ricardo had said he liked it when she bought it. She clasped a thin gold chain around her throat and was putting on earrings when Ricardo came out of the bathroom. He had a white towel wrapped around his waist and was scowling.

"I cut myself shaving," he said with great annoyance, and Susan jumped up.

"Oh dear. Let me see it."

"It's all right. But I can't find the alcohol."

"It's in the closet," she said immediately, and went to fetch it for him. He took it from her and went back into the bathroom. He left the door open, and as he raised his hand to apply the cotton swab to his chin Susan saw the muscles in his back ripple. Then there was a knock on the door and she went to let in the girl who baby-sat for Ricky every evening.

They had dinner in the hotel dining room and were joined by Joe Hutchinson and his wife. The extra people relieved the tension between Ricardo and Susan a little and Susan found herself chattering away in a manner quite foreign to her usual quiet self. Ricardo was pleasant although he seemed a little abstracted. They said good night to the Hutchinsons in the lobby and Ricardo said, "Let's go for a walk along the beach. I don't want to go in yet."

"All right," she agreed instantly. "I'm sure Barbara won't mind being out a little late."

It was a beautiful night. The moon hung over the water, huge and silvery, trailing a wake of shimmering light in the dark ocean. Susan took off her high-heeled sandals and Ricardo took off his jacket and loosened his tie. They walked in silence for some time, Susan conscious with every nerve in her body of the man beside her. At first they saw a few other couples but then they came to a stretch of beach that was deserted. Ricardo stopped. Susan halted as well and turned to look at him. Barefoot in the sand, she had to look a very long way up. "Do you want to go back?" she asked.

"Not yet." He spread out his jacket. "Let's sit down."

Without a word she dropped gracefully to the sand. She clasped her arms around her knees and gazed at the moon. "It's so lovely," she said dreamily.

Then he moved, and the sky was blotted out. "So are you, *querida*," he said, and started to kiss her. She slipped her arms around his neck and when he laid her back onto his jacket, she went willingly, kissing him back, caressing the back of his neck with loving fingers. His lips moved from her mouth to her throat and she looked up at the moon as she felt the warmth of his mouth against her bare skin. The huge silver globe shone serenely down on them and Susan smiled a little. "Diana, the moon goddess, is watching us," she whispered softly. His mouth moved to her breast, and through the thin cotton of her dress her nipple stood up hard. She closed her eyes and slid her fingers into his hair, holding him against her. "Ricardo," she breathed.

"Mmm," he answered, his voice muffled by her body. He slipped a hand under her skirt and began to caress her bare leg. For the first time Susan realized what he intended.

"Ricardo!" she said in a very different tone, and tried to sit up. He moved easily so his body was across hers and, locking his mouth on hers, he stifled her protests. Susan was horrified. They were lying right out in the open. Anyone could come along. "Ricardo," she hissed when he finally took his mouth away, "stop this. Now. This instant."

"I don't want to." His mouth was moving along the curve of her throat. His hand slid up her leg to her thigh. "Love me," he whispered and kissed her again, softly this time, gently, coaxingly.

"Not here," she muttered against his mouth. But her body was trembling, calling to him.

He pushed her bodice down and his mouth found the fullness of her breasts. His hand moved further up her leg. Her body quivered, reveling in his touch. For a minute she swayed on the edge of surrender. "Susan," he said, his mouth moving against her. "*Amada.*"

"Ricardo," she whispered unevenly, and the word was enough to tell him that he had won. She whimpered with pleasure as his weight pressed her back against the sand, her arms going up to hold him, her nostrils filled with the scent of him. Her body arched to the demanding urgency of his and they moved together in the shattering climax of passion while the silver moon looked down, silent, beautiful, and indifferent to human desires.

After a long while Ricardo rolled over on his back and stretched. Slowly, reluctantly, Susan opened her eyes and came back to reality. She looked at her husband and felt weak with love. "Darling," she said softly, tentatively. She longed, with every fiber of her body, to hear him say he loved her.

The moonlight clearly showed her his face. It looked bright, triumphant. "I knew I could make you want to," he said. "Little puritan." He laughed.

Susan felt struck to the heart. Was this all he was going to say to her? She sat up and rested her face on her knees, her hair swinging forward to hide her face. "We'd better get dressed," he was saying. "No point in pushing our luck."

"No," she replied numbly. "I suppose not."

He talked cheerfully as they returned along the beach, and when she shivered he hung his jacket around her bare shoulders. His good humor appeared to be completely restored by her surrender on the beach. It was Susan, who had surrendered because she loved him so helplessly, who was left feeling betrayed and forlorn.

They returned to Connecticut at the beginning of April and on the sixth the Yankees opened the season at the stadium. Susan went to the game and sat in a box with a few of the other wives and children. It was a Sunday afternoon and the huge ball park was crowded. Out in center field the World Championship banner fluttered in the breeze and the sun was warm on her head.

When Ricardo came to the plate, the whole stadium rose in ovation. He gave his famous, disarming grin, stepped up to the plate and cracked a single into left field. "God, but he makes it look easy." It was Linda Fatato, wife of the Yankee pitcher speaking. "Sal always says one of the best things about being on the Yankees is that he doesn't have to pitch to Rick." Susan smiled in acknowledgment and looked at her husband as he took a lead off first base. There he was, she thought, the most conspicuous and most elusive of men. He performed with utter naturalness in front of thousands and yet his deepest self remained a mystery. Susan had no doubt that there were subterranean depths to Ricardo. She had met many people who were all on the surface; what you saw was all there was. Ricardo was not like that. He was like an iceberg—the important part of him remained submerged. She listened to the roar of the crowd as he jogged out to center field and thought that her husband was one of the most solitary persons she had ever known.

With the beginning of the baseball season Susan's life took on a more stable pattern. She had her room back to write in, and Maria was there to take Ricky off her hands for a few hours every morning. She found she was able to write and the book started to take on shape and depth.

She would have been perfectly happy if her relationship with Ricardo had been more secure. As it was, there were times when she felt closer to him than she had ever felt to any other human, when it seemed they were together in a way she had never found with anyone else. It happened when they made love, of course. But it was there at other times as well. The evenings, for instance, when they would listen to music, she curled on the end of the sofa and Ricardo stretched out with his head in her lap. Then the utter perfection of Bach, so pure and so clear, seemed to be merely the echo of what there was between her and this man whom she loved.

But there were other times as well, the times when he seemed so far away, so inexplicable, so beyond the reach of her understanding. His initial tolerance of her writing had given way to barely concealed impatience. He did not attempt to infringe on her time, but she was aware, always, of his irritation, his disapproval. Consequently she was very careful not to overrun the time she had set for herself, even though there were times when she was caught up and working well and wanted very much to stay for another hour. But she didn't. She would put down her pen and physically take herself downstairs even if her mind was still wrapped up in another world.

One morning, at the end of May, for the first time, she let herself believe what she knew in her heart of hearts: she had something publishable. When she came downstairs to lunch she was still floating in a cloud. Ricardo had spent the morning mowing the lawn. He had a night game that evening and was leaving directly after it for a two-week road trip. Susan smiled at him a little absently and went to get Ricky from the playpen. She carried him out to the kitchen and put his jars of food in a baby dish to warm them up. Ricardo followed her and began to tell her something and she listened for a few minutes without really hearing him. She had an opening sentence for her next chapter forming in her mind.

"Susan, are you listening to me?" The edge on his voice was what caught her attention.

"I'm sorry, Ricardo." She sounded contrite. "What were you saying?"

"I was telling you that the men are coming to excavate for the pool this week." His face was dark with annoyance. "I won't be here, if you remember, and you must see to it."

"I'm sorry, darling," she repeated. "I was thinking of something else. I'm paying attention now. What do you want me to do?"

He proceeded to give her instructions and she listened carefully, but she could tell from the clipped tone of his voice that he was still irritated. "You've made out a list of your schedule for me, haven't you?" she asked at the end of his lecture. "In case I have to get in touch with you?"

"Susan." He looked even more annoyed. "I have just told you, very clearly, what you must do."

"I know that, Ricardo," she said with gentle dignity, "and I understand what you've said. But I just want to be sure I can get in touch with you. Suppose something happened to Ricky, for instance? You wouldn't want to wait to find out until you called at night, would you?"

"No." He watched as she put a bib on Ricky and propped him up in the high chair. "I've left a schedule and a list of hotels and phone numbers on my desk," he said.

"Good." She spooned some pureed vegetables into Ricky's mouth. "I do wish you didn't have to be away so much," she said as she wiped Ricky's chin with a cloth.

"Do you?" he said. He was standing just behind her and she could feel his eyes on the back of her neck.

"Don't forget Miss Garfield will be in on Thursday," he added. "She's the woman I engaged to take Mrs. Noonan's place." Mrs. Noonan, the woman who handled Ricardo's mail, had retired to Florida with her husband.

Susan turned to look up at Ricardo. "Is there anything I need to tell her?"

"Not really. Just make her feel at home. I went over everything with her the other day when she was here."

Ricky yelled and she turned back and fed him another spoonful. Ricardo smiled—she could hear it in his voice—and said, "I'm hungry, too. When is lunch? Where is Maria?"

"Maria's downstairs doing the laundry and lunch will be ready in twenty minutes."

"I'll go shave first." He walked to the kitchen door. "Have you packed for me yet?"

"Not yet. I'll do it after lunch, after Maria puts away the laundry." She turned her head. "Oh, and Ricardo, if you're going upstairs, will you please take your jacket with you?"

"Of course," he replied with absolute courtesy.

Later, when she went upstairs after lunch to pack his suitcase, she saw that he had indeed carried his sweat jacket upstairs. He had also deposited it in a heap on the bed. Susan saw it, frowned and then laughed. "Oh well," she said out loud, "I suppose I mustn't expect miracles. It *was* upstairs. It wasn't on the floor. It'll probably take the rest of my married life to get him to hang it in the closet."

On Thursday the doorbell rang promptly at nine a.m. and Susan called, "I'll get it, Maria!" and went to the door. She had been waiting to greet Miss Garfield and make sure she had everything she needed before disappearing upstairs to her desk. She opened the door and found herself confronting a tall, slim, gorgeous creature who couldn't have been a day over twenty-five. The vision smiled and said, "I'm Vicky Garfield. I've come to work on Rick's correspondence."

"Oh," said Susan blankly. "Yes. Do come in." She held the door open wider and the other girl walked over the threshold. "I'm Susan Montoya," Susan added quickly. "My husband isn't here, but I'll be glad to show you around and help you get started."

"Thank you, Mrs. Montoya." Vicky Garfield smiled. She was at least five feet eight inches tall and she had pitch-black hair and violet eyes. She wore a slim, smart dress and elegant sandals. Next to her Susan felt small, insignificant and frumpy. "Rick explained he would be on the road," Miss Garfield was going on, "and he showed me what he wanted and where to find things when I was here the other day."

That was the second time she had called him Rick. Susan cleared her throat and glanced down at her own dungaree skirt and ancient espadrilles. Her hair needed a wash and she had put it into pigtails for the morning. She felt ridiculous. "Well, then, you know where the study is," she said faintly.

"Yes. Perhaps you could just help me locate this week's correspondence."

"Of course." Susan led the way to the study. Ricardo's desk was in its usual immaculate order. He was as meticulous about his business papers as he was careless about his clothes. "The letters are kept here." Susan pointed to a large wire bin. "Most of them are fan letters from kids, but there are also a lot of requests for appearances, for commercial endorsements and so on. But my husband explained all that to you."

"Yes, he did." The girl smiled politely at Susan. "Thank you, Mrs. Montoya. I suppose I'd better get to work."

Susan smiled back with equal politeness. "If you want anything, coffee or tea or something to eat, Maria will be happy to help you. Have you met Maria?"

"Yes, the other day."

"Oh. Well—good luck, Miss Garfield." Susan closed the study door and went to the stairs, her mind in a whirl. *Where* had Ricardo found that gorgeous creature? And why hadn't his wife been at home when he interviewed her?

She cast her mind back, trying to recall when Ricardo had told her he'd hired a replacement for Mrs. Noonan. It had been about a week ago, she remembered. She had been out for the afternoon, having lunch and going to the new exhibit at the Yale Art Gallery with Maggie Ellis. He'd told her when she got home that he had found someone. She frowned. He'd said she came from an agency. "A modeling agency, most likely," Susan now muttered with unusual waspishness. She did not get very much accomplished on her book that morning.

Miss Garfield finished at two o'clock and sought Susan out before she left. "I've put aside all the mail that needs Rick's personal attention and answered the rest," she said. "Do you want me to stop at the post office and mail it?"

"If you would be so kind," Susan responded formally. "Were there enough stamps?"

"Yes. But we're running low on the pictures that Rick wanted included in all answers to his fan mail. Shall I order more?"

"Yes. Yes, I suppose you should."

"All right, then." Miss Garfield gave her a brief, impersonal smile. "I'll see you next week, Mrs. Montoya."

"Yes." Susan's widely set gray eyes did not reflect her own answering smile. "Yes, Miss Garfield, you will."

"Miss Garfield came today," she told Ricardo when he called that night. "She seems very competent. She is going to order some more pictures—she said you were running low."

"Am I? That's the sort of thing Mrs. Noonan always saw to. Evidently Vicky is going to be all right."

He'd called her Vicky. "Yes," said Susan, a little hollowly. "So it seems."

"Have they started work on the pool?" he asked.

"Yes, they came today at last." She filled him in on what had been happening around the house, told him that Ricky was cutting a tooth and listened to his report on tonight's game.

"I miss you," she said softly as he was preparing to hang up.

"I miss you too, *querida*," he said and the dark tones of his voice were like a caress. "I'll miss you even more in a few hours," he added, and now she could hear the familiar amusement. "As a roommate, Joe doesn't compare with a wife."

"Why?" she asked blandly. "Does he snore?"

"I'll explain it to you when I get home." The note of amusement deepened. "In fact, I'll *show* you."

"You do that," she said gently. "Good-bye, darling."

He chuckled. "Good-bye. I'll call you tomorrow."

He hung up and Susan sat quietly for a few minutes staring at the phone. Then she went to pick up Ricky, who was fussing in his playpen. Later, she would watch the game on television. At least that way she would be able to see him. She closed her eyes and rested her cheek against her son's dark silky head. Her stomach muscles were taut and she felt as if someone were squeezing her heart. She loved Ricardo so much. If only she could rest secure in the knowledge that he loved her too.

But he didn't. To love someone meant to share oneself with the beloved, and that Ricardo did not do. She doubted if he ever had with anyone—certainly he did not with his mother or his sisters. But, then, they were only women. Women, in Ricardo's view, had been made for specific purposes—for sex, for motherhood, for ministering to a man's other appetites and needs. In response, men provided women with material comfort and security. That was the view her husband had about marriage—the view he had of her, his wife. She supposed it was a conception that had a lot to recommend it. She could always count on his recognizing his obligations toward her. She knew that he would always, unhesitatingly, put himself between her and any danger the world might threaten her with. If he was autocratic he was also invariably gentle. He had a temper but she had long ceased to fear it. He never allowed it to go beyond mild annoyance and irritation. She wasn't important enough for him to get really mad at her, she thought a little desolately, just as she wasn't important enough for him to confide in. And she couldn't push herself on him. Some things had to be given freely or not at all. She pressed her lips against Ricky's downy head and felt tears sting behind her eyes. Ricky squirmed, seeking her breast, and shakily she laughed. "All right, sweetheart. Mommy will feed you." Blinking hard, she carried the baby into the other room.

Chapter Eleven

Ricardo hadn't been home above a few hours before Susan asked him, "Where did you find Miss Garfield? Didn't you tell me she came through an agency?"

"No, I did not." He gave her a brief, dark look. "You were probably thinking about your book and not listening to me. She's Frank Moyer's daughter."

"You never told me that," Susan said positively.

"I did too." His eyes closed a little and he rested his head against the back of his chaise longue. They were sitting out on the patio in the warm sun. Ricardo had flown into New York early that morning after a night game in California. He had not had much sleep.

Susan looked at his relaxed figure, clad now in running shorts and an old T-shirt. He had the strongest legs of anyone she had ever seen: long, deeply tanned, black-haired and hard as iron. She leaned back in her own chaise and squinted into the sun. "Frank Moyer," she said idly. "Isn't he the man who runs the Y?"

"Yes. I mentioned to him that I was looking for a new secretary and he suggested Vicky. She's in the process of getting a divorce and I guess she's found time hanging on her hands."

"Oh." Susan's eyes swung back to her husband. "Why is she getting a divorce?"

His lashes lifted and his astonishing large brown eyes regarded her speculatively. "Why all this interest in Vicky Garfield? You aren't jealous of her?"

Susan bit her lip and then, ruefully, she smiled. "Yes, I am. She makes me feel like an untidy little shrimp. The last time she came I even put on makeup and a dress—but it didn't help."

His eyes glinted and a faint smile touched his mouth. "Vicky is getting a divorce because she found out her husband was having an affair with his secretary."

Susan's eyes widened. "He must have been mad," she said. "I mean, *look* at Vicky."

"I have, *querida*," he murmured wickedly, and she frowned. "And what I see," he went serenely on, "is a foolish young woman who runs off to the divorce court at the least sign of trouble." He closed his eyes again. "Women have no sense at all," he said sleepily. Ricardo did not approve of divorce.

"It seems to me Vicky's husband is the one with no sense," Susan said severely. "If he loved her and wanted to keep her, he should have kept his hands off his secretary."

The brown eyes opened again. "Now you are the one who sounds foolish." He held out his hand. "Susan," he said, his voice soft and dark. "let's drop the subject of Vicky. Come here."

She went over to sit on the edge of his chaise longue. "I thought we'd put some steaks on the grill for dinner," she said. "Are you hungry? Do you want a snack first?"

"I'm hungry," he answered. He was holding her hand

and now his fingers moved caressingly over the thin skin of her wrist. "But not for food."

"I see," she whispered, and, leaning down, she kissed him, slowly and lingeringly. When she raised her head they were both breathing a little more quickly.

"Let's go upstairs," he said.

"All right," she answered, all thought of Vicky Garfield and her divorce swamped before the rising tide of heat in her blood.

Susan's mother had a party a few days later and both Susan and Ricardo attended. Mrs. Morgan had invited a large crowd of friends, colleagues and neighbors and she had carefully consulted Susan about Ricardo's schedule before she set the day. He had very few days off and Mrs. Morgan was anxious to have her son-in-law present.

Susan had given her mother a date and the party had been scheduled. Ricardo, who knew no one, was soon the center of a large, attentive group and Susan wandered off a little to see if she could do anything to help.

"Susan," said a male voice that sounded oddly familiar. "I've been waiting for you to come."

Slowly Susan turned and looked at the boy—man now, actually, who was facing her under the big maple tree. "Michael . . ." she said wonderingly, "is it really you?"

A familiar wry smile touched his mouth. "It's really me."

"I can't believe it," she said slowly. "It's been so long."

"I know. Too long." His narrow, sensitive face looked much older, she thought. His light blue eyes flashed a look at Ricardo and then came back to her. "I only came because Dad said you would be here . Can we sit down and talk?"

"Of course," she replied instantly. "Let's go to the grape arbor."

She was still there forty minutes later when Ricardo came looking for her. "Ah, there you are Susan," he said as he came up to her. "I thought you'd gotten lost."

"No." Michael had risen as Ricardo approached and now Susan got up too. "This is Michael Brandon, Ricardo," she said, in introduction. "We grew up together. Michael, my husband, Ricardo Montoya."

Ricardo put out his hand, and after a barely perceptible hesitation, Michael took it. Ricardo said something pleasant and as Michael replied Susan studied the two men before her. Michael only stayed for a few more minutes and ten minutes later Susan saw him leaving the party.

"You're very quiet," Ricardo said to her as they drove home later. "Is it because of that boy you were talking to?"

She sighed. It was a relief to be able to talk about it. "Yes. He's changed a great deal. I must admit he's made me feel very sad."

"You said you grew up together?" His voice sounded detached, impersonal.

"Yes. He was always a year ahead of me in school— from nursery days on up. And we were always good friends."

"Just friends?" he asked.

"No." She stared out the window at the dusk. The trees of the Merritt Parkway were rushing by them. "You're going to get a ticket if you don't slow down," she said automatically, and the car slowed. "He was a

brilliant boy," she went on softly, "but he was unhappy.
Rebellious. He didn't get on with his father or his stepmother. He was—oh, angry and hurt and he struck out
at others because he was so unhappy himself. I understood that, you see. I understood *him*. With me he
could be himself." She rested her head against the high
seat behind her. "I've always felt I failed him. I cared—
but I didn't care enough to give him what he wanted,
what he needed."

He grunted and she shot him a quick look. "Not just
sex—though there *was* that too. He wanted me to run
away and marry him. He'd gone to Harvard, and he
was wretched there." She sighed very softly. "He was so
brilliant. He made high seven hundreds on both his
college board SATs. And then he failed out of college."

"He must have wanted to fail out," Ricardo said noncommittally.

"Yes. I was finishing high school and he wanted us to
run away. I didn't want to give up college, give up my
own life. What it comes down to is that I didn't love
him enough."

"What has he been doing?"

"Oh, Ricardo," the words were a cry of pain, "he's
just been drifting around, working on oil rigs, doing
odd jobs. He's gotten so—quiet. All the fight seemed
to be knocked out of him. Talking to him made me feel
like crying."

"It's sad to see a good mind wasted, but you mustn't
blame yourself, Susan. A man must find his own way.
Either he has the strength to make it, or he does not."

"No," she said, after a minute in a very low voice,
"that may be true for you, Ricardo, but it isn't true for
everybody. I *know* my being with him would have made

a difference." She looked out the side window once
again. "Poor Michael," she almost whispered.

They finished the rest of the drive in silence.

Ricardo left for another quick road trip the following
week, and the day after he left Martin Harrison called
Susan to ask her out to lunch. She was pleased to hear
from him and accepted gladly.

It had been quite a while since she had been into
New York and she dressed with care and pleasure: a
softly woven peach-colored suit and a creamy cotton
and linen blouse set off her own coloring quite satisfac-
torily, she thought. In fact, she felt quite as sophisticated as Vicky Garfield as she stepped into the
vestibule of the restaurant Martin had chosen and gave
his name to the maître d'.

He was at the table and waiting for her. "Susan." She
had forgotten how southern his voice was. "You look
marvelous," he said, and sat down again as the waiter
seated her.

"Thank you, sir." The gleam of admiration in his hazel eyes was very pleasant. She grinned. "It's fun, coming into New York for lunch. It makes me feel very
sophisticated."

"Does it?" The waiter reappeared and Martin asked,
"Would you like a drink?"

"Yes." She frowned thoughtfully. "I think I'll have a
Bloody Mary." Martin ordered a martini, and as the
waiter went away he looked at Susan with smiling eyes.

"Do you want to feel sophisticated?" he asked.

"Well, it's nice for a change. I spend most of the
time smelling like milk and baby powder."

"Tell Rick to take you out more," he recommended
laconically.

The waiter arrived back with the drinks and set them on the table. Susan raised her glass and said, "Cheers. It's good to see you again."

"It's good to see *you*." He took a swallow of his martini. "I would have called you sooner but I got the distinct impression that Rick was not overly enamored of our friendship."

Susan's eyes widened. "Don't be silly, Martin. Ricardo's not like that."

He smiled a little lopsidedly. "I would be, if you were my wife."

"No, you wouldn't be," she answered serenely. "You'd be happy to know that I had a friend whom I liked very much."

He was studying the olive in his drink. "How is the writing coming along?" he asked abruptly, changing the subject.

"Well . . ." she let out her breath on a long note, and then proceeded to tell him.

"This was very lovely," she said as she finished her coffee an hour and a half later. "I do thank you so much, Martin."

"I meant what I said earlier, you know," he said. "You ought to get Rick to take you out more."

She smiled gently. "Ricardo has a very busy schedule at the moment, I'm afraid. And he really doesn't *like* going out all that much. But we do see people, you know. As a matter of fact, I'm having a party in two weeks—just a backyard picnic. We've built a new pool. I was hoping you'd come."

"I'd love to," he answered immediately. "When is it?"

"June twenty-eighth."

"I'll write it on my calendar," he promised.

"Good."

"Can I get you a taxi?"

"No, thanks. I'm going to do some shopping while I'm here." She gave him a charming, rueful look. "Ricardo has this new secretary who is so elegant that I feel like a frump every time I look at her. I've decided I need some new clothes."

He looked down at her fair shining head. "You could never look frumpy," he said gravely.

"You haven't seen Vicky Garfield," she retorted. She rose up on tiptoe and kissed his cheek. "Thanks again. We'll see you soon."

"Yes. Soon." He stood in the doorway of the restaurant and watched as she walked away down the street.

Martin duly presented himself at the Montoya residence in Stamford on June twenty-eighth. He parked his car on the wide circular drive behind a lineup of other cars and walked around the house toward the sounds of voices and laughter.

There were about twenty people on the patio and several in the pool. Susan saw him standing there and came across to greet him. "You are looking very fragile and very beautiful in that raspberry dress," he said, and she smiled, not knowing how it lighted up her widely set, luminous eyes.

"I'm so glad you came," she said simply. "There are quite a few people here you must know. Come along and let me introduce you around."

It was a very casual, pleasant party, with food spread on a table in the shade of the patio and a bar where guests could help themselves. Rick came over to greet him and stayed to chat for a while. Martin, who was tall himself, was uncomfortably conscious of the superior height and strength of his host. Ricardo was wearing lightweight khaki slacks and a navy Izod shirt and he looked muscular, lean and very tough. His manner was pleasant but Martin was aware of a cool look in the great dark eyes that made him feel distinctly wary.

There was a little stir among the Yankee players who were standing by the bar and Martin and Ricardo turned to look. A stunningly beautiful girl, tall and slim and raven-haired, was coming out to the patio. "Excuse me," Ricardo murmured to Martin, and went over to greet the new arrival. The girl smiled up at him radiantly, and put a hand on his forearm. They spoke together for a few minutes and then Ricardo took her over to the bar to get her a drink and introduce her to the people there. Martin looked for Susan.

He found her deep in conversation with a silver-haired distinguished-looking man and an equally distinguished-looking woman of approximately the same age. As he watched, the woman said something to Susan and she turned toward the bar. The black-haired beauty had accepted a drink from Ricardo and was smiling perfunctorily at the men who were being introduced. That one is only interested in Rick, Martin thought, and he turned back to Susan. She was excusing herself, and as Martin watched she crossed the patio toward her husband. Martin watched in admiration as she greeted the newcomer with gentle dignity. Next to the tall, magnificent, dark-haired splendor of her husband and the other woman she looked very small and slight and fragile. With a sudden flash of insight, Martin realized that this must be the Vicky Garfield who Susan said made her feel like a frump.

A middle-aged Spanish-looking woman came out of the house and crossed to say something to Susan. As Martin watched, Susan excused herself and disappeared inside. Vicky Garfield slid a hand into Ricardo's arm and drew him away toward the pool.

"Mr. Harrison?" a woman's voice said at his elbow. He turned and found the distinguished woman Susan had been talking to regarding him with a smile. "I'm Helen Morgan," she said, "Susan's mother."

"Mrs. Morgan." He put out his hand to take her extended one. "How nice to meet you."

It was a successful party in that all the guests appeared to have a very good time. Vicky Garfield hung on Ricardo the whole time, but it was not awkward because Susan did not appear to mind nor did Ricardo appear to take it very seriously. He seemed to be in a relaxed mood, his eyes sparkling with good humor and amused comprehension as he looked down into Vicky's gorgeous face. He did not seem at all smitten, Martin thought. He said something of the sort to Susan.

"I know that," she responded quietly. "She flatters him and he enjoys it. That's all."

He looked at her closely. "After all, in Rick's book, that's what women are for," he said with sudden insight. "Isn't that true?"

Susan was afraid it was all too true, but she wasn't about to say so to Martin. "Not necessarily," she answered coolly. She looked up at him out of remote, gray eyes.

"Where have you gone?" he asked very gently after a moment.

"What do you mean?"

"I mean that you can retreat into yourself faster and put up a No Trespassing sign more successfully than anyone else I've ever known. It can be rather— disconcerting."

Her face relaxed a little. "I'm sorry. I just don't feel like discussing my husband."

"All right, that's fair enough. Now, what about letting me see your book?"

"Oh, Martin." She looked abruptly very young and very vulnerable. "I'm getting cold feet."

"Nonsense. We discussed this at lunch. If it's any good, I'll tell you. And recommend it to my agent. If it isn't any good, I'll tell you that too." He looked at her soberly. "You didn't just write it for yourself, Susan."

She wrinkled her nose. "I know. Well, come along. It's in my study. I've made you a copy."

He grinned. "Good girl," he said, and followed her through the french doors and into the house.

"It went well, I think," Susan said to Ricardo much later, after the last of the guests had driven away.

"Yes, I think so." He smiled a little. "You have the knack of making people feel comfortable, *querida*."

"Thank you," she said in a low voice.

He yawned and sat down in one of the patio chairs. "I have a sore throat from talking so much."

She sat down herself on a chaise longue and stretched out her legs. "Vicky was such a good audience, I expect you couldn't help yourself."

It was quite dark now and the only light came from the family room through the patio doors. She felt rather than saw him look at her. "She is a beautiful woman," he said. "It's second nature to her to be a good audience for a man." His tone was casual, dismissive.

Susan stared up at the starry sky. No, she thought, Vicky Garfield was not important to him. Which was not to say that he wouldn't sample what she was so clearly offering. After all, he had as much as said he thought marital fidelity was strictly for women. "I shouldn't make the same mistake with Vicky that her husband made with *his* secretary," she said coolly, warningly.

There was a moment of startled silence. Then, "Susan!" He sounded delighted. "You're jealous."

"No, I'm not." There was a pause. "Well, maybe I am," she amended. "You have to admit she's hardly subtle."

"She doesn't intrigue me, *querida*." She saw him move in the darkness and then he was sitting on the edge of her chaise. "You are the one who intrigues me. What were you doing with Harrison for such a long time in the house?"

She was astonished that he had noticed their absence. "I gave him my book to read," she said a little unwillingly. The subject of her book always seemed to cause constraint between them.

"I see."

She looked up, trying to read his face. "I can trust him to tell me if it's any good or not, you see. I—I *need* to know, Ricardo."

"I see," he said again.

She went determinedly on. "If it *is* good, he's going to recommend it to his agent."

There was a silence for so long that it became an almost tangible presence between them, then as last he spoke. "I don't make any pretense to possessing Harrison's critical ability, but you never thought to show it to me first?"

She was dumbfounded. "I never thought you would be interested."

He flexed his shoulder muscles almost wearily. "No, I suppose I haven't been very supportive, have I?"

"You've let me have the time to work," she protested. "I *have* appreciated that, Ricardo."

He stood up. "It's late and you must be tired."

"Yes." She let him help her to her feet.

"I rather expected your friend Michael to be here to-night," he said as he locked the french doors.

"I asked him. But he didn't want to come." She sighed. "I don't think seeing me again made him very happy."

"It was not seeing you, *querida*. It was seeing *me* that bothered him."

"Poor Michael," she said.

"Poor Michael, indeed." He took her arm. "Come to bed." She leaned against him gratefully as they went up the stairs together.

Chapter Twelve

A strange man arrived immediately after breakfast the following day and spent the morning closeted in the study with Ricardo. He was a little abstracted over lunch and Susan didn't ask him any questions. She had long since learned that any questions from her would invariably be met by a brief, "It was business," answer. If Martin thought she could hang out a No Trespassing sign, she reflected wryly, he should see Ricardo in action.

The day was pleasantly cool and Ricardo asked her if she'd like to take Ricky and go down to the Stamford Nature Museum. She was delighted by the idea and they packed the baby, the car seat and the stroller into the station wagon for the five-minute drive. Ricky was fascinated by the animals on the small farm and Ricardo and Susan enjoyed them almost as much. After walking about for an hour, they sat down by the lake to watch the ducks and Ricky fell asleep on the grass. "The man who was here this morning was from Latin American Watch," Ricardo said as he slowly threw bread to the birds. "It's a human rights organization that deals solely with Latin America. They've asked me to be on their board of directors."

Susan looked curiously at his expressionless profile. "I see. And what did you say?"

He turned to look at her and the set of his mouth was grim. "I said I'd think about it. I've been involved behind the scene for a few years, but . . ."

Somehow Susan was not surprised that a human rights organization was one of Ricardo's "business" connections. "But what?" she prompted as his voice trailed off.

"I don't have just myself to consider anymore," he said a little roughly.

"I see," she said, and now she *was* surprised.

"It would involve some trips," he was going on. "And I won't be very popular in some circles."

She hadn't thought of that. Abruptly she remembered the latest headlines from Central America and shivered. He could be in danger. If she knew Ricardo, he would go into this thing wholeheartedly if he went in at all. "You'll probably wind up on everyone's death list," she said faintly.

He laughed but sobered almost immediately. "It won't be as bad as that, Susan. I'm too prominent a figure to be picked off easily. But I want to be honest with you. It will involve me traveling about a bit, and it will probably involve some nasty accusations, too."

She thought again of the unmarked graves and unknown prisons all over the troubled countries of Latin America. The thought of Ricardo lying in one of them made her feel physically sick. "And if I say I don't want you to do it?" she asked uncertainly.

"Don't you?" he responded bluntly.

Nervously she tore at the grass with unsteady fingers. He wanted to do it, she thought. He might do it even if she objected. But he was asking. For the first time, he was asking.

She kept her eyes on her own hands but she felt him there beside her. They were such complete opposites, she thought. The strong and the weak, the courageous and the fearful, the adventurous and the timid. Her whole instinct was to keep him safely home by his own hearth. She clasped her hands around her knees and cleared her throat. "If you want to do it, then you should," she said, she hoped firmly.

She could feel some of the tension drain out of him. "Do you mean that?"

"Yes." She turned to look at him. "I hope you have a good insurance policy," she added lightly.

He grinned. "It won't come to that, *querida,* I promise."

"I'll hold you to that," she replied a little tartly. "No matter how good the policy, you're worth a lot more to me alive than dead."

His large brown eyes sparkled. "I hope you're not just referring to financial matters."

She remained grave. "Naturally, I'm referring to financial matters. What else would I be referring to?"

"I have no idea," he replied, and chuckled at her look. "I'm not a fish to always rise to your bait."

She made a face at him. "It's getting late and you have a game tonight."

"That's true." He yawned and stretched and rose to his feet with easy grace. "You collect the baby and I'll collect the junk," he said. She had to blink away a sudden tear before she could move to obey his instructions.

Two days after the party Martin called and asked if he could come up to Connecticut to see Susan. "Of course," she responded breathlessly.

"I could come up tonight. I have an appointment this afternoon."

"Tonight will be fine. Oh," she added belatedly, "Ricardo has a night game. He won't be home."

"I know," Martin responded briefly. "I'll see you later, Susan."

Susan did not mention the phone call to Ricardo. She would tell him Martin's verdict later, she thought. The house was quiet, with Maria gone and Ricky asleep, when Martin arrived at about eight o'clock. Susan brought him into the family room and gestured him into a comfortable chair. She herself took the sofa. He was carrying her manuscript and her eyes kept going back to stare at it. "Well?" she said tensely. "What did you think?"

"I thought it was going to be good, Susan," he said deliberately. "Knowing you, I was sure it would be publishable. But I never expected this."

Her gray eyes searched his. "You liked it?"

"I thought it was wonderful. Extraordinary, actually. Where the hell did you learn to write like this?"

Her eyes began to glow. "Oh, Martin, do you mean that?"

"I mean every word of it." He was deadly serious. "You were Kate, of course?"

"Yes." She spoke carefully, hesitantly. "It's not all autobiographical, Martin. The central complication is fiction. But I *did* have an older sister like Jane—beautiful, joyous, intelligent."

"What happened to her?" he asked curiously.

"She died in a car crash two years ago. It was so terribly tragic. Sara was so gifted, so lovely. It just wasn't fair. I suppose in a way this book is my tribute to her."

"But you realize, of course," he said softly, "that the interesting character is the child."

"Kate? Well, of course, she's the filter through which the action is seen. . . ."

"She's the interesting character," he repeated, very definitely. "It doesn't surprise me at all that *she* is the one who grew up to marry the hero."

Susan felt her skin flushing. If only he knew why Ricardo had married her . . . "But you liked it?" she got out.

"I thought it was superb. There are a few rough patches, perhaps, but Susan, I really think it's the best first novel I've ever read."

She glowed with pleasure. "Oh, Martin, it means so much to me to hear you say that! I *thought* it was good, but then I didn't really know." Her small face was alight with happiness. "*Thank* you."

"Thank you for showing it to me." He looked down at the manuscript on his knees. "May I show it to my agent? I'm quite sure he'll be interested."

"Of course you may." She gave a little shiver of excitement. "I'm so *happy.*"

He smiled a little crookedly. "Suppose you let me tell you a little about the publishing world," he offered. "You're such an innocent."

Susan might be an innocent, but Ricardo most definitely was not. She would leave all the business arrangements up to him. However, she did not think it would be tactful for her to say as much to Martin and so she smiled and said softly, "That would be very nice, Martin."

They talked about publishing and then about her book again and Susan found herself telling him a little about her own childhood. Before they knew it, it was almost midnight.

"I'd better get going," Martin said as he glanced in deep surprise at his watch. "I had no idea it was this late." He stared at Susan for a minute, his eyes taking in her slender figure clad in a soft, smoky-blue summer dress. "I can never keep track of the time when I'm with you," he said quietly.

Susan smiled at him a little sleepily. "I know. I talk your ear off." Her hair shimmered in the soft light of the lamp and her eyes looked wide and dark and mysterious. "You've been such a good friend to me, Martin," she said.

"I'm afraid friendship is not the emotion I feel for you," he responded a little harshly. "Surely you've sensed that?"

She had been curled up on the end of the sofa and now she sat up and swung her legs to the floor. The corner of her dress stayed caught under her for a minute and he had a brief glimpse of a bare, golden-brown thigh before she pulled it firmly down.

"Susan." He moved to sit beside her on the sofa. "Surely you've guessed by now that I'm in love with you."

Susan stared at him in dumb astonishment. He picked up her hands and bent his head to kiss them. "Please, Martin," she said a little breathlessly. "Don't."

"I tried to stay away from you," he was going on, his voice muffled by her hands. "I didn't call you for months, but then I couldn't stay away any longer. And once I saw you again, I was lost."

"Oh Martin," Susan said in great distress. "I had no idea. And you shouldn't be saying these things to me. I'm not free to listen. You know that."

"You could be," he answered, and still retaining his grasp of her hands, he looked up. "I know it sounds almost ludicrous," he said, "to think that any woman could prefer me to Rick Montoya. But I think I'd be a better husband to you. I understand you, you see." She stared at him out of enormous eyes and slowly, very slowly, she shook her head. "God, Susan," he groaned, "I love you so much." He slid his hands up her bare arms to grasp her shoulders. "Will you at least think about what I've said?"

But Susan wasn't listening. The sixth sense that always told her when Ricardo had entered the room caused her to turn her head and look at the doorway. Her husband was standing there watching them. His face was expressionless but at his side his fists were slowly opening and closing. "Ricardo!" Susan said breathlessly, and Martin dropped his hands from her shoulders.

"Martin was just leaving," she said, and stood up.

"I see," Ricardo answered. He did not sound angry but Susan's eyes were on his clenched fists. Her heart was hammering so hard she thought she would faint.

Martin was very pale. He too got to his feet. "Do you want me to go?" he asked Susan.

She glanced once more at Ricardo before she turned to Martin. "Yes," she said tensely.

Martin hesitated, obviously unsure if he should leave her alone with her ominously silent husband.

Susan was icy with fear but she managed to speak calmly, quietly and with authority. "Martin. Go, please. Now." She stared at him, willing him to obey her, and after another moment's hesitation, he did. Ricardo was still in the doorway and so he went out the french doors to the patio. They could hear the sound of his feet on the stone. Then, a few moments later, came the sound of his car starting up.

Susan hadn't realized she was holding her breath. She let it out now and turned to look at her husband. His hands had relaxed but she saw the little telltale pulse beating in his right temple. "I'm sorry," she said softly. "It was my fault. I should have seen it coming and I didn't."

Still he said nothing and she crossed the room toward him. She was not physically afraid now that Martin had gone. She knew Ricardo would never hurt her. But she had been terrified for Martin. She stopped in front of her husband. "You have a right to be angry," she said humbly. "It was very stupid of me."

"Stupid not to have timed this better?" he said deliberately.

She stared up at him. He had been hurt and now he was trying to hurt back. "Do you think I've been unfaithful to you?" she asked.

He looked down into her clear, truthful eyes. After a minute his face relaxed a fraction. "No, I suppose not," he said. "What was he doing here?"

"He came to bring back my book." All the joy Martin's words had given her were effectively destroyed by this sequel. She had to break through to Ricardo. She couldn't bear the way he was looking at her. "Ricardo," she said, "darling." She put her arms around his waist and laid her cheek against his chest. He was stiff and unyielding under her hands. "We talked about my book," she said, "and then, just as he was leaving, he broke down and said he was in love with me." The look in Martin's eyes came back to her. "He meant it, I think. Poor Martin." She turned her face into Ricardo's shoulder. The scent of him, the feel of him, drove all thought of Martin from her mind. "I'm so sorry," she said, her mouth pressed against his shoulder.

After a very long minute his arms came up to circle her lightly. "He has been in love with you for a long time," he said. "Apparently you were the only one who didn't see it."

The relief she felt at the feel of his arms about her was tremendous. "Did you?" she asked.

"Of course."

She closed her eyes. "Why didn't you warn me?" she murmured.

"I didn't think I had to. I thought all women had a sixth sense for something like that."

It was true, she thought, tightening her arms about his waist. She should have known. But she was so absorbed by Ricardo that she didn't see other men very clearly. "It's bad enough being married to a femme fatale," he was going on, "but an innocent femme fatale is murder."

"A femme fatale? I?" She was so astonished her voice squeaked.

"You." Very, very briefly his cheek came down to touch her hair. Then he released her. "What did Harrison have to say about your book?" he asked.

She longed quite desperately to feel his arms about her once again, but he had put her away from him very definitely. "He liked it," she said.

"I was sure he would." Ricardo sat down in his favorite chair and stretched out his legs.

A thought struck her. "Ricardo, do you suppose he was only saying that because—because of how he feels about me?" she asked in dismay. She dropped down onto an ottoman at his feet.

"No, I don't. What exactly did he say?" She told him,

and when she had finished he nodded slowly. "I'm not exactly one of Harrison's admirers," he said then, "but I don't think he'd mislead you on something like this."

"Not deliberately, no. . . ."

"Why don't you let me read it?" he asked.

"I'd love you to read it," she responded instantly. "If you're sure you want to?"

In response he held out his hand. "No time like the present," he said laconically.

She got up from her ottoman and went to retrieve the manila envelope from the sofa. "You don't mean to start reading now?" she asked as she gave it to him. "It's after midnight."

"I'll sleep late tomorrow," he said, and slid the manuscript out of the folder.

She was utterly disconcerted. She had been sure he would want to make love to her tonight, to assert his rights in the face of another claim. And here he was, putting his legs up on her ottoman, making himself comfortable for a long stay. "Well," she said uncertainly, "I guess I'll go up to bed."

"Um." His eyes were on her manuscript. "You'd better. One of us is going to have to get up with Ricky tomorrow."

Very very slowly she trailed off to their room. The whole scene after Martin had left had been very anticlimactic, she thought crossly. Once she had convinced Ricardo of her innocence, he had totally lost interest. And she had been sure he was going to murder Martin! He didn't care, she thought miserably, as she undressed upstairs. So long as she remained sexually faithful to him, he didn't care about her other feelings. She should have let him stew for a while. It would have served him right. She got into bed and curled up under the sheet.

She remembered Ricardo's hands, opening and closing so menacingly. No, she thought soberly. On second thought, she had acted in the only possible way. Ricardo had only been a hair's breath from punching Martin. Susan didn't have any illusion as to Martin's chances should such a situation have come to pass. She shivered and burrowed deeper into her pillow. In retrospect, she had gotten off very lightly. And he was even reading her book. She yawned. When you came to think of it, she reflected sleepily, that was really something. She closed her eyes and in two minutes she was asleep.

Ricardo was beside her when she awoke the following morning. She looked for a minute at his dark head on the pillow next to hers and then her eyes traveled down to his strongly muscled shoulders and back. His skin looked very dark and coppery against the white of the sheets. She remembered the feel of his skin against hers, the hard demanding urgency of his body pressing her down into the softness of the bed. Desire ripped through her like a rowel of pain. She closed her eyes, took a deep breath and then slid out of bed. Down the corridor Ricky was crying and she slipped her feet into terry-cloth slippers and went along to her son's room. "Good morning, sweetheart," she said as she opened the door. "Were you calling me?"

Ricardo didn't awake until almost eleven, an unheard of hour for him. He was capable of functioning on far less sleep than she was and was usually up by seven-thirty at the latest. "Good morning," she said brightly as he came down the stairs dressed in old jeans and a light blue knit golf shirt. "You slept well."

He grimaced and rubbed his head. "Too well. Do you have any coffee?"

"Come out to the kitchen and I'll make you some." Maria was on vacation for two weeks and Susan was doing all the chores and the cooking. He followed her out to the shining, modern, white Formica kitchen and sat down at the table. She put coffee in the Farberware instant perk and plugged it in. "Well, don't keep me in suspense," she said. "What did you think of it?"

"I think it is beautiful," he answered simply.

Her heart thudded, skipped a beat and then began to function again. "Do you mean that?" she almost whispered.

"Yes." He looked at her steadily, his brown eyes dark and oddly grave. "I know I'm not a literary type like Harrison, and I read mostly nonfiction these days, but I did take a few Lit courses in college. I know what good writing is. And your book is good. Very good." She smiled at him from across the room, a smile of pure happiness. "It was about Sara, wasn't it?" he asked.

"Yes." She leaned back against the counter. "I wanted to try to capture her, to show what she was like—the warmth, the brightness, the vivid charm of her. It was something I felt I had to do. I wanted to do. For Sara and for Mother."

"And you were Kate," he said quietly.

"Yes." The coffee had stopped perking and she poured him a cup and brought it over to the table. She set out milk and sugar and then poured a cup for herself and came to join him.

"Such a shy, sensitive little girl," he said softly. There was a pause. "And so lonely."

Her head was bent, and she was gazing intently into her coffee. "It isn't easy to be the only weed in the flower garden," she said lightly.

"I think, rather, it was the other way around." He

sounded very somber and, startled, she raised her head. "You must publish it," he said, changing the subject.

She hesitated. "Martin said I should get an agent. He offered to recommend me to his." She bit her lip. "Ricardo, I think I should talk to Martin. He left last night on such an—unpleasant—note. I owe it to him to at least see him and explain." She could feel the heat flushing her cheeks. "I'm dreadfully afraid I led him on," she confessed. "I didn't mean to, but if I'm honest I have to admit he could easily have misinterpreted my actions. I—I do *like* him, you see."

"Yes." His eyes were dark and inscrutable. "I see."

"Then—then you don't mind if I call him?"

"Just this once, Susan." There was a warning note in his voice and she responded hastily.

"Of course. I promise I won't see him alone again."

His long lashes half fell, screening his eyes. "I'm hungry," he said. "I could use some breakfast."

She rose instantly. "What would you like? Eggs? Bacon? Toast?"

"It all sounds good." He watched in silence as she fixed his breakfast, and when it was put in front of him he said, "Thank you, *querida.*"

She was standing next to him and bent to drop a light kiss on his thick shining hair. *"De nada,"* she said. Her head cocked. "There's the prince, waking up from his morning nap. I'd better go up to him." Ricardo watched her slight figure move swiftly to the door. It wasn't until she was out of sight that he picked up his fork and began to eat.

Chapter Thirteen

Susan's interview with Martin left her feeling distressed and guilty. She hated to be the cause of someone else's unhappiness and, clearly, she had made Martin very unhappy.

"I shouldn't have spent so much time with you in Florida," she said wretchedly. "I shouldn't have come into the city to have lunch with you. I wouldn't have misled you the way I did if I had been single. All I can say is that I thought my marriage made anything more than friendship between us impossible."

"Not everyone takes marriage so seriously," he had said.

"Well I do."

"And Rick?"

"Ricardo as well. We are married and we plan to stay married, Martin. I'm sorry, but there it is."

She had spoken the truth to Martin, she reflected as she rode home on the early-afternoon train. Ricardo had not married her because he loved her, but he did take his marriage seriously. It was one of the reasons they had been able to make it work. He might not love her, but he respected her position as his wife and the mother of his son. She could not imagine any circumstances under which he would run off to the divorce courts. If he found another woman whom he desired more than her, he would simply make arrangements on the side. Her position would always be secure.

She felt unutterably depressed by the time she got off the train. Ricardo was waiting for her at the station, and as she got into the station wagon next to him she felt like bursting into tears. What did she care about position? It was his love she wanted.

"How did it go?" he asked as they maneuvered through downtown traffic.

"Terrible," she said mournfully. "Poor Martin. I felt so wretched for him. He was really quite serious, I'm afraid."

He grunted. "And what about your book?"

"I'm to call his agent tomorrow. That part at least looks promising."

"Good."

Susan turned around in her seat to smile at Ricky, who was securely belted into his car seat in the back. "How did you make out with the prince?" she asked. It was the first time she had left Ricardo in charge of the baby for more than an hour.

"Very well," he answered peacefully. "I paid bills and answered mail all morning and he zoomed around in that walker you bought him. We managed very well." He shot her a quick, sidelong look. "I even changed his diaper. Twice."

She laughed. "Bravo. Shall I pin on your medal now or later?"

He kept his eyes on the road although a faint answering smile touched his lips. "If you can keep awake until I get home tonight, you can reward me then," he said.

They didn't speak again until they reached home. "I

think I'll take a swim before dinner," Susan said as they got out of the car. "The city is like a furnace today and seeing poor Martin has really thrown me. I *hate* to make people unhappy."

"I know you do." Very briefly he touched her cheek. "I think I'll join you. It has been hot today."

They swam for an hour, taking turns swimming Ricky around. The baby loved the water and cried whenever they tried to take him out. "Enough," Ricardo finally said. "I have a game tonight and I won't have the energy for it if I don't sit down for a few minutes." Ricky yelled as his father plunked him down and promptly got his legs up under him to crawl toward the pool again.

Susan snatched him up. "Life has certainly become peppier since Ricky learned to crawl," she said. "We can't leave him here, Ricardo. Get the playpen from the house."

Ricardo wrapped a towel around his waist to keep his bathing trunks from dripping on the carpet and went in through the french doors. He was back in a few minutes carrying the folded-up playpen, which he proceeded to set up in the shade of the umbrella. Susan took off Ricky's wet suit, put a dry Pamper on him and deposited him in the playpen with some of his toys. "Now," she said, "take a nap." Ricky kicked and fussed and both his parents sat down and ignored him. In ten minutes he was asleep.

"I hope he stays as easy to handle as he gets older," Susan said to Ricardo with a smile. "Somehow, though, I doubt it."

"I doubt it too," he answered dryly.

He stretched out on the chaise longue and closed his eyes. Susan regarded his relaxed figure for a minute in silence and then she sighed. "I wish you weren't going away again tomorrow," she said wistfully. He opened his mouth to answer and she said hastily, "I know, I know. It's your job. You tell me that every time. But that doesn't mean I won't miss you."

"Will you, *querida*?" His eyes were still closed.

"Yes, I will."

"That's good." He sounded very sleepy and, annoyed, Susan closed her own eyes.

She must have dozed off, for when she woke Ricardo was gone. After checking on Ricky, who was still sleeping, Susan went into the house. The only sign of her husband downstairs was a wet towel draped over one of the kitchen chairs. She picked it up and went upstairs. Ricardo was in the shower. Susan looked at the clock. It was almost time for dinner. Hastily she pulled off her own suit and put on a pair of navy shorts and a yellow Izod shirt. She tied her hair at the nape of her neck with a yellow ribbon, thrust her feet into sandals and ran back downstairs to put the chicken on the grill and the rice on the stove. When Ricardo came downstairs ten minutes later she was able to say, "Dinner will be in half an hour. I think I heard the paperboy come by a few minutes ago."

He went out to get the paper and sat on the patio reading it as she took Ricky upstairs to change him. When she came back down the rice was done. "I think we'd better eat in the kitchen, Ricardo," she called as she threw a salad together and heated up Ricky's food. "I going to have to feed Ricky as we eat. He's starving."

He came out and took a place at the table. Susan strapped Ricky into his high chair and served up the food. "I'm spoiled rotten," she said as she tried to eat and feed Ricky pureed carrots at the same time. "Maria takes so much off me. I almost forgot to put dinner on."

"I could have gotten something at the ball park," he said. "I didn't want to wake you. You looked tired."

"I was," she admitted. "And depressed, too." She sighed. "Poor Martin."

"Do you know, *querida*," he said, and a curious look of quiet gravity came over his face, "I live in growing dread of one day hearing you say, 'Poor Ricardo.' "

Ricardo didn't go on the road trip after all. A pitch from the Orioles ace relief pitcher connected with Ricardo's head and he ended up in the hospital. Susan, who had been watching the game on TV, was frantic. He had lain still for so long and then she couldn't see him because he was surrounded by trainers and teammates. When the announcer said, "He's moving! He's getting up!" the rush of relief was so overwhelming that she nearly fainted.

Ricardo walked off the field and a runner went to first base for him. Ten minutes later the phone rang. "Susan?" said a male voice. "This is Chuck Henderson." It was one of the team coaches. "Were you watching the game?" he asked.

"Yes," she said tensely.

"Rick seems fine," he said quickly. "Dr. Hastings is going to take him over to the hospital for an X-ray—he most probably has a concussion—but I'm sure he'll be fine. He asked me to call you and tell you that."

"Are they going to keep him overnight, Chuck? He shouldn't drive. Does he want me to come in and get him?"

"They'll keep him overnight." Chuck was positive about that.

"Oh. Will you ask Dr. Hastings to call me after they've checked him over?"

"Sure thing, Susan. Try not to worry. He took a hard crack but the batting helmet absorbed most of the shock. He'll be fine."

"Okay. Thanks for calling, Chuck."

"I'll have Doc Hastings call you later," he promised again. "Try not to worry too much."

"Okay," she said again, and slowly hung up the phone.

The ball game was still on in the family room when she went back inside. "It was a fast ball that got away from Richards," the announcer was saying. "Montoya went down like a shot." Susan switched the TV off and started pacing. She was still on her feet two hours later when the phone rang again. She picked it up on the first ring.

"Hello," she said sharply.

"Mrs. Montoya?"

"Yes. Is this Dr. Hastings?"

"That's right. Rick's going to be fine, Mrs. Montoya, but he has a concussion and the hospital wants to keep him for a day or two."

"I see. How—how serious is the concussion, doctor?"

"He took a good knock. He's got some ringing in his ears and he's dizzy and nauseous. But there doesn't appear to be any serious damage."

Doesn't appear to be. Susan swallowed hard. "When can I see him?"

"You can come in tomorrow if you like."

"Where exactly is the hospital, doctor?" she asked, and wrote down the directions he gave her. It was two when she finally got into bed and nearly five when she finally fell asleep. She was up at seven-thirty and put in a phone call to her mother. Mrs. Morgan was shocked when she heard Ricardo had been hurt and promised to drive down immediately to take care of Ricky so Susan could go to the hospital.

Ricardo looked very white under his tan, and his cheekbones seemed to stand out under his skin. "Oh darling," she said as she went to stand next to the bed. "How do you feel?"

"Lousy," he said frankly. "My head hurts like hell." He moved his head restlessly on the pillow. "Who's staying with Ricky?"

"Mother. She came right down after I called. Can I get you anything?"

"I'm thirsty."

She poured a glass of water for him. His hand was unsteady and she said softly, "Let me hold it." He relinquished the glass to her and sipped it slowly. Then he leaned back and closed his eyes. "The ball got away from Richards, Susan," he said. "He wasn't throwing it at me deliberately."

"Tell that to your aching head," she said a little acidly, and pulled a chair up next to the bed. He smiled faintly. "I'm glad you're here," he murmured. In a few moments he was asleep.

The hospital released him after two more days and he went home for a week. Susan was so glad he was better that she waited on him hand and foot. At the end of the week he went back to the hospital for a checkup and was pronounced fit to play. He immediately made plans to fly up to Boston where the Yankees were starting a four-game series with the Red Sox.

"Can't you at least wait until the team comes home?" Susan protested.

"This is an important series, Susan," he answered. "We were six games up on the Sox when this road trip started and now we're down to three. We can't lose this series."

Susan had not protested any further. What Ricardo had said was true—the Yankees were missing his presence badly. The pennant race had heated up and Ricardo had to play if he was fit. So she packed his suitcase, drove him over to get the limousine to the airport and kissed him good-bye with a smile. She even managed to refrain from telling him to be careful.

The Yankees and the Red Sox split the series in Boston, leaving New York with its three-game advantage, though Ricardo got only one hit in the entire series, a little pop fly that fell just out of the right fielder's reach. He performed brilliantly in the field, however, and the announcers spoke excusingly about his injury so Susan didn't think too much of his unusual lapse.

The slump continued throughout the entire two-week homestand, however, and by then it seemed the whole world had become aware of Ricardo's failure to perform at bat. Newspaper articles were written on the subject. The announcers talked of it constantly. Ricardo's batting average plummeted and the Yankees dropped to two games behind Boston. And always, rarely said outright but constantly implied, was the innuendo that since being hit on the head, Ricardo was afraid of further injury. It was the only reason it seemed anyone could find to account for this most consistent of all players falling into such a catastrophic slump.

It was anguishing for Susan to watch him and yet she had never admired him more than now, when under the most intense pressure from fans, newsmen, coaches, players and most of all himself, he continued to maintain a composure and a courtesy that was nothing short of heroic. He never lost his temper, never allowed an expression or a gesture of anger or despair to escape as he repeatedly struck out or popped out or grounded out and returned quietly to the dugout. To all the myriad questioners he replied simply, "I don't know what's wrong."

Susan didn't know either, but she was utterly certain that fear of injury was not the cause of Ricardo's problem. He received advice from everyone on the team and he tried it all: he changed his stance, he shortened his grip, he moved closer to the plate, he moved further from the plate, but nothing seemed to help.

He did not speak of his slump to Susan as, apart from listening to their suggestions, he did not speak of it to his teammates. Joe Hutchinson called her one day to see if Ricardo was being more open at home than he was in the clubhouse. "Ricardo is a very private man, Joe," Susan said slowly. "He has never been one to talk about his problems or his feelings."

"I know. But, Susan, I really think that's a big part of his present problem. He can't, or he won't get what's bothering him off his chest. I know when I was in a slump last year the only thing that snapped me out of it was talking to people—to my wife, to the other guys—and especially to Rick." He paused. "Can't you try to get him to open up a little?"

"I'll do what I can, Joe," Susan responded quietly. But when she hung up the phone she knew that she was not the one who could open this subject with Ricardo. She trembled to think what must lie behind his apparently unruffled self-command, how the proud and passionate inner man must be feeling in the face of such continual and public failure. She could never be the one to try and breach that self-command. It had to be Ricardo who spoke first. All she could do was be as sensitive as she possibly could to his moods, and to all his other needs.

He never spoke to her of the slump but she sensed in him a need for her company. It was a small consolation, a hidden flower in the wasteland, the fact that in this, the most profoundly distressing time of his career, he did not turn away from her. He didn't want to go out, refused even the simple distraction of a movie that she thought might be good for him. He seemed happiest just sitting quietly with her—around the pool in the afternoon, listening to music at night. Susan thought that he felt comfortable with her because she was a woman and so not one of his peers, his equals.

The team left for another road trip and Ricardo's slump persisted. Susan got to the point of feeling ill every time he came to the plate. How could he stand it, she wondered despairingly. How could he go up there, time and time again, endure the taunts of the fans, the implications of the sports reporters, the doubts he must see in the eyes of his teammates? Where did he find the courage? Where did he find the strength of will?

The team got into New York in the early afternoon and Ricardo was home in time for a swim before dinner. Susan had heard from her agent the day before that he had found a publisher for her book but she had hesitated to tell Ricardo last night on the phone. It did not seem the time to remind him that he had a successful wife. She did tell him over dinner and he seemed to be geniunely pleased, asking her for the details of the contract with a thoroughness she could not begin to answer. "I think you'd better read it when I get it," she said. "I haven't the foggiest idea of who has what rights. I expect it will all be in the contract. Mr. Wright seemed to think it was a good deal."

"He's supposed to be a good agent," Ricardo admitted. "I checked on him. Still, it's always wise to look things over personally."

After dinner they watched an old movie on TV. Ricardo was very quiet and seemed to be paying attention to the screen, but Susan could sense the tension in him. They went upstairs after the news and Ricardo was in the shower when Ricky woke up and began to cry. He was cutting a tooth and having a very difficult time of it. So was Susan. She gave him some Tylenol and walked him and then rocked him, and finally he fell back to sleep. When she went back into her own bedroom, Ricardo was asleep as well. Susan undressed without putting on the light and slipped quietly into bed so as not to disturb him. She had thought he looked strained and tired and was sure he wasn't sleeping well.

She awoke at three in the morning to find him gone. She got out of bed, and clad only in her thin cotton nightgown, she went downstairs to look for him.

He was sitting in the dark on the patio. He turned his head when he heard the door open and said, "What are you doing out of bed in the middle of the night?"

"Looking for you," she replied, and went to lay her hand lightly on his bare brown shoulder. The muscles under her fingers were rocklike with tension. Susan felt like throwing herself into his arms and weeping, but that was not what he needed. He needed to release some of that terrible tension. She thought she knew what part of the problem was, at any rate. He had been gone for two weeks. Drat Ricky and his tooth, she thought. She put both hands on his shoulders and began to massage them gently. He closed his eyes. "Mmm. That feels good."

She continued with the massage until she felt him relax a little. Then she bent forward so her cheek was against this and her hair swung across his face. "Why don't we go back upstairs?" she murmured. "Ricky is finally asleep."

"Are you trying to seduce me, Susan?" he asked. He sounded grave.

"Yes." She kissed his cheekbone. "I am. If you reject me, I'll be very insulted."

"I would never want to insult you," he said, and stood up. He was wearing only his pajama bottoms as usual and he towered over her in the darkness. She moved closer and put her arms around his waist. He held her very tightly. "I missed you, *querida*," he breathed.

She kissed his chest and then, lightly, delicately, she licked his bare smooth skin. She could feel the shudder that ran all through him and without another word he picked her up and carried her into the house and up the stairs to their bedroom.

She closed her eyes as his weight crushed her into the mattress. His mouth on hers was hard and hungry and his kiss drove her back hard into the pillow. She felt his terrible urgency, his barely controlled desperation. His hands hurt when they gripped her delicate flesh. He groaned and she could sense him making a terrific effort to get himself under control. She opened her eyes. She wasn't ready but it was not her needs that concerned her at the moment. She loved him very very much. "It's all right, darling," she whispered. "You don't have to wait."

His dark eyes looked into hers for a very brief second and then he buried his face between her neck and shoulder. He held her close but his hands now felt more gentle. After a minute one of them slid down her shoulder to her breast and began, very lightly to caress it. Then he turned his head and began to kiss her throat. Her own hands moved slowly over his back. "Ricardo," she murmured.

His hand moved down to her stomach and then moved again. She gasped, pressing up against him. He locked his mouth on hers and continued to caress her until she whimpered. Her mouth softened and he said her name, cupping her breasts in both his hands. She opened her eyes and they stared at each other for a minute out of passion-narrowed eyes. Then she put her hands on his hips, pulling him toward her, over her. She arched up toward him, her breasts filling his hands as she urged him to fill her body, to complete her, to finish what he had started.

He drove into her and something in her answered to the hungriness in him, blazing up for him in a bonfire of wild sweetness and ecstasy.

"Do you know you always make love in Spanish?" she asked him a long time later. Her head was pillowed on his shoulder and his hand was sifting gently through her hair.

"Well, it's my first language, after all," he replied. "It's the language we almost always spoke at home— even when we lived in New York."

She sighed with contentment and after a minute his hands left her hair and moved to her back. Susan's eyes half closed and she rubbed against him a little, like a cat being stroked. His hand moved from her back down to her hip and delicious quivers of anticipation began to run through her again. "That was like manna in the desert," he murmured into her ear. "Shall we do it again?" Very gently his fingers caressed the delicate flesh on the inside of her thigh.

"Mmm," said Susan, moving slightly. "Let's."

Ricardo did not get much sleep on his first night home, but he looked a great deal better as he left for the ball park the following day. Some of the strain at least was gone from his face.

Susan felt better too. It was ineffably sweet to her to know that Ricardo had refused to use her simply to slake his own need. Even though she had given him permission, he had held back and waited for her. He was such a wonderful man, she thought. If only he could break out of this ghastly slump!

Chapter Fourteen

It was Friday night and the Yankees were opening a four-game series with the Red Sox. Boston was four games ahead of them in the pennant race and this series could be crucial. If the Yankees lost, it would be very difficult psychologically as well as statistically for them to ever regain the lead.

Susan's heart was heavy as she turned on the set at eight o'clock to watch. At this point she thought she knew what Ricardo's problem was, but she didn't know how to help him overcome it.

He had lost his confidence. It was as simple as that. He had had a few bad days, which everyone—even Ricardo—had to have once in a while, but because they came right after the accident, people had begun to doubt him. And so instead of simply shrugging and riding out the slump, as she was certain he would have done in any other circumstances, he had tried to prove that he was okay and he had tried too hard. The more he tried, the more tense he became. And the more tense he became, the more impossible it was for him to hit. It was a vicious cycle. The answer was to restore his confidence, but Susan didn't know how to do that. She was the last person he would listen to on the subject of baseball. She had never even watched a game until she had married him.

There was quiet in the stadium as Ricardo came to the plate for the first time. The usual wild cheering his presence had always provoked was replaced this time by a distinctly uneasy silence. There were no boos, no catcalls as there had been on the road. Nor were there any cries of encouragement; just silence. The Yankee fans all seemed to sense the magnitude of what was happening. Ricardo took two strikes and then swung at a bad pitch and grounded it to the first baseman. There was still that eerie silence in the ball park as he returned to the dugout.

He struck out the second time he was up and popped out the third. When the Yankees came to bat in the bottom of the ninth inning, the score was tied at two—two. Joe Hutchinson was the first batter and he singled to center. Rex Hensel, the shortstop, sacrificed him to second. The third batter, Buddy Moran, hit a towering fly to left that was caught at the fence by Boston's Hank Moore. It was two out, the winning run was on second and Ricardo was up. Susan watched him swing his bat and start to move from the on-deck circle toward the plate. Then he paused and looked back at the dugout toward the manager. Frank Henry was coming off the bench and picking a bat out of the rack. Astonishingly, the announcer's voice came over the P.A. "Batting for Montoya, Frank Henry, number nineteen."

A roar went up from the stadium and Susan could hardly see the set through the tears in her eyes and the ache in her throat. This was the final humiliation, being pulled for a pinch hitter in the kind of crisis situation Ricardo had always excelled in. She scarcely heard what the announcers were saying, but the TV camera picked up Ricardo as he sat on the dugout bench. Bert Diaz was beside him, looking upset. Ricardo's face was unreadable.

"That's gone!" the announcer cried loudly, and the camera followed the flight of the ball as it dropped about ten rows back in the right-field stands. The camera then swung to a grinning Frank Henry as he jogged around the bases. His teammates were waiting for him at home plate and the first man to shake his hand was Ricardo.

"Now, there is class," the TV announcer said quietly. "Any other athlete I know would have gone down to the locker room. But not Montoya. I hope to God he can lick this slump. The game can't afford to lose a man of that caliber."

It was after one o'clock when Susan heard Ricardo's car come into the driveway. Ricky had woken up again with his tooth and she was upstairs, rocking his crib, trying to get him back to sleep. Ricardo didn't come upstairs, and when Ricky finally went off some fifteen minutes later, Susan went quietly downstairs. She was wearing a thin summer nightgown and matching peignoir and her bare feet made scarcely any sound on the carpeting.

She found Ricardo in the family room. He was sitting with his elbows on his knees and his knuckles were pressed hard against his forehead. He was rigid with tension. Susan thought her heart would break. "Ricardo," she said out of an aching throat. "Darling, I'm so sorry." She crossed the room to him and he turned in his seat and blindly reached for her. His arms were clamped about her waist, his face pressed against her breasts. "Susan," he groaned. "*Dios*, Susan. I am so scared."

She held him tightly, her lips buried in his hair. "I know, darling, I know," she whispered.

With his face still pressed against her, he began to talk. She had never seen him vulnerable before. She held him close and listened as he poured out his fears, his uncertainties, letting her inside his defenses where no one had ever been before. He held nothing back and in her heart was a strange mixture of pain and aching joy. "Maybe I *am* afraid of getting hurt," he groaned at last in anguish. "I don't know. *Dios*, Susan, I don't know anything anymore!"

She rested her cheek against his smooth dark hair and closed her eyes. She had been right all along, she thought. He was suffering from a catastrophic loss of confidence. Somehow, she had to help him restore it. For the first time he had turned to her and she mustn't fail him now. She took a deep, steadying breath and said calmly, "I know what the problem is, Ricardo."

After a minute his arms loosened and he looked up at her. "You do?" he asked blankly.

"Yes. I haven't said anything because—oh because I was afraid you'd think I was silly."

"*Dios*," he said. "But what is it?"

She looked him directly in the eyes, her own clear and steady and utterly truthful. "You're taking your eye off the ball," she said.

He sat up straight. "What!"

"It's so elementary that I think it needed an amateur like me to pick it up, Ricardo. I thought awhile ago that that might be the problem—simply because I know that was always my problem in tennis when I began to go off my game. And I've watched you for several weeks now. You're so hung up with your stance and your feet and your swing that you simply aren't watching the ball."

He stared at her, a look of dawning wonder on his face. "Can it be?"

"Absolutely. I'll bet you a million dollars that if you go up to the plate tomorrow, stand any way you like and simply watch that ball, you'll hit it."

"I'm not watching the ball," he repeated slowly. "You know, you may be right."

"I know I'm right. It's what's thrown your timing off. You had a little slump in Boston, which was perfectly natural since you hadn't played for a while, but then you started fiddling around with your natural stance. And you got so hung up on fiddling that you began to take your eye off the ball. So of course the slump went from bad to worse."

He sat back in the chair and stared over her head, obviously thinking hard. "I think you're right," he said after a few minutes of silence. "I think that's exactly what happened."

"It is," she said positively.

His large brown eyes focused once again on her face. "You should have told me sooner," he said.

"I would have, but I didn't think you'd listen," she said hesitantly. "After all, what do I know about baseball?"

"You know something more important in this case," he said. "You know me." He shook his head and laughed. "Taking my eye off the ball. I can't believe it."

Susan hadn't seen that smile in weeks and her stomach clenched now at the sight of it. Dear God, she thought, he had actually believed her. She was still standing in front of him and now he reached up and pulled her down onto his lap. She put her arms around his neck and nestled to him. His body felt warm and relaxed against hers. "I'm a genius," she murmured. "It's time you appreciated that."

"I have appreciated you for quite some time now, *querida*," he said softly into her hair.

Susan closed her eyes. Please God, she prayed, let this work. She had no idea if Ricardo were watching the ball or not. She simply thought he needed to feel he would get a hit and then whatever it was that was wrong would correct itself. If this didn't work, he'd never listen to her again. She couldn't bear that, not now when for the first time she was beginning to think that perhaps he did love her after all. He had trusted her tonight. He had let her in. It simply *had* to work.

They stayed like that peacefully, for a very long time. There was no need to talk, no need to make love even; it was enough that they were quiet and together. Later, upstairs in their bedroom, Ricardo did make love to her with a heartstopping tenderness and passion that drew from her a seemingly bottomless generosity of surrender and of love. She could give to him forever, she felt. There was no one else like him in the world. He fell asleep peacefully in her arms and it was Susan who spent a sleepless night, praying as she had never prayed before, for Ricardo and for their marriage. So much depended upon what happened that afternoon.

Ricardo left for the stadium early to take batting practice. It was Saturday and the Yankees were playing an afternoon game. Susan put Ricky in for his afternoon nap and switched the TV on at two o'clock to watch. She felt sick with apprehension.

Ricardo was the first man to come to bat in the bottom of the second inning. The Red Sox had Paul Beaulieu, their premier pitcher, on the mound and he had retired the first three Yankees on strikes.

The announcer spoke as Ricardo came up to the plate. "I understand Murphy wasn't going to play Montoya today—he thought perhaps what Rick needed was a break from the pressure. But Rick asked him for one last game." Susan dug her fingernails into her palms. They had been going to bench Ricardo.

The first pitch was a strike. "That was a fastball on the outside corner," the announcer said. "Beaulieu has *very* good stuff today."

There was silence in the ball park as Beaulieu went into his windup. He delivered the pitch and Ricardo swung.

Crack!

Susan knew the sound and watched almost in disbelief as the ball arched into the upper stands. The stadium rose to its feet, screaming hysterically. The Yankee dugout emptied and the whole team was lined up at home plate waiting for Ricardo. "You'd think Montoya'd just won the World Series!" shouted the announcer over the din.

Ricardo's face was serious as he shook the hands of his teammates. It wasn't until Joe Hutchinson slapped him on the back and said something that a smile dawned. At the sight of that familiar grin the noise, impossibly, became even greater. "I think we've got the old Rick back," one announcer said.

"I hope to God you're right," the other responded fervently.

By the time the game was over it appeared the first announcer had been right. Ricardo went three for four and doubled in the winning run in the bottom of the eighth. The slump was over.

Marv Patterson, one of the Yankee announcers, always had an after-game show when the Yankees played at home and he announced excitedly in the ninth inning that Ricardo was to be his guest. Ricky was crying for his dinner by now and Susan ran out into the kitchen for his high chair, plunked it down in front of the TV and fed him as she watched.

Patterson's introduction was so laudatory it was almost embarrassing and Ricardo's face, as he listened, held the look of faint amusement that was so familiar to Susan that it made her heart turn over. He hadn't looked like that in months. Finally Patterson wound up his panegyric and turned to his guest. "What happened today, Rick?" he asked. "I don't think I've ever seen anyone break out of a slump more dramatically."

Ricardo grinned. "You've probably never seen a more dramatic slump, either."

The announcer laughed. "You're right. It was— awesome."

"It was catastrophic," Ricardo replied cheerfully.

"But what *happened* to cause you to break out of it?"

"My wife solved the problem," Ricardo said. "Last night she told me I wasn't watching the ball."

Marv Patterson stared. "Not watching the ball?" he repeated.

"Yes. It was as simple as that."

"And *your wife* picked it up?"

"That's right." Ricardo looked very serious now. "She's an amazingly observant person, my wife. It comes from being a writer, I guess."

"Is she a writer?" Marv Patterson asked interestedly.

"Yes. Her first novel will be published this spring. It's

called *The Flight* and her editor said it was one of the finest first novels he's ever read." Susan stared at her husband in utter astonishment. He was actually bragging about her book!

Marv Patterson was talking to Ricardo now about the pennant race and Susan spooned fruit and vegetables into her son's eager mouth and continued to stare at Ricardo's face on the screen. Never, as long as she lived, would she be able to figure him out.

She was in the kitchen when he came home, and when she heard the door slam she ran out into the hall and flung herself into his arms. "You did it!" she cried joyfully. "I knew you could!"

He swung her off her feet and held her tight. "It was that, more than anything else, that saw me through." He kissed her quick and hard. "The luckiest day of my life was the day a snowstorm blew you to my door," he said, and set her back on her feet.

She laughed unsteadily. "Mine too." She looked up into his face and intoned portentously: "I got the 'man who, more than anyone in our time, has assumed the stature of a hero, an athlete of almost mythic proportions. . . .' "

"Cut it out," he said good-naturedly. "So you watched the postgame show?"

"Of course I did." A terrible din came from the kitchen and Ricardo looked around in alarm. "Ricky's playing in the pot closet," Susan explained, and led the way into the kitchen. Their son was sitting amid a collection of pots and pans and he was banging blissfully. "He's just discovered it," Susan said with a laugh. "It beats all his other toys by a mile in his book."

They didn't get a chance to talk quietly until after

dinner and after Ricky's bedtime. Then they went together into the family room and sat on the sofa, Susan in the corner and Ricardo stretched out with his head on her lap. He closed his eyes. "Hmm," he said. "This is nice."

Susan's fingers gently touched his hair. "Mother called today," she murmured after a while. "She invited us to a benefit dance for the hospital. I said I didn't think so but that I'd get back to her. She was annoyed. She said we're worse than hermits, that we never go anywhere."

His eyes stayed closed. He was clearly enjoying the touch of her hand. "We can go if you want to," he said.

Susan sighed. "I suppose we should. It isn't just the slump that's kept us home. We didn't go anywhere before it happened—as Mother pointed out to me."

He opened his eyes. "*Querida,* I'm sorry. I didn't realize that I was turning you into a hermit. Your mother's right. I should take you out more."

Susan smoothed his thick straight hair back from his forehead. "I've never been a social butterfly," she said. "I think it's you Mother is concerned for. You used to go to a lot of parties, or so she informed me."

"I went to parties—and not a lot of them—because I had no one I wanted to stay at home with," he said softly. He reached up for her hand and drew it down to his mouth. "I don't like to go out now because I have to be away so much that when I'm home I don't want to have to share you."

"Oh darling," she whispered. "That's lovely. I'm glad you feel like that." He held her hand against his cheek and she said, cautiously, "Do you know, you sounded almost proud of my book today? You pushed it shamelessly."

He grinned. "I thought I did a very good sales pitch. I got in the title, and when it's coming out." He arched his head back a little so he could see her. "And I *am* proud of it. I'm proud of you."

She looked into his face out of wide, wondering gray eyes. "I always had the impression you didn't like me to write," she said simply.

He relaxed his head once more into her lap. "Yes, well, it had nothing to do with your writing, really," he said a little gruffly.

"But what was it, Ricardo?" she asked curiously.

"It was when you wrote you always seemed so far away from me," he explained awkwardly. "I don't mean physically, but . . ."

His voice trailed off and Susan said, very gently, "Yes, I see."

He laughed a little self-consciously. "I used to think of a poem I studied once in a Lit course in college. It was about a knight who falls in love with an elfin queen and awakens to find himself alone in a cold, empty world."

It took Susan a minute but then she said, "Keats. 'La Belle Dame Sans Merci.'" She quoted softly:

> And I awoke, and found me here
>   On the cold hill side
> And this is why I sojourn here
>   Alone and palely loitering,
> Though the sedge is withered from the lake,
>   And no birds sing.

"Yes," he said, "that's the one." He held her hand tighter. "I know I'm not the kind of man you admire, the kind of man you thought you would marry. I'm not literary or intellectual. But I love you. I can't imagine what life would be without you." He added, a little shakily, "I'd be 'poor Ricardo,' I'm afraid."

"Not the sort of man I admire," she repeated incredulously. "Ricardo, I've never admired anyone more in my life than I've admired you these last months. Can you possibly understand how proud I've been to be your wife, to know that you are the father of my son? But I had no idea how you felt about me. I thought you were just making the best of a difficult situation."

He sat up and swung his legs to the floor. "Are you serious?" he asked in amazement.

"Well . . ." She bit her lip. "Yes." As he continued to stare at her she added defensively, "After all, we hardly knew each other when we married."

"That's true, I suppose." He ran a hand through his hair. "It's hard to remember the time I didn't know you. For so long now I've felt closer to you than to anyone in the world. I never thought I *could* feel like this about anyone. I never used to feel lonely, but now, if I ever lost you . . ."

His voice stopped and he looked at her. "Oh darling," Susan whispered, and reached up with gentle fingers to smooth the lines from his forehead. "You won't ever lose me. I plan to stick like glue. And even if sometimes my mind is a million miles away, my heart is always, always yours."

"Do you mean that?" he asked gravely.

She reached up and laid her lips gently on his. "I admire you, I love you, I worship you, I adore you," she murmured against his mouth. "What else can I say to convince you?"

"Well." His arms came up to hold her. "You could try showing me."

"I'd love to," she whispered back.

"How about right here?" His eyes sparkled at her with laughter.

She knew he expected her to protest, to insist they go upstairs to the bedroom. "Why not?" she said sweetly, and, sliding her arms around his neck, she pressed the whole length of her body against his.

His reaction was instantaneous and she found herself lying back on the sofa with Ricardo above her. "Kiss me," she whispered. He did and it was long and slow and quite astonishingly erotic. "Do you remember that first time?" she murmured when he moved his mouth down the slender, delicate lines of her throat.

"Mmm," he said huskily. "I'll never forget it."

"I think I knew then what could be between us," she went softly on. "I can remember thinking, I must be crazy, I don't even know this man. But you bewitched me. You always will."

There came the cry of a baby from upstairs and Susan stiffened to listen. "Let him cry for a little," Ricardo said. "At this particular moment, I need you more."

"Ricardo," she said, and let him press her back into the sofa cushions. Her hands went up to hold him close. She had never been happier in her entire life. Ricardo was right; Ricky would simply have to wait.

SUMMER
STORM

Chapter One

I t was a beautiful day in early May when Mary O'Connor came out of the heavy oak door of the university's Freemont Hall. She paused for a minute on the top of the steps and surveyed the scene below her. The green lawns of the New England campus were heavily speckled with students in various states of undress, reclining under the dogwood trees and cramming for final exams. Mary turned her own face briefly upward to feel the warmth of the sun and someone behind her said, "Dr. O'Connor?"

Mary turned, recognized the student, and repressed a sigh. He was a very large, very amiable, not very clever young man who had, for reasons she could not fathom, decided to fall crashingly in love with her. Considering the fact that the highest mark she had given him all semester was a C, his devotion was a mystery to her.

It was not a mystery, however, to Bob Fowler (the large student) or, indeed, to at least a dozen other men, both young and old, who had come in contact with Mary Catherine O'Connor during the year she had been teaching at this university. It was not, regrettably, her Ph.D. in literature or the impressive scholarly reputation she had acquired upon the publication of her book last year that was the cause of all this male admiration. Rather it was the fact that she was twenty-six years old and beautiful.

As she stood now, poised on the top of Freemont Hall's steps, male heads in the area swung around instinctively. It was an attention Mary scarcely noticed, she was so accustomed to it. She stood listening to Bob Fowler for a few minutes with exemplary patience, shook her head in refusal of his offer to carry her briefcase to her car for her, turned resolutely away from him and started down the steps.

There was a blinding flash of light and instinctively she stopped and looked toward its source. There was a photographer standing at the bottom of the steps and as she looked at him the camera flashed again, twice. "Who are you?" Mary demanded.

"Mary O'Connor? *Doctor* Mary O'Connor?" the photographer answered crisply with a question of his own.

"Yes, but . . ."

"Thank you, doctor." The man sent her a smile and turned to climb back into his car. She hesitated, then shrugged her slim shoulders and watched him drive off. It was probably someone from the campus newspaper, she decided.

Ten days later Mary was once again coming out of Freemont Hall where she had her office. It was an extremely warm day and she was wearing the jacket of her beige poplin suit slung casually over one shoulder in order to get the cooling benefit of her short-sleeved navy polka-dot blouse. There were several students clustered on the stone landing outside the building and they were all talking in excited whispers.

"I'm dying to go talk to him," Mary heard one girl saying. "I wish I had the nerve."

"But what can he be doing *here*?" said a male voice. "Have you heard anything about a movie being shot on campus?"

Slowly Mary looked down the stairs to the man who was the cause of all this excitement. He was leaning against the hood of a smart red sports car and looked around him casually, as if he owned the place. He seemed entirely unaware of all the watching eyes, entirely at his ease. Mary supposed that when you possessed one of the most famous faces in the world, you got used to being watched. "Damn," she said under her breath.

Bob Fowler looked around and saw her. "Dr. O'Connor," he said enthusiastically, "take a look at who's standing there at the bottom of the stairs. It's Christopher Douglas!"

"So I see," she replied coolly, and once again surveyed the tall slim man leaning against the red car. He was looking off down the campus toward where an impromptu soccer game was going on on one of the lawns and his splendid, arrogant profile was clear as a cameo. As she watched he seemed to lose interest in the game and turned back to the building in front of him, looked up, and saw her. Instantly he pushed himself off the car and stood upright, moving unselfconsciously and with all the lithe grace she remembered so well. He kept his dark eyes on her the whole time she was descending the stairs, unaware, as was she, of the breathlessly watching students.

She stopped in front of him and looked up. She had forgotten how tall he was, but then she had not seen him in almost four years. "Hello, Kit," she said to her husband. "What are you doing here?"

He didn't answer for a minute but stood looking gravely down at her. "You're wearing your hair differently," he finally answered, "but otherwise you haven't changed."

"Nor have you," she replied, returning his regard. One forgot, she thought to herself, inwardly not half so calm as she hoped she appeared on the surface, one forgot he really looked like this. Extreme, completely male beauty is a very rare phenomenon, and Christopher Douglas had been blessed with it in abundance. "What are you doing here?" she repeated, clutching more tightly at her briefcase.

"I came to see you." The movies, she thought, had never done justice to his voice. It took the theater to allow him its proper range. "I had no idea of your home address," he was going on, "so I tracked you down here. I have to talk to you, Mary. Something has come up."

She knew, instantly, why he had come. There was a very strange feeling in the pit of her stomach as she said, "I don't live very far from here. Do you want to follow me home? My car is parked in the faculty lot— over there." She gestured to an eight-year-old Buick and he nodded.

"All right. That's your father's old car, isn't it?"

"Yes. Daddy passed it on to me a few years ago." He waited for her to move away before he opened the door of his red car and got in. She backed slowly out of her space, moved into the narrow road that crossed the campus, and drove toward the main gate. The small red sports car followed.

* * *

"This is very nice," Kit said as he followed her in the front door of the small white clapboard house.

"I'm only renting it," she answered, putting her briefcase down in the hall and leading him into the living room.

He looked around him slowly, taking in the furnishings. "You've still got the rocker," he said. "And the drop-leaf table." His long fingers caressed the wood of the table lovingly; he had stripped and refinished that table himself.

"Yes." She bent her head, not looking at him. "Can I get you a drink?"

"I'll take a beer, if you've got one." He sat down on the sofa, which was new and held no memories, and stretched his long legs in front of him.

"Yes, I have beer. I keep some in for Daddy when he comes to visit." She walked into the kitchen, hung her jacket over one of the kitchen chairs, and opened the refrigerator. She was annoyed to find her hands were shaking. She opened the beer, got out two glasses and then poured herself a stiff Scotch. She brought his beer into the living room, got her own drink and went to sit in the rocker.

"How *is* your father?" He sipped his beer and regarded her inscrutably over the rim of the glass.

"Fine. He hasn't retired, but at least he isn't accepting new patients anymore. He and mother actually went to Europe for a month earlier this spring." She ran a finger around the rim of her glass. "I think they finally feel they've got me off their hands."

"You landed yourself a very good job," he said, "in a very prestigious university."

She shrugged. "It was about time." She changed the

subject. "You're looking very fit. California life must agree with you—you're dark as a gypsy."

"The weather is good," he agreed. He took another sip of beer. "Even you might tan a bit out there."

"Me?" She glanced down at her bare arm. "I doubt it. I've never had a tan in my life. Sunburn now, that's different."

He looked at her for a moment in silence and then said, slowly and deliberately, "I have never seen skin as beautiful as yours."

Damn him, damn him, damn him, she thought. "It's Irish skin," she answered lightly and took a gulp of Scotch.

"Irish eyes too."

She put her glass down with a sharp click and stared at him. "All right, Kit, we've traded compliments and upheld the social amenities. Now perhaps you'll tell me why you came here." She sounded annoyed. "You could have gotten my address from Mother, you know. You didn't have to look me up right on campus, in front of a gaggle of star-struck students. How am I going to explain that?"

"I didn't like to call your mother," he answered a little grimly.

She picked up her glass and took another swallow of Scotch. Better to get it said and done with, she thought. "I imagine you're here about a divorce." Her voice to her own ears sounded hard and flat.

"Is that why you think I've come?"

"I can't imagine any other reason. In fact, I can't imagine why you didn't divorce me years ago."

"I might ask you the same question."

He had the darkest eyes of anyone she had ever known. She found it difficult to keep looking at them and gazed instead at her elegant foot, sensibly shot in a plain navy pump. "I thought I'd leave it to you," she mumbled.

"*You* were the one who threw me over," he replied. "*You* were the one who said you would never live with me again."

"Mmph," she said.

"For an English scholar you're damned inarticulate." His voice sounded distinctly amused.

She glared at him. "I didn't divorce you because a divorce isn't going to make any difference to me. You know that. *I* can't marry again. But you can, so if you want a divorce I'll give you one. I don't believe in being a dog in the manger."

"Do you know, I thought that might be it," he said softly. "So there isn't anyone else?"

"Good God, Kit," she replied irritably, "you know my family. The O'Connors are more Catholic than the pope. No, I'm stuck with the single life." She looked at him challengingly. "And I find it very much to my taste. One marriage was quite enough for me, thank you."

"I see. So you plan to hide yourself away in a cloister for the rest of your life."

"The university is hardly a cloister. And I am not hiding away. I have work to do. It's the work you are doing that really counts in life—surely you of all people will agree with that."

"I would have—five years ago." His face was still reserved, quite unreadable. Before she could ask what he meant he went on. "I didn't come to ask you for a divorce."

"You didn't?" He had, as always, thrown her off her balance. "Then what did you come for?" she asked for the third time.

"Was there a photographer around the school last week bothering you?"

Really, she thought, his habit of answering a question with a question was very annoying. "Yes," she said shortly.

"He was from *Personality.*"

"What!" *Personality* was the most notorious scandal sheet in the country.

"I'm afraid so," he answered bleakly. "Have you ever seen the paper?"

"I've seen it in the supermarket. I read the headlines while I'm waiting on line."

"Well, your picture will be gracing page one next week," he said. Then, rather inadequately, "Mary, I'm sorry."

She was staring at him in stunned horror. "Are you serious?" He nodded. "I see." She swallowed hard, remembered her Scotch and picked it up. It was empty. "Damn," she said.

"Make yourself another," he suggested.

"No." She shook her head. "Another one of those and I'll be on my ear. Do you want another beer?"

"No."

"All right," she said tensely. "You'd better explain."

He ran a hand through his thick black hair in a gesture that was achingly familiar. "Yes," he said. "That's why I came."

"I don't know how closely you have followed my career," he began slowly, "or if you have followed it at all, but you must have realized that no one in Hollywood knows that I am married."

She had in fact read everything about him that came her way and she had seen all his pictures, but she wasn't going to tell him that. "Certainly, no one has ever disturbed *me*," she replied. "Until now, that is."

"I know. And I didn't want you disturbed, which is precisely why I kept my mouth shut. I don't give many interviews, you know, or go in for talk shows or things like that, so no one has had the opportunity to pin me down on my marital status. Everyone just assumes I'm single."

"You mustn't be terribly popular with the media if you are so unforthcoming," she said lightly.

He smiled, teeth very white in his tanned face. "I'm not." The smile faded. "I learned exactly what the media can do to you when I was making my first picture." There was a note of bitterness in his beautiful voice. "But then you know all about that."

She was staring in fascination at the toe of her shoe. "Yes, I remember."

"So, naturally," he resumed his story evenly, "if a reporter thinks he's got a good bit of gossip about me, he's keen to use it. I don't know how, but someone from *Personality* found out about you."

Her eyes traveled slowly from her toe to his face. "You can't squash it?"

"No. I only found out about it because my cleaning lady's daughter is a typist at the paper. She told me about it yesterday. I thought that the least I could do was warn you."

"How much do they know?" Her voice was barely a whisper.

"Not everything." He leaned forward. "They know we were married and that we split up after all the newspaper gossip about me and Jessica Corbet. That's all."

"Are you sure?" Her lips were white.

"Yes."

"I—see. Do they know we're still technically married?"

"Oh yes, that's the juiciest info of all from their point of view. Christopher Douglas's secret wife and all that rot."

"Oh, Kit, *why?*" she almost wailed. "*Why* did this have to happen?"

"I'm sorry, Mary," he repeated.

"You should have divorced me ages ago," she said. "Why didn't you?"

"Because I didn't want to," he answered coolly. "Like you, I saw no necessity. You are the only woman I have ever wanted to live with permanently."

"You didn't want to live with me," she contradicted him in a low voice. "You just wanted to sleep with me. Unfortunately, you had to marry me to do that." He pushed his hand through his hair once more and she smiled a little at the gesture. "I don't blame you, Kit, not anymore. I was as much at fault. I shouldn't have married you."

"Well, you did," he said in an odd voice, "and here we are." He looked slowly around the room and his eyes stopped at the overflowing bookcase. "Are you happy, Mary? Do you have what you want?"

"Yes," she answered, ignoring the pain that had unaccountably appeared around her heart. "I've made a place for myself in a world I've always loved. Yes, I'm happy."

"I'm glad. But surely you take a break from academia once in a while? What are you doing this summer? Not more research?"

"No." She lifted her chin proudly. "This summer I've been invited to lecture at Yarborough."

His head came up, poised and alert. "Have you really?"

Yarborough College was a very small school on the shores of a New Hampshire lake. It had, however, over the past ten years acquired considerable national prominence because of its summer dramatics program. The head of the drama department, George Clark, was a bit of a genius, and the small campus theater was a gem of acoustical and dramatic engineering. The combination of the two had produced the Yarborough Summer Festival, in which top drama students from all over the country were given the opportunity to work in a theatrical production with a few noted professionals. Each year the festival did one play and concentrated on one period of theatrical history A prominent scholar of that period was always invited to lecture and the college gave graduate credit to all the drama students who attended.

"They're doing the English Renaissance this year," she said, "and as you know that's my period. So, for the price of a few lectures, I'll have a lovely New Hampshire vacation."

"What play are they doing?"

"They're being very ambitious. It's *Hamlet*."

"*Hamlet*? And who is to play the lead?"

"Adrian Saunders," she said, naming a young English actor who had made a hit in a recent British series run on public television.

"Ah." He smiled at her, the famous devastating smile that was calculated to turn every woman's bones to water. "It sounds like fun."

She rose to her feet and he rose also. "I think it will be."

He stood for a moment, looking down at her. "I'm

afraid you're going to be bothered, Mary. Just refuse to answer all questions. Don't worry about being polite. Refuse all interviews. It will all die down in a short while, I promise you."

"I suppose so." She sighed and then suddenly became very formal. "Good-bye Kit. It was kind of you to have come." She did not offer him her hand.

"I'm sorry it was on this particular business," he replied gravely. "Do you know, no one has called me Kit for years." He turned and walked swiftly out the door.

She heard his car door slam and the engine start up. In a minute he had backed out of her doorway and had disappeared up the street. Mary sat down in her pine rocker and looked blindly at the sofa where he had sat. She had not felt so upset since the last time they had met.

She would have been even more upset if she had heard the conversation Kit had with his agent early the following day. "Chris!" said Mel Horner genially when his secretary informed him who was on the phone. "What are you doing in New York?"

"Never mind that Mel," Kit replied. "I want you to book me into the Yarborough Festival this summer."

"What!"

"You heard me," Kit replied testily. "I want to work at the Yarborough Festival. They're doing *Hamlet*, with Adrian Saunders."

"But if they have Adrian Saunders for Hamlet, what will you . . ." The agent's voice trailed off in bewilderment.

"I'll play whatever they've got left." His client's voice was clear as a bell over the three-thousand-mile connection. "Laertes, Claudius, the gravedigger—I don't care."

"But Chris," his agent expostulated, "that is exactly the sort of thing you always avoid like the plague. The media will swamp you, wanting to know why you're taking such a small role . . ."

"Goddammit, Mel," Kit said savagely, "I don't want a lecture. I want you to get me into that festival. I don't care what I play, or how much money they offer. I just want *in*. Is that clear?"

"Yeah," said his agent faintly. "I'll get on it right away."

"Good," said Kit, and hung up the phone.

Four days after Kit's visit the storm broke over Mary's head. *Personality* hit the stands with a picture on the cover of her standing on the steps of Freemont Hall. "CHRIS DOUGLAS MARRIED!" screamed the headline. "Wife University Professor!"

"Huh," said Mary when she first saw it. "I wish I *were* a professor." Then her phone started to ring and it didn't stop until the end of the term when she fled the campus and went into seclusion.

She went to Nantucket, where her oldest brother had a summer cottage. Her sister-in-law was in residence with the three children and Mike came out from Boston on weekends. Kathy was a warm and intelligent person who had the tact to leave Mary to herself and not burden her with unwanted sympathy. Mary played tennis with Kathy and went bicycling and swimming with the children. There was no television in the cottage and the only paper Mary saw for two weeks was the local *News*. It should have been a thoroughly relaxing time for her. She was with people she loved and who loved her, and she was doing all the recreational things she liked best to do. It was therefore disconcerting to find herself so restless and dissatisfied.

She knew what was bothering her—more precisely, she knew *who* was bothering her. She had thought she was over him. She had put him out of her life and her work and that, she had thought, was that. She had convinced herself that her happiness lay with things of the mind, not with a dark, slim man who had once torn her life apart and almost destroyed her in the process.

The day before she was due to leave Nantucket for Yarborough it rained. After lunch Mary took an old brown raincoat of Mike's and went for a walk. She went down to the beach and there, with the rain falling on her face and the waves crashing on the sand, she thought back to those innocent undergraduate days of five years ago when she had first met Christopher Douglas.

Chapter Two

S he had heard of him long before they met. He was in the graduate drama school at her university in New Haven and had been something of a celebrity on campus for over a year. For one reason or another, Mary had never been to any of the drama productions in which he had starred. She herself was very busy, and in the English department something of a celebrity in her own right. She was, for example, the only undergraduate ever allowed to take the famous graduate seminar of the university's leading professor of Renaissance literature. Mary O'Connor, ran the talk in the English department, had all the marks of a real scholar.

Her commitment to her work scared off a number of boys who would otherwise have wanted to take her out, but she didn't lack for dates. At twenty-one, tall and slender, with long black hair, dazzling pale skin and absolutely blue eyes, she was stunning enough to be forgiven for her brains. She was the youngest of five children and, her brothers and sisters all said affectionately, the smartest. That was why her mother had relented and allowed her to attend a secular, coeducational university. Both her older sisters had gone to a Catholic college for women and upon graduation both had taught school for two years and then married.

"Mary Kate is different," her sister Maureen had told her mother. "For one thing, she's ten years younger than I am and seven years younger than Pat. That's two generations in today's age, Mom. She shouldn't be bound by the same rules we were." And her conservative, apprehensive, but deeply caring mother had relented. Mary had gone to school in New Haven, only a few miles away from her native Connecticut town but worlds away in outlook and philosophy.

She had loved it. And she had not, as her mother had feared, been "corrupted" by bad influences. At the beginning of her senior year she still did not smoke pot or get drunk every weekend; and she was still a virgin.

It was shortly before the Christmas break that a boy she had been dating invited her to see the drama-school production of *Twelfth Night*. "Christopher Douglas is playing Orsino." he told her, "and he's supposed to be terrific."

"Okay," said Mary casually, "I'd like that."

She went, and her whole life changed.

She would never forget the first time she laid eyes on Kit. The lights in the theater had dimmed, the curtain had slowly risen, and there he was, alone in the center of the stage, reclining carelessly against some brightly colored cushions. The first thing she had noticed was his voice. It came across the footlights, effortlessly audible, deep and velvety with just the suspicion of a drawl.

> If music be the food of love, play on,
> Give me excess of it, that, surfeiting,
> The appetite may sicken, and so die.

She listened, breathless, caught in the magic of that voice. Then he rose and moved toward the front of the stage and she really looked at him for the first time. He was a splendid young male, beautiful and tall, slim-hipped and black-haired, with a virility whose impact she felt even across the distance that separated them. She sat rooted to her seat throughout the entire performance. She had never dreamed, she thought, that a boy like this could really exist in the world.

Afterward she and her date, whose name she never afterward remembered, went out for something to eat. They stopped around first to see a friend in one of the dorms, so they were late getting to the local eatery they had made their destination. When they came in the door the place was crowded. Her date had taken her arm and was steering her into the room when someone called his name. They turned and saw a tableful of students eating pizza and drinking beer. One of the students was Christopher Douglas. The boy who had called to them spoke for a minute to her date and then, as they were turning to leave, her escort said to Kit, "We just saw *Twelfth Night*. It was terrific."

"I'm glad you liked it," the beautiful voice replied pleasantly. He looked at Mary and stood up. "Why don't you two join us? I'll round up a few extra chairs."

Before she quite knew what was happening, Mary found herself sitting next to Him. "Did you like the play as well?" he asked her.

"Yes, I did," she answered. "Very much. Your interpretation of Orsino was fascinating."

He raised a black eyebrow. "Oh?"

She subjected him to an appraising blue stare. "If you were even the *slightest* bit effeminate," she said at last, "you couldn't have gotten away with it."

He grinned appreciatively. "Do you know the play?"

"Yes. The English Renaissance is a particular interest of mine."

"Ah. An English major."

Her date caught his last words and leaned across her. "Not just an English major, a summa cum laude English major."

Mary flushed with annoyance. "Perhaps I ought to tattoo it on my forehead in case any one should miss the fact," she said lightly. The remark passed completely over the head of her date but *he* looked at her even harder.

"Hey, Kit," called one of the students from further down the table. "I meant to ask you if you'd seen the latest production at the Long Stage."

"No," he answered, easily pitching his superbly trained voice down the length of the table, "I haven't." A jukebox was playing and a few couples were up in a small dance area. "Would you like to dance?" he said to Mary.

"Why, all right," she replied, startled, and he took her by the hand and led her out to the floor.

"I'm afraid I didn't get your name," he said, drawing her competently into his arms.

"It's Mary O'Connor. Did I hear someone call you Kit?"

"Mm." His mouth wore a faint smile. "After Kit Marlowe, the Elizabethan playwright. Jim thinks I look the way he must have."

Mary thought of Marlowe, brilliant, poetic, and dead in a barroom brawl at the age of twenty-eight. She laughed. "He may be right."

He pulled her closer until she could feel the whole hard length of his body pressed against hers. The music was slow and dreamy. Mary felt herself relaxing against him, relaxing into him. "Do you live on campus? Can I take you home?" he murmured into her ear.

The music stopped and she pulled away from him. "No, you may not take me home," she said with what she hoped was firmness. "I came with someone else and *he* will take me home."

She turned and made her way back to their table. Her date looked both grateful and relieved when she sat down and immediately began to talk to him. They stayed for another thirty minutes during which time she could feel Kit's dark gaze boring into the back of her head. When they got up to leave she smiled generally around the table and refused to meet his eyes.

She thought to herself as she undressed and got into bed that she had behaved like a child. He must think that no one had ever suggested going home with her before. She should have been funny and casual and made a clever remark. The problem was he unnerved her so much that she *still* couldn't think of a clever remark. She thought of the feel of his body against hers and of her reaction. The problem was, she thought, he scared her to death.

He called the next day and asked her out. She said she was busy. He named another time and she said she was busy then too.

"Doing what?" he asked.

She thought he was being rude and answered repressively, "I'm working on a paper." She would have liked to tell him that what she did was none of his business. She didn't, however, because she was almost constitutionally incapable of being rude herself. Her parents, she thought regretfully, had brought her up too well.

"When is the paper due?" he asked relentlessly.

"The day before Christmas recess. Then I go home." That should give him enough of a hint, she thought.

"I'll call you after the vacation then," said the beautiful voice in her ear and she stared at the phone in astonishment.

"I'll probably be busy preparing for finals," she got out.

"I'll call you," he said firmly and hung up.

She went home for Christmas and tried not to think about Christopher Douglas. She went out with a boy she had known since high school who was also home on holiday and she found the dates strangely depressing.

"You don't look very happy, honey," her father said to her as she came into the living room one night after saying good-bye to her escort in her car.

"I don't know, Daddy," she replied with a sigh. "It's just that I'm so *sick* of mediocre boys."

"Mediocre?" he queried with a grin.

"Well, they're nice enough, I guess. It's just that they don't interest me much. And lately it seems everyone I go out with starts to talk about marriage. *Why* do men always want to get married?"

He laughed. "Does Dan want to marry you?"

"I think so," she answered gloomily.

"I always thought you liked Dan."

"Oh, I like him. But he's so—so conventional. His talk, his ideas, his clothes, his car. I don't think in all the years I've known him that he's ever once surprised me."

"Well, then," her father said gravely, "clearly you oughtn't to marry him."

"No." She sighed. "I don't think I'll ever marry. I think I'll devote my life to scholarship. It's much more satisfying than going out on all these boring dates." She trailed gracefully upstairs, leaving her father with his head buried in the newspaper, his shoulders shaking.

She got back to college on Monday and by Friday he still hadn't called. She was unreasonably annoyed. If people said they were going to do a thing, then they ought to do it, she thought. She refused two dates for Saturday night and was sitting in her room reading *Tamburlaine the Great* by Christopher Marlow when she was called to the phone. He was down in the lobby. Would she care to go out with him for a bite to eat?

"All right," she heard herself saying, "I'll be down in five minutes." She brushed her long hair, dusted some blusher on her cheeks and put on lipstick. She changed her jeans for a pair of corduroys, picked up her pea jacket and went downstairs to the lobby.

They had a wonderful time. She had thought they could have nothing in common, but by the end of the evening she felt she had known him forever. She didn't quite know what she had expected—a "film" star type personality, she supposed, to go with his looks. But he wasn't like that at all. He was, in fact, the nicest boy she had ever met. The nicest man, she corrected herself, as she said good night to him sedately in the lobby of her dorm. He was twenty-five, four years older than she, and centuries older in experience she was sure. She did not invite him up to her room.

Mary shivered a little; the Nantucket rain was turning colder and she got up and began to walk slowly down the beach. It was painful, looking back like this; painful to look honestly and see how cocksure and how foolish and how young she had been. And yet she knew, as she reflected on the self-absorbed adolescent she had been, that she could not have handled things any differently from the way she had. Her only alternative had been to simply say good-bye and refuse to see him. And that was something she had not been able to do.

They had reached the crisis point in their relationship rather quickly. He wanted to go to bed with her and she would not. He was very persuasive, and every sense she owned was screaming for her to give in to him, but there was a hidden core of iron in Mary's character and on this issue he came up against it.

"But, Mary, why?" he asked, his lips moving tantalizingly along her throat. They were both in the front seat of a car he had borrowed and the car was parked in front of her dorm. He wanted to come up to her room.

"No, Kit," she said, and his mouth moved to find hers once again. She closed her eyes; nothing she had ever experienced had prepared her for the way she felt when Kit kissed her. His hand slid inside her open coat and began to caress her breast.

"I want you," he said. "I want you so much. Mary— let me come upstairs."

"No," she said again.

"God damn it, why not?" Frustrated passion was making him lose his temper.

She gave him the same answer she had given all the other boys, the answer that had stood her in such good stead for four years. "Because it's a sin," she said and stared resolutely out the front window.

"What?"

That was the answer she usually got. "You heard me. It's a sin. Against the sixth commandment—you know, the one that says, 'Thou shalt not . . .'"

"I know what the sixth commandment says," he replied irritably. He looked at her, trying to make out her expression in the dark. "Are you serious?"

And in fact she was. Then, as now, she was as oddly simple in some ways as she was bafflingly complex in others. Sex before marriage was a sin and she wouldn't do it.

He had tried to change her mind. By God, he had tried. He would have succeeded too, she thought, if she hadn't been so careful about where she would go with him. He was as hampered by lack of opportunity as he was by her own resistance. You can't make passionate love in the middle of a crowded student party—or at least not if you are as private a person as Kit was. You could do quite a few things at a movie, but certainly not what you ultimately wanted to do. He didn't own a car, and on the few occasions when he suggested borrowing one, she had said she had other things to do.

He stopped calling her and for a month she didn't see him. It was pure hell and it was then that she came to the reluctant realization that she loved him. It was a terribly upsetting recognition. They were of two different worlds, really, and she feared and mistrusted his. Those worlds had touched briefly here at college but in June they both would graduate, and like two meteors on opposite courses, they would grow farther and farther apart as the years passed, never to touch each other again. She would continue her studies and, with luck, land a teaching job in a decent university. He would make it big in acting; she had no doubt at all about that. He had the looks, the talent, and the drive. Most of the boys she knew traveled through life in a pleasant cloud; they did things because they seemed like good things to do at the moment. Not Kit. He knew exactly what he was doing and exactly where he was going. And he was going to the top. There was no place for her in the future he envisioned for himself.

In March she learned she had been awarded a fellowship for graduate study. Kit was offered a job with the Long Stage, a regional theater based in New Haven that often sent productions on to Broadway. He called her up to tell her the good news and to congratulate her on her award. Her heart almost jolted out of her body when she heard his voice and she agreed to go out with him for a drink to celebrate.

They went to Guido's, the place where they had first met. Kit ordered a pizza and—as a special treat—a bottle of wine instead of the inevitable beer.

"I've located a small apartment in a decent area of New Haven," he told her, his strong white teeth making quick work of the pizza. "It's in a two-family house. Not very elaborate, but it's clean. And cheap. And I have yard privileges." He looked at her out of brooding dark eyes. "You could move in with me while you're working on your degree."

"No," she said.

"Christ, sometimes I think that's the only word you know."

She put her wineglass down. "You shouldn't have called me up. I shouldn't have come with you." There were tears in her eyes. "I'll get a cab back to my dorm."

"No." His long fingers shot out and closed over her wrist. "No, sit down, Mary."

Slowly she obeyed him and while she fished around

in her purse for a tissue he began to talk. "I'm bound and determined to stick to acting. You know that. It's what I want to do most in life. It's what I think I can be *good* at. I have a job at present but the money stinks. I have no family to fall back on if I lose it. I've gone through school on scholarships and loans and my net worth is a debit account."

He looked at her and his flexible mouth was taut and grim. "You don't know what it means to need money. You come from a comfortable New England home. Your father is a doctor and your mother belongs to all the right clubs and committees. Your sisters and brothers are pillars of the community. You have brains and beauty and integrity. You're probably right to run like hell from me. You ought to marry a lawyer or an engineer. Someone like your brothers, who can give you a big house in a nice New England town where you can teach in the local college and raise your kids to play on the local little league team."

She sniffled into her tissue. "You seem to have my life all planned out for me."

He paid no attention to her interruption but went on, his face dark and intense. "My own future is uncertain, to say the least. I have no business asking any girl to tie herself to me—and especially not you." She was looking at him now, her face as somber as his. "But I love you," he said. "This last month has been hell."

"I know." Her words were barely a whisper. "I love you too." She looked down at his lean hard hand, which was clasped tensely about his wineglass. "Why especially not me?" she asked.

"Because of all the things I've just said. You aren't cut out to be an actor's wife. And for you, marriage would be a serious business."

She kept her eyes on his hand. "Yes." A strand of long black hair had fallen forward across her cheek and she pushed it back behind her ear with a slow, unconsciously seductive gesture.

"So, given all that," he said harshly, "will you marry me?"

With almost palpable effort she dragged her eyes away from his hand and looked up at his face. She moistened her lips with her tongue. "Yes," she said. "I will."

Kit burst upon her quiet, conservative, academically oriented New England family rather like a bombshell. Her mother, obviously worried about the proposed marriage between her youngest daughter and this extraordinary boy, spent a good deal of time during the long weekend they stayed with her trying to probe Mary's feelings. Mary was certain she was regretting the nice woman's college she had wanted her daughter to attend. Kit would not have come into her orbit if she had been safely cloistered at Mount Saint Mary's.

"You are so *unalike*, darling," she said cautiously to Mary. "You are so intelligent. Learning has always mattered so much to you."

"Kit isn't exactly stupid, mother," Mary replied patiently. "He has a B.S. in mathematics from Penn State, you know."

"Mathematics?" Her mother looked astonished.

"Yes. He got into acting when he joined a student production at Penn for a lark and he ended up deciding he liked it better than math. But he finished his degree. It took him six years to do it, because he had to work, but he finished. He *does* finish what he starts, and he is a very good actor. He'll make it."

"Suppose he does, darling." Her mother's voice was troubled. "Will you like that sort of life? The publicity is ghastly. And I'm sure most of those people in Hollywood take drugs. And the divorce rate . . ."

"I know all that, Mother, and believe me I've thought about it." Mary smiled a little ruefully. "But I love him. What else can I do?"

Her mother's face relaxed a little. "Your father seems to like him," she said hopefully.

Mary grinned. "You know, Mother, I've decided the worst thing you can do is to decide on the sort of man you *don't* want to marry and the sort of life you *don't* want to lead. The minute you do that, God looks down on your smug little plans and says, 'Ah-ha, I'll fix her.' And he did just that. He sent me Kit."

"He is—rather awesome." For the first time there was the hint of laughter in her mother's voice.

"I don't know what he is. I only know that there he is and I've got to be with him."

"Well, then, darling," said her mother briskly, "shall we plan for a wedding in June?"

Kit was rather startled to find that his nuptials were to be celebrated with as much pomp as Mrs. O'Connor clearly envisioned. But it wasn't the trimmings he objected to so much as the delay.

"June!" He groaned. "Are you going to make me wait until June?"

Mary's eyes always seemed to get at least two shades bluer whenever she looked at him. "Yes, I'm afraid I am."

"But what does it matter, since we're going to be married anyway." His voice had dropped to the husky note that always made her heart begin to race. "What difference can a wedding ring make?" he coaxed.

"It isn't the ring. It's the sacrament," she said patiently. "Oh, Kit, I've explained and explained . . ."

"I know." He had glowered at her dauntingly. "I can't think clearly anymore. And it's all your fault."

She had bit her lip and then giggled. "Darling, you look so funny . . ." And he had stalked off in high dudgeon.

They were married the week after graduation in the church where Mary had been baptized, and there had been a reception for two hundred people on the lawn of the O'Connor family home. They were to go to Cape Cod for their honeymoon, but after they left the reception Kit got on the highway going west rather than east.

"Hey," said Mary in a startled voice. "You're going the wrong way."

"No, I'm not," he replied calmly. "We're going to spend tonight in our own apartment. We can leave for the cape tomorrow."

"Good heavens, why did you decide to do that? We're all booked into the cottage in Chatham."

He gave her a sidelong glance that emphasized the remarkable length of his lashes. "I have no intention of driving five hours on my wedding day," he said. "I'm saving my strength for other things."

It took a minute for his words to register, but when they did she felt a strange shiver deep inside her. "Ah," she got out, she hoped calmly, "I see."

Their apartment consisted of a bedroom, living room, and eat-in kitchen. It was sparsely furnished, mostly from the O'Connor-family attic. The bedroom, however, did boast a double bed with a beautiful maple headboard, and it was to this room that Kit steered her as soon as they were in the door. He put their suitcases down with a thump and went to pull down the shades.

When he had performed this task to his satisfaction, he turned to look at his wife.

She was wearing a blue seersucker shirt-dress and sandals. Her long hair, which reached halfway down her back, was tied loosely at the nape of her neck with a blue ribbon. She looked back at him, raised a black eyebrow and said, "Well? Are you going to show me what you've been making such a fuss about for the last six months?"

He tackled her. She was standing next to the bed and his rush toppled her backward so she was lying on the white Martha Washington bedspread with him on top of her. She began to laugh. He growled and bit her ear. She laughed harder. "I love your subtle technique," she got out breathlessly through her mirth.

"Oh, so you like subtlety?" He slowly pulled the ribbon out of her hair, dropped it on the floor, and bent his head to kiss her. Her mouth opened under his and her arms went up to circle his neck. Always before, she had put a barrier between them, always there had been the awareness that she would let him go so far and no farther. Today the barrier was gone.

When he raised his head and spoke, his voice was husky and his breathing uneven. "And now," he said, "let me see what I've got here." He began to unbutton the front of her shirt-dress. She lay perfectly still, gazing up at him out of darkened eyes. In a minute he had skillfully bared the upper part of her body; her skin was flawless, her breasts perfect. "Almighty God," he muttered. "You're so beautiful." Very gently, almost tentatively, he touched the single small beauty spot that lay near the nipple of her right breast. His light touch sent an electrifying sensation through her entire body.

"Kit," she whispered. "Darling."

He bent to kiss the beauty mark and his hands began to move caressingly on her body. "My princess," he said. "My beautiful Irish witch." He unbuttoned the rest of her dress and then his hands were tugging on the elastic of her half-slip and panties. Instinctively she stiffened and he began to murmur endearments again while his mouth and his hands touched and caressed her. There was extreme tenderness in his voice and in his hands, and sweet cajolery, and the hypnotic quality of rising passion. When Mary's body arched up against his, he released his hold on her only long enough to tear off his own clothes.

She clung to him, swept along on the tide of rising desire. Her brain, that sharp, critical, well-trained arbiter of her life, was swamped by the purely physical sensations Kit's touch aroused. He was murmuring to her and blindly she obeyed his instructions, needing him desperately to assuage the throbbing ache he had created within her. He loomed powerfully over her and she held him tightly, heedless of the pain, stunned by the unexpected searing intensity of the pleasure. He was saying her name over and over; dimly she heard him through the waves of sensation that were sweeping her body. "I love you," she whispered as she felt them coming to rest. "I love you."

They lay still together for a long minute and she ran her hands over the strong muscles of his shoulders and back, feeling the light sheen of sweat that clung to him. His heart was hammering; she could feel the heavy strokes as she felt the heat of his body and the laboring of his breath. She was a little awestruck at the thought that she had been able to do this to him. And when she thought of what he had done to her. . . .

After a while she murmured, "Do you know, this is the first time I've ever understood *Anna Karenina?*"

He laughed, a soft dark sound deep down in his throat, and raised his head to gaze into her face. The look he gave her was brilliant, full of amusement and triumph. "I hope you're not planning to throw yourself under a train?"

Her lips curved and she felt her heart turn over with love. "You know what I mean." She traced the outline of his mouth. "I never understood what love of a man can do to a woman."

He kissed her fingers and then her throat. "You're so generous, Princess. It's one of the reasons I love you."

They lay quietly together, content and peaceful. Then Mary whispered, "I ate hardly anything at the reception and I'm starving."

He yawned and sat up. "Great minds think alike. I've just been contemplating calling out for a pizza."

"Yum." She sat up as well. "With sausage."

"With sausage." His eyes narrowed a little as he looked at her. "I warn you, though, the pizza is just an interlude. I haven't finished with you by a long shot."

"Oh?" She opened her blue eyes very wide and looked limpidly back at him. "You sound very sure of yourself."

He leaned closer. "Shouldn't I be?" There was a hint of laughter in his voice, and more than a hint of confidence. He looked like a man who knew what he wanted and knew also that what he wanted he would get.

It was unnerving, the reaction that look and voice produced in her. She waited a minute before she replied, very softly, "Go call for the pizza."

They left for the Cape the following day and stayed

for a week. It was a blissfully happy honeymoon followed by an equally happy summer spent in their small
apartment, painting the walls and making the rounds of
tag sales to find furniture. They were deeply in love
and deeply happy.

It was a happiness that lasted exactly seven months.
They both worked hard and they had practically no
money, but they had each other. "I'm going to write my
doctoral dissertation on 'One Thousand and One Ways
to Cook Hamburger Meat,'" she would say as she
dished up another plate of their staple food.

"What's wrong with hamburger?" he would demand.
"It's nutritious, it's tasty, and it's cheap. The perfect
food. You're a genius to have discovered it." And they
would laugh and eat their dinner and fall into bed.

The idyll ended on January 6 when she went to the
doctor and found out she was pregnant.

Chapter Three

"**B**ut I *can't* be pregnant," she had protested to the doctor, a gynecologist who was a friend of her father's. "I'm on the pill." On some issues, Mary was *not* more Catholic than the pope and this was one of them. Both she and Kit had agreed that children were something to be put off for the future.

The pill was not infallible, Dr. Murak told her gently, and she was most definitely pregnant. About three months along, actually. He told her not to worry, that he would be glad to take care of her. She was Bob's girl, after all, and there would be no charge. He had known her family for years and did not make the mistake of mentioning an abortion.

Kit was not so perceptive. After five minutes of incredulity, anger, and general agitation, he suggested that she get an abortion. Nothing in her entire life had ever shocked her more.

"But, Christ, Mary, we can't *afford* a baby," he stormed angrily. "I don't have a dime to my name. I work crazy hours—and so do you. What's going to happen to your fellowship if you have a baby? You'll have to give it up."

"Then I'll give it up," she had replied grimly.

"I don't want you to give it up!" he shouted. "I didn't marry you to make you give things up!"

"Would you rather make me a murderer?" she shouted back.

He thrust his hand through his thick hair, causing it to fall untidily over his forehead. "It isn't murder," he answered in a more controlled voice. "It's a perfectly legal operation."

"Oh God," she said, pressing shaking hands to her mouth and staring at him with horrified eyes. "How can you say this to me? You're talking about *our baby*." And she began to cry, harsh wracking sobs that hurt her throat and chest. After a minute he put his arms around her.

"It isn't that it's not important to me," he said, a note of quiet desperation in his voice. "It's that it's too important. A child needs security and he can't have security if there's no financial stability."

She was stiff within the circle of his arm, refusing the comfort of physical contact that he was offering. "Money isn't that important." She sobbed. "It's love that matters."

"You can say that," he answered grimly, "because you've never known what it's like to need money and not to have it." She was trying desperately to control her sobs and her body shook with the effort of containment. He held her for a minute and then said wearily, "All right, sweetheart, please don't upset yourself like this. We'll have the baby. I don't know how the hell I'm going to manage it, but I will. Somehow, I will."

They had patched the quarrel up, but a bitter seed had been sown. And then in March he got an offer to test for a role in a new film being shot by one of Hollywood's leading producers.

"He was in New Haven three weeks ago and saw me in the Tennessee Williams revival we're doing. He's making the movie version of *The Russian Experiment* and he wants me to test for the role of Ivan."

"Oh, Kit, how marvelous!" *The Russian Experiment* had been the blockbuster novel of the previous year, and they had both read it. It was a sophisticated combination of suspense, intrigue, and political and metaphysical speculation. Ivan was a young anarchist whose brooding and bitter presence had been a thread woven throughout the entire fabric of the novel. It would be a fabulous part if Kit could get it.

He had gotten it. The producer had liked his test and, with much hullabaloo about "discovering a new Brando," had signed him to a contract.

He had gone to California to make the movie and she stayed in Connecticut. He didn't want to take her away from her fellowship and then there was the baby. They both agreed it would be far more sensible for her to wait until the summer, until after the movie, after the baby, after the papers and finals, and then they would decide what they would do and where they would live. They closed up their apartment, stored their furniture in her mother's attic, and she went back home to live.

The female star of *The Russian Experiment* was Jessica Corbet, an actress of international repute. She was beautiful and talented, and at thirty-two had gone through two husbands and several highly publicized affairs. According to the papers, she began a new one with Kit.

At first Mary didn't believe it. She was sophisticated enough to know that ninety percent of the gossip blazoned across the headlines of movie scandal sheets was untrue. If Kit had been more faithful about calling her, if he had written with any regularity, perhaps she would not have begun to doubt.

It was a terrible experience for her. She had been brought up in a close-knit, loving, and supportive family, and all her relationships had hitherto been deeply secure and unquestioned. When once the first trickle of doubt about Kit had been let in, it seemed as if the entire foundation of her marriage began to crumble. He hadn't really wanted to marry her, she thought. She had forced him into it by refusing to sleep with him. He didn't really want a wife. And he certainly didn't want a baby. He had made that very clear.

There was never any mention in the scandal sheets or the gossip columns that she read so feverishly of the fact that Christopher Douglas had a wife. It didn't occur to her that he might be trying to protect her. It did occur to her that he didn't want her anymore, was embarrassed to admit that America's hottest new sex symbol had a pregnant wife at home.

Whenever he called, which was not very frequently, he sounded distracted and very very distant. She couldn't ask him about any of the things she was reading in the paper. She could only be polite and cool and distant herself.

She finished her term at school and got, as usual, high honors. At the end of June, three weeks early, she went into labor. Her mother and father took her to the hospital and then tried to get hold of Kit. He wasn't at his apartment. He wasn't at the studio. Finally Mrs. O'Connor got his agent on the phone. Kit had gone off to Jessica Corbet's ranch for the weekend, he told Mary's distressed mother. He would see if he could contact him.

After 8 hours of labor, Mary's baby was born dead. The cord had caught around his neck during the delivery and he had strangled. Dr. Murak was devastated. "There was nothing I could do," he kept saying to Dr. O'Connor. "Nothing, Bob. It was just one of those freak things."

Mrs. O'Connor finally got hold of Kit at his apartment a day later. He flew into New Haven on the first flight, but when Mary opened her eyes to see him standing at her bedside, she had said only, "Go away. I never want to see you again." And she hadn't, until *Personality* had discovered her existence and precipitated his arrival on her doorstep.

The rain had stopped and she looked up at the gray Nantucket sky and saw a patch of blue over the water. The storm was passing over. She lifted her head, her wet black hair slicked back, and stood for a long time, staring at that blue sky. The storm always passes, she thought, if one only has the fortitude to wait it out.

It had been a year before her storm of grief and guilt over the loss of her baby and the failure of her marriage had begun to abate. It had been a terrible year and sometimes she thought the only thing that had saved her sanity was her work. She threw herself into her studies with a feverish and grim intensity. By day, working in the library or attending classroom lectures and seminars, she kept the agony at bay.

It was at night that it overwhelmed her, and she would cry silently in her solitary bed. She blamed Kit. He became her scapegoat; on him she hung all the responsibility for their failure. *He* had run out on her when she needed him. *He* had not wanted the baby. It was desperately important that her consciousness should have someone else to take responsibility, because deep in her subconscious, she blamed herself. Although she tried, she could never forget that her first reaction to news of the baby had been dismay. That had changed, and as he had grown inside her her feelings had become warm and protective. But initially, she had not wanted him. Deep, deep inside her, her Irish Catholic upbringing was saying that God had punished her for that initial rejection. And the more she felt this the more feverishly she tried to blame Kit. Lying awake night after endless night, she began to understand what Thoreau had meant when he said "The mass of men live lives of quiet desperation."

She had thrown herself into her work and her work had saved her. None of her professors or her fellow students had ever mentioned Kit to her again. They behaved to her with the scrupulous and impersonal respect that her scholarly achievement commanded in their world. It was a world she clung to: a quiet and traditional place where only intellectual things counted.

In two years time she had her Ph.D., and the following January the university published her doctoral dissertation as a book. It established her scholarly reputation immediately. She was offered a job at a prestigious Massachusetts university and knew, if she produced as she was fully capable of doing, she would be given tenure. She had achieved a place for herself, a place worthy of reverence, and she had thought her life was settled.

And then Kit had come back.

Nothing had really changed, she told herself as she walked back to her brother's cottage through the brightening day. She still had her job. The university had stood behind her: her colleagues had been supportive and unquestioning, her students had been fiercely protective, the university security force had acted as her bodyguards. It would all die down and by September be forgotten.

Only she would not forget. She had seen his movies; why, then, she thought despairingly, should seeing him again in person have had such an effect on her? When she at last reached the cottage, her face was once again wet, but not this time from the rain.

She left Nantucket the following day and went back to her own house to do laundry and repack for her three-week sojourn in New Hampshire. She arrived home on Saturday night and was to leave again Monday morning. Sunday afternoon, taking a break from the ironing board, she called her parents. Her father answered the phone.

"Hi, Daddy," she said cheerfully. "It's me. How are you doing?"

"We're just fine, honey," he answered. "How are you?" There was a cautious note to his inquiry that puzzled her.

"Great," she replied. "The weather on Nantucket was super and Mike and Kathy and the kids were just what I needed. So sane, if you know what I mean."

He chuckled. "I don't know if I'd call my grandchildren sane, precisely, but I know what you mean."

"I feel like a bird on the wing. I had wanted to get down to see you and Mother but I leave for Yarborough bright and early tomorrow morning. I won't see you until August, I guess."

"You're still going to Yarborough?"

"Of course I'm still going to Yarborough. Daddy, what's wrong? You sound funny. Is mother all right?"

"Your mother's fine," he assured her. "She'll be sorry she missed your call. She's out playing tennis with Sue Bayley. The town tournament starts next week and they've entered the doubles competition."

"Oh. Well, wish her luck for me and give her my love. I'll send you a postcard from Yarborough."

"Yes, you do that." Her father's voice came strongly now over the wire. "Have a good time, honey. And— give the place a chance, will you? Remember, things aren't always what they seem to be."

"You sound like Hamlet," she replied in a puzzled voice. "Are you sure everything's okay at home, Daddy?"

"Positive."

"All right, then, Daddy, I'll say good-bye for now."

"Good-bye, Mary Kate. Call us if you need us."

"I will. Good-bye." She hung up the phone and stood staring at it doubtfully for a full minute. What on earth had gotten into her father?

Chapter Four

Yarborough College was set on a crystal-clear lake in the foothills of the White Mountains. It had been founded eighty years ago as a small men's liberal-arts college and had managed to survive with much of its original character intact. It offered its students—who now included women—an excellent academic program coupled with one of the best ski schools in the country. In the summer it ran its now-famous drama school and festival. Of the last five productions to come out of the festival, three had gone on to Broadway.

Mary had never been to Yarborough herself but she had seen pictures of the campus and she was looking forward to the idyllic peace and security promised by such a lovely setting. Her own schedule called for her to deliver one hour-and-a-half lecture a day. Her students, who were all also involved in the production of the play that opened at the beginning of August, would receive six graduate credits for the summer school. The stipend she was to receive for giving the lectures was nominal, but room and board was included, and her lectures covered material she knew thoroughly and so had not taken a tremendous amount of work for her to put together. All in all, she was looking forward to relaxing in the beautiful New Hampshire summer.

As she turned in to the gates of the campus she was surprised to see a crowd of people standing on the drive. She braked the car and someone shouted, "It's her!" Cameras started to flash and questions were shouted. Very frightened, Mary gripped the wheel of the car and a man in a guard uniform opened her door and said, "Move over, Dr. O'Connor, I'll drive you in."

Obediently she slid over and in a minute the man had the car moving briskly forward. The reporters all jumped aside, and as the car moved up the drive another guard firmly slammed the huge iron gate shut.

"My God," said Mary faintly. "What was that all about?"

The guard smiled briefly. "You're Mrs. Christopher Douglas, aren't you?"

"Are they *still* harping on that?" she said incredulously.

"They've been here for almost a week now, I'm afraid. Nasty lot." The car came to a halt in front of a venerable old brick building and a slim, wiry man came running down the steps. "Here's Mr. Clark," said her escort.

"Dr. O'Connor?" The director of the festival opened the door of the Buick and Mary got out and offered her hand.

"Yes. Hello, Mr. Clark. What a fuss at the gate!"

"Isn't it terrible?" he replied, looking not at all distressed. "I've put you in one of the summer cottages we had built a few years ago especially for the festival. I'll drive with you over there and we can unload your luggage. Then, if you like, I'll give you a quick tour of the campus."

"That sounds great," Mary agreed. The guard got out of the car and she and George Clark got in.

"Turn left at the bottom of the drive here," he said and she accelerated slowly.

The cottage she had been alotted was charming: small and rustic, with a bedroom, a sitting room, and a screened-in porch. "Meals are served in the dining room," Mr. Clark told her. "I'm afraid we all eat together: professionals and students alike. It's supposed to be part of the charm of the program."

She smiled reassuringly. "I'm sure it is, Mr. Clark."

"George, please," he answered. "We're very informal here in the summer."

"Then you must call me Mary." She looked around her. The row of cottages was set in the side of a hill and surrounded by huge pines. The sparkle of the lake was just visible through the trees. "It's like a summer resort," she said, half humorously.

"I hope you are going to enjoy yourself," he replied with a warm smile. "We didn't ask you here just to work."

They walked around the campus and Mary found herself liking George Clark very much. He was not precisely good-looking but his narrow face and quick, nervous hands were oddly attractive. They talked about her lectures and she told him a little of what she had planned. He was pleased and encouraging and told her something about the students she would be working with.

"How is the play shaping up?" she asked curiously. "You've been rehearsing for a week now, haven't you?"

"Yes. And the most damnable thing has just happened. We've lost our Gertrude."

"Oh no," she said with sympathetic concern. Gertrude was Hamlet's mother in the play and it was

a central role. "You had Maud Armitage, didn't you?
What happened?"

"She broke her ankle on the tennis court."

"Good heavens."

"That is putting it mildly. I have a New York agent
scouring the earth for a replacement—hopefully an actress who has done the part before. Time is getting
short. It's only three weeks until we open. That's the
one great drawback of this summer school—there just
isn't enough time."

"Well, it's Hamlet who is really important," she said
soothingly. "How is Adrian Saunders managing?" They
were walking up the path leading to the building that
housed the English and drama departments, and at
these words of hers he stopped dead. "Is something the
matter?" she asked.

"Is it possible you don't know . . . ?" He was staring
at her in stunned surprise.

"Know what?" Her voice was sharp with alarm.

"Adrian Saunders backed out at the last minute," he
said slowly. "He got a movie offer and of course he
wanted to take it. So we got someone else to play
Hamlet."

She felt a warning prickle of apprehension. "Who?"
she asked tensely and was not surprised when the answer came.

"Christopher Douglas."

Her first impulse was to run. She went back to her
cottage and set for a long time on the front porch, her
hands clasped into tense fists, staring out at the pines.
Two things finally got her on her feet and into the bedroom to unpack. One was the knowledge that if she
backed out now, George Clark would be left without a
teacher for his course. The other was her father's ad-

vice about giving Yarborough a chance. Obviously he had known Kit was going to be here. And he had not told her, had let her come in ignorance of what she would find. Her father, she remembered, had always liked Kit.

So she unpacked, showered and changed into a blue shirt-dress, and made her way slowly over to the dining hall. Sherry, George had told her, was served before dinner in the recreation room of the dining hall. She opened the door of the spacious, high-ceilinged room, stepped over the threshold and saw him immediately. He was surrounded by a pack of girls and seemed to be listening patiently to what one of them was saying. It was such a familiar pose to her: the turn of his head as it bent a little toward the favored person, the clear-cut profile. . . . He looked up and saw her. He dropped his fan club instantly and came across the room, moving like a panther with long, graceful, silent strides.

He stopped in front of her and she said, "I didn't know you were here."

"Yes," he replied. "So George told me." His eyes on her face were as black as coal. "Would you have come if you'd known?"

"No." She stared at him and her lovely full mouth tightened with temper. "*Why*, Kit? You knew I was lecturing here. There was a crowd of reporters at the gate when I came in. It's going to be horrible."

"I thought it was time I tried something more serious," he replied. "And I wanted to get back to the stage. When my agent called and told me the Yarborough Festival needed a Hamlet quickly, I took it. I knew you'd be here, of course, but as the truth of our relationship has already leaked, I didn't see what harm could be done by my coming too."

She glared at him, her back rigid. "There's no harm to you, of course, you're probably used to people shouting at you and snapping your picture every time you go around the corner. I, thank God, am not accustomed to being perpetually hounded in such a fashion. And I don't *want* to get accustomed to it. I am absolutely furious with you for doing this to me."

Her eyes shot blue fire at him. Infuriatingly, he grinned. "Now, now, don't get your Irish up, Princess." A man appeared at her elbow and he said, "I don't think you know Mel Horner, my agent. This is Dr. O'Connor, Mel, of whom you have heard much."

Princess. He used to call her Princess when . . . "How do you do, Mr. Horner," she got out and offered her hand. Somewhere a bell rang and they were all moving into dinner. She found herself between George Clark and Frank Moore, a nice boy from Kit's old drama school who was to play Laertes. Kit was sitting opposite her, flanked by the pretty student who was to play Ophelia and a young art student who was working on the set. She was also very pretty.

Everyone but Mary had been in residence for a week and they all seemed to be quite comfortable with each other. The girls were obviously overwhelmed by Kit and hung on his every word with breathless attention. Mary sat quietly and let the conversation flow around her.

"What did you think of the costume sketches, Chris?" George asked.

"I liked them." Kit took a sip out of his glass. He was drinking milk. "I think not quite so much velvet, though? We may be in New England but it is summer after all."

"True," George agreed. "And the lights can get pretty hot."

A little silence fell as Kit attacked his pot roast. He had always been a good trencherman, Mary remembered. He ate little breakfast and lunch, but he liked his dinner.

"I've wanted to ask you something about your last picture, Chris," said Carolyn Nash, the pretty Ophelia. "Did you *really* do your own stunt work?" She had large, pansy-brown eyes and they were directed worshipfully up at his dark face.

"Yes." He smiled a little ruefully. "I must say I kept on suggesting they get a professional stunt guy in, but the director never saw it that way. Unfortunately."

"Why not?" asked Mary suddenly. There had been some very dangerous scenes in his last film, she recalled.

"Saving money, I expect," he replied and ate another forkful of meat.

Mel Horner snorted. "Don't you believe it. They didn't get a stunt man because no one else looks like Chris. More important—no one moves like he does. But he was quite safe, Dr. O'Connor, I assure you."

Mary was intensely annoyed. "I'm quite sure that Kit can take care of himself," she said sweetly.

At her use of that name the two girls' heads swung around and they stared at her, big-eyed and speculative. "Kit?" said Carolyn on a note of inquiry.

Mary stared at him in exasperation. "It's a nickname for Christopher," he said blandly and smiled kindly into Carolyn's small face.

She looked like a kitten that has just been stroked. "Why do you say Chris was safe doing those stunts?" she asked Mel innocently.

"He's much too valuable a property for a production company to allow anything to happen to him," Mel said bluntly. "There aren't many stars around these days whose very name guarantees a stampede at the box office."

Kit shot a look at his agent and Mary said even more sweetly than before, "I suppose that's true."

Black eyes stared at her face for a minute and then he asked, with precisely the same intonation she had used, "And did you graduate summa cum laude *again*?"

She looked thoughtfully back and then, suddenly, smiled, "I'm sorry."

He made a brief gesture with his hand. "Okay." And he went back to eating his dinner.

"I don't know how you stay so thin and eat so much," complained Mel, looking with envy at his client. Mel had a very pronounced potbelly.

"He basically only eats one meal a day," Mary replied absently. She realized what she had said and flushed. "At least he did."

"I still do." There was definite amusement in Kit's deep beautiful voice.

"I have a friend in one of your courses, Dr. O'Connor," Frank Moore said to her and she turned to him in relief.

"Oh? Who is that?"

"Jim Henley."

"Oh, yes." Mary smiled. "I know Mr. Henley. He's in my senior seminar."

"I have to confess I wrote and asked him what you were like when we knew you would be giving the lectures this summer."

"Oh?" She sipped her water.

"And what did this Jim Henley say?" asked Kit mischievously.

"He sent me back a telegram." Frank grinned. "It had only two words on it: Drool Drool."

Kit laughed and so did Mel Horner and George Clark. Mary, who had developed a technique for dealing with drooling male students, said coolly, "Did he? How disappointing. I thought Mr. Henley had the makings of a scholar."

Frank Moore flushed and George Clark and Mel Horner sobered immediately. Only Kit still had a wicked glint in his eyes.

"That's the girl," he said encouragingly. "I bet that cool expression really keeps them at a distance."

She bit her lip. The trouble with Kit, she thought, was he always could make her laugh. She wrinkled her nose at him. "It does."

His eyes laughed back at her but after a minute he turned to Mel Horner. "By the way, Mel, I want you to arrange a press conference. Tomorrow afternoon will be as good a time as any I suppose."

Mel Horner's mouth dropped open. "A press conference?" he almost squeaked. "You never hold press conferences. I've been begging you for years . . ."

"Well, I will hold one tomorrow," said Kit with ominous calm. "What's more, I think the rest of the cast should be there. And George as well."

"Are you serious, Chris?"

"I am perfectly serious. It's the only way to put all these unfortunate rumors to rest. I do not," he said with devastating simplicity, "want the press to disturb my wife."

Chapter Five

Tuesday morning Mary delivered her first lecture. There were thirty-five students in the festival program, some of them members of the cast and the rest involved in other aspects of the production. She knew that the young eyes watching her so assessingly were more interested in her relationship to their leading man than they were in her academic record. Well, she thought grimly, they were damn well going to be in for a shock.

The first thing she did was to hand out a reading list. Eyes popped open and a male voice asked incredulously, "Do you really expect us to read all these books?"

The speaker was the tall, broad-shouldered, blond boy who was playing Fortinbras. Physically a good foil for Kit, she thought, before she answered, "Certainly I do. You are all receiving six graduate credits for this summer school. I rather imagined you would expect to work for them."

"Well, we *are* working," replied the boy. He gave her a lazy, charming grin. "I don't at all object to sitting in class with you, Dr. O'Connor. In fact, it's a pleasure. But between rehearsals and daily lectures, I really don't see how we can possibly get all this reading done."

Mary looked severely into the handsome, boyish face. "That, Mr. Lindquist, sounds to me both unscholarly and insincere. Are you *quite* sure you wish to remain enrolled in this summer school?"

There was absolute silence in the classroom. Then Eric Lindquist said quietly, "Yes, I'm sure. I apologize, Dr. O'Connor."

"Your apology is accepted." She glanced around the class. "Are there any further questions? No? Good. My topic for today is the place of drama in Renaissance England." The students obediently picked up their pens.

The press conference was held that afternoon in the recreation room of the dining hall. Mel Horner, taking full advantage of his client's unusual mood, had made a few telephone calls, and as a result there were representatives from the New York press and the wire services as well as the usual fan and scandal sheets. George Clark served as a general host, and while they were waiting for Kit to arrive, he and the other cast members circulated among the press, answering questions about the production and even more questions about Mr. and Mrs. Douglas.

"I don't know much about her at all," Frank Moore said cheerfully to an inquisitive reporter. "She's supposed to be a terrific Renaissance scholar. I haven't read her book yet, but it made quite a stir in the academic world. If today's lecture is anything to go on, the reputation is deserved. She knows her stuff. What's more—she makes it interesting."

George Clark, the only one besides Kit and Mel Horner who knew the real circumstances behind Kit's presence at his festival, lied gamely. "No, it was a complete accident. Neither of them realized the other was coming to Yarborough."

"How do they act toward each other, Mr. Clark?" shot an eager woman reporter.

"As two civilized people," snapped George in return. He was beginning to realize why Kit did not give press conferences. He noticed a small movement at the door and then Kit came quietly in. He was dressed casually in a navy golf shirt and tan pants and he stood in the doorway, making no sound and slowly looking around the room. Gradually, without his seeming to do anything at all to attract it, the attention of the room swung his way and the place erupted into chaos. George Clark suddenly found himself a little shaken at the thought of directing Christopher Douglas. Magnetism like that was something that came along perhaps once in a generation.

Mel Horner stepped to the mike that had been set up and spoke into it. "Now, ladies and gentlemen. Mr. Douglas will be happy to answer your questions, but they really must come one at a time." He looked nervously at Kit and thought, I hope the hell he keeps his temper.

He did. He put on what Mel afterward told him was perhaps the finest performance of his career. He disdained the microphone and pitched his celebrated voice to an easily audible level. "I thought perhaps that first I would explain a little about my marital situation since it seems to have provoked such universal interest." He didn't sound at all sarcastic and he smiled charmingly before he went on to give a very edited account of his marriage: "We were both students and too young. It simply didn't work out." The coincidence of himself and Dr. O'Connor—he scrupulously called her

Dr. O'Connor the whole time—both working at the Yarborough Festival this summer was just that, a coincidence. He had not realized until after he took the role that she would be lecturing here. "So you see," he concluded disarmingly, "it has all been a tempest in a teapot."

"But why didn't you ever get a divorce, Chris?" asked the man from *Personality*.

"Neither of us ever got around to it, that's all. If I had wanted to marry again, I would have. I'm sure we'll do something permanent eventually. We've just both been rather busy these last years."

"Why did you keep your marriage such a secret?" It was the eager young lady from one of the wire services.

He shrugged. "It was over with before I became established. The subject never came up. And I certainly didn't want Dr. O'Connor bothered by a lot of unnecessary questions." He gestured beautifully around the room. "As has happened."

"Is that why you're holding this press conference? To protect—ah, Dr. O'Connor?" It was a man from a New Hampshire paper.

Kit looked at him thoughtfully. "Partly. I feel guilty about having caused her all this trouble. But I was hoping, too, that there might be some interest in my tackling such a formidable role. After all, I haven't done any theater in five years and my movie roles have hardly been of this caliber."

"How do you feel about Hamlet?" asked the man from the Associated Press and from then on the conference moved into theatrical areas. Kit wandered around the room, chatting pleasantly, patiently answering questions, utterly relaxed, utterly charming.

"I don't believe what I'm seeing," muttered Mel

Horner to George Clark. "*Chris* of all people. He hates things like this."

"John Andrews was right, of course," replied George soberly. "He's doing it to protect Mary."

Mel looked at him accusingly. "You haven't told anyone that Chris asked to come here?"

"Of course not!"

"Good. The fat would really be in the fire if the press found that out."

"Or if Mary did."

"True." Mel Horner sighed. "What a shame to waste a woman like that in the classroom. That skin! Those eyes! She could make a fortune in the movies."

George grinned. "Somehow, gorgeous as she undoubtedly is, I cannot see Mary in the movies."

Mel Horner thought for a minute. "I suppose you're right," he replied gloomily. "The problem is I can't see her as Chris's wife either, and I'm afraid that that is what he wants."

They both looked at the slim, dark man who was sitting casually now on the arm of a chair talking to a New York theater critic. "He seems a very decent sort," said George Clark, "but it's a hell of a life, isn't it?"

Mary stayed as far as possible from the press conference. Her brief experience with the media after the bombshell of her marriage had dropped had been enough to permanently scar her sensibilities. What a life Kit must lead, she thought, with a flicker of genuine horror. Still, he had known what it would be like and he had gone after it with a single-minded intensity, ruthlessly sacrificing everything else to this one driving ambition. Having been one of the things sacrificed, she hoped that at least to him the result was worth the price.

She spent the early part of the afternoon in the library and then, when she thought the press must be gone, she changed her clothes and went down to the lake. The college had almost half a mile of lakefront property, with a dock, an area of lawn chairs, and a volleyball court. Mary sat down in one of the chairs and stared out at the sparkling water.

"The press conference went very well," said a rumbling voice in her ear, and she turned to see Alfred Block, the actor who was playing Claudius, Hamlet's uncle. Block was a well-known actor from the Broadway stage who had never managed to break into movies. He was in his middle forties, with dark brown hair that was beginning to thin. His eyes were gray with the hint of a slant that was oddly surprising in his otherwise Anglo-Saxon face.

"It's over then," she replied with a restrained smile. "I thought it would be safe for me to emerge from my hiding place."

"Where do you hide, Mary, when you want to escape?"

"The library, where else?" she replied lightly, not liking the way he was looking at her. There were two young students stretched out on the dock, both wearing bathing suits and showing a lot more flesh than she was in her khaki shorts and plaid shirt. Why didn't he go leer at them, she thought with exasperation. Alfred Block had cornered her over coffee in the recreation room last night and she had heard more about him and his career than she ever cared to know. She was afraid the man was going to make a dreadful pest of himself and was wondering how best to handle him when Kit arrived.

"Thank God that's over," he announced, as he flopped down on the grass at her feet and closed his eyes.

"Don't let us disturb your rest," said Mary testily.

"I won't," he mumbled, his eyes still closed. She stared at him for a minute as he lay there on the grass with his feet crossed, his hands clasped behind his head, his eyes closed against the sun. She was suddenly intensely aware of him, of the rise and fall of his chest with his even breathing, of the beat of the pulse at the base of his tanned throat, of the latent power in the length of his lean body. . . . She took a deep breath and reached out to kick him in the ribs with her sneaker-shod foot.

"Hey!" he yelled indignantly, and sat up.

"I want to hear what happened at the press conference," she said sweetly.

"That hurt." He rubbed his side and glared at her reproachfully.

"You're tough," she answered even more sweetly. "You run along the tops of moving trains, you hang from cliffs, you punch out thugs, how can a little nudge in the side hurt you?"

"That was more than a nudge." He looked at her speculatively. "You've seen my movies." His voice was soft, dangerously soft, and the glint in his dark eyes was more dangerous still.

Mary was absolutely furious with herself. "Yes," she snapped. "I've seen your movies."

"I should imagine," put in the insinuating voice of Alfred Block, "that all the world has seen your movies,

Chris. Especially that last little adventure film. *How* much money has it grossed?"

The two girls who were sunning themselves on the dock had been slowly moving their way ever since Kit had arrived. Hearing Alfred's question, one of them eagerly volunteered an answer. "I read in *Variety* that it may eventually be the biggest-grossing movie ever."

"Really?" Mary looked at the girl, glad of any excuse that would direct her attention away from Kit. "Has it done that well?"

"Oh, yes." The young face glowed at Kit. She was a very pretty girl, golden brown from the sun, with long, sun-bleached hair and widely spaced green eyes.

He looked back at her with pleasure, his eyes going over the smooth expanse of tanned young skin. He turned back to Mary. "You're going to be red as a lobster if you stay out too long in this sun."

Devil, thought Mary, amused in spite of herself. She met his eyes and made a face. "I'm afraid you're right." She held out an arm and regarded it appraisingly. "It's just turning nicely pink." She leaned back in her chair. "However, before I go, what happened at the press conference?"

"I think I put to rest all their speculation about you and me, if that's what you mean."

"Yes, that's what I mean. Will they—go away now?"

He shrugged. "Most of them." He looked up suddenly and his eyes locked with hers. It was almost as if he had touched her. "You'll be safe," he said deeply.

She pushed herself to her feet. "Good," she replied through a suddenly dry throat and knew, as she walked up the stairs from the lakefront lawn, that so long as he was around she wasn't safe at all. She would simply have to keep out of his way, which considering the small size of the school and the fact that they took all their meals together, was not going to be easy. What she needed, she thought, was someone to act as a buffer between her and Kit. She thought about the various possibilities as she slowly climbed the hill that led to her cottage in the pines. Not Alfred Block—he was too nasty; not Frank Moore—he was too vulnerable; not Eric Lindquist—he was too cocky. George. The name flushed into her brain and she smiled with satisfaction. Of course. He was very nice, intelligent, talented—and old and sophisticated enough not to think she meant more than she really did.

She arrived at her cottage and went in to shower and change for dinner in a suddenly confident frame of mind. Kit thought he was so damn irresistible—well she would show him. The stinker, she thought, as she blew her hair dry. I'll fix him for coming here and putting me in this horrible position.

Chapter Six

M ary put her plan into action at dinner. She made
sure she entered the dining room with George,
and it seemed very natural when she took a seat beside
him at the table. During dinner she devoted almost her
entire attention to his conversation, and under the
heady spell of her blue eyes, he seemed to grow at
least two inches.

Mary never flirted. Whenever she wanted to charm
a man she simply sat quietly, looked beautiful, and listened. It was a devastating technique and had soothed
the wounded breasts of many affronted male professors
who had originally objected to the appointment of so
young a woman to the faculty of their illustrious university.

Back in the recreation room she sat on a sofa, allowed George to bring her coffee, and for the first time
that evening looked directly at Kit. He was standing
against the great brick fireplace, holding a cup of coffee and he was, as always, surrounded by a crowd of
girls. Across the shining blond and brown heads their
eyes met. Mary, not a bad actress herself, produced a
cool indifferent smile, leaned back and crossed her
long and elegant legs. George returned with her coffee
and she greeted him with a noticeably warmer smile.

Carolyn Nash, following the direction of Kit's eyes, said, "Dr. O'Connor sure surprised us this morning. She gave out a reading list as long as my arm. The worst part of it is, she seems to expect us to actually *do* the reading."

Kit's eyes came back to her pretty face. "Of course she does. Dr. O'Connor takes her job seriously."

"Well, so do I. But my job is to play Ophelia."

"You have Ophelia's lines down letter perfect," he said, "so you don't need to spend time on them. Have you always been such a quick study?"

She blossomed under his attention and was about to answer when another girl, the sun-bleached girl from the lake, broke in. "You're the one with the long part, Chris! The longest part Shakespeare ever wrote. I think it's marvelous that you have so much of it down already."

He replied absently and continued to stand there, islanded by adoring girls, his real attention somewhere else. Mary's shoulder-length hair had drifted like black silk across the cushion she was leaning against; her relaxed, slender body in its green summer dress was half sitting, half reclining on the soft, cushiony sofa. She tipped back her head and laughed at something George Clark said to her. As Kit watched, Alfred Block drew up a chair next to Mary's sofa and broke into the conversation. After five minutes the group was joined by Frank Moore.

Mary yawned daintily, put down her empty cup and rose. She shared a general smile among her admirers, made a remark Kit couldn't hear, and moved to the door. Three men hurried to open it for her. She left, alone. Kit dropped his retinue and went after her.

She was going up the path through the pines that led to her cottage when he caught up with her. He didn't say anything, just fell into step next to her and continued the uphill climb. Finally she could stand the silence no longer and said, "I don't believe your way lies in this direction."

At that he reached out and grasped her arm, forcing her to stop. They had come out of the woods by now and were on the paved road that ran along the front of the five summer cottages alotted to various members of the festival staff. The road was lit by a single light posted high on a wooden pole and he stopped her under its pale illumination. With hard fingers around her wrist he held her left hand up to the light. "You're still wearing my ring," he said. "You're still my wife, and by God you're going to act like it. Leave poor George alone. You'll knock him right off his feet and you don't want him. You're only using him to teach me a lesson."

He was perfectly right of course and his perceptiveness made her furious. She jerked her hand away from his. "Leave me alone," she said in a trembling voice. "I was doing just fine until you came bulldozing your way back into my life. You knew I was going to be here when you came. If you don't like what you see, then you'll just have to lump it."

She turned to leave him and he reached out and caught her once again, this time by the waist. She twisted against his grip, struggling to get away from him, and he pinned her arms behind her, holding her so that she faced him. Mary felt the brief impact of his body against hers and she stiffened. She stared up into his dark dark eyes. "What do you want, Kit?" Her voice sounded breathless and she hoped he would put it down to the struggle.

His eyes, darkly lashed and unfathomable, looked back at her. "You," he said. "I want you." They stayed like that for a long minute, their eyes locked, their bodies scarcely an inch apart. His eyes were unfathomable no longer; no woman with a single normal instinct could fail to recognize what was glimmering there now. Her eyes fell before that look.

"I thought that was it," she said in a low voice. "When George told me you were here, I knew you had come to persecute me."

"I don't want to persecute you, Princess." His voice was deeper than usual, dark and husky. He released her wrists and slid his hands up her bare arms to her shoulders. "I want you to come back to me. Be my wife again. I do want you most damnably." And he bent his head and kissed her.

It was like coming home again. It was that feeling that frightened her most, frightened her more than the flooding sweetness of her unplanned response. The feel of his arms around her, his body hard against hers, his mouth on her mouth . . . When she was with him like this it was the only time she stopped thinking and just felt.

But he hadn't brought her quite that far yet. Some remnants of sanity still remained, enough at any rate to enable her to pull free of his embrace. "No," she said, unsteadily but definitely. "No. We tried it once and it didn't work. I'm not going to put myself through that hell again."

He pushed his black hair back off his forehead. "You never gave me a chance. I was *not* having an affair with Jessica Corbet. That was all media hype."

She stared at him incredulously. "Are you serious? The yacht—the trip to Rome—you were alone with her all that time and you never made love to her? You can't possibly expect me to believe that."

"That was *after*," he replied stubbornly. "After you told me you never wanted to see me again, after I wrote you two letters and never got an answer. Then I thought, hell, I might as well be hung for a sheep as a lamb. But while we were really married, I was faithful to you."

"Faithful?" There was unmistakable bitterness in her voice. "Do you call it faithful to call once every two weeks and talk for three minutes? Do you call it faithful to never even *attempt* to explain what was behind all the headlines. What the hell did you expect me to think?"

"I expected you to trust me. You never asked me about Jessica at all."

"No." She stepped away from him a little farther. "No. And I'm not asking now. Your private life has nothing to do with me any longer."

"It's that goddamn pride of yours," he said savagely.

"Pride is about all you've left me, Kit!" she flashed back. "My pride and my job. It took me a long hard time to regain the one and to earn the other and I'm not risking either again."

"You kissed me back just now," he said. "You can't pretend you're indifferent to me, Mary."

"We always did strike sparks from each other. It's what got us married in the first place. But marriage is more than making love, Kit. You and I may be good at that part of it, but we were dismal failures at the rest."

"We're older now," he said persuasively.

"I know, which is why I have the sense this time to say no and mean it." His face looked as bleak as winter and she sighed. "It wasn't all your fault, Kit. You're right, I was too proud to ask you to explain, too proud to show you how hurt I was. Perhaps now I'd do things differently. But you can't turn the clock back, Kit. We had our chance and we blew it. The people we were then don't exist anymore."

"I don't believe that," he said. "Mary . . ." There was the sound of laughter down the path. "Hell!" he said explosively under his breath.

She looked up at him sadly. "There really isn't anything else to be said. And I would appreciate it if in future you had a thought for my reputation. What are people going to think when they meet you coming down the path from my cottage?"

"They won't think a thing," he replied and after a minute produced a faintly mocking grin. "I have the cottage next to yours."

She did not get much sleep that night. Somehow she had not expected him to be so direct in his approach; she had not expected him to want her back as his wife. She had thought that, as always, he simply wanted to sleep with her.

As she lay awake into the small hours of the morning, however, the realization came to her that that was what he did want, that that was what marriage meant to him. It was not what it meant to her, however. She had grown up a great deal in the past four years and she knew that they had failed previously because both of them had been too self-absorbed to reach out of their own needs and desires to consider the needs and desires of the other. Kit had been so intent on his career that everything else, including her, had gone down before that drive like grass under a roller. He was so—single-minded. He always had been.

She would have to be the one to give in. If a marriage is to be successful, she thought, at least one partner must put it first. All those theories about men and

women in equal partnership sounded lovely, but she
had never seen it work successfully. One career had to
give, one personality to yield. Particularly if there were
children. You couldn't have your cake and eat it too,
she thought bleakly.

What it all came down to was that what he offered
her wasn't good enough. She loved him, she admitted
that in the darkness and the privacy of her solitary bedroom; she would never feel for another man what she
felt for him. She even understood why he was the way
he was. He had always been on his own; his mother
had died when he was very young and his father had
remarried and then died a year later, leaving Kit in the
care of an indifferent stepmother. He had grown up
learning how to fend for himself and he had learned to
be ruthless. Once he decided what he wanted, he went
after it; and if anything came between him and his desire, he walked over it without rancor and without pity.
It had been like that with the baby. And then with her.

Now he had decided he wanted her again. He
wanted her to leave her home, her family and friends,
the peaceful fulfillment of her work—and for what? To
live a life she loathed and feared, where you couldn't go
out to dinner without being followed and photographed,
where every shiver in your relationship was blazoned
across the front pages of horrible newspapers, where
there was no peace and no silence. And for what? For
the nights that could make the universe shudder? But
what of the days? And the long, lonely times when he
was gone on location. And the other women, beautiful
and available, always so tantalizingly within his reach?

No. No. No. She would never go back to being Mrs.
Christopher Douglas.

Chapter Seven

Mary finally fell asleep about four in the morning and three hours later her alarm rang. She felt heavy-eyed and sluggish as she made her way down the path to the dining room. She collected coffee and a muffin from the buffet and sat down at an empty table. There was no sign of Kit.

She finished her coffee and went to get a second cup. When she arrived back at her table it was to find she had company. Eric Lindquist was sitting there, and as she reseated herself he gave her his endearing boyish grin. The Sunshine Kid, Mary thought sourly, and started on her second cup of coffee.

"Have you heard who George snagged to play Gertrude?" he asked enthusiastically.

"No. Who?" She was not in a talktative mood.

"Margot Chandler." Mary's eyes widened and he laughed. "I'm not kidding, Dr. O'Connor. Margot Chandler has actually consented to play Hamlet's mother."

"She's too young," Mary said incredulously.

"Not really. She must be at least forty-five. Well preserved is the proper word for her, I think."

"Has she ever done any stage work?"

"Not to my knowledge." His grin widened. "This is definitely a 'Hollywood Goes Arty' summer at Yarborough."

"Kit has played Shakespeare on stage many times," Mary said astringently and suppressed a sudden urge to smack the handsome young face across from her. There was nothing on earth worse than a condescending twenty-two-year-old, she decided.

"Actually, I know he has. He had a damn good reputation at drama school—they still talk about him. But I'm certain as hell that Margot Chandler hasn't ever put her luscious mouth around a Shakespearean phrase."

"What on earth was George *thinking* of?" Mary asked despairingly.

"Well, he didn't have a whole lot of time to pick and choose. And apparently La Chandler has decided that her days of playing sexy leading ladies are numbered and so she had better look for a new metier for her talents. I shouldn't be at all surprised if Liz Taylor's big hit in *The Little Foxes* galvanized her. And, then, few women would pass up the chance of acting with Chris." His blue eyes were widely innocent in his suntanned face.

"As his *mother*?" Mary asked ironically. Eric grinned. He rather overdid that boyish smile, she thought cynically, and rose. "I'll see you in class," she said.

"Sure thing." He paused. "Mary," he added tentatively.

She stopped, turned and looked at him. She had always maintained a carefully formal relationship with all her students. It had been necessary. She was only a few years older than most of them and she was well aware of her own sexual attractiveness. But everyone at the summer school was on a first-name basis and she was here for too short a time for any of the boys to have a chance to become overly familiar. So she smiled briefly at Eric, nodded, and went on her way.

* * *

Her lecture on the Elizabethan concept of tragedy went very well. The students seemed resigned to the fact that she expected them to work and a few even became quite enthusiastic in a discussion she initiated on the concept of catharsis as it applied to Shakespearean tragedy. After the class was finished they all disappeared in the direction of the theater. Mary's lecture went from nine to ten-thirty and after that they rehearsed.

Mary took her books back to her cottage and decided to run into town to the drugstore. Accordingly, she got into her car and headed toward the college gates. There didn't appear to be any reporters around and she drove in a relaxed frame of mind. She did her shopping and was coming out of the store when the now-familiar flash went off. She stared for a moment in angry frustration at the man who was now approaching her. He had curly brown hair, a crooked nose, and was wearing a shirt that was halfway open, showing what Mary thought was a disgusting amount of hairy chest. She hated men who didn't button their shirts. He trained a smile at full tooth power straight at her. "Hi," he said ingratiatingly. "I'm Jason Razzia, free-lance writer and photographer. I'm planning an article on you and Chris, Mrs. Douglas. I wonder if I could talk to you for a few minutes."

"I have nothing to say to you, Mr. Razzia," she replied coldly. "And I do *not* wish to have my picture taken. I would appreciate your going away and leaving me alone."

"Aw, come on now, it's my livelihood, you know," he said coaxingly. "Just a few short questions. Like is it true that you and Chris are getting back together again?"

"No, it is *not* true," she said firmly. "I wish I could make you understand that there is no story here, Mr. Razzia. Mr. Douglas and I have ended our relationship and we have no intention of resurrecting it. That is all. Good-bye. And please go away." She walked to her car, got in and slammed the door. He took two more pictures of her before she drove away.

Mary was seething as she drove back to school. For the past month of her life she had felt positively hunted and it was all Kit's fault. He could have played Hamlet out in California somewhere. Why did he have to come to Yarborough to do it?

She worked for an hour or so in the library after lunch, looking up some material for an article she was planning on Elizabethan songbooks. As always, the academic discipline soothed her nerves and she was in a calmer frame of mind when she walked down to the waterfront later in the afternoon. Rehearsal had ended and the lawn was filled with people, some swimming, some playing volleyball and others simply soaking up the sun. Mary had her bathing suit on under a terry-cloth sundress, and when she reached the waterfront she stood to unzip the cover-up while her eyes automatically searched the area for Kit. She didn't see him and so she dropped her dress on a chair with her sandals and towel and made for the lake.

There were a few students stretched out on the dock as she walked out to dive off and the male eyes all regarded her approvingly. She wore a plain navy maillot suit that showed off her slender figure tastefully but unmistakably. Her skin was like magnolia petals. She pulled her black hair back on the nape of her neck and secured it with an elastic band. Then she dove into the water.

It was cold. She came up gasping for breath, treaded

water and looked around her. There were three rubber boats floating about in the water near her, two of them occupied by couples and one apparently empty. The lake was not very wide at this particular point and there was no sign of other boats. Mary struck out for the other side.

She was an excellent swimmer, not fast, but strong and steady. The youngsters on shore watched her unwavering progress toward the far side of the lake. And they watched as well the yellow rubber boat that followed her.

Mary didn't see the boat until she was three quarters of the way across. She paused then to tread water and get her bearings, and almost the first thing she saw was Kit leaning on the oars of the boat. "Where did you come from?" she demanded.

"I was snoozing in the boat when I saw you take off across the lake. I thought I'd follow to make sure you didn't get run down by a passing motorboat. There *are* some around, you know."

"Are there? I didn't see any." She was a little out of breath and was beginning to tire. "If you don't mind, I won't stay here chatting," she said pleasantly.

"Why don't you climb in? The water's cold and you've had quite enough of a swim for one day I should think."

He was right. It had been a longer swim than she had anticipated. "All right," she said and swam over to the side of the boat. She put her hands on the side. "I hope I don't swamp you."

"You won't." He moved to the far side of the boat to help balance it, and Mary pulled herself out of the water and into the rubber dinghy. She sat down and shook water out of her eyes. "Have a towel," he said hospitably, and gratefully she reached out and took it. She dried her face, pulled the elastic band out of her hair and began to towel it.

"I bit off more than I was ready to chew," she said candidly.

"You would have made it," he replied, moving back himself to the center of the boat.

"Oh, I know that. But I would have been tired. And then I would have had to go back." She finished toweling her hair and looked at him closely for the first time. He was wearing only bathing trunks, also navy, and around his neck hung a St. Joseph medal. She had given him that medal for his birthday four years ago. He caught the direction of her stare and his hand went up to finger the medal. "I still have it," he said. "I don't know if I really believe in it, but I've always worn it. It's about all I've got left of you."

Her eyes dropped. "Don't, Kit," she said softly. There was silence as the boat drifted and then she said, "I hear Margot Chandler is to be your mother."

He laughed. "Isn't that a surprise? I suppose she's getting too old for glamour-girl parts."

"Can she act?" Mary asked bluntly.

"It won't matter, I think," he replied thoughtfully. "Gertrude is hardly a complex character. In fact, in some ways she resembles many California women: beautiful, loaded with sex appeal, essentially good-natured, but shallow. I have a feeling all Margot Chandler will need to do is play herself. She'll probably do very well. And the theater is small enough that voice projection needn't be a problem."

Mary was silent for a minute, digesting what he had just said. Then she smiled mischievously. "Eric

Lindquist says that this production should be labeled " 'Hollywood Goes Arty.' "

Kit's answering smile was rueful. "He's exactly the sort of kid I'd like to punch in the nose."

"I know," Mary answered longingly. "That boyish grin . . ."

He began to row the boat toward the far side of the lake. "You never did appreciate youthful male arrogance," he said. "You knocked it out of me fast enough."

"You were never really arrogant," she said quietly. "Just determined." She watched him row, watched the smooth ripple of muscle across his arms and chest. He was so slim that his impressive set of muscles always came as something of a surprise. He had gotten them working in a warehouse, he once told her. It had been one of the many jobs that put him through school.

The boat was almost on the shore and Mary noticed, with surprise, a strip of sand along the water's edge. "I didn't know there was a beach here."

"I noticed it yesterday and I thought I'd take a look. I don't think it's private property—there's no dock or boat at any rate."

Mary had been brought up on the shore of Long Island Sound and a beach always beckoned to her. Kit jumped out of the boat into waist-high water and she followed without hesitation. They towed the boat to shore and walked out onto the sand.

"This has been put here by someone," she said, wriggling her toes luxuriously. "It's too fine to be native."

Kit was looking through the trees that surrounded the small sand crescent. "I think I see a house. It must be private property after all. I suppose we'd better go."

"Yes," she said regretfully. It was so peaceful and sheltered and quiet here. She walked back to the water and helped Kit push the boat out. He got in first and had reached out a hand to help her when a man with a camera jumped out from behind some trees on their left and began snapping furiously. Kit swore and made a motion to get out of the boat.

"No, don't!" Mary cried. She was in the boat by now. "Just push off. Please, Kit."

He hesitated a minute and then did as she asked, propelling the small dinghy with hard furious strokes away from the shore and the intruder.

"Goddamn parasites," he said. "Bloodsucking bastards." He was in a quiet, concentrated rage and his own fury served to dampen hers.

"It was a man called Jason Razzia," she said in a low shaking voice. "I met him this morning in town. He said he was doing a story about—us."

"Razzia," he said with loathing. "I know him. A freelancer. The scrapings of a particularly rancid barrel. He's made me his pet project lately."

"Is it like this all the time?" she asked dazedly. "Don't they *ever* let you alone?"

"It's worse now than usual," he replied, a bitter twist to his mouth. "Most of the time, when I'm going about my work, they leave me alone. I have a house that's pretty well isolated out in a canyon, and photographers don't bother to camp at my door. It's you who are the interest now."

"Don't I know it," she returned even more bitterly. "All because you decided you had to play Hamlet at Yarborough."

"I wanted to play Hamlet," he said.

"You could very well have played Hamlet in California," she retorted.

He went on as if she had not interrupted. "And I

wanted to see you again." He stopped rowing, rested his hands on the oars and looked at her. "Do you think the pursuit by media hounds is the worst part of living in California? Well it's not. The worst thing is the artificiality of so much of the place, the superficiality of so many of the people. Not everyone. There are some fine and talented people—people who are interested in doing good things. Like Mark Stevens, who directed my last film. But somehow I always have the strangest sensation of touching many people without being touched in turn myself." He smiled a little crookedly. "When I saw you again in May it was as if I had come home again."

It was exactly the feeling she had had when he kissed her, and his voicing it now jarred her unpleasantly. She frowned, not wanting to hear this, not wanting to respond to it. He was so clever, she thought. He knew just what to say to get to her. "You can't go home again," she said fiercely, staring at his feet. His toes were so straight. Hell, she thought, why did everything about him have to be so damn beautiful? She looked up into his face. "Thomas Wolfe wrote that many years ago, and it's true."

"Mary." He leaned forward and put a hand on her knee. "Listen to me, sweetheart . . ."

The sensations emanating from that lean brown hand reached all the way to her loins and stomach. "No!" she said violently. "Leave me alone!" And, precipitously, she dove off the boat and swam back to shore under the interested eyes of the assembled students.

She didn't linger on shore but slipped into her sandals, pulled her dress on over her wet suit, and headed for her cottage. This was the second day in a row she had fled from the lake because of Kit, she thought, as the screen door closed behind her. How on earth was she going to manage three weeks of this?

She was afraid of him. She was afraid of what the sight of him did to her, afraid of the memories his presence stirred in her mind and her heart and her body. It would be so easy, so fatally easy, to slip back into their old intimacy. It had happened this afternoon. When he had rowed her to that beach she hadn't murmured a protest. It had been so natural—he had always been interested in exploring places he hadn't seen before and she had always gone along. When they had been at the cape. . . . God, she mustn't think of the cape.

She stripped off her wet suit and got into the shower. When she got out she put on a white terry-cloth bathrobe and went to lie on the bed. Why was she reacting this way, she asked herself desperately. Come on, she thought, you're supposed to be smart. You're not just a quivering mass of hormones; you're supposed to have a brain. Use it.

She stared at the ceiling and she thought. She thought of what he had said to her this afternoon and of how her hostility toward him dissipated the moment they were together again.

Together again. The last time they had been together had been before he went to California. They had not had a long marriage, but it had been a deeply intimate one. She understood what he had said this afternoon about no one really touching him. She had felt that way too. Quite probably she was the single human being who knew him best in the world. In California he would always feel he had to guard his tongue. He had not guarded it with her.

That was the problem. They had lived together so closely, had filled each other so completely—and then he had gone away. Except for that brief moment at the hospital she hadn't seen him again. All her bitterness had been directed at him in absentia. She had no experience of being around him and being hostile, or even indifferent. Her experience in being with him, the relationship she was so afraid of reprising here at Yarborough, had been profoundly close and satisfying.

He had chosen the life he had, she thought stubbornly as she dressed. At one time she had been willing to share it with him, but no longer. No longer was she willing to give up her gentle world of literature, scholarship, and teaching. She was not willing to surrender her happiness—happiness based on security, familiarity, understanding, respect—for the harsh, publicity-hungry world of film, for marriage to a man she loved but did not trust. He had ridden roughshod over her once; she could not bear it if he ever did that to her again. No. Better to keep one's hand from the fire if one did not want to be burned.

The conversation at dinner was mainly about Margot Chandler and her amazing decision to come to Yarborough to play Gertrude. None of the professional cast had ever worked with her; they were mainly theater people and Margot Chandler's success had been solely in films.

"I've never met her," Kit offered at one point, "but I've heard she's inclined to be somewhat temperamental."

"Most big film stars are," said Alfred Block with a sneer. Mary looked at him closely. It really was a sneer.

"I didn't think anyone actually did that," she said in amazement. "I thought it only happened in books."

Everyone at the table looked puzzled, except Kit, who chuckled.

"Did what?" asked Frank wonderingly.

"Sneered," replied Mary. "He really did sneer. Curled his lip and everything. I thought it went out with Dickens."

George started to laugh and Alfred Block looked uncomfortable. "*Chris* certainly isn't temperamental," said Carolyn Nash both earnestly and adoringly.

"No, he's not," replied George, sobering. "Not that he can't be damn stubborn when it suits him." He stared across at his star who regarded him imperturbably in return.

"Too much stage business is distracting," Kit replied calmly. "I don't have to be constantly doing things in order to keep people watching me."

It was true and George knew it better than anyone. He smiled. "Stubborn," he repeated. "And—sometimes—right."

Mary kept to her plan of the evening before and stayed by George when they went into the recreation room. "You don't," she asked with tentative hopefulness, "happen to play bridge, do you?"

Melvin Shaw, the veteran English actor who was playing Polonius, jerked his head around. "Bridge?" he inquired. "Did someone mention bridge?"

"Yes," said Mary. "Do you play?"

He did. And so did George. And so—surprisingly—did one of the students who was working on costumes. She was an attractive no-nonsense girl who had impressed Mary in class with her intelligent questions; her name was Nancy Sealy.

The four settled down happily for the evening. Safe, thought Mary, as she raised George's bid by a heart. Kit did not play bridge. It was not one of the accomplishments highly valued in the Philadelphia neighborhood where he had grown up.

"I'll walk you home," George offered when the second rubber ended and Mary, remembering last night, accepted with a smile. Kit had left the rec room some time ago, but she couldn't be sure that he wasn't lying in wait for her somewhere on the path to her cottage.

She wasn't exactly free of him, however, as George apparently wanted to talk about his star. "Chris is a bit of an enigma, isn't he?" he said as they walked slowly up through the pines. He's not at all what I expected him to be."

"Oh?" said Mary.

"To be frank, I wasn't sure I wanted him. We've worked hard here to establish a reputation as the best summer theater in the country and I didn't want to risk it on the whim of a Hollywood star who fancied he could do Shakespeare."

"Why did you take him then?" Mary asked curiously.

"Timing, for one thing. When Adrian Saunders backed out I had to replace him fast."

"You could have gotten someone from the legitimate stage without too much difficulty."

She saw George's teeth gleam in the darkness. "Yeah. I know. I guess I just couldn't resist it."

"Having a superstar, you mean?"

"No. His voice. I just couldn't resist that voice. I went to see his last film again and that was what got me, that beautiful, flexible voice. He's the only American actor I know who really has the voice for Shakespeare. It seemed such a waste to hear it shouting 'Shoot, goddamn it'—which seemed to be his biggest line in that very unliterate film."

Mary laughed. "He did a lot of Shakespeare at drama school, George. I wouldn't worry."

"We're going to have every major critic in the country here for opening night, Mary," he said rather grimly. "As you said earlier, Chris isn't just an ordinary Hollywood actor. He isn't even an ordinary Hollywood star. He's a superstar. They'll be here to see if he really ought to be taken seriously or to see him fall on his face. It's his face, after all, that has been his ticket to success so far, not his acting."

"I always thought he was quite good in his films," Mary said quietly.

"He was. But they were hardly demanding."

"No, I suppose not." They had reached her cottage by now. "I have a bottle of Scotch tucked away," she said. "Would you like a nightcap?"

"Sounds good," he said, and came in after her. She got ice from the small refrigerator in the sitting room and poured two drinks. The night air was chilly on the porch so they sat down inside, Mary on the Early American sofa and George in a chair facing her.

"How are rehearsals going?" she asked, sipping her drink and drawing her legs up under her.

"Not bad at all. He won't fall on his face, if that's what you mean. He does know his stuff. In fact, I find him surprisingly professional."

"Why shouldn't he be professional?" she inquired frowningly.

"No reason. I suppose I thought he'd be rather the way he described Margot Chandler—temperamental. But he's not. And he has surprisingly little vanity. That probably amazed me most of all."

"He grew up in a tough Philadelphia neighborhood," said Mary with a small smile. "His looks were more a handicap than anything else. In order to hold his own he had to learn to do everything better than anyone else. And the two things they did in that neighborhood were fight and play basketball. He never learned to value his looks, that's for sure."

"Basketball?" said George on a note of inquiry.

"He went to Penn State on a basketball scholarship." She held her drink between her two palms and looked down into its amber depths. "He broke his thumb and was out for half the season in his sophomore year. That's when he tried out for a part in the college play. He got it and he was hooked. He threw up the basketball scholarship and went in for acting."

"I see," said George quietly. Then, unexpectedly, "You still wear his ring."

"Yes." A slight flush warmed her cheeks. "Technically we're still married. And a wedding ring is good protection."

"Hmm." George looked at her speculatively. "Half the women in this country would give their eyeteeth to be married to Chris Douglas."

"Well, I belong to the other half," she replied lightly.

"He still loves you. You must know that. He watches you all the time."

Unexpectedly she raised her eyes and he found himself thinking that he had never seen such utter blueness before; there was not a hint of gray or of green in those eyes. They were clear and darkly lashed and absolutely blue. "I know," she said tensely. "He follows me, too. And I don't want him to. I would never have come to Yarborough if I thought Kit was going to be here."

"Is that why you've been so attentive to me?" he asked wryly.

The blue gaze never wavered. "Yes," said Mary candidly. "I need protection."

"From your husband?"

She hesitated. "Yes," she repeated finally. "He is my husband, that's true. But we haven't lived together for over four years and I've told him I will never live with him again. If he wants a divorce he can have one. I just want him to leave me alone."

"I don't think he will, Mary," George said. "In fact, I think the main reason he came here was not to play Hamlet but to see you."

"I'm beginning to think so too." Mary suddenly felt very tired. "I was fool enough to tell him where I'd be for the summer, so I suppose part of it is my own fault."

"Why are you so afraid of him?" George asked innocently. "If you mean what you say, all you have to do is say no and keep on saying it. Chris can hardly kidnap you."

Mary sighed, put down her glass and stood up. "I suppose you're right. But sometimes I feel like King Canute standing on the sand and forbidding the tide to come in. Nothing that I say will make any difference." She smiled. "Good night, George."

"Good night, Mary. And thanks for the drink."

She stood at the screen door and watched him go off down the path. As she turned to go in the house she noticed a figure on the porch of the cottage next to hers. It was too dark to see anything but his outline but she knew he was watching her. Childishly she stuck her tongue out at him and slammed the cottage door as she went inside. Good God, she thought as she unzipped her skirt. I'm really regressing if I've descended to this. Wearily she undressed and went to bed.

Chapter Eight

The next day Margot Chandler arrived at Yarborough. Mary first saw her at a cocktail reception George hastily threw together for the professional staff and the cast that afternoon. It was held in a lovely elegant old room in Avery Hall. Mary put on a white linen suit with a hot-pink blouse and walked uncomfortably on high heels down through the pines. She was frankly curious. She had only seen one or two of Margot Chandler's films, but over the course of the years, and the course of numerous husbands, the star had become something of a national institution. She represented, to Mary's mind, The Hollywood World. What would she be like?

She was, to begin with, exquisite. Small and delicately made, she wore a simple black dress that Mary realized must have cost the earth. She may have been forty-five but she most certainly did not look it. Her pale hair was soft and shining, her skin was fresh and unlined, her figure slim and flexible. "Good heavens," said Mary, as she was introduced by George, "no one is ever going to believe you're Hamlet's *mother.*"

The perfect Chandler teeth showed in a charming smile. "I was a child bride, of course." she said delicately. Kit was standing next to her and she raised her famous green eyes to his face. "I don't think I had expected such a large son, though." The top of her blond head came only to his shoulder. She put her hand on his arm. "Darling, I should so like to introduce you to my secretary. He is a great admirer of your films and is quite *longing* to meet you." She cast a brief smile in Mary and George's direction before she deftly steered Kit off toward another corner of the room.

"Well," said Mary in some amusement as she watched the small feminine figure tow Kit's six feet three skillfully away. "So that's Margot Chandler. It was a brief meeting, of course, but most interesting."

George chuckled. "God help me. I have to direct her."

"Darling," Mary purred, putting her arm on his sleeve and looking up at him through her lashes. "Would you mind terribly getting me a drink?"

"Cut it out," said George inelegantly. They walked together toward the table that had been set up as a bar. "She's not living on campus, you know. Too terribly rustic."

"Oh dear. Where is she staying?"

"The Stafford Inn. It's the poshest place in the area. Not posh at all by her standards of course—she called it 'rather a hole' but the best we can do locally."

Mary sipped her drink and smiled absently at Adam Truro, the boy who was playing Horatio. "Will she be eating with us?"

"Tonight she is," George replied. "Somehow I rather doubt that the college cuisine is going to be up to her standard, but I did emphasize our atmosphere of family coziness here at Yarborough."

"I'll bet she's just going to love it," Mary said dryly and George made a comic face.

* * *

Margot Chandler did in fact accompany them to the dining room that evening. The meal was roast chicken with gravy, mashed potatoes, and peas. She looked at it with wide-eyed incredulity. "Darling," she said reproachfully to George, "I can't eat this. Think of the calories."

"I'm sorry, Margot," said George. "I suppose the food here is rather caloric. The kitchen staff is used to cooking for hungry youngsters, I'm afraid."

"Perhaps I'll just have a word with the chef," Margot murmured gently and disappeared in the direction of the kitchen. When she returned it was with a white-uniformed waiter who removed her plate. She reseated herself and smiled seraphically around the table.

Kit, who was already halfway through his dinner, said with amusement, "Are they fixing you something else?"

"Yes. The chef, such a dear man—he speaks only Spanish you know—quite understood my problem." The chef apparently did, for shortly thereafter he appeared himself carrying a new plate that contained a grilled steak with a beautiful salad on the side. The Chandler eyes flashed in gratitude and Mary watched in some awe as the chef nearly fell over himself protesting to her that in the future he would be pleased—ecstatic actually—to cook for her whatever she might desire. Margot answered in lovely liquid Spanish and the chef departed with a majestic flourish. Dinner resumed.

"I've admired you for years, Miss Chandler," said Eric Lindquist with a charming boyish smile. He had maneuvered successfully to be at the same table with The Star.

"Have you?" Margot looked speculatively for a minute at Eric's handsome, suntanned face. She smiled. "I'm sorry, I'm afraid I've forgotten your name."

"Eric Lindquist," he said. The admiration in his blue eyes was blatant. "I'm playing Fortinbras."

"Oh, yes." She took a dainty bite of her steak and turned to Kit. "I'm counting so much on you, Chris darling, to get me through this play. The thought of my own daring quite terrifies me." She gazed up at him out of wide and helpless eyes. It was quite clear that Eric Lindquist held no interest for her and for the remainder of the meal she skillfully, charmingly, and mercilessly monopolized Kit's attention.

Mary said little but watched thoughtfully as Margot went into action. When they all went into the rec room after dinner, she found herself alone with Margot for a minute as George and Kit went to get them coffee. Margot looked at Mary speculatively, taking her in from the top of her black head to the tips of her patent-leather pumps. "You're married to Chris?" she asked bluntly.

Mary felt her temper rising. She did not like that look at all. "Yes," she said shortly.

"But you don't live together?"

"No."

"I see." Margot smiled at her charmingly. "You are a teacher here, I understand."

"That is correct, Miss Chandler."

The men returned and George handed Mary her cup. Margot smiled dazzlingly at the two males and said, "Isn't it just marvelous, a woman intelligent enough to teach college. You must be very smart, Mary."

Mary smiled back even more dazzlingly. "Yes," she said, "I am."

"She graduated summa cum laude," said Kit, dead-pan, and Mary shot him a look.

The Chandler nose wrinkled. "Summa cum . . . What does that mean?"

"It means that Mary is very smart indeed," said George with a smile.

"Mary, George." It was Melvin Shaw's English accent. "How about some bridge?"

"Wonderful," said Mary with alacrity. In Melvin she had tapped a deadly serious bridge player—he even had Master's points, he had told them last night. She saw he had Nancy Sealy in tow. "George?" he asked again.

George cast a quick look at Margot and Kit. She looked smooth as cream; he looked a trifle grim and the dark eyes that looked back at George held a definite message. "Isn't there someone else who could make a fourth?" George asked Melvin.

"No. No one who can play worth a damn."

"Oh, well in that case . . ." George allowed himself to be towed off, casting an apologetic glance back at Kit, who looked like thunder. Margot immediately put a hand on his arm and began to talk to him.

As Mary sat down at the card table she involuntarily glanced over to where her husband stood with Margot. They made a striking couple, her small, feminine fairness against his towering male darkness. But no matter how delicate and fragile she might appear on the surface, Mary was sure that underneath Margot was a cool, tough customer. She looked closer to thirty than forty, but her sophistication and assurance came from years of power, years of handling men to her own advantage. She seemed to be handling Kit very well. The scowl was gone and he was laughing. After a few minutes they left the room together.

"Mary" said Melvin in exasperation as she played a card. "That was my queen. You just trumped your own partner."

"Oh dear," said Mary, trying to recall her wandering wits. "Sorry, Mel. I wasn't paying attention."

"Well, please do so," he said severely.

"Yes, I'll try." And she stared resolutely at her hand.

For the next two days Mary scarcely saw Kit, George, Alfred, or Margot. "Hell," George had muttered to her as their paths crossed briefly on Friday, "she doesn't even know her lines. And she needs her hand held constantly. I'm going to tear my hair out."

The fact that Margot was proving a disrupting force among the cast was confirmed by Carolyn Nash, who sat down next to Mary at the lakefront on Saturday afternoon. "She's a pain in the neck," said Carolyn forthrightly in answer to Mary's question as to how Margot was doing. "She hangs on Chris like a leech, and every time George moves her off center stage she cries."

"Oh God," said Mary. "What a mess. But is she any good, Carolyn?"

"I don't know," the girl grumbled. Then, unwillingly: "She may be all right. Chris has been coaching her about her voice. It's a little thin and high." She sighed. "He's incredibly patient with her. I'd like to give her a good swift kick myself."

"Yes, well you aren't a man," Mary murmured.

"That's true. She's very beautiful."

"Very."

They looked at each other and laughed ruefully. "I must say," confessed Mary, "that I really didn't believe women like that existed. I thought it was all part of the Hollywood myth. She actually calls people 'darling.'"

"She lays it on so thick you can't believe it," said Carolyn in amazement. "I mean, I admire Chris enormously. I think he's wonderful, actually. But she . . ."

"I know. She makes Scarlett O'Hara look subtle." They both laughed again and felt much better for having shared their mutual dislike of La Belle Chandler, as Mary called her nastily. They neither of them bothered to reflect that Margot's chief sin in both their eyes was that since she had arrived, she had totally monopolized Christopher Douglas.

Sunday morning Mary arose early and decided to go to Mass first and have breakfast afterwards. She put on her blue shirt-dress and espadrilles and got in the car. It was the first time she had ventured off campus since Wednesday when she had been accosted by Jason Razzia. She looked cautiously around as she drove out of the college gate but there was no one around. She made it to church without incident and on the way back to college stopped to pick up the Sunday papers. The store she stopped at was a small food market that had a lunch counter as well where they served coffee, donuts, and sandwiches. Sitting at the counter having a cup of coffee was her nemesis. Razzia jumped up the minute he saw her.

"Hi there, Mrs. Douglas! You and Chris done any more boating? Or has Margot Chandler been keeping him too busy?" Mary ignored him and went to the cash register to pay for her papers and the few groceries she had picked up. "She's between husbands right at present, you know, and may be in the market for a younger man. It seems to be the new fad."

Mary gritted her teeth, collected her change, and stalked to the door. "You're a good-looking dame," came the revolting voice from behind her, "but Margot is supposed to be pure dynamite. Better watch out."

Mary longed, with a passion that curled her fingers, to turn and smash him across his hateful face. She climbed into her car and relieved her feelings slightly by slamming the door hard and pretending that Jason Razzia's fingers were in the way.

She got back to college, to safety, she thought as she drove in the gates and went to have breakfast in the dining room. She took her papers along, and over her second cup of coffee she opened the theater section of the *Times*. The headline jumped out at her: CHRISTOPHER DOUGLAS TACKLES HAMLET. She put down her coffee cup, folded the paper, and read:

During the past ten years some of the most interesting and daring of our theatrical ventures have come out of Yarborough College's Summer Drama Festival. Last year George Clark, the festival's talented and innovative director, sent on to Broadway a very smart and excruciatingly funny production of Sheridan's eighteenth-century classic *The School for Scandal*. Two years before we had Louis Murray and Merrill Kane in a very fine and passionate *Antigone*, a play that was distinguished by Mr. Clark's excellent use of the chorus. This year, with a piece of casting that takes one's breath away, Mr. Clark is presenting Christopher Douglas in *Hamlet*.

Hamlet is perhaps Shakespeare's most fascinating and demanding character. The actor who portrays Hamlet places himself in a position of inevitable comparison to the great actors of our century: John Gielgud, Laurence Olivier, and Richard Burton to

name a few. The challenge is daunting. Mr. Douglas
first of all is an American, and no American actor in
recent memory has risen to the challenge of Shakespeare in any way comparable to the British. Sec-
ondly, Mr. Douglas's main experience has been in
movies. He had stage experience as a student, and
was in fact given his first screen test on the basis of
a performance at New Haven's Long Stage, but the
fact remains that the greater part of his career has
been spent in films.

It has been a phenomenally successful career, one
hastens to add. There is not another screen actor
performing today who can equal his popularity. His
films invariably make back their initial investment in
the first month of showing. But is that admittedly
astonishing record enough to enable him to under-
take so demanding a role as Hamlet?

One's immediate reaction is to say no. No, the
man who starred in *Raid on Kailis,* that glossy, adventurous blockbuster, is not the man who can play
Hamlet. Which is not to say that Mr. Douglas was
not very fine in his last film. He was. He has a
screen presence that is possibly unsurpassed by any
other actor in recent memory: a really beautiful face
in the classic sense, a lean and splendid body and a
voice that most actors would sell their souls for. Perhaps that is the problem, perhaps he has so much
going for him that it is too easy for him to sit back
and let the façade do all the work.

And yet . . . one remembers Ivan of *The Russian
Experiment.* It was his first role and his best, and

hinted at possibilities within him yet to be explored. In his recent films he has portrayed the popular modern hero: casual on the surface, tough and self-sufficient underneath. He has done it charmingly, effortlessly, and has managed at the same time to convey a sexual quality that is remarkable considering the restraint of most of his love scenes. But in Ivan we had something more: a depth and complexity hinted at, but palpable. The man who played Ivan *may* be able to do Hamlet.

Mr. Douglas apparently thinks himself that it is time he moved on from the world of popular movies into something more challenging. He could not, however, have picked a more formidable role. One applauds his courage. And awaits the outcome.

There was the sound of a chair being pulled out and Mary looked up to see Kit sitting down with a cup of coffee. "Have you seen the *Times*?" she asked immediately.

"No, I haven't." He sipped his coffee. "Good morning."

She wrinkled her nose slightly. "Sorry. Good morning. And read this article." She handed it over and picked up her own cup, her eyes on his face as he read. When he had finished he put it down and looked thoughtful.

"I don't know what whim brought you to Yarborough, my friend, but you've put yourself behind the eight ball, haven't you?" she said tensely.

"Have I?" he replied calmly.

"Yes. George said the first-night audience would be packed with critics waiting to see if you were going to fall on your face. Apparently he was right." She tapped the paper with a long, nervous finger.

"Everything Calder said here is true, you know. I did coast through my last three movies. It was all I had to do, really." His eyes were black and inscrutable as he watched her face.

"I know." She looked at him very seriously. "Why did you take those parts, Kit? They surprised me. I thought, after *The Russian Experiment,* you would hold out for something more serious."

"Can't you guess?"

"No."

He smiled crookedly. "Money, my dear. Filthy lucre. I wanted to put enough of it in the bank so that I'd never have to worry about it again. And I've done that. I had ten percent of *Raid On Kailis,* you know." He pushed his coffee cup away. "I'm not ashamed of those films. They were well done, they were fun, they were exciting without being violent. They weren't terribly serious, I'll agree, but they served a purpose. They entertained millions."

"Yes," she said slowly. "I know that." She gave him a worried look. "But you are going to have to come up with a helluva Hamlet to beat the image you've made for yourself. The critics won't incline toward leniency."

"Are you concerned about me, Mary?" he asked softly.

"Yes. I am. The rehearsal time is too short. You're working with students. And Margot." Her voice altered imperceptibly as she said that last name and he grinned.

"She's going to be all right. All George has to do is put her at center stage and she's happy."

"How about you?"

He looked sardonic. "I don't need the center of the stage."

Her throat was suddenly dry. "Kit"—unconsciously she leaned toward him—"can you do it?"

"I think so. If I want to." His voice was soft and very deep. "Is it important to you that I succeed?"

"Yes." Her voice in return was barely a whisper. "Yes, it is."

"Mind if I join you?" said George's cheerful voice.

"Of course not," returned Mary after a minute, forcing a smile.

Kit turned his splendid raven head toward George and favored him with a cold stare. "You're up late," he said disapprovingly.

"It's Sunday," replied George mildly, tucking into his plate of scrambled eggs. "My day of rest."

"Why don't you go over and hold Margot's hand for a while?" asked Kit disagreeably.

"It's not my hand she wants to hold." George refused to be ruffled by his star's evident bad temper. Kit gave up trying to intimidate him and turned to Mary.

"How about a game of tennis?" he asked.

"Tennis?" She looked at him incredulously. "You never played tennis before. You said it was a sissy game."

He grinned a little. "I was being defensive. I didn't want you to teach me to play because I knew you'd beat me."

She gave him a long blue stare. "And now you think I can't?"

"I don't know," he returned frankly, "but at least it'll be a contest."

"I'll meet you at the courts in half an hour," she said.

"Fine." He smiled pleasantly at George. "See you later," he said and strolled casually out of the dining room. Everyone present, including George and Mary, watched him go.

Half an hour later, dressed in a white tennis dress and carrying her racquet and a Thermos, Mary arrived at the tennis courts. There were four of them, each with a concrete rubberized surface and all four were presently in use. Mary went to sit next to Kit on the bench and looked at him appraisingly. He was wearing white shorts and a light blue shirt.

"How good are you?" she asked speculatively.

He glanced sideways down at her, his lowered lashes looking absurdly long against the hard male line of his cheek. "You'll find out."

"We're through now," said Nancy Sealy as she came over to the bench with the girl she had been playing. "You can have our court, Mary."

"Thanks." Mary flashed the girl a smile and bent her head to unzip her racquet cover. That look of Kit's had disturbed her, and as she took the court she tried to ignore the suddenly accelerated beat of her heart.

They warmed up for five minutes, then Kit said, "Shall we start? You can serve first."

"Okay." She put one ball in the pocket of her dress, picked up another, and went to stand at the service line. Mary had been playing tennis since she was eight years old. Her parents belonged to a golf and tennis club and she had always spent hours every summer on the courts. She wasn't a powerful player, but she was extremely steady and accurate. She tossed the ball high in the air and served. Kit returned it deep to the baseline with a hard forehand shot. Mary, who had moved in, missed it. She stood for a minute looking at him in surprise, then went to serve again. This time she put it on his backhand side and his return, while deep, was not as hard. She sent it back with her own smooth, classic forehand and eventually took the point.

She eventually took the game as well, but it took three deuces before she was able to put it away. Then Kit moved to the service line.

The ball boomed across the net and was by her before she had finished getting her racquet back. "Good grief," she said. "What was that?"

"Was it in?" he asked.

"What I could see of it was."

"Good." He grinned. "My problem is that all too often it isn't."

It was an extremely strenuous set. Kit made up in power what he lacked in accuracy and Mary's wrist was aching from returning his shots. It took them an hour to reach 6–6.

"Shall we play a tie breaker?" he asked as he came to the net to hand her the balls.

"Why don't we quit now?" she replied. "That way we both win."

"We neither of us win, you mean," he contradicted.

She made an exasperated face. "You're so bloody competitive. All right, we'll play a tie breaker."

"No." Unexpectedly he put the balls in his pocket. "No, you're right. We'll quit while we're both ahead."

"I'm dying of thirst," she confessed as they walked off the court together. They had been playing in the full sun and her face and hair were damp with sweat. She looked at Kit and saw that his shirt was soaked. "I brought a jug of water with me," she said, gesturing to the Thermos tucked under the bench. "I'll share it with you."

They sat down together on the bench in the shade

and Mary poured the water. She had only one cup so she drank first, refilled it, and passed it to him. "You always think of everything," he said as he accepted the cup.

"Well, I've been playing tennis for a lot longer than you. If you ever get more consistency on that first serve, though, you'll make mincemeat of me. It's vicious."

"Yeah. When it goes in."

"You're not missing by much. You just need more practice. You could use a little more work on your backhand too."

"Mmm."

She hooked several wet tendrils of hair behind her ears and smiled ruefully. "My wrist hurts. It was like returning cannonballs."

He didn't answer for a minute and she poured herself some more water. She could feel his eyes on her. "What we need is a swim," he said at last. "What do you say?"

She thought of the cool clear lake. "I say that sounds good."

"Great." He stood up and picked up both their racquets and the water jug. "Let's go change into bathing suits."

"Okay." She fell into step beside him, her own long lithe stride almost the equal of his. A little voice inside her said she oughtn't to be spending time with him like this, that it was dangerous. Nonsense, said Mary silently to that uncomfortable little voice. There will be a million people around the lakefront. How can it possibly be dangerous?

They didn't go to the school lakefront. When she came out of her cottage dressed in a suit and terry-cloth cover-up, she found Kit sitting on her front steps. He wore bathing trunks and an ancient gray college sweat shirt that she recognized. "Good God," she said before she thought. "Do you still have that thing? I should have thought you'd have some designer sportswear by now."

"There's nothing wrong with this sweat shirt," he returned amiably. "There aren't any holes in it, are there?"

"No." She smiled at him, unaware of the affectionate amusement in her eyes. "In some ways you haven't changed at all. You never did give a damn about clothes."

"I like them clean and comfortable. As long as they meet those two requirements, I'm satisfied." They had begun walking down through the woods and at this point he veered off into the pines. "I've found a nice spot on the lake—a little cove. It's on college property so we won't be trespassing. Come on."

"But Kit," she protested as he plunged off through the trees. "I don't want to . . ."

He stopped and turned. "For God's sake, stop acting like a nun about to be raped. Come on!"

"Don't be crude," she snapped in return, but she followed him off the path and down through the woods. After about five minutes they came out of the trees and there they were on the shore of the lake. "Oh Kit," she breathed. "It's lovely."

"Great for fishing," he said with satisfaction. "I was out here at five this morning and it was beautiful."

"Did you catch anything?"

"You'll be eating it for dinner," he replied with a grin.

He dropped his towel and stripped his sweat shirt off. She began to do the same. "Daddy certainly made a convert out of you," she said, her voice muffled by her cover-up as she pulled it over her head. "Nothing, but nothing, would get me out of bed at five in the morning."

"Does your father still have the boat?"

"Yes." She looked away from him to the sparkling lake water. Kit had loved to go out with her father on those early-morning fishing expeditions. She had thought sometimes that he enjoyed her father so much because he had never really known his own.

"Race you in," he said.

"Okay." They both headed for the lake at a run and their diving bodies went into the water at almost the same instant. The two sleek black heads emerged close together and they yelped simultaneously, "It's freezing!" The lake here dropped off steeply after the first few feet, and though they were not far from shore, Mary found she was over her head. She treaded water and looked around.

They were in a small cove, protected from the college waterfront by a promontory of pine trees. Mary could hear some of the students shouting and laughing as they played volleyball, but they were hidden from her view, as she was hidden from theirs.

They swam for perhaps ten minutes and then, by unspoken mutual consent, headed back to the shore. Mary picked up her towel and silently watched Kit as he dried himself vigorously. He was not watching her, he was looking off down the lake, and so she let her eyes linger on the smooth brown expanse of muscled shoulders and back, the strong brown column of his neck. He finished drying himself and spread out the towel on the patch of grass that grew beyond the trees. He lay down, put his hands behind his head, and closed his eyes against the sun. "Tell me about Hamlet," he said.

She spread her own towel next to his, sat down and rummaged in her canvas bag for a comb. "What do you want to know?"

"I find him hard to figure out. He vacillates so—one

moment he's full of energy, vowing to avenge his father's murder, and the next he's in a blue funk, unable to do anything at all."

Slowly she combed the tangles out of her wet hair. "That's the Hamlet problem in a nutshell. It's not the typical Elizabethan revenge tragedy at all. The conflict in *Hamlet* is within the hero, not outside him."

"As I understand it," Kit said, "according to the code of the revenge tragedy, Hamlet is supposed to murder his uncle because he's discovered that his uncle murdered his father. An eye for an eye and all that. And he doesn't seem to question the morality of the code. He seems to think he ought to murder his uncle. God knows, he has reason enough to hate him. Aside from killing Hamlet's father, he's stolen the throne from Hamlet and married his adored mother. Hamlet keeps *saying* he hates Claudius, that he wants to kill him, but every time he has a chance, he flubs it."

Mary finished with her hair and returned the comb to her bag. "Haven't you talked about this with George?"

"Yes. He's inclined toward the Olivier interpretation, that Hamlet's feelings for his mother are what get in the way. But I think there's something more."

Mary wrapped her arms around her knees. "He's a terribly complicated character," she said slowly. "He doesn't know himself why he is incapable of acting. I think it stems from his state of mind, myself."

"The first soliloquy, you mean.

Oh God! God!
How weary, stale, flat, and unprofitable
Seem to me all the uses of the world!

Kit's beautiful voice lingered on the words, drawing out all the vowel sounds in a way that sent a sudden shiver down her spine.

"Precisely," she said after a minute's silence. "What is the point of acting in such a world? It won't bring his father back, it won't make his mother chaste, it won't restore the innocence of his love for Ophelia. Yet consciously he feels he *must* act. The contradiction puts a terrible strain on his mind."

"He can be a nasty bastard."

"Yes. He's dangerously close to the edge at times. And yet, there is a basic beauty and goodness about him that shines through all the torment."

"Hmm. I can see why he's considered such a challenge."

"The ultimate challenge for an actor, it's said." She turned a little to look at him. "Are you afraid, Kit?"

His eyes remained closed. "Yes," he said. "To do it well I'm going to have to reveal myself as I've never done before. Yes, you could say I'm afraid."

She didn't say anything but kept looking at his quiet relaxed face. She had told him he hadn't changed, but that wasn't true. There were faint lines at the corners of his eyes and a look about his mouth that hadn't been there before. He looked older. He looked as if he had suffered. She was conscious of deep surprise as she thought this and his eyes opened and looked into hers. "Lie down here with me," he said softly, and her heart began to hammer in her breast.

Chapter Nine

"No," she said. She dragged her eyes away from his and turned so her back was to him. "If you start that, I'll leave."

"Will you?" He reached up and caught her arm, levering her back with the strength of his wrist until she was lying beside him on the spread towels. In a minute he had rolled over and pinned her down, his mouth coming down on hers in a hard, hungry kiss whose intensity pressed her head back against the striped towel and into the ground. At the touch of his mouth all her defenses melted. She was hardly aware of when the tenseness left her body and her mouth answered to the demand of his.

"Mary." His voice was a husky murmur in her ear. "I love you. Don't you know that?"

"Do you, Kit?" She looked up into his face so close above her own. "I don't know what I know anymore," she said and lightly ran her finger over his cheekbone.

He bent his head and kissed her throat. "Come back to California with me."

She closed her eyes. The urge to give in to him was tremendous. "I can't," she whispered. "It isn't my kind of world, it never could be."

"You can bring your own world with you," he said and sat up.

At his withdrawal she felt alone and bereft. After a minute she opened her eyes to gaze up at him. "What do you mean?"

"I mean there are universities in California—damn good ones too. Why couldn't you teach at one of them?"

"Teach?" she said weakly.

"Yes. Or write. Isn't that what you like to do best? Your book was excellent—as I'm sure you know."

Her eyes widened. "You read my book?"

His eyes were smiling at her. "You saw my movies."

"Yes." How could such dark eyes look so softly tender? She sat up and leaned her forehead on her knees. "You'd want me to go on teaching?"

"Of course I want you to go on teaching!" He sounded almost violent. "I've always wanted you to fulfill your potential. I would never stop you from doing that. That's why I was so upset when—when you said you would give up your fellowship."

He had shied away from mentioning the baby and she too avoided touching that particular pain. "I don't know, Kit. It's too hard to combine careers. I've seen it happen over and over again. Someone's always got to give."

Her hair had begun to dry in the sun and a strand of it swung forward over her cheek. He reached out and gently pushed it back off her face. "If you like," he said, "I'll move east."

Her eyes were great blue pools in her clear, fine-boned face. "Do you mean that?"

"Yes. I don't think I could manage Massachusetts. I'd

have to be closer to New York. Maybe Connecticut again if you want to stay in New England."

"I don't know," she said again and heard the uncertainty in her own voice.

"Will you think about it?"

"I—yes."

He smiled at her. "Good girl." He rose to his feet and held a hand out to her. "Time for lunch," he said lightly, and she put her hand in his and let him pull her to her feet. "Your nose is red," he said as he picked up the towels.

"Rats. My sunscreen is in my bag. I forgot to put it on." She peered at her shoulders. "I'm really not the California type, Kit."

"I'll build you a screened-in porch," he said. "Come on."

"All right," she answered irritably, annoyed by his haste. "What's the big rush? Are you *that* hungry?"

"Yes, I am." He looked at her, a wicked gleam in his dark eyes. "But not for food. If we stay here any longer, you'll find out what I *am* hungry for."

"I'm coming," she said quickly and picked up her bag.

He raised an eyebrow but said only, "Follow me, Stanley," as he walked into the pines.

Her nose *was* red and so were her shoulders. She decided to make herself a peanut-butter-and-jelly sandwich and spend the afternoon on her porch reading the papers. It was difficult, however, to concentrate on the problems of the Middle East and Latin America. The problems of Mary O'Connor Douglas seemed so much more urgent.

She had told him she would consider going back to

him. She couldn't believe she had said that, but she had. She had meant it too. She must be insane.

Of course he hadn't meant what he said about coming east. She knew Kit too well. His career came first with him; he had only said that to get under her guard. And he had got under her guard—damn him.

Part of her longed for him, longed for him and ached with missing him. And part of her feared him, feared what would happen if he turned away from her again as he had once before. She didn't know if she could dare to risk it again.

At about four o'clock George appeared at her door and she invited him in for a drink. He left at five and she went in to change for dinner. There had been no sign of Kit all afternoon and she found herself looking forward to seeing him at dinner.

He wasn't there. Nor was Margot Chandler.

"Where are Chris and Margot?" Carolyn Nash asked George, and Mary could have kissed her for her bluntness.

"Chris went over to the Stafford Inn this afternoon to work with her," George replied calmly. "I expect they're having dinner there."

"Just who is the director around here, George?" Alfred Block asked insultingly. "Ever since the Queen Bee arrived it seems as if Chris is taking over. *He* tells her what to do, how to stand, how to speak."

"That's true," put in Eric Lindquist. He gave George a sunshiny smile. "I haven't liked to say anything, but . . ."

"You creeps!" said Carolyn indignantly. "It isn't Chris's fault if she hangs on him like a parasite. He's only thinking of the good of the production."

Mary was startled and a little alarmed. She had no

idea there was such discord in the ranks. She looked at George, who did not seem the least perturbed by what was being said. He looked so high-strung and nervous, she thought, that his calm was a perpetual surprise to her. He said now, pleasantly but firmly, "*I* am the director of this play, no one else. And I have a leading lady to deal with who is extremely nervous about her first stage role. She will do very well if only we can instill some confidence in her. Chris is the person who has had the most success doing that, and I am grateful to him for his effort. But when it comes down to what happens on that stage, I am in charge. And I would suggest that none of you forget it." He went back to eating his dinner.

Mary looked at him in admiration. He glanced her way, caught her look, and winked. She smiled a little in return and pushed some food around on her plate. She wasn't hungry. The idea of Kit and Margot together quite took her appetite away.

They played cards after dinner. If nothing else, Mary thought, this summer will have improved my bridge game. By ten o'clock she had a headache, however, and excused herself to go to bed. Melvin Shaw, who hated to see the best player after himself disappear, protested. But she rose, said firmly, "Good night, Melvin," and prepared to leave.

"Shall I see you to your cottage?" George asked.

"No. I really am tired and headachy," she said. "I'll see you tomorrow."

"It's probably the coming storm that's put you out of sorts," said Nancy Sealy. "It's amazing how the weather affects one."

"Is there a storm coming?" asked Mary sharply.

"There's supposed to be," the girl replied. "I heard it on the radio before I came down to dinner."

"Oh," said Mary faintly. "I see. Well, good night everyone."

The night was cool as she stepped out into the darkness, and there *was* the feel of a storm. Mary hurried up the path, anxious to reach the shelter of her cottage. Kit's windows were dark and his car was gone.

Once she was inside she undressed quickly and got into bed. She felt strung-up and tense. There was going to be a thunderstorm. She knew it, could feel it, and hated it.

When she was fourteen years old, Mary and a friend had been walking home from the tennis courts when a sudden thunderstorm had come up. They were taking a shortcut across a field and the lightning had been terrifying, shooting in jagged bolts from the sky. Mary had been frightened, but she remembered what her father had once said about getting caught on a golf course in a thunderstorm. "We should lie down flat!" she shouted to her girlfriend.

"Yuck. The ground is soaked," her friend had replied. "I'm going to run for it."

The sky had lighted up. "Not me," said Mary, who had great faith in her father's wisdom. She had dropped to the ground as the other girl began to run across the field. A bolt of lightning had been attracted by the upright, running figure. The girl had been killed instantly, and ever since then Mary had been petrified by thunderstorms.

It didn't actually begin until about midnight. There was distant rumbling for about half an hour and then it started to rain. A bolt of lightning lit up the night outside Mary's window and a few seconds later came a sharp crack of thunder.

Wrapped in a blanket, she crawled out of bed and went to hide in the corner of her bedroom. She was huddled there, shaking uncontrollably, when she heard a voice from the sitting room calling her name. She tried to answer but a crack of thunder drowned her out. Her bedroom door opened and Kit stood there, dressed in jeans, and a sweat shirt. He saw her almost immediately. "Oh, sweetheart," he said gently. He crossed the room and sat down on the floor beside her. "You're perfectly safe, you know. If it hits anything it'll be one of the trees, not the cottage."

"I—I know," she stuttered, turning with a great rush of gratitude into the warm safety of his arms. "But somehow knowing doesn't seem to help."

He held her closely, drawing her into the shelter of his body, knowing from past experience that this more than his words would comfort her. She closed her eyes and pressed against him, not even noticing the wetness of his shirt under her cheek.

The storm lasted for about twenty minutes, during which time they stayed huddled together on the floor. Then it began to abate, the thunder sounding more distant, the lightning flashes less bright. Finally all that was left was the rain, beating steadily against the roof and the windows.

"It's all over," said Kit's voice gently.

"Yes." Her tense, cramped muscles relaxed a little. She tried to laugh. "I feel so stupid, but I can't seem to help it."

"I know." His hand was moving slowly, caressingly, up and down her back. His cheek was against her hair. She closed her eyes and rested against him.

"You knew I'd be a basket case." It was a statement not a question.

"Yes. I thought I'd better come over and check on you. It was a nasty storm."

"Mmm." It wasn't fear she was feeling now but something else. His hand continued its smooth rhythmic stroking and she drew a deep uneven breath.

"Mary," he said and she looked up. He bent his head and began to kiss her, a deep, slow, profoundly erotic kiss. She lay back in his arms, her head against his shoulder, her arms coming up to circle his neck. His lips moved from her mouth to bury themselves in her neck. His hand slid under her pajama top and cupped her breast. "Mary," he muttered, "my princess, my Irish rose . . ."

The love words, the touch of his mouth, his hand, shattered whatever resistance she had left. "Let's get into bed," he murmured.

Her will to deny him had totally left her; she felt herself giving up, giving way. "All right," she whispered, and he got to his feet, pulling her up with him. He picked her up and laid her on the bed and stood beside it for a minute as he stripped his shirt off and undid the buckle of his jeans. She had left a lamp on and she watched him in its dim glow. Then he was beside her, his long fingers undoing the buttons of her pajama top, going to the elastic at her waist.

He touched her bared flesh and she felt him as a flame of desire, a flame that burned deep within her; and deep within her rose the urge to answer him, to satisfy him, to give to him and hold nothing back for herself. "Kit," she whispered, and he kissed her again, his long lean body hard and heavy now on hers. Her own body remembered the feel of him all too well, and quite suddenly she wanted him as badly as he wanted her. There was no one like him, nothing else in the world like this. "Kit," she said, urgently now, and then "Ah . . . h," as he buried himself deep within her. She shuddered as the piercing, quivering, throbbing tension began to mount within her. Her fingers were pressed deep into his back, white with pressure.

"Mary, baby, love." As one they moved together in profound, shuddering, ecstatic passion.

Afterward she was utterly still, lying quiet under the weight of his body, and he was still with her. After a long time he stirred and shifted his position. "I'm too heavy for you."

"No," she said. "You're not."

He looked down at her with dark, warm, peaceful eyes. "Go to sleep, Princess," he said, and turned her over on her side, the way she liked to sleep, and pulled her into the warmth of his body. She closed her eyes and in two minutes was deeply asleep.

Mary woke early the next morning to the sound of the birds. She turned to find Kit lying beside her, his chin propped on his hands, his brow lightly furrowed. He turned his head slightly when he heard her move and his eyes, meeting hers, were uncertain and wary.

He had taken advantage of the situation last night and he was evidently unsure of what her reaction would be in the clear light of the morning after. If I had half a brain, Mary thought, I'd tell him to get out. She felt her lips curving in a smile. "I knew I'd be like King Canute," she said.

His face dissolved into laughter. "Why King Canute?"

"He was the fellow who ordered the tide not to come in."

He was still laughing. "God, Mary, I love you. There isn't another woman alive who would drag in King Canute at a moment like this."

"He's very appropriate. Alas."

"Don't say 'alas.' " His face had sobered. "It's been such hell, being around you, wanting you . . . It reminded me a little of when we first met, only this was so much worse." He moved closer, put an arm across her and buried his face between her breasts. "Wanting and wanting and not having," he said, his lips moving on her bare flesh as he spoke. Then, deeply, fiercely, "Wanting what was mine." He rubbed his cheek against her and she protested a little as the roughness of his beard scratched her tender flesh. He rested his head on her breast and she gently ran her fingers through his touseled black hair.

"It's not like this with anyone else," he said.

"I'm afraid I can't return the compliment," she replied a little acidly. "I haven't got your standard of comparison."

He chuckled. "Thank God for that."

Her fingers continued to move caressingly through his hair. "You'd better go," she said. "I don't want anyone to see you leaving here."

"Why not? We're married."

"Yes—I know." Her fingers stilled and he raised his head to look at her. His nostrils looked suddenly tense.

"I thought you were coming back to me."

"I . . ." She looked up into his face. It was hopeless, she thought. She was weak with love for him. "I suppose I am," she said helplessly.

His face relaxed and the eyes that looked down at

her were so dark, so unbearably beautiful. "Then I don't give a damn who sees me," he said and began to kiss her again. He didn't leave for another hour.

She lectured that morning on Hamlet, and as she talked about the problems of the play and the characters she kept seeing Kit's face. What had he meant, she wondered, when he had said that to play Hamlet well he would have to reveal himself?

She did not want anyone at school to know they had gotten back together again. "Please, Kit," she had said just before he left her that morning. "I need a little time to adjust myself. I can't bear the thought of all these people looking at me the way they will look if they know." Color had stained her cheeks and her voice had trailed off.

He had frowned. "If it was up to me, I'd simply move right in here. There isn't any need for explanations. We're married."

"I know. But I'm not ready yet. Please, Kit," she had said again, this time a little desperately, and he had given in.

She didn't quite know herself why she was so reluctant to make public the fact of their reconciliation. It had something to do with the fact that she was hardly reconciled to the reconciliation herself.

She knew how she felt about him, but she didn't quite trust his feeling for her. He wanted her and he was very adept at getting what he wanted. But would he continue to want her or would it be, as it had been before, a case of out of sight out of mind.

She would have to move to California; she had reluctantly come to that conclusion. He might do an occasional stage play, but the bulk of his work was in the movies and the movie industry was in California. She wanted to be separated from him as little as possible; she remembered all too vividly what had happened the last time they were separated.

She should see a doctor about birth control; that thought crossed her mind a few times during the week that followed. If they kept on the way they were going, she was sure to get pregnant. She would love to have Kit's baby, but she wasn't sure what his reaction would be. She was afraid to ask him. That topic by unspoken consent was taboo between them.

She should send in her resignation to the university as well, but she procrastinated about that too. She felt as if her whole life were off balance and a little unreal; the only reality was the night, when her bedroom door opened and Kit came in.

"It's the strangest feeling, hearing people talk about Chris Douglas," she said to him as the dawn came up on Saturday morning. "I keep thinking, That's *Kit* they're talking about, my husband, the man who neglects to shave before he comes to bed and scratches me all up with his beard."

He gave a warm, sleepy chuckle. "Poor love. I'll shave tomorrow night."

She kissed the top of his head where it lay pillowed on her breast and then went back to her original thought. "I just can't seem to reconcile *that* person, Movie Star Christopher Douglas, with you. It's very peculiar."

"No, it's not," he answered. "Everyone else sees the façade, the reputation, the good nose and the straight teeth. You see *me*. You always have. That's what I love about you. You see right through to the heart of people. Phoniness and sham simply collapse in front of you."

She was silent for a long time. "I think that's one of the nicest things anyone has ever said to me," she said at last.

"Um." She felt his eyelashes against her skin as his eyes closed. Outside the birds began to sing.

"It's getting late," she said. "I hear the birds."

" 'It is not yet near day,' " he answered sleepily. " 'It was the nightingale, and not the lark, that pierced the fearful hollow of thine ear.' "

"Kit!" She laughed and shook him a little. "Stop quoting *Romeo and Juliet* and get up."

"No," he answered simply.

" 'It was the lark, the herald of the morn; no nightingale,' " she quoted back severely.

"You're a spoilsport." He sat up, yawned and stretched. "For how much longer do you mean to keep me creeping in and out of your bedroom in the dead of night? I'm getting too old for such exploits." He got out of bed and picked his jeans up from the bedside chair.

"Until after the play opens," she answered, pushing her hair off her forehead. "I know you think it's silly of me. *I* even think it's silly of me. But I can't help it."

"For a smart woman you can be awfully illogical." He pulled a shirt over his head.

"I know," she replied a little glumly.

"Look, Mary." He sat for a minute on the edge of the bed. "You and I have got to talk. It's no good thinking we can talk at night; I've got other things on my mind when I come in here."

"I'm a little distracted myself," she murmured.

He grinned and kissed the tip of her nose. "Let's go out somewhere for dinner tonight."

"Kit, I would love that," Mary replied fervently. The

endless bridge game had gotten on her nerves this last week, but she hadn't known how to get out of it.

"Great. I'll find some quiet spot and make a reservation. Not, I hasten to add, in my own name."

"Will it be all right?" she asked as second thoughts struck her. "What will you tell George?"

"I will tell him that I am taking my wife out to dinner," he said with wicked simplicity, got up off her bed and left.

Chapter Ten

Mary took her time dressing for dinner that evening. She had spent the whole afternoon in the library, hidden away from the press of people she was feeling so acutely this week. It was difficult to behave around Kit as she had last week, when she had been determined to keep him at a distance, and she was afraid her changed feelings were obvious. She felt, with what was perhaps hypersensitivity, that everyone was looking at them, and wondering.

She wore her white linen suit, the dressiest outfit she had brought with her, and took pains with her hair, blowing it dry carefully so it feathered softly back off her face and curled smoothly on her shoulders. At precisely seven o'clock she heard a horn toot outside, and she picked up her black patent leather purse and went out the door.

"How crass," she said as she got into the car. "Honking the horn for me. You might have knocked on my door."

He grinned. "When I was a kid I always longed to pick up my date by blowing on the horn. Unfortunately, I could never afford a car."

"Poor deprived darling," she murmured sympathetically. "Well, if you want to enact your adolescent fantasies, who am I to stop you?"

"Do you want a punch in the nose?" he asked amiably.

She laughed. "Not really. Where are we going?"

"A place George suggested. The Elms, it's called. He said the food is good and the customers are mostly local people."

"Good," said Mary. "You can usually count on New Englanders not to bother you."

It was her first experience of going out with Kit since he had become famous. He parked the car himself in the restaurant lot, and they walked up the stairs of the old clapboard inn and into the lobby. "Mr. Michaels," Kit said pleasantly to the hostess. "I have a reservation for seven-thirty."

The woman's eyes widened as they took him in. She looked nervously at her reservation chart. "Yes, c-certainly," she stuttered. "Come right this way, sir."

Mary was thankful to see it was a corner table, but the walk across the room seemed endless to her. One or two people glanced idly up as they passed and then froze as they recognized Kit's face. It was not a face, Mary thought ruefully as she sat down and regarded him across the table, that one was likely to mistake. He had picked up the menu and for a minute she regarded him, trying to see him as others must, as these people throughout the dining room, all peering surreptitiously at their corner, must see him. She looked and saw a tall, very tan, leanly built man in a lightweight gray suit. His hair was black as coal, black as night, black as hers. He looked up and she smiled a little to herself. She could never see him dispassionately; it was impossible.

"Do you know, I believe this is the first time I've ever seen you in a suit," she said. "It becomes you."

"That's true. I didn't own one when we were married, did I?" The waiter appeared at his elbow and he asked her, "Do you want a drink?"

"Yes. I'll have a vodka martini on the rocks."

"I'll have a whiskey sour," Kit told the waiter.

When the man returned with their drinks he put the martini in front of Kit and the whiskey sour in front of Mary. They exchanged a glance of secret amusement, and after the waiter had gone, Kit changed the drinks. "It's so embarrassing, having a hard drinker for a wife," he said mournfully.

She sipped her martini. "I can't help it if you only like sissy drinks."

"I wasn't brought up in a nice alcoholic middle-class family. I developed a taste for beer at an early age, and I haven't changed."

"You like milk even better," she said.

"Good God, Mary, don't ever let that get out," he said in mock horror. "Think of my rough-and-tough reputation."

She smiled at him, a warm and beautiful smile. "I'll protect your secrets to the death."

"Will you?" He put a hand over hers on the table. Involuntarily she glanced around. At least half the restaurant was looking at him. She pulled her hand away and felt the color flush into her cheeks. "Ignore them," he said. "They're behaving very well, really. After a few minutes they'll stop looking."

She sat back and tried to relax. "I suppose you're used to it by now."

"You never really get used to it. It's just something

you have to live with." He glanced over her shoulder. "Ah," he said. "Here it comes."

A man appeared at their table carrying a pad and a pencil. "Mr. Douglas," he said a little nervously and with a definite New York accent. "Would you mind giving me your autograph? It's for my daughter. She just loves your pictures."

As Mary watched, a still and guarded look of cold courtesy settled over Kit's face. It was the mask, she realized, behind which he must have learned to hide from a continual public scrutiny. "I'm sorry," he said coolly, "but I don't give autographs when I am not working."

The man looked nonplussed and backed away a little. "Sorry," he said. Kit nodded coldly and after a minute the man turned and left.

"You were rather brutal," Mary murmured after a minute.

He looked at her. "If I had signed that paper, we'd have had the whole damn restaurant over here for autographs. Now they'll leave us alone."

"Yes," said Mary, a little unhappily. "I suppose that's true."

He smiled at her expression. "You were brought up to be polite. I wasn't. Actually, I don't believe in being polite."

Mary sighed. "I'm learning, believe me."

"Let's order," he said, and handed her the menu.

The meal was delicious and Mary felt herself relaxing as they ate and drank the bottle of wine Kit had ordered to go with it.

"I've decided I'll move to California with you," she said as she savored a perfect filet mignon.

His face blazed into happiness. "Do you mean that?"

"Yes. I can probably work at the UCLA library without any trouble. I don't know about teaching, though. I'd better keep flexible so I can adjust to your schedule."

"Listen to me, Mary." He was deadly earnest. "I want you to have your own life. I do not want you to sacrifice what you want to do for me. If you want to teach, teach. It's what you're trained for."

"Actually, I wasn't," she returned slowly. "I was trained for scholarship. Scholars usually teach so they can eat, not necessarily because they like it."

His eyes were looking deeply into hers. "Did *you* like it?"

Her lips curled a little at the corners. "Not particularly," she said.

His eyes smiled back. "Money isn't a problem, sweetheart. We have plenty of that. If you want to write books, you go right ahead. You don't have to worry about a roof over your head. You can have a housekeeper—a cook—a secretary—whatever you want."

Mary blinked. "Goodness. Do you have all those people?"

"No. I have a housekeeper who is extremely crabby but a good cook. We'll have to find another house, though. You'd hate the one I have now."

"Why?"

"It's ghastly," he said cheerfully. "I bought it from some starlet—bought it furnished. I kind of just close my eyes to the inside of it. I took it because it was isolated and I liked the view."

"But why didn't you redo it?" she asked wonderingly.

"I don't know. It didn't seem as if it was worth the effort."

"How long have you had it?"

"Three years."

"Three years!" She stared at him in astonishment. "You've lived in a house you hate for three years and haven't tried to change it?"

He grinned a little lopsidedly. "It was just a place to hang my clothes and park my car. It never felt like a home. No place feels like a home if you're not there."

"Oh, Kit." The words were barely a whisper. She put down her fork and looked at him. "I'll make a home for you, darling."

"I'd like that," he said simply. "Are you sure you don't mind giving up your university job? Won't you miss the contact with all those famous academics?"

"I don't think so," she replied thoughtfully. "I think I might do better at a younger, less venerable institution. All the professors at my place are so—stodgy."

"Even Leonard Fergusson?" He sounded incredulous. Leonard Fergusson was the chairman of her department and a world-renowned scholar.

"I think he's getting old," she replied frankly. "He suffers from a certain inflexibility of thought, which sometimes approaches petrification. He also frequently exhibits a disturbing inability to recognize what century he is living in."

He threw back his head and laughed. "How on earth did he ever hire you?" he asked when he had got his breath back.

"The English department didn't have enough women. They have only *one* tenured female professor, can you believe it? I was to be his second token woman."

"Well, one thing California isn't is stodgy," he said

cheerfully. He put down his knife and fork and looked with satisfaction at his empty plate. "That was good."

Mary was only halfway through her steak. "Tell me about California," she said.

"It can be lovely," he answered promptly. "I think this time I'd like to look for a house on the ocean. Would you like that?"

"I'd love it," she answered.

"Maybe I'll get a boat. Like your father's."

Her lips curved tenderly. "That would be fun."

"Yes, it would be. It could be a very decent life, Mary. Not everyone in California is a flake, or a drug addict, you know. Or a movie star."

"Contrary to what my mother thinks," she murmured, and he laughed. "But would we have any privacy, Kit?" All through dinner she had been aware of the watching eyes that surrounded them.

"Money can buy an awful lot," he said a little bitterly. "It can even buy privacy."

"I suppose so," she replied dubiously.

Coffee was served. As she drank it she tried once again to ignore the pressure of watching eyes.

"Have you finished?" Kit asked.

"Yes," she said. They rose and walked back across the restaurant floor—through the battery of staring eyes.

She watched him as he drove back toward campus, watched his long-fingered, sensitive hands as they competently held the wheel, watched his profile, watched his mouth. There is a curious combination of ruthlessness and vulnerability about that mouth, she thought. "What do you think of Margot Chandler?" she asked curiously.

He smiled a little in the darkness of the car. "She's not a bad sort, really. I've met worse."

"What does that mean?"

"It means that she's basically a decent person, that she means no harm to anyone, and that she has an affectionate heart."

"Oh," said Mary rather blankly.

He glanced at her sideways. "What do you think of her?"

"I don't know," she answered carefully. "Her surface is so bright and hard that I haven't been able to get through anywhere. She's the most sophisticated person I've ever met."

"Sophisticated," he said thoughtfully. "Yes, I suppose that is a good way to describe her."

"What word would you use?" she asked, looking at him closely.

"Worldly," he answered promptly. "Like so many Hollywood people, she believes that good can come out of evil, that lies might be better than truth, that the end justifies the means."

"Good God," Mary said faintly. "I thought you said she was basically decent."

"She is—basically. But she's been corrupted. The world does that to people—and the Hollywood world more than most, I suppose."

"You sound very cynical."

They had reached the college gates by now and he swung in, accelerating smoothly up the long drive. "I'm not, really." They came to a halt in front of his cottage. It was about ten-thirty. "How about a walk?" he asked.

"That sounds marvelous," she returned. They had always loved to walk together, and being carless, they had done a lot of it in their early married life. "Let me change my clothes first," she said.

When she came back out of her cottage in sneakers and jeans, she found he was before her, similarly attired. "I found a nice path up through the woods the other morning," he said. "It's too dark to take it now, but I'll show it to you sometime."

She shook her head at him. "You missed your calling, Kit. In some other age you would have been an explorer."

"I would have loved that," he said as he took her hand. "Do you know, I was thinking of doing a movie about David Livingston?" They began to walk down the road together.

"Livingston," she said slowly, on a note of surprise. She thought for a minute. "He was quite a complicated character. Was he a saint or an egomaniac? Or a combination of the two?"

"I should think a good movie would show him as a little of both."

"Yes. Do you have a script?"

"Not yet. I've been thinking of setting up my own production company. I'd have to borrow some money. There's no way I'm going to touch all my nice safe little investments. But I have a few million free to play around with."

"A few million." She laughed. "I can't quite take it in, Kit. When I think of all the hamburger we used to eat!"

"I know." He put his hand, which was still holding hers, into the pocket of his windbreaker. "But they were the happiest days of my life—those hamburger days."

"Yes," she said. "Mine too."

The sound of music drifted to them. It was coming from the direction of the rec room. They could hear a chorus of lusty young voices raised in song.

"Do you want to go over there?" she asked.

"No." He grimaced a little. "I thought perhaps the college atmosphere here would make me feel like a student again. Instead it's made me feel a million years old."

She laughed. "You aren't exactly a geriatric case, darling, but I know what you mean."

They walked down to the lake and sat for a while in the empty lawn chairs, looking out at the still water. Then they walked back toward the cottages, sometimes talking, sometimes silent, their steps, from long practice, in perfect unison. The students were still singing in the rec room when Mary and Kit walked together into her cottage and went to bed.

Mary woke as the first gray light of dawn was filling the room. She looked at Kit, sleeping peacefully beside her in the double bed. It frightened her a little, what the sight of him did to her. When she was near him she was no longer Dr. O'Connor, the cool, clear-thinking, intelligent, dispassionate scholar. That persona, so carefully built up and nurtured for the last four years, crumbled like straw at the touch of his hand.

She had burned her last bridge last night when she told him she would go to California with him. All that was left now was to send in her resignation. The university would have no problem replacing her; half the academic world would give their right arms for the chance to teach there. And Leonard Fergusson would have confirmed all his prejudices about the untrustworthiness of women teachers.

Why was she so reluctant to write that letter? For she was, and in the gray morning light she realized that she still wasn't completely easy about her decision to go back to Kit. She adored him, but she didn't quite trust him and she hadn't quite forgiven him either. They never spoke about the baby and she knew that until they did, until they laid that sad little ghost to rest, that their marriage would never rest on solid ground. Yet for the life of her she could not bring the subject up. The wound had almost healed, but the scar still ached.

"Good morning," said a deep sleepy voice in her ear.

She turned her head and smiled at him. The smile was a little painful but he didn't seem to notice. "One of the things I've missed most is the way you warm up the bed," she said after a minute. "It's chilly sleeping alone."

"If it's up to me, you'll never sleep alone again," he answered.

She sighed a little and snuggled down under the covers next to him. "That was a melancholy sound," he murmured, and putting his arms around her, he pulled her close. She rested her head against his shoulder and put an arm around him in return. The muscles of his back felt hard and strong under her hand. They were neither of them wearing any clothes.

"This is not a position that is conducive to rest," he murmured after a minute.

"No? I'm comfortable." She closed her eyes.

"Are you, sweetheart?" His hand began to move slowly up and down her back, curving down now and then to caress her hip. She felt a throb deep within her.

"Don't do that," she said.

"All right," he answered softly. "How about this?" He knew exactly where to touch her, exactly how to arouse her. But for some inexplicable reason she did not want to make love now. She pulled away from him a little, but that only gave him room to bend his head and begin to kiss her breasts.

She lay perfectly still as he caressed her body, willing herself to stay separate and apart from him, trying to ignore the rising tumult of her senses. She did not want to give him what he wanted from her; this time at least she would make him take it. She had already given him too much.

"Mary . . ." His shoulders over her blotted out the rest of the room. "Love me," he whispered. She looked up into his eyes, black and glittering; his face was hard with desire. The angry core of separateness within her began to dissolve under his look. They stayed poised like that for a long minute, their eyes locked together. "Love me," he said again. And very very slowly she opened her legs.

As the power and the wonder of him came into her she closed her eyes. It was impossible to deny him, to deny herself; and she arched up against him, lost as always in the flooding majesty of his love. Passion flamed through her blood and thought receded as together they scaled the heights and came, shudderingly, to rest together.

He lay for a long time afterward with his arms locked tightly about her, as if he felt her slipping away and he would hold her to him, by force if necessary.

"It's getting late," she said at last.

"All right." He let her go and rolled over on his back. "For how long are we going to go on playing this game, Mary?"

She put her arm across her eyes to block out his darkly impatient face. "Let me tell my parents before we do anything public," she said.

"Will you call them today?"

"All right." She took her hand away and watched him dress. She felt suddenly ashamed of herself. After all, as he kept pointing out so reasonably, they *were* married. She was behaving like an idiot. She slipped out of bed, pulled her white terry-cloth robe around her and belted it. "Poor darling," she said. "I know I've been unreasonable. I'll call them today, I promise." She put her arm through his and walked with him to the door.

"I may sound like a terrible male chauvinist, but it bothers the hell out of me to see you with other men and not be able to show myself as the 'man in possession.'"

"That does sound terribly like a male chauvinist," she said softly. "But I love you anyway." He had opened the porch door and was standing framed in the doorway. She reached up on tiptoe to kiss him. His arms came around her.

There was a flash of light and then another one. Mary felt Kit's body stiffen and then he pushed her away from him. She stared in numbed astonishment. Out on the road in front of them was Jason Razzia, with his camera.

Kit cursed under his breath, a word she had never heard him use before. His eyes were wild with anger, and with the swiftness of a panther he was down the porch steps and running toward the photographer.

Jason Razzia backed up toward the woods as he saw Kit coming. Then he turned to run, but he wasn't quick enough. A lean, hard hand shot out and grabbed him by the shoulder. The other hand pulled the camera from him and sent it smashing down against a rock.

"Hey!" said Razzia. "You can't do that."

"I just did it," said Kit. "And I'll smash your head in the same way if you don't clear out of here." His searing anger had such force that for the first time since childhood Razzia found himself physically afraid of another person. He tried to pull away from Kit's iron grip.

"I'm g-going," he stuttered. Murder was looking at him out of Kit's dark eyes.

"And stay away from my wife," said Kit between his teeth. His voice was low and absolutely menacing. "If I catch you anywhere around her, I'll kill you. Do you hear me?"

"Yeah, Chris. Yeah, I hear you. Sorry. I'm going . . ." Razzia was shaking now and Kit shoved him toward the woods.

"Get out of here, you scum." Razzia ran.

Slowly, very slowly, Kit swung around and looked at his wife. She was still in the doorway of the porch and he could see from where he was standing that she was shivering. He cursed again, silently, bent to pick up the shattered camera, and then walked back to where she stood. Instinctively, she backed away from him. He stopped. "It had to happen in front of you," he said. Anyone who did not know him would not have heard the fierce anger that lay under the flat tone. "Any other woman in the world would have gotten a cheap thrill out of that. But not you."

Mary's eyes were dark in her white face. Her hands were clutched, protectively, on the front of her robe, holding it together. Kit had himself under control now, but he still wore the menacing aspect a male assumes when he is really angry. She was afraid of him.

"Let's go inside," he said in a calmer voice.

"No." She backed up onto the porch. "No. It's no good, Kit. I couldn't stand it. Photographers snooping around, peeking in my bedroom window. It's horrible!"

He followed her into the porch. "You don't mean that. One little incident like this can't make any difference between you and me."

"It does," she replied shakily.

His hand grasped her shoulder and she winced at the pressure of his fingers. "You only say that because you're upset."

"I am upset," she said. "But I mean it. I can't go back to you, Kit. I can't."

He let her go. His mouth looked taut and thin. "I'm not going to beg you, Mary." His voice was deeply bitter.

"I don't want you to."

"If this if your final decision, I'll abide by it."

"Oh, God, Kit," she cried. "Will you please just *go*?"

He dropped his hand from her shoulder, turned and walked out the door. She went inside and collapsed in a shivering heap on the sofa.

After a long time she got up and went in to shower. It was Sunday, she realized in stunned surprise. She would have to go to Mass.

She dried her hair, put on a print summer-dress, and walked out to her car. She felt numb. It was a state that continued all through the first part of the Mass, as she automatically made the responses, standing and sitting and kneeling like an automaton.

When she came back from communion, she knelt and bowed her face between her hands. It was quiet in the church, with only the organ playing. Dear God, she prayed, help me. What have I done?

It isn't true, she thought, eyes closed, shut in on herself, it couldn't be true that she had rejected Kit simply because a photographer had taken their picture. That ugly little scene had been the catalyst, not the cause, of her decision. Nor had she sent Kit away because he had punched out the despicable Razzia. It was something else, she realized.

Communion was over and the congregation stood for the final blessing. As the rest of the people in the church filed out Mary knelt back down. Once more she bowed her head. Her reaction to Kit this morning, she thought, had its roots deep in the past. She loved him, yes, but there was a dark side to his nature that she had encountered before and it was that aspect of him that she had recoiled from this morning.

He had come into her life five years ago like some splendid young god, sweeping her off her balance, out of her safe, familiar setting and into the passionate, ecstatic world of sexual love. But she had found, as had so many unfortunate Greek maidens before her, that it is dangerous to love a god. Gods, as classical literature should have taught her, tend to look out primarily for their own self-interest.

Kit had looked out for his, and at her expense. Contrary to what he claimed, he didn't need her. He was the most frighteningly self-sufficient person she had ever known. If something or someone got in his way, he smashed it, as he had smashed that camera this morning.

In the dim quiet of the church she looked up at the statue of the Virgin on the side altar. She was holding the infant Christ in her arms. Looking at that serene image of motherhood, Mary recognized that she had never forgiven Kit for suggesting an abortion to her.

When the baby had died she had felt that he had almost willed it to happen. It still lay between them. It always would. And that was why she had rejected him this morning. Very slowly she rose to her feet and walked out of the church.

She went back to the college and worked on Elizabethan songbooks all afternoon. When she went over to the dining hall for dinner, she devoutly hoped that Kit would not be there. He was. She saw him standing by the fireplace as soon as she walked into the rec room. Tonight he did not turn to look at her.

He didn't sit at her table for dinner either. Mary, seated between George and Alfred Block, was aware in all her nerve endings of his tall dark figure at the table next to hers, but she forced her eyes and her outward attention to George and Alfred and the students who were sitting with her.

After dinner they went back into the rec room and there it was even worse. To the onlooker, she supposed, they were no different than they had been all last week: polite, civilized toward each other, indifferent. But last week they had been playing a game. This was for real.

"We missed you at dinner last night, Chris," Mary heard Carolyn say to him.

"Mary and I went into town for dinner," he replied coolly. "It made for a change."

They had all known that, of course. The two of them couldn't have been absent together without causing a great deal of speculation. "Are you two getting back together again?" asked Eric Lindquist sunnily.

"As a matter of fact"—and here Kit's eyes met hers—"we were discussing a divorce."

She felt as though someone had hit her over the head with a brick. His eyes were coal-black and inimical. She put her hand up to brush a nonexistent strand of hair off her cheek. Everyone was staring at her. "I suppose it's time we did something about this unorthodox situation," she said. She went to pick up her coffee cup and discovered her hand was shaking. She hastily put it down again. "How about some bridge?" she asked Melvin Shaw. She managed to play for two hours without remembering a single card she had in her hand.

Chapter Eleven

The play was due to open the following Saturday night and for the remainder of the week George worked his cast hard. It was the only thing in the whole dreadful week that Mary had cause to be grateful for. Kit spent almost all his waking hours in the theater and Mary was spared the achingly painful sight of him for most of the day. He skipped dinner a few nights as well; the same nights that Margot was absent. She supposed, Mary thought dully, that she should be grateful for that as well.

The result of the heavy rehearsal schedule was that Mary had too much time alone. Ordinarily she would have relished the opportunity for solitude in such lovely surroundings, but in her present emotional state she needed the distraction of other people. When she was by herself, she tended to think of Kit. It didn't do any good to think of Kit, she didn't want to think of Kit, but she did think of Kit. Continually. She took to spending her afternoons in the library working on the Elizabethan songbooks. If it was not the vacation she had envisioned, at least it was better than continually brooding about what could not be helped.

On Thursday she slipped into the dark of the theater and sat down in a chair in the back row. It was the first time she had ever come to a rehearsal. She hadn't meant to come today, but the pull had been too strong. She didn't think anyone had noticed her entrance.

Kit was halfway through the third soliloquy. Carolyn Nash, as Ophelia, was at stage right, kneeling in silent prayer, her back to Kit. Mary thought the scene looked rather awkward, and George apparently had come to the same conclusion. She heard his voice calling, "Hold up a minute, Chris!" He got up from his chair in the front row and went to the edge of the stage. In a minute he had jumped up, and Mary watched as he re-arranged Carolyn so that she was turned more toward the audience. He was saying something to her, but Mary could not hear him. He walked back to the edge of the stage and jumped down. "Let's try it again," he said. Kit walked off the stage. "All right," George called. "Now."

Very slowly Kit came back on, his head bowed, his eyes on the ground. The scene looked very strange to Mary. Both Kit and Carolyn were wearing jeans and sneakers. In a low yet perfectly audible voice Kit began. "To be, or not to be, that is the question."

Mary listened carefully, all her senses trained on the man on stage. His voice is like no other actor's, she thought. The voice alone would get him through. He looked up and saw Ophelia. Mary sat forward on the edge of her chair. She was curious as to how George would stage the "nunnery" scene.

It was not as physical as many she had seen. It was, if anything, restrained. George stopped it once to say to Kit, "*You've* got to generate the intensity of this scene, Chris. It would be easy for me to let you toss Carolyn around and throw the furniture, but I'm not going to do that. For one thing, I don't want Carolyn all bruised up."

"Thank you, George," the girl put in with a grin.

He smiled back at her. "And more importantly, I want to establish the feeling that Hamlet is *holding in*. He's a keg of dynamite about to explode. He doesn't explode—yet. But you've got to give out vibes, Chris. You've got to be scary."

Kit had been listening courteously. Now he nodded. "Yes. I see."

"All right. Let's take the scene from where you look up and see her."

They began again. Someone came over in the dark and sat down next to Mary. "You haven't been in here before," said the unmistakably English voice of Melvin Shaw.

Mary smiled a little and wished he would go away. "No."

"What do you think?" he asked her.

"What do *you* think?" she returned. "You've done a lot of Shakespeare. You've seen how this production is shaping up."

"I don't know quite what I think," he returned slowly. "To be frank, I wasn't at all pleased to discover that Chris had replaced Adrian Saunders. I almost pulled out."

"Why didn't you?"

"I believe in sticking to my contracts, for one thing. And George has acquired a rather good reputation recently. A reputation that is deserved, incidently. He has a great deal of respect for the play as it is written. But any *Hamlet* lives or dies by the actor who plays the lead."

"Oh," said Mary. "Kit sounded good to me," she added cautiously.

"He needs more fire," said Melvin Shaw. "He's got all the equipment to do the part. He's the only American actor I've ever known who has a genuine feel for the language. He's got the intelligence. But does he have the soul?"

"I think he does," she said defensively.

"Well, my dear, Saturday night will tell us." He smiled at her. "I'm looking forward to our bridge game this evening."

Mary's heart sank. "So am I," she answered hollowly.

George began to call for Melvin, and as soon as he had walked down the aisle Mary slipped out of her seat and out the theater door.

She begged out of the bridge game that night. Kit and Margot had been at dinner and she felt she couldn't bear to spend the evening playing cards and listening to Margot play up to Kit. "I have a headache," she said to Melvin with an apologetic smile. "I think I'll have an early evening."

He looked extremely glum. "I'll turn in too, then. Good night, my dear."

She turned and found George beside her. "I'll walk back with you," he said.

"All right." The night was chilly and she put her arms into her sweater as they went up the hill to the cottages.

"What did you think of our rehearsal this afternoon?" he asked.

"I didn't think you saw me," she returned in surprise.

"I have a sixth sense where you're concerned," he

said. She didn't reply and after a minute he repeated, "What did you think?"

"I was there for less than half an hour, but from what I saw I thought it looked good. Are you pleased?"

"Pretty much. It's coming together. Alfred has surprised me. He's very strong as Claudius."

"Well that's good," she answered. They had reached her cottage. "Claudius needs to be strong."

He smiled down at her. "Will you invite me in for a drink?"

She hesitated. She hadn't missed George's comment earlier about having a sixth sense where she was concerned, and she didn't want to lead him on. On the other hand, she knew she wouldn't sleep at this early hour and she did not fancy spending the next few hours alone.

"Of course," she said. "Come on in."

She mixed Scotches and went to sit on the sofa. "I thought Carolyn did well this afternoon," she said as soon as he was seated in the wing chair.

"Yes. She has the kind of fragile prettiness one needs for Ophelia. And she can act. I think she'll be one of those who make it."

Silence fell. Her throat felt dry and she sipped her drink. They were both studiously avoiding talking about the one person they were both thinking about. George brought the subject up first. "I don't know if Chris is going to come through or not."

"How do you mean?" Her voice sounded husky and she took another swallow of her drink.

"There's something missing. He has everything down; he hasn't put a foot wrong on stage all week. But . . ." He frowned a little, trying to find the right words.

"Melvin said he needed more fire."

"It isn't just that, either. The damnable thing is, I feel as if he has it and is holding it back. But I may be wrong."

"Well," she said weakly. "I suppose Saturday night will tell."

"It certainly will. There will be critics from three TV networks, two national magazines, and the *New York Times* in the audience. I usually get the critics sometime during the course of August, but this is shaping up into a regular opening night.

"God have mercy," said Mary.

He grinned. "It's not God's mercy we need, but John Calder's. He's the *Times* theater critic and he's the one who will decide our fate. If he likes it, we'll almost certainly get a Broadway run."

"Broadway," she said. "My goodness."

He put his drink down and came over to sit next to her on the sofa. "I'm tired of talking about the play," he said. "I want to talk about you."

Her blue eyes widened and she looked a little warily into his face. "What do you mean?"

"Is it true that you and Chris are getting a divorce?"

There was a barely perceptible hesitation and then she said, quite firmly, "Yes."

"I am very glad to hear that." He took her drink from her unresisting hand. "You are driving me absolutely crazy," he said. And kissed her.

His mouth was warm and hard and insistent on hers. She was quiet in his arms, letting him kiss her but giving him very little response.

"Mary," he said shakily and touched her cheek.

"Oh George," she said sadly. "I didn't mean this to happen."

"I should imagine it must happen to you all the time." She had been looking at the open collar of his shirt, but when his words registered she raised her eyes to his face. At the flash of blue a muscle flickered alongside his mouth. "I don't mean that you try to be provocative," he said. "Quite the contrary, as a matter of fact. But you're quite a special lady. Any man would want to get near you."

"No one ever has," she replied in a low voice, "except Kit."

"Whom you are going to divorce."

"I—yes."

"I don't want to rush you, Mary, but I should like so much to be more to you than just a friend."

She looked searchingly into his narrow, clever, attractive face. She liked George very much. She had thought once she would marry a man very like him. "I had no idea you felt like this," she said honestly.

"I thought for a while there that you and Chris were going to get back together."

"I thought so too. For a while." She took a deep breath. "I love him, George. I think I always will. But I can't live with him."

He was staring intently at her face. "Why not?"

"Oh—reasons," she replied evasively. "But the thing is, I'm just not interested in anyone else. Not that way, at least. I like you very much, but . . ."

Her voice trailed off and he finished her sentence for her, ". . . as a friend."

"Yes," she said. "I'm sorry it sounds so trite."

"Look here," he said strongly. "I hope you aren't planning to spend the rest of your life alone just because your marriage didn't work out."

"That's what Hamlet advises Ophelia," she replied a

little bitterly. " 'What should such fellows as I do, crawling between earth and heaven? We are arrant knaves all; believe none of us. Go thy ways to a nunnery.' "

"Don't be an idiot," he snapped. "This is the twentieth century, not the sixteenth. And Ophelia was a simp."

Mary's lips curled at the corners. "She was, rather, wasn't she?"

"Mary," he said, his voice a note deeper than usual. "Beautiful, beautiful Mary. Listen to me. . . ."

"No." She pulled back from him and stared with somber eyes across the room. "No, George. Please don't upset me by saying things I don't want to hear. It isn't just my feelings for Kit. There are religious reasons, too."

"All right." He sounded suddenly very weary. He got to his feet. "But don't run away from me? Will you promise me that at least?"

She smiled a little. "Yes."

He stopped for a minute and held her face between his hands. "I can be a very patient man," he said softly and kissed her forehead before he turned and left the room.

Friday was the last day of class. Technically there was nothing to hold Mary any longer at Yarborough. She could grade her papers at home and telephone the marks to George. After telling herself all week that she couldn't wait to get away, it was distressing to find herself so reluctant when the moment of release finally arrived.

She had to be here on opening night; she had to see for herself how Kit was going to fare. It was as simple as that. When it came right down to it, she thought in grim amusement as she stuffed the final essays into her briefcase, wild horses couldn't drag her away.

She spent all day on her porch, reading essays and grading them. When she went down to dinner it was to find Kit, Margot, Melvin, Alfred, and George missing. They were in the theater going over the scene in Gertrude's bedroom, Carolyn told Mary. George had sent over for sandwiches.

Mary felt the tension in the dining room. It was quieter than usual and the only talk that was introduced had to do with the play. "Poor Chris," said Frank Moore as the main course was served. "I know *I'm* exhausted—we worked on the fencing scene all day long. And he's still going strong. I don't know how he does it."

"And keeps his temper," put in Adam Truro. They ate for a few minutes in silence and then Adam volunteered, "John Calder is going to stay at the Stafford Inn. George says it's the first time a New York critic has ever come for his opening night."

"If the play does go to Broadway," breathed Carolyn, "I wonder if they'll replace all the students?"

"We have to get to Broadway first," said Eric Lindquist. "And we all know who that depends on." He looked in the direction of the theater and the whole table unconsciously followed his lead.

"I wonder what he's thinking," said Frank, and no one asked to whom he was referring.

"He's so calm." Carolyn's eyes were large with wonder. "He must know how his whole professional reputation is at stake, but you'd never know it to look at him. He hasn't any nerves at all."

Oh yes he has, thought Mary to herself. She remembered other opening nights. The calmer Kit appeared the more uptight he really was. She found herself completely unable to eat her dinner.

Saturday was interminable. Even the Elizabethan songbooks couldn't capture Mary's attention. There was an early dinner served at five o'clock. Everyone was present in the dining room and the atmosphere was brittle with tension. Kit was there this time, looking cool and collected. Mary found herself at the same table with him and she listened as he made Carolyn laugh with a joke and flattered Margot outrageously until some of the strain left her face. He seemed utterly relaxed, utterly nonchalant. Mary wondered if she were the only one to notice that he had eaten scarcely a bite of his dinner.

The meal was almost over when Carolyn repeated the judgment she had voiced about him yesterday. "Honestly, Chris, I don't think you have a nerve in your whole body."

"I believe Hemingway called it 'grace under pressure.'" Mary said quietly. She had scarcely spoken at all during the course of the meal.

Kit's eyes involuntarily found hers. She smiled at him, a sweet and beautiful smile. "Good luck," she said softly.

He didn't answer but nodded his dark head at her, his eyes grave and a little abstracted.

After dinner Mary went back to her cabin to change. It was six o'clock. The hour and a half before curtain time stretched before her. She tried to read a magazine but couldn't concentrate on more than one sentence at a time.

Finally it was time to dress. She put on a raspberry

linen sundress with a pleated bodice and full skirt. A
string of pearls around her neck dressed it up as did
pearl-button earrings. Her hair fell loosely to her shoulders, satiny black, softly curling It was cooling down
so she put a white piqué jacket over her bare shoulders. She didn't know if it was the evening air or ner-
vousness, but she was shivering by the time she
reached the theater.

She had a seat in the third row and looked around
her, trying to pick out the critics. The lights were dim-
ming when George slipped into the seat next to hers.
"That's Calder there," he murmured in her ear.

Mary stared at the gray head in front of her. "Oh."
The lights went out and she closed her eyes, breathing
a wordless prayer of supplication. When she opened
them the curtain was slowly rising, revealing Dan Palmer
and Mark Ellis, two of her students, dressed as soldiers.
"Who's there?" said Mark sharply. The play was on.

Mary sat tensely throughout the first scene. George
had handled the ghost very skillfully, she thought, using shadows and a tape recorder. The stage was cleared
and then, with a fanfare of trumpets, the court swept
on.

In center stage, on twin gilt chairs, sat Alfred Block
and Margot Chandler—the King and Queen. Sur-
rounding them was a mass of courtiers dressed in
bright clothing: Melvin Shaw as Polonius, Frank Moore
as Laertes, Carolyn Nash as Ophelia, and various other
students. In the corner, apart, wearing severe black,
was Kit. Alfred began his speech:

"Though yet of Hamlet our dear brother's death
The memory be green, and that is us befitted
To bear our hearts in grief . . ."

Alfred's voice was strong, his bearing dominant, but Mary's whole attention was focused on the still, black figure in the corner. Gradually, as the scene went on, she realized that she was not alone in her reaction. The people seated around her were watching Kit as well. Finally came the line she was waiting for: "But, now, my cousin Hamlet, and my son—" said Alfred.

Kit didn't look up, didn't move, but his whole tense figure seemed to quiver at the words. "A little more than kin, and less than kind!" His beautiful voice was edged with bitterness and scorn. Next to her Mary heard George let out his breath, as though he had been holding it for a long time.

George's confidence seemed to increase as the first act progressed. At the end of it—as Kit said despairingly:

> "The time is out of joint, O cursed spite,
> That ever I was born to set it right!"

—George leaned over and whispered to Mary, "He's pulling it off. He didn't have this in rehearsals."

At the first intermission it seemed that the audience agreed with George. Mary wandered around the lobby, assiduously eavesdropping, and general opinion seemed to be that Kit was remarkably good. As Mary heard one lady say to her friend, "My dear, that voice! I think I could listen to him recite the telephone directory and be happy."

The audience settled back in their chairs and the play resumed. It opened with Act III, the "To be or not to be" soliloquy, and the nunnery scene. And it was then that Mary, and the rest of the audience as well, began to realize what it was that they were seeing. Kit seemed to have himself under iron control. His voice was harsh and low; only twice did he forget himself and begin to shout. But the force of emotion he generated was overpowering: the anger, the pain, the furious sense of betrayal, it was all there. You have to be scary, George had told him. He was.

And he was so much more. He reached into the heart of the character and laid bare all the anguish that underlay Hamlet's wild and enigmatic behavior. The blighted ideals, the betrayed love, the aching uncertainty, and above all else, the poignant and unbearable loneliness. His big scene with Margot, the one that George had rehearsed and rehearsed yesterday, was absolutely shattering. When it was over, Mary realized, a little dazedly, that Kit had been right about Margot. She made the perfect Gertrude: lovely, sexual, affectionate, but shallow. The power of the scene came from the contrast between her grief and repentance, which manifested itself in easy tears, and his, which was harsh and violent, tearing apart his heart and his mind.

The intermission that followed this scene was different from the first one. People were quiet now, almost subdued. No one showed a disposition to linger over his cigarette and stillness had fallen over the auditorium even before the lights had begun to dim for the opening of Act IV.

The last two acts were stunning in their emotional impact. What moved Mary more than anything else was the way she could see aspects of Kit's real character coming through the words and emotions of Hamlet. When he leaped into Ophelia's grave after Laertes, his bitter searing anger reminded her vividly of the morning he had gone after Jason Razzia.

The final dueling scene with Frank Moore had the audience on the edge of their seats. "Frank fenced on his college team," George murmured in Mary's ear. "That was one of the reasons I chose him for Laertes."

Kit's fencing was a match for Frank's. He must have put in long hours of practice, thought Mary, as she watched the swords flashing on stage. The final moment had almost arrived: the infuriated Laertes, unable to break through Hamlet's guard, stabbed his unsuspecting opponent between bouts with his sharp and poisoned sword. There was a moment of breathless silence as Kit looked down at his wounded arm and realized for the first time that Laertes was playing with a sharp sword. His eyes narrowed, his breath hissed between his teeth, and he advanced on Laertes, sword up.

The two men began to fight again, not in a sporting contest this time, but for blood. The clash of swords and the heaviness of their breathing were the only sounds in the entire theater. Finally Kit, with a strong skillful stroke, struck the sword from Laertes hand. Bending, he picked it up. Slowly he held out to Laertes his own sword, which was blunt and harmless. His face was implacable, and Laertes, knowing as he did that the sword Kit retained was not only sharp but also tipped with deadly poison, was forced to accept. The fight resumed.

Mary's hands were clasped tensely in her lap. She knew what would happen, even knew the exact words that would be spoken, but when they came, when Kit cried out in a terrible voice of mingled anguish and fury:

"O villainy! Ho! let the door be locked.
Treachery! Seek it out,"

she felt her hand go, involuntarily, to her throat.

It stayed there throughout the remainder of the scene, as Adam Truro, playing Horatio, clasped the dying Hamlet in his arms. His broken voice uttering the famous farewell, "Good night, sweet prince, and flights of angels sing thee to thy rest!" brought stinging tears to her eyes.

There was the sound of drums and Eric Lindquist, blond, handsome, boyish Eric, playing Fortinbras, came marching in. His clear blue eyes swept around the stage, littered with the corpses of Laertes, Gertrude, Claudius, and Hamlet. He reared his golden head: "I have some rights of memory in this kingdom," he said clearly, "which now to claim my vantage doth invite me."

The contrast was devastating: the brilliant, tortured, complex Hamlet and this sunshiny boy who saw in the cataclysmic ruin before him only his own advantage.

The muffled drums began to roll and four students stepped forward to lift Kit's still body up, high in the air above their heads. Eric's voice rolled out across the audience, over the drums:

"Let four captains
Bear Hamlet like a soldier to the stage,
For he was likely, had he been put on,
To have proved most royal; and for his passage
The soldiers' music and the rite of war
Speak loudly for him."

The soldiers carrying Kit moved slowly up the scaffolding that represented the castle steps. In the distance a gun began to shoot. They reached the top of the scaffolding and stood still, Kit's body still raised high above them. The curtain fell.

For fully half a minute there was not a sound in the theater. Then the clapping began, at first a ripple, then a growing tide as the curtain calls began. Tremendous applause greeted the supporting cast, with Margot getting the biggest hand of all. Then, out on to the stage to join his fellow performers, came Kit. The theater erupted in a storm of acclaim. He smiled, bowed, and held out his hands to Margot and Carolyn. The curtain came down but the clapping refused to subside. At last it came up again to reveal Kit, alone on the stage. The audience rose to its feet in thunderous ovation. Mary felt herself crying. It was the most overwhelming tribute she had ever heard an audience bestow on a performer. She turned to look at George. His face was glowing. "You did it." He seemed to be talking to Kit across the avalanche of sound. "I wasn't sure if you would, but by Christ you pulled it out. Best goddamn Hamlet I ever saw."

Mary picked up her purse to fish for a tissue. "And you directed it," she said shakily.

"No." He shook his head and looked at her. "No one directed what Chris did tonight. That he did all by himself." He grinned. "The SOB was saving it up. And I was scared to death. Wait until I get my hands on him." The crowd was beginning to move toward the exits. "I'm going backstage," said George to Mary. "Coming?"

"Not just yet," she replied. "You go ahead." As he walked toward the front of the theater she took her place in the crowd that was leaving by the rear exit.

Chapter Twelve

She went back to her cottage and sat down in the living room. She understood now what Kit meant when he had said that to do Hamlet well he would have to reveal himself. In order to portray the emotions he had this evening he had first to have felt them. And then he had to show what he had felt up there on the stage.

Kit was a very private person. His strong feelings about his privacy had always been a source of despair to his agent and to the various publicity people who had been associated with his pictures. Mary understood that part of him, that passionate feeling of not wanting to be exposed, written about, journalized. For such a man to do what he had done tonight—the sheer blazing courage it had taken to get up on a stage and reveal all *that*—shook her profoundly.

She felt that for the first time since she had known him she was seeing him as he really was. She had never associated him with any weakness. He was so splendidly male, so tough and strong, such a dominant lover; he had seemed invulnerable to her. But tonight she had seen something else. She had seen a man who knew what it was to love, to be rejected, to be betrayed, and above all, to be alone.

For the first time she considered the possibility that she had failed him more deeply than he had failed her. She had never given him a chance. She had driven him away, and in so doing she had hurt him badly. She had seen that tonight, in the scene with Ophelia.

She thought of all that she had seen tonight and she felt humbled and ashamed and cowardly. She had been so afraid of being hurt herself that she had taken no thought for the hurt she might be inflicting. And she claimed she loved him. Poor Kit, she thought. He deserved better. He had told her once that she saw through to the heart of him, but that wasn't true. If she had, she would not have sent him away without giving him a chance to explain.

He would be tied up with the cast party for a while, but she didn't want to see him in a crowd of people. And she wanted to see him tonight—she felt she must see him tonight. She left her cottage and walked resolutely next door to his, went in and curled up on the sofa, prepared to wait.

He came about an hour later. There was a frown on his face as he pushed the door open; the light had warned him someone was waiting for him. "It's only me," she said quietly from the sofa.

"Mary!" He sounded surprised and a wary look came over his face. "What are you doing here?" He came into the room and dropped rather heavily into the wing chair. She noted with a pang of anxiety that he looked very tired.

Now that she faced him she didn't quite know what to say. He looked so weary. She said with a curious note of huskiness and uncertainty in her voice, "I only came to tell you that if you still want me back, I'll come. But if you tell me to get out, I certainly won't blame you."

He closed his eyes. All the muscles in his face went rigid. When he opened them again he said, "Do you mean it this time? I don't think I can take it if you change your mind again."

Tears began to pour down her face. "Oh, darling, I'm so sorry. I've been so horrible. And I love you so much. Please, please take me back." She wasn't sure who made the first move, but three seconds later she was in his lap, locked in his arms, her head buried in his shoulder. She continued to cry. "I've been so afraid of you, afraid of loving you," she got out. "You hurt me so much before."

"I know I did," he replied. His own voice was husky with emotion. "Mary"—his arms tightened, his lips were in her hair—"I was so sorry about the baby, sweetheart, I was so sorry."

Her body was shaking with sobs but she made no attempt to stop them. She felt as if a hard knot that had been lodged within her for four years was slowly dissolving and washing away with her tears. "I blamed you," she said into his shoulder.

"I know," he repeated. "I knew, as soon as I got that call from your mother, that I had made the biggest mistake of my life in neglecting you. All the way in on the plane, I knew it in my bones."

"But why, Kit? Why didn't you ever call me? Why did you just—disappear?"

"It was unforgivable. I know that now—I knew it as soon as I got your mother's call. But I was like a man driven, Mary. I pushed everything that wasn't my career to the back of my mind—and that included you. I knew this was my only chance to make it and I just grabbed everything that could possibly be useful. Even Jessica Corbet. I didn't go to bed with her, but I didn't try to squash those rumors either. I think I must have been a little mad."

"Your only chance?" Her sobs were lessening now and she lifted her head to look at him. "What do you mean?"

"I mean that if I hadn't made it with *The Russian Experiment*—if I hadn't gotten another picture with a good salary out of it—I was going to quit acting."

Her eyes were great blue pools of astonishment. "Quit acting! But why?"

"Because I was going to be a father and I was damned if I'd have my kid raised the way I was. I had to give him financial security. And I was damned if I was going to let you stop your studies because we couldn't afford a baby-sitter. I have a math degree—I was going to see if I couldn't get a job in computers."

"Computers!" She couldn't have looked more horrified if he had said he was going to run numbers. He smiled a little at her expression. "But why didn't you tell me?"

"Because of the way you look now," he replied. "And I thought that if I put everything I had into it, that I *would* make good in Hollywood. And I did. But in the process I lost everything that mattered." He put his cheek against her hair and held her to him. "I lost my son. And I lost you." There was a long moment of silence, then he said, as if he found the words difficult, "Where did you bury him?"

She felt a fierce pain about her heart at what she had shut him out from. "In St. Thomas's, next to my grandparents. I'll take you there if you like."

"Yes," he said very low. "I'd like that."

She closed her eyes. "I was such a beast," she whispered.

"No, you weren't. You weren't in any state to listen to explanations. I realized that and that's why I did what you asked and left. After I thought you had had a chance to recover a little, I wrote you. I wrote you twice, telling you just what I've told you tonight. But you never answered."

"I tore the letters up."

"I see." His voice was flat.

"I told you I blamed you." She took her head out of his shoulder and spoke somberly. "If there's one thing the Irish know how to do, Kit, it's nurse a grudge. I'm really not a very nice person. I don't know why you even want me back."

He smiled at her and there was pain as well as tenderness in his look. "No, you're not 'nice.' You are intelligence and integrity, beauty and passion. It's like touching solid ground in a quagmire to touch you again."

She cupped his face between her hands. "I never really thought you needed me," she said. "Not like I needed you."

"You seem to have gotten along fine without me," he returned. His face was very still between her palms. "You have your job, your family."

She kissed him. "I was operating on half a heart." She kissed him again and felt him begin to smile.

"I know. All these years I've felt as if something of me was left out. It's only when I'm with you that I feel that I'm a whole person again."

She sighed and snuggled, if possible, even closer. "To think we owe all this to that wretched magazine," she murmured.

"What magazine, sweetheart?"

"The one that found out we were married and spread my picture all over the front page. If it hadn't been for that, you would never have come to see me. And I would never have told you I was working at Yarborough."

"True," he sounded a little cautious.

"You did come to Yarborough because you knew I'd be here, didn't you?"

"Yes."

"I thought the whole setup was too neat to be a co-incidence," she said complacently.

"Actually, I called my agent right after I saw you." He was speaking slowly, carefully, as if testing her reaction: "I told him just to get me in, I'd play any part. It was only luck that Adrian Saunders got that movie offer. Otherwise I might have been stealing one of the student's parts."

She sat back on his lap and stared at him. "Good heavens, I'd no idea you'd done that. I thought that when the part became available you'd taken it because you knew I would be here."

"No." He looked measuringly into her eyes and seemed to be reassured by what he saw there. "I have another confession to make."

She compressed her lips a little. "What is it?"

"I was the one who leaked the story of our marriage to *Personality*."

"You what!" Her eyes were wide with incredulity.

"I leaked the story," he repeated. "I was desperate to see you again and I couldn't think of any reason for me to present myself. And then, too, I thought that making the marriage public would force you to do something about it. You hadn't even tried to get a legal separation, so I hoped that maybe there was a chance you'd consider coming back to me."

"You stinker," she said, but the lines of her mouth were soft.

He grinned. "It worked."

"Why couldn't you just have come to see me?"

"Would you have listened to me if I'd arrived at your doorstep, hat in hand?" He looked at her skeptically.

Her lips curled a little. "No, I suppose not. I was too well armored in all my grudges."

"Well, the course I took was crude. I'll admit that. But it was effective." He smoothed her hair back from her forehead. "Do you know something?" he asked in a kind of astonishment. "I'm starving."

"Of course you are," she answered, sympathetically. "You didn't eat a bite of your dinner." She pushed herself off his lap and stood up. "I have some peanut butter and jelly in my fridge. Come on and I'll make you a sandwich."

He stood up and staggered a little. "Ow! I think you cut off all the circulation in my legs."

"You're so romantic," she murmured. He hobbled around the room for a bit and she watched him, smiling. When he finally came to a halt she said, "Bring your toothbrush and pajamas and a change of clothes."

He swung around with no suggestion of stiffness at all. "What did you say?"

"You heard me," she returned serenely. "I won't even push you out in the morning."

He heaved a great dramatic sigh. "Thank God for that. I've come to the conclusion that I'm really a very domestic type. All this creeping about in the dead of night doesn't appeal to me at all."

It was true, she thought, as she watched him collect his things. He looked like every woman's dream lover, but he had been happy as a clam refinishing furniture and painting walls in their first apartment. And he had not been indifferent to the thought of fatherhood; quite the contrary. If he had been willing to give up acting for it, he took it very seriously indeed.

She thought back to that dreadful argument they had had when she first told him she was pregnant. She remembered how angry he had been when she said she would give up her fellowship. It had upset her dreadfully, that anger. She had not realized that it sprang from his great and generous love, from his passionate desire to see her free to fulfill the promise that was in her. He still felt the same way. She remembered how concerned he had been when she had said she would give up teaching.

They walked together in companionable silence back to her cottage. He sat down and stretched his long legs in front of him while she made the sandwiches and poured two glasses of apple juice. He looked at her in admiration as he bit into the peanut-butter-and-jelly sandwich.

"You're wonderful," he said. "You always have whatever's needed right on hand."

She laughed at him. "Just like the mother in *The Swiss Family Robinson*."

"Well," he replied dryly, "not quite."

He finished his sandwich and yawned. Mary did the same. "I'm dead," she said. "You use the bathroom first and I'll clean up these crumbs." In five minutes they were both in pajamas and in bed. In seven minutes they were asleep.

* * *

Mary woke to find the sun streaming into the bedroom. She had been so tired last night that she hadn't closed the shade. She hopped out of bed, drew the shade down, and got back in next to Kit. The New Hampshire morning was chilly and she snuggled down comfortably under the covers. He was still asleep and she curled up against his wide, warm back, closed her eyes and dozed.

Half an hour later he stirred and rolled over. She propped her cheek on her hand and looked down into his face. He gave her a sleepy smile and yawned. "What time is it?" he asked.

"Nine-thirty," she replied. "I feel very decadent."

"You haven't started to be decadent yet, sweetheart," he said with slow amusement.

She tried to look severe. "Everyone will be looking for you."

"Let them look," he murmured. "Kiss me." His voice was very deep and she seemed to feel it in her bones. She bent her head to him. His mouth was gentle under hers; their kiss was infinitely tender. He made no move to touch her. She raised her head and looked down into dark dark eyes. As she stayed where she was suspended over him, he slowly raised his hand to touch her hair. "It's like silk," he murmured. "All of you is like that. Silky and soft . . ." His eyes narrowed and they stared at each other.

Beyond his fingers tangled in her hair he had not touched her. Her body was crying out for him but she too deliberately held herself back, their denial feeding their desire as effectively as any caress could have done. "Take your pajamas off," he said and her hands moved, shaking, to obey him. Their eyes never separated as they both slowly divested themselves of their nightwear. "Now lie down next to me," he directed and she did as he asked, stretching out beside him, her beautiful body positioned for his love.

His hand slid across her stomach and cupped her breast. "Do you want me to wait?" he whispered.

"No," she whispered back, her body on fire for him. "I want you now." She arched up toward him and he came into her hard, his hands gripping her so strongly that he bruised her skin. But she did not object, clinging to him tightly herself, her mouth crushed under his, her whole body shuddering with the pleasure he was giving to her.

They finally lay quietly, breathing hard and still linked together. It was a long time before she found the composure to say, "Now *that* was decadent."

"Um," he answered. "Did you like it?"

"Wow," she said simply, and he chuckled.

"Stick around awhile and we'll try it again. Maybe we can improve."

"I'm always interested in improvement," she replied and he kissed her throat.

"I'm glad to hear that."

They stayed in bed until noon, at which time hunger forced them to get up. "I tell you what," said Kit, yawning and stretching, "I'll go into town and get coffee and donuts and the papers. We can eat here."

"That sounds great." She was watching in admiration as his muscles bunched when he stretched. "I have to get to Mass yet," she added, "but they have one at five this afternoon."

"Well," he conceded slowly, "I might be ready to let you leave by then."

She laughed, got out of bed and bent to pick up her

pajamas. "I'm getting dressed," she said firmly. "You lecher."

He grinned. "I have a lot of time to make up for." He watched her folding her pajamas to put them in the drawer. "You always did wear the sexiest nightwear," he murmured. "Flannel pajamas."

"When you live in New England you opt for warmth," she replied serenely, putting them away. "I never could see the point of a sexy nightgown anyway. I bought one for our honeymoon, you remember, and all it did was wind up on the floor."

His teeth were very white in his dark face. "True." He headed for the shower. "I won't be long."

She put on her terry-cloth robe and went out into the living room to finish tidying up. It was a good thing the maids didn't work on Sunday, she thought as she poured herself a glass of apple juice. They would have gotten a shock if they had opened the bedroom door half an hour ago!

Kit came out of the bedroom wearing navy cotton pants and a red-striped rugby shirt. "I'll be back shortly," he said. "Don't run away."

"I won't. But neither do I think I'll accompany you out to the porch."

He laughed. "No use borrowing trouble," he agreed. After he had left, Mary went in to take a shower.

He was gone for almost an hour and she was on the point of having more peanut butter and jelly for breakfast when she heard his car pull up in front of the cottage. He came in carrying a bag in either hand. "Coffee," he said, putting one bag down on the table. "Donuts." He put down the other bag.

"Thank heavens," Mary replied, taking out a container of coffee. "I was about to have a caffeine fit."

He sat down next to her on the sofa and picked up his own coffee. "I ran into George as I was driving out, that's what kept me."

"Oh? What did he have to say?" She sipped her coffee with obvious pleasure.

"He gave me this." Kit reached into his pocket and pulled out a folded sheet of paper. "It's John Calder's review, the one that will appear in the *Times* tomorrow morning. He dropped a copy of it off with George before he left this morning."

Mary put her coffee down and took the papers from him. There was more than one typed sheet and she spread them out and began to read. The first sentence allayed her anxiety: "A milestone in American theater occurred last night with the Yarborough Festival's production of *Hamlet* with (with the single exception of Melvin Shaw's Polonius) an all-American cast." She glanced up at Kit quickly but he was calmly munching a donut. She looked down and continued to read. There was praise for George, for his "sensitive and perceptive" handling of the staging and the relationships among the characters. Carolyn was singled out for her "bewildered and delicate Ophelia," Frank for his "simple, gullible, likeable Laertes," and Alfred for his "authoritative Claudius." Calder devoted a whole paragraph to Margot's "light-minded, light-hearted, light-skirted Gertrude."

The second half of the article concentrated on Kit. "If anyone had doubts about the acting ability of Christopher Douglas," she read, "they were laid to rest last night." Mary went through the remainder of the article in growing jubilation. When she had finished she looked back to the one sentence that had lodged in her mind and read it out loud: "Quite possibly the finest

Shakespearean performance ever delivered by an American actor." She put the article down and turned to him with glowing eyes. "Oh, Kit!"

"Nice, huh?" he said nonchalantly

"Nice? It's marvelous. And it's true. You were—oh, I can't find the right word. But I cried and you know I don't often do that."

He put down the dregs of his coffee and looked at her with warm, dark eyes. "Did you cry, Princess? That's the biggest compliment of all." She smiled at him a little mistily. He smiled back and said, "I'm afraid I've eaten all the donuts."

"You haven't!" She leaned forward and grabbed the bag. There was one left and she appropriated it firmly. "I imagine George was thrilled," she said around a mouthful.

"He was feeling pretty good. He's sure we can go to Broadway if I want to."

"Do you?"

"What do you want to do?" he returned. "Would you like living in New York for a few months."

"Sure," she said recklessly. "I could always work at the Columbia library if I wanted to."

His brow cleared. "In that case, I'll do it. It will help enormously, when I try to borrow money to do a picture of my own, if people are reassured that I really *can* act."

"Do you know," she said thoughtfully, "Daddy might lend us some money. He's always looking for a good investment."

"Yes, well I haven't worked out the details yet. But I will. I have no intention of overspending my own budget."

She smiled a little abstractedly. "Speaking of Daddy, I think I'd better call home and break the news."

"Mel flew in this morning," he said in a seeming non sequitur. "He and George have set up a press conference for this afternoon at three. The TV people will be there. I said I'd come."

"Then I most certainly better call home," she said decisively.

"You don't mind if I announce that we're back together?"

She leaned over and kissed his cheek. "I'll come with you." She picked up the phone. "But first . . ."

He sat quietly next to her as she dialed the familiar number. Her mother answered on the third ring. "Hi Mother," she said.

"Mary Kate! Darling, how are you?"

"Fine. Listen, Mom, sit down. I have some news that may surprise you. Are you sitting?"

"Yes," came the faint response.

"Kit and I are getting back together again."

"Oh, Mary Kate, I'm so glad!" was the surprising reply. "I've been praying all month that this would happen."

Mary stared at the receiver. "You have?"

"Yes. And your father too. Is Kit there?"

"Yes."

"Put him on. I want to talk to him."

"Okay." Mary held out the phone to him. "She wants to talk to you."

Kit looked a little warily at the receiver. He took the phone in a distinctly apprehensive manner and she smiled to herself. He had always been a little nervous around her mother. "It isn't that I don't like her," he had once said to Mary. "I do. It's just that she's so proper. Every time she looks at me, I'm sure I'm eating with the wrong fork or something." He said now into the phone, "Hello Julia, how are you?"

Mary couldn't hear her mother's response, but from the expression on Kit's face she gathered that it was satisfactory. "I wasn't sure how you would feel about it," he said. There was silence as he listened to the voice on the other end and then he grinned. "Yes, well I've been chasing her mercilessly for three weeks and she's finally given in." Silence. "I feel the same way," he said. "Okay, fine, I'd love to talk to him." Pause. "Hi Bob. Yes. Well, I'm happy about it too. Oh, the play went well. Looks like we'll be going to Broadway." Long long pause. "Thank you very much," said Kit quietly. Then, "I'll put your daughter on."

She took the receiver. "Hi, Daddy."

"I'm so happy for you, Mary Kate."

"Me too." She laughed a little. "I don't think I realized how *un*happy I've been all these years."

"Well, your mother and I did, honey, and that's why we're so pleased you and Kit have decided to try it again. I always thought you had something special."

"We did. We do."

"Great. When can we expect to see you?"

"Hold on a minute." She put her hand over the phone and said to Kit, "Do you want to stop off and see my folks after you've finished here?"

"Sure," he said.

"Daddy? Kit is tied up here until the end of August, but we'll come for a weekend after that. Yes, the play was terrific. Kit was fantastic. The rave reviews should start on the TV news tonight. Okay. That would be lovely. How about next weekend? Good. We'll see you then. Bye now."

She hung up the phone. "They're coming up to see the play next weekend."

"Great. Better book them into the Stafford Inn."

"Yes. What time did you say the press conference started?"

"Three o'clock." He looked at his watch. "Half an hour from now. God, where did the day go?"

"If you can't remember," she said dryly, "I'll be very insulted."

"You'll have to remind me," he murmured. "Tonight."

"You're insatiable." She stood up and brushed donut crumbs off her lap. He leered. "*And* a donut thief," she added. "What does one wear to a press conference anyway?"

"I'm wearing exactly what I've got on," he replied equably.

She looked at him critically. "You might shave."

"I might do that," he conceded.

She looked down at her jeans and bare feet. "I have to change, that's for sure." He didn't move. "Well, come on," she urged, "don't just sit there staring at me! Do you have your razor here?"

"No."

"Well then go and get it. Or better still, shave over there. I could use the bathroom." And she shoved him out the door.

The rec room was crowded with people, television cameras, and still-photographers when Mary and Kit walked in together. George was talking with a network television critic when he looked up and saw them. It seemed the whole room made the discovery at the same time, for suddenly cameras began to flash and TV equipment to roll. Mary looked startled and George watched as Kit put a protective arm around her shoulders. He felt a deep pain around the region of his heart as he looked at the pair in front of the fireplace.

They made a striking couple, both tall and slim and black-haired, Kit's bronzed masculinity a foil for the magnolia creaminess of his wife. Mary had regained her poise and was smiling a little. She looked cool and composed, as if she had done this sort of thing every day of her life. Kit had dropped his arm but the impression of unity they gave off was very strong.

So she had gone back to him, George thought dully. He really wasn't all that surprised. How could he—or any man—hope to compete with Chris Douglas? The hell of it was, thought George as he moved closer to the fireplace, he liked Chris. He would like him much better, however, if he wasn't married to Mary.

"Yes," he heard Chris saying in response to a question, "I'd accept an offer to go to Broadway. But only if my coworkers—including Mr. Moore and Miss Nash— are invited as well."

George looked quickly across the room to where Carolyn and Frank were standing together. The expressions on their faces brought a reluctant grin to his own. Yes, it was very difficult to dislike Chris Douglas.

Mary was talking now. "I'm not quite sure what my future teaching plans will be," she answered a woman reporter's question. "So much depends on my husband's schedule." She sounded sweet and demure and George saw Kit give her a quick, amused look.

There was another question and then Kit was signaling to George to come and join them. As he came slowly forward Mary turned the blue of her eye on his face. He smiled a little crookedly at what he saw there.

A reporter asked him a question and he turned to answer it.

At four-fifteen Kit called a halt. He and Mary made a gracious but determined exit, and as they were walking back up through the pines she heaved a sigh of relief.

"I know," he said. "But I do that sort of thing very seldom."

"Why did you do it today?" she asked curiously.

"I thought it would help George and the festival."

She leaned her head against his arm for a minute. "I have to get moving to church."

"I'll come with you," he said.

She stopped and stared at him. The only time he had ever gone to church with her was the day they were married. "You don't have to," she said faintly.

"I'd like to. I've done a lot of thinking in the last four years and that was one of the things I thought about."

"Oh, darling." Her face was radiant. "It would make me so happy."

He took her hand and began to walk again up the hill. "Well, that's what I want to do," he said. "Make you happy."

She raised their linked hands and kissed his fingers. "You do. You do."